PRAISE FOR THE WORK OF JULIE KAEWERT AND THE BOOKLOVER'S MYSTERIES!

" 'Publish and perish' seems to be the rule in the world of London publisher Alex Plumtree. In *Unbound*, Alex plunges into another deadly plot. . . . If the idea of a murderous political society operating within the Society for the Preservation of Rare and Antique Books isn't entertaining enough, Kaewert offers a complex puzzle within a puzzle and lots of insight into the daily life of a small, quality publishing house—which is the real charm of the book."—*Publishers Weekly*

"Murderous. You'll have fun with the booklore and the history."—*Booknews* from the Poisoned Pen

"Sure to appeal to any mystery lover, *Unbound* illustrates how the publishing world can be most competitive—and most deadly."—*Women's Magazine*

"Publishing can get pretty deadly in England, as evidenced in Julie Kaewert's engaging and complex thriller."—*San Francisco Chronicle*

"*Unsolicited* is very much an old-fashioned, classical English mystery that, but for a few modern twists, could have been written in the

days of Michael Innes or Nicholas Blake."
—Tom and Enid Schantz, *The Denver Post*

"*Unsolicited* is an action-packed, suspenseful thriller, with a mystery that grows downright spooky before it is all very satisfactorily wrapped up in an exciting man-against-the-sea climax. There's never a dull page in this international page-turner. We hope to hear from Kaewert again. She is good!"—*The Denver Post*

"I was thoroughly captivated by this book. As I read, I was reminded more and more of the early Dick Francis novels. . . . Like Francis, Ms. Kaewert writes about a milieu about which she is familiar, and this adds to the realism of the novel. I recommend *Unsolicited* highly!"—*Mystery News*

"A roller-coaster ride of thrills."—*Ocala Star-Banner*

*Available from Bantam Books

UNPRINTABLE

JULIE KAEWERT

BANTAM BOOKS
NEW YORK TORONTO LONDON SYDNEY AUCKLAND

Unprintable

A Bantam Crime Line Book / November 1998

Crime Line and the portrayal of a boxed "cl" are trademarks
of Bantam Books, a division of Bantam Doubleday Dell
Publishing Group, Inc.

ISBN 0-553-57716-6

Published simultaneously in the United State and Canada

Bantam Books are published by Bantam Books, a division of
Bantam Doubleday Dell Publishing Group, Inc. Its trademark,
consisting of the words "Bantam Books" and the portrayal of a
rooster, is Registered in U.S. Patent and Trademark Office and in
other countries. Marca Registrada. Bantam Books, 1540 Broadway,
New York, New York 10036.

For Annalisa.

ACKNOWLEDGMENTS

This book could not have been written without the help of many extraordinarily kind people. Tom Parson of Denver, in the tradition of fine printers, went out of his way to demonstrate the art of hand printing, lend me rare books, and explain the intricacies of the history and culture of printing. Nancy Missbach, Denver bookbinder and general biblioexpert, provided advice, information, and an introduction to Tom. John Windle, rare-book dealer in San Francisco, kindly advised on many issues. My brother-in-law, Dr. Steve Harrington of Duluth, provided medical advice. Tom and Enid Schantz of the Rue Morgue Mystery Bookshop in Boulder provided invaluable advice, as usual, as did Barbara Peters of The Poisoned Pen in Scottsdale. Thanks to Kathy Saideman for sharing her awe-inspiring skills.

As for the British contingent, Howard Mills of Boulder served nobly and skillfully as a local British English consultant-cum-editor/fact checker, and saved the book from hopeless American clangers. Rachel Knoedler did the same and was kind enough to introduce me to Howard. Peter Bear, RIBA, of London, provided generous on-foot reeducation on the neighbourhood of Clerkenwell, and vital fact-checking. Stuart Gulleford of the Campaign for an Independent Britain graciously answered questions about the European Union and checked facts. As usual, my tolerant friends Pat Jackson and Sally Freeman frequently shared their time and news from across the pond, as did Timothy and Kathryn Beecroft.

Finally, sincere thanks to still more people who made the book possible day by day and week by week: my Alex Plumtree-like husband, Bill, for pleasantly bearing with me; babysitter extraordinaire Elizabeth Lehnert; and my extremely helpful and supportive writing group of Karen Lin, Janet Fogg, and Jim Hester. I'm grateful to Roxane Perruso, Dan and Nancy Fleming, Kathy Klatman, and Floyd and Elaine English for their vital assistance. The friends who encouraged me at a difficult time know who they are. I will never forget their kind encouragement.

Special thanks are due Laura Blake Peterson, Kate Miciak, and Amanda Clay Powers for their continuing patience, sense of humour, and expert guidance.

UNPRINTABLE

CHAPTER ONE

Be not the slave of words.

THOMAS CARLYLE

THERE'S NOTHING LIKE THE JOY OF PLACING PRISTINE handmade paper in a press, clicking bits of type into a composing stick, and breathing the exotic aroma of oil-based ink. Nothing, that is, except perhaps changing the history of Europe.

Alarm bells should have rung when the deputy prime minister phoned me at the Press one balmy March day.

"Alex Plumtree? Guy Ferris-Browne here. I admire your work at Plumtree Press tremendously. Listen—I know this is a bit sudden, but . . . are you free for lunch today?"

I sat up a bit straighter. It wasn't every day that the humble phone lines of Plumtree Press were graced by the nation's second-in-power. Ferris-Browne was also minister for the environment, but the politician's greatest fame had come from his bold leadership of the Labour Party's European Union enthusiasts.

How could I possibly refuse lunch with the man? "Yes—yes, of course, Deputy Prime Minister. I'd be delighted."

"Good! Fine. Members' Tea Room, one o'clock. Cheers," and he was gone.

I hung up the phone and glanced down at my clothes. Tweedy jacket, corduroy trousers, a tie. Could have been worse. Rummaging on my desk top, I unearthed my diary. "Damn!" I muttered. *Victor Fine, two o'clock* was scribbled on that day's page. Fine was a fellow Bedford Square publisher at Rollancz, a long-established Socialist publishing house. He'd kindly agreed to share the secrets of their hugely successful Left Book Club, a politically oriented series of books purchased by subscription. Though I was not a Socialist, I *was* a bibliophile and was actively considering starting such a club for fellow book-lovers.

I checked my watch: noon. Just time to make it. "Lisette," I said, rounding the corner of her sunny domain, "would you ring Victor Fine and postpone our two o'clock meeting? Please? Guy Ferris-Browne just rang—he wants me for lunch."

"Well, well." Lisette, who was not only my best friend's wife but deputy prime minister of Plumtree Press, smiled mischievously. In the thick French accent that hadn't improved in over two decades on English soil, she said, "No doubt 'e wants to offer you a position in the government. 'Ow would you like to be addressed, sir? Do you wish me to curtsy?" She came out from behind her desk and did just that.

"Very funny, Lisette. I don't know when I'll be back; apologise to Fine for me, will you?"

"Of course, your 'ighness. Will there be anything else?"

"Stop that!" I joked, and dashed down the stairs, nearly colliding with our postman and general dogsbody. "Sorry Derek," I threw over my shoulder, as he righted his tottering pile of post.

"Oy! Where's the fire, mate?"

"Westminster!" I replied, flying out the door. Later I would reflect that Derek had been oddly prophetic.

Forty-five minutes later I stood peering through the door of the Members' Tea Room. I'd been here only twice before in my life. It had recently been redecorated in a clubby style, after the ceiling had fallen in on the esteemed members of the House of Commons.

A Conservative MP who'd found multimillion-pound success as a novelist passed me on his way to the tea room. The smile that beamed from the back covers of thirty-five million paperbacks suddenly trained its magnificence on me. I smiled back.

"Plumtree," boomed a voice from behind me. A hand fell on my shoulder, and I found myself standing face-to-face with my host. Ferris-Browne was an attractive man with a distinctive mane of thick grey hair, tastefully tamed. He matched my height of six feet four inches and positively reeked of power—more so in person than on television. "So good of you to come."

"Not at all. My pleasure, sir."

He steered me off down the hall. "We're not eating at this ghastly place, old chap. Actually, we're popping round to Number Ten."

Surprised, I followed. I'd never been inside the prime minister's residence before, though the PM had been a close friend of my father's. We walked over the road and along Parliament Square to Parliament Street, toward the gates that marked Downing Street. The gates opened as if by magic at Ferris-Browne's approach, into the cloistered cul-de-sac housing Number Ten. The deputy PM did his best to put me at ease, chatting sociably about a collector's boxed set we'd just published at the Press. It contained three works featuring one of London's lesser known but more intriguing neighbourhoods, Clerkenwell. "Superb printing. Excellent design," he enthused. "Who printed it for you?"

"A Clerkenwell shop, in fact. Amanda Morison, of Amanda's Print Shop."

"Not the Morison of Pelican Press, surely?"

"The same." I knew instantly that Ferris-Browne had to be a fine-printing enthusiast if he knew about Stanley Morison. Beloved by connoisseurs of type everywhere, Morison was a 1920s printer and publisher who had single-handedly resurrected and reproduced the most classic typefaces, making them available to modern-day printers. "Stanley Morison was Amanda's great-uncle."

"Ah." The door with the brass numeral 10 on it swung open as we approached, the constables on either side nodding at us impassively. Ferris-Browne steered me up a flight of steps and into a capacious conference room. The table was laid for three.

We had no sooner entered the room than the prime minister himself, Graeme Abercrombie, joined us. Abercrombie was a small, genial man with salt-and-pepper hair and a broad face. He gave one the impression of a friendly dog—comfortable and comforting. Immediately behind the PM was a giant of a man with disconcertingly white-blond hair and eyebrows. A bodyguard, I thought.

"My old friend Maximilian's son." Abercrombie clasped my hand in both of his famous ones. He looked momentarily taken aback; my dark hair, blue eyes, height, and facial features were so like my deceased father's that I regularly startled people. But Abercrombie quickly recovered, gazing into my eyes as if trying to read something there.

"I'm delighted to see you again, Alex," he continued warmly. "The last time I visited the Orchard, you were all of ten years old. Knowing your father, he never told you, but he helped me with my platform and funding when I first stood for Parliament. In those days"—he sounded almost wistful—"I was a Conservative moderate."

"It's wonderful to see you again, Prime Minister. I still have the copy of *Treasure Island* you sent me—it was very kind of you."

It all came back to me: two and a half decades ago, in our sitting room, Abercrombie had seemed taller and thinner but just as friendly. I recalled my father telling me, after Abercrombie left that night, that there *were* honest politicians, and Graeme Abercrombie was among the best of them. Having met the man and played hide-and-seek with him in the garden, I'd volunteered to go door-to-door with leaflets for him. Abercrombie had sent me a lovely edition of *Treasure Island* for my troubles, nicely inscribed. I could still recall agonising over the thank-you note to the new PM after he'd won.

"I'm sorry your father died so young, Alex." Abercrombie sighed. "For all our sakes." Then with a wave of his hand he dismissed the blond giant, and the three of us were alone.

The prime minister indicated that I should sit, and put himself on the other side of the table with Ferris-Browne. "Guy says you're going to help me survive this election," he said, and tucked into his salad.

Everyone in Britain knew that Abercrombie had been forced to call an election over the EU issue. In barely one month's time he would know whether he had sufficient support to remain Prime Minister. It had been an eventful year in British politics, even before the explosion of the EU issue: Abercrombie's young Labour predecessor, Anthony Flair, had been unceremoniously thrown out of office in the wake of a massive financial scandal.

"I haven't told him yet, Graeme," Ferris-Browne interjected.

"Ah, then I will. You see, Plumtree, we need public opinion to be galvanised *with* us and *against* Dexter Moore."

Dexter Moore was the anti-environmental, anti-EU, ultra-Conservative who would be the only real contender against Abercrombie in the April election. I'm sure I wasn't the only person who was incredulous that Moore had been swept into the highest level of British politics—merely on the strength of his opposition to the European Union.

Something had happened to the stoic people of Britain since they'd begun to perceive a threat to their independence from the EU. Not only did they want to prevent Economic and Monetary Union; they wanted out of the entire entangling alliance. What had begun as the Common Market had somehow evolved into the European Union, without people realising what had happened. The European courts in Strasbourg now overrode Parliament and the decisions of the English courts. The EU was now demanding allegiance for defence purposes, and Britain's NATO membership was about to go out the window.

In response to this sudden perception of trickery on the part of the government, the people of England had begun to display almost pathological patriotism, bursting into emotional renditions of "Land of Hope and Glory" with little provocation. Evidently a fair number of Britons were willing to roll to the Right again—even to someone like Dexter Moore—to keep England forever England. I personally couldn't have been lured into Moore's camp for the sake of forestalling the EU. But I *was* opposed to the thought of drinking beer in litres, and paying the barman with Eurocurrency bereft of the stolid profile of Her Majesty.

"We want you to do what you do best," the prime minister continued.

I raised my eyebrows, a forkful of chicken on its way to my lips.

"Publish a book."

Relief and confusion swept over me in equal measures. I could do that, certainly; but how would publishing a book help Abercrombie stay in office?

"You've heard of Lord Chenies's latest novel, *Cleansing*, I'm sure."

My heart sank. The best-selling literary novelist Nigel Charford-Cheney, also Lord Chenies, was a fellow parishioner of Christ Church Chenies. While the rural village that bore his family's name had changed over the years from Cheneys to Chenies, his lordship's surname complicated a bit by marriage, remained Cheney. I'd known him since childhood. The first chapter of *Cleansing* had been published by a serial publisher—Lord Chenies's son, Malcolm—to universal disapproval. Lord Chenies was one of the nation's most luminous literary lights—every novel in the last ten years a best-seller—but he'd made the mistake of going political with this book. If the first chapter was any indication, it was ultra right wing in the most odious way, appearing to condone violence on England's downtrodden. All the top publishers had refused it, and finally Lord Chenies's own son had taken it on.

My mind raced. They wanted *me* to publish *Cleansing*? They probably knew that I was well-acquainted with Lord Chenies . . . but what about Malcolm Charford-Cheney? Wasn't he already doing the dirty deed, chapter by horrid chapter?

"You see, Plumtree," piped up Ferris-Browne, "we think people will be so appalled by attitudes like Lord Chenies's, they'll come rushing over to our side. When they see the ugliness of Dexter Moore's attitude exposed, they won't believe they ever considered voting him in. It must be done quickly, of course; we'd want the book to be reviewed no later than next month. And of course no one must know we've been involved, unless you feel it necessary to tell a trusted colleague or two at the Press."

I saw in that moment exactly what the trade-off was. For publishing this book, I would be reviled, badly reviewed, even hated. My name would be mud. I would be assumed to be of Dexter Moore's, and Lord Chenies's, ilk. In exchange, I would become part of the PM's inner circle, someone vital to his campaign. Also, not insignificantly, I would reap the benefits of an automatic best-seller. With Lord Chenies in our stable, Plumtree Press's literary credibility would skyrocket overnight.

Still, there were seemingly insurmountable difficulties. Not least of these was the fact that I wanted this book nowhere within miles—sorry, kilometres—of my trade catalogue. Frowning, I wiped the corners of my mouth with a serviette. "You know I'd like to help you. But how can you be certain the book would turn people away from Moore? It seems to me it would only give credence to his prejudices, by publicising them further. Besides, Malcolm Charford-Cheney has the contract."

"I hear Malcolm and his father have had a bit of a disagreement," Ferris-Browne said. "Lord Chenies is not entirely pleased with Malcolm's handling of the novel. He would be most receptive, I think, to another offer—from a respectable publisher."

Ah. So the esteemed minister had already done a bit of groundwork.

"As to your doubts about the book's effectiveness in swaying public opinion," he went on, "people have already turned away from Dexter Moore since the first chapter was released; you've seen the media reaction yourself." He shot me a reassuring smile. "Trust me, Plumtree—this sort of thing is my speciality. I did it well enough to get Abercrombie into office, didn't I?"

I couldn't deny the truth of that, and smiled uncomfortably at his mild reprimand.

"Now," Ferris-Browne continued smugly, "I have an idea to make this controversial best-seller more palatable. How about using the heraldry—fictional, of course—of the aristocratic protagonist's family, maps of their country estate, and so forth, in breathtaking colour plates? You could publish a collector's edition, to look like your Clerkenwell books. Your friend Amanda Morison could do the job. Leather covers, leather slipcase—handmade paper. I can see it now. Lord Chenies would surely jump at the chance."

The cost of such a book would be mind-boggling. I didn't hold it against him; people often forgot that book publishing was a business, not a playground for literary and aesthetic whims. But his next suggestion surprised me.

"You could charge a bomb for the collector's edition." Ferris-Browne displayed remarkable business acuity for a bureaucrat. "And of course the trade edition could be printed anywhere, however you see fit. We're not asking you to lose money."

"I'd be grateful in the extreme, Plumtree," the prime minister declared, leaning forward, looking me directly in the eye. "I wouldn't ask this if it weren't absolutely vital. And I wouldn't ask it if I didn't think . . . well, let's just say it would be to your benefit in the long run."

I knew nothing of the true nature of Ferris-Browne, but I did trust Abercrombie. My father, after all, had held him up as a paragon in the world of politics. So even as I wondered why Abercrombie had faltered in his last sentence, and feeling certain I'd missed vital subtleties, I took a deep breath and said yes.

There was immediate approbation and back-slapping; then both men stood and politely ushered me out. I saw the prime minister move down the corridor with the waiting Nordic giant as Ferris-Browne took me down the stairs and out of the front door. Lunch had been over before it began, gastronomy clearly taking a back seat to efficiency in such dire political days.

"One more thing, Plumtree," Ferris-Browne said as we stood at the kerb. "In the interest of confidentiality, this must never be discussed over the phone. See if you can get some sort of press release out to the papers about it. When I see an article in the paper, I'll know we're on." A warning echoed somewhere in the back of my mind; he was distancing himself, and the PM, from me. Smiling,

Ferris-Browne told a waiting chauffeur in a Bentley to take me back to Bedford Square, and that was that.

Safely ensconced in the luxurious back seat, I had a sinking feeling. What had I done? I fell back on my reliable test: what would my father have said? He had never, to my knowledge, failed to do the right thing, nor had he shirked responsibility. He'd instilled in me a sense of duty that had brought me back from leading sailing holidays in the Mediterranean to run the family publishing company upon his death. As I considered, I knew that my father would have helped his old friend. And he'd have done virtually anything to keep a man like Dexter Moore out of Number Ten.

We'd travelled halfway to the West End before I reached this conclusion. Stabbing a button on the armrest, I spoke to the driver through a speaker system. "Sorry, would it be possible for you to take me to Clerkenwell Green instead?"

I needed to speak to Amanda. She would think I'd lost my mind, but she might appreciate the custom. Small fine-art printers didn't have a licence to print money.

I was deposited at Amanda's doorstep on Clerkenwell Green. Now this "green" was a paved street like any other, but it had been a favoured site for Socialist rallies as far back as the fifteenth century. Amanda met me at the door to her shop, wide-eyed as she watched the PM's Bentley roll away. Such motors rarely made their way into the largely Socialist, though increasingly trendy, world of Clerkenwell.

Her expression demanded an explanation. "It's a long story," I said. "Some day."

"Hmm," she said. "Well, come in. Coffee?" As always Amanda was no-nonsense, assertive, and composed. A blend of businesswoman, artist, and political activist, she was tall and wiry. Her hair hung in a thick copper-coloured plait down her back and she wore her unvarying uniform of a peasant skirt, a gauzy blouse, and a leather waistcoat.

I followed her inside, through a veritable tunnel of printer's cabinets containing her legacy of precious fonts. A pungent wave of heady chemical fumes hit me; the print shop always reeked of solvent and inks.

I saw Amanda's assistant—printer's devil, in the trade—Bruce, running something on the platen press. "Hello, Alex!" he shouted in greeting, while working the treadle. I waved, watching him insert sheets of paper into the slot between bed and platen with impressive speed. He left the sheet of paper there just long enough for the inked type to hit it, then whipped it out, deftly adding it to a pile of printed sheets. Incredible. So impressed was I with Bruce's craftsmanship and obvious fondness for making books that I had long since forgotten to be shocked by his nose ring, pierced eyebrow, and green hair.

The phone rang; Amanda hurried to answer it. As she spoke in curt monosyllables to her caller, I looked round the shop with affection. Walking through Amanda's door was like stepping into the past. As other printers abandoned traditional hand-printing methods for more modern ones, Amanda snapped up their fonts, cabinets, and machinery. Everything she owned was a minimum of fifty years old and coated with more than enough London grime to prove it. Yellowed tray labels lovingly hand-printed with font names from Arrighi to Zapf looked as if they'd been splashed with everything from tea to etching acid in their time, as had the volumes stacked haphazardly atop the cabinets—such riveting tomes as *Printing and the Mind of Man*, *Five Hundred Years of Printing*, and *The Practise of Printing*. For some months now I had been envious of her complete set of *The Fleuron*, seven beautifully printed volumes of essays on the art of printing issued by Stanley Morison and the much-revered Francis Meynell of Nonesuch Press.

Something happened to me every time I set foot in Amanda's shop; the inky smells, the soft *ca-chunk* of the

smooth-running handpress, transported me to the barn at
the Orchard. There my father had lived out his secret
dream of being a printer. I smiled at the thought of that
place, at the image of my father working the treadle of the
smooth-running press with a practised rhythm.

It was in the barn, on a steamy summer's day, that he'd
taught me about the "kiss"—the printer's term for the impression made by metal type into the paper. "The kiss
should be just enough to make an impression, mind you,"
he'd said, eyeing his latest effort from the verso, "never too
heavy." He'd winked at me, knowing that at the tender age
of twelve I was attaching another meaning to his words.
Then of course he'd used the opportunity to educate me
on that other, more important sense of the word "kiss"
and all to which it might lead. In such ways my father had
managed to associate the printed word with life's most vital lessons.

Small wonder I'd ended up a book publisher.

Amanda hung up the phone with a bit of pique. I
joined her at the coffee-making worktop, noticing again
the wooden floors she'd scrubbed until they looked almost
bleached, and the William Morris quotes she'd stencilled
on the walls. Morris, one of the finest printers ever to
grace England's soil, had founded the country's first socialist publishing house practically next door, near the
Marx Library. Amanda had painted the quotations to run
around the room just under the ceiling, in a bold black-
letter Gothic typeface:

> *I really am thinking of turning printer myself in a
> small way. . . . I began printing books with the hope of
> producing some which would have a definite claim to
> beauty . . . books which it would be a pleasure to look
> upon as pieces of printing and arrangement of type. . . .
> Nothing can be a work of art which is not useful; that is to
> say, which does not minister to the body . . . or which does*

*not amuse, soothe, or elevate the mind. . . . That thing
which I understand by real art is the expression by man of
his pleasure in labour. . . . Educate, agitate, organise.*

Amanda poured hot water onto the pile of instant grounds
in each mug and stirred more fiercely than was strictly necessary. I wondered what was wrong; she had yet to speak
since her phone call.

"Amanda," I began, "I've come to see if you'd like to
take on another special edition."

"Really?" she asked, cheering slightly. She sat at her
desk and waved at the extra chair. "What's the book?"

"That's the only drawback; you're not going to like
the book. But the collector's edition will need plenty of
expensive colour plates, and I think we should run it on
the Vandercook, if it's all right with you." She nodded.
Book enthusiasts loved to be able to see where the print
sank into the paper, and her Vandercook proofing press
had an immensely heavy cylinder that made for a nice impression. "I think we'll need to print five hundred or so."

"What's the book?" She eyed me suspiciously.

"Before I tell you, I want you to know there's a good
reason. I wouldn't ask it otherwise. All right?"

"Uh-oh."

"It's Lord Chenies's novel, the one his son, Malcolm
Charford-Cheney, has started to print serially. *Cleansing*."

She blanched. "I see."

"I don't agree with his politics at all, but it'll be a best-
seller. And it is fiction, after all."

"Right." The scepticism in her tone was obvious. But
she sighed and glanced toward yet another grimy machine
in a corner. "You know I can't afford to refuse. I'll use the
monocaster." Amanda's monocaster was a machine that
allowed her to produce her own bits of type. The machine
shot molten lead into moulds, or matrices, then popped
the "sorts," or individual pieces of type, right out. That

way she could make enough type to set an entire signature at once—a signature usually being a group of sixteen pages printed on one sheet—rather than just two pages at a time. Few printers had enough loose type in one font to set an entire book. If Amanda wanted, she could even have someone create matrices for a private font all her own.

"Lovely," I said. "I still need to work out the details, but this needs to be done in a hurry. I'll be happy to pay you a rush fee."

She raised her eyebrows. "How much of a hurry?"

"I need finished books inside of a month."

She nodded grudgingly. "I can do that." The least hint of a smile pulled at one corner of her mouth. "Don't suppose we'll be printing this one with kenaf and soy."

I smiled. Amanda, a serious environmentalist, preferred to work with paper made mostly from a hemp called kenaf—technically *Hibiscus cannabinus*. It destroyed fewer trees than wood pulp-based paper. And soy ink was kinder to the environment than oil-based. We both knew that for those reasons, Lord Chenies, ever opposed to environmentalism, would insist on wood-pulp paper and petroleum-based ink for his special edition. The joke was on him, really; hemp or cotton rag paper would last virtually forever, whereas paper containing wood would yellow and grow brittle relatively quickly. At least Amanda had retained her sense of humour, I thought.

"Done, then." I might have stayed another moment or two to chat, but I sensed that she was troubled, and not just by the thought of printing *Cleansing*. The phone call?

"I'll shoot off. There's work to be done. Thanks for the coffee—ring me with your estimate?" She nodded. Bruce caught my eye and nodded a good-bye, miraculously managing to maintain his paper-shuffling and treadle rhythm at the press.

Amanda saw me to the door. "Thanks for the business, Alex. But next time bring me a good Socialist author." The Clerkenwell boxed set had been much more to her liking.

I smiled. "I don't think so. The boxed set is being nicely balanced by Lord Chenies; but after this, Plumtree Press will remain strictly *apolitical*. Victor Fine and his archenemies at the Conservative League can have it."

"No one's apolitical, Alex—no one."

The grimness of her last words haunted me as I made my way back to Bedford Square. I chose to walk, first along Farringdon Road to Clerkenwell Road, then up the hill to Hatton Garden. Strolling down the street lined with diamond merchants, passing Hasidic Jews in their long dark coats and formal hats, I reflected that it wouldn't be long before I'd need a wedding band for Sarah. August twenty-ninth couldn't come soon enough. I felt a surge of high spirits at the thought of ringing her; it was the high point of every day.

At the moment my fiancée, Sarah Townsend, was skiing as an extra in *Plunge!*, a film featuring her friend Jean-Claude Rimbaud, the star who made the world's fair sex swoon. I wasn't wildly ecstatic over her choice to stay with Rimbaud's film entourage at the Swiss ski resort of Verbier for the filming, especially in these last months before our marriage. But Sarah, having left her position at a European investment bank, worked for Jean-Claude now, managing his private charitable foundation. She insisted that they were nothing more than friends.

I tried not to worry about it . . . too much.

Back at the Press, Lisette teased me mercilessly about what she called my top-secret meeting with Ferris-Browne. But even she was impressed to learn that I'd had lunch with Graeme Abercrombie—at Number Ten. "You're *not serious*!" She made me tell her everything—had I seen the PM's wife? What colour were the carpets? What did we have for lunch? Mineral water? Really? What sort?

I felt uncomfortable *not* confiding in her completely

about the purpose of the meeting; Lisette and her husband, George, had been my closest confidants for years. What's more, I knew she could tell I was keeping something from her. Still, it wasn't strictly necessary to tell her; perhaps the fewer people who knew, the better. As I retreated to my office, she muttered, "I suppose now you are going to be the bloody James Bond of Bedford Square."

Laughing, I tossed over my shoulder, "Guess that makes you Moneypenny."

Lisette's good-natured but colourful abuse followed me back to my door. Too late, I caught my mistake and grimaced. I'd have to be careful joking about Lisette playing Moneypenny to my Bond; things had changed since her husband left in the midst of a raging midlife crisis. He'd signed on for a year with Médecins avec Avions, a group of physicians who flew round the world ministering to the world's ill and impoverished.

Sinking into my desk chair, I thought it was just like George: even in the midst of a reckless midlife crisis, he found a way to help people. Everyone but his own family, that is. A sharp twinge of sadness struck when I thought of his boys, seven and nine. I only hoped they didn't think his tight-lipped departure was somehow their fault. All things considered, Lisette had coped quite well. George had left barely a month after the Stonehams' move to Chorleywood. Since then Lisette and I had grown much closer. I'd felt it necessary to step in to fill the gap with the children, and I drove her to and from work most days. We talked along the way. At least one night a week I had dinner with her and the boys, and I tried to make it to their football games.

At first I'd been merely bewildered by George's abrupt abdication of his responsibilities; lately I'd grown quite peeved with him. It would take some time to get over the fact that he'd deserted me in the year that our pair was going to finish first in the Henley Regatta. We'd trained for years toward that goal, and just when it was within reach, he'd done a bunk. It was still enough to make my blood boil. I hadn't bothered to train at the rowing club since he'd left.

I often wondered if it was right to be this close—this *emotionally* intimate—with my best friend's wife. No doubt Sarah wondered, too, though to her credit she'd never mentioned it. On the other hand, Lisette was, along with Ian Higginbotham, my closest business associate. In my absence, she ran Plumtree Press. Ours was a business relationship; it didn't matter that it was a male-female one. But it wouldn't do to make remarks about Bond and Moneypenny; their relationship depended upon distinctly sexual overtones, even if Bond resolutely failed to act upon them.

Shaking my head at the complexities of life, I resigned myself to the fact that it was time to ring Lord Chenies. I braced myself as I dialled his number. Conversation with his lordship was anything but easy, let alone pleasant.

"Who is it?" he answered, in the gruff, grating voice that so resembled that of the Prince of Wales. The man was a study in perpetual irritation, an impression accentuated by his failure to speak in full sentences.

"Alex Plumtree, m'lord."

A grunt. "Plumtree. Getting on famously with your chum Martyn Blakely. Fine job."

Good heavens! A compliment? From Lord Chenies? My old friend Martyn Blakely had recently been called as vicar of our church, Christ Church Chenies. Lord Chenies lived just through the gate from the church in the story-book fourteen-fireplace Chenies Manor. Evidently Martyn had made an excellent first impression.

"What do you want?" Lord Chenies demanded.

Sadly, I reflected that most people probably called him to ask for something—most likely money.

I decided to meet bluntness in kind; no point beating about the bush. "I want to know if you'll let me publish *Cleansing*, m'lord, with a slipcased collector's edition of five hundred to precede the trade paperback printing." I named what I'd decided was a suitable figure for an advance, though it was ten times the largest I'd ever offered. Beads of sweat broke out on my upper lip at the thought of earning back that much money on a single book. *Cleansing* had jolly well *better* be a best-seller. . . .

Silence. Then, "Malcolm get on to you?"

Fortunately I'd had years of practise breaking his lordship's code. One simply supplied the first word of each sentence, and sometimes the second, for him.

"No."

"Argy-bargy last week. Didn't keep promises publishing Chapter One. Took it back. Never publish another work of mine in his life. Changed my will."

Embarrassed at being privy to the intricacies of his family life, I pondered what to say next. "So, er, contractually, there won't be a problem with Malcolm?"

"Damn well better not be. Told him we're through. Finished. Every sense of the word."

"Right. Well, then. Are you interested in my offer?"

"Yes."

"Good. Mind if I look in with the contracts on my way home tonight?" Startled, I realised I'd acquired his habit. "We'd like to move along fairly quickly. Do you have a copy of the manuscript?"

" 'Course I do. Come for a drink—show you some of my books. Sevenish." Then, before he replaced the receiver, I heard, "Ha! Young Plumtree—my publisher." *Bang.*

"Thank you very much, m'lord," I said to the dead telephone.

Three hours later I stood on his doorstep and rang his bell, glancing at my surroundings appreciatively. Chenies, I reflected, was the perfect rural village, virtually unchanged since the seventeenth century. Cottages surrounded Lord Chenies's manor house and the perfect Chiltern flint church nestled at the manor's gate. A world-renowned inn, the Bedford Arms, sat conveniently near, and the whole village was tucked safely within a wide border of fields—divided, of course, by hedges.

Lord Chenies had achieved notoriety lately for his stance on matters environmental as well as literary. Yesterday the familiar facade of Chenies Manor had adorned the local weekly newspaper accompanied by a story about Lord Chenies ripping out his hedges the day before it became illegal to do so. The *Chorleywood Communicator* had dutifully reported on the local chapter of hedgerow preservation vigilantes, known as Hedges in Transition (HIT), which had taken great offence at Lord Chenies's actions and painted him as the Great Satan. Helena Hotchkiss, a Chorleywood acquaintance of mine and national director of HIT—not to mention the enormously politically correct founder of a rain-forest homeopathic pharmaceuticals firm—had written the venomous article herself. As I stared at the gaping trench where his hedges had been, his lordship opened the door.

"Damn bleeding hearts," he said, following my gaze.

There was no good answer to that greeting; I remained silent. I'd been in the manor house often before, but didn't recall it being so spartan. The air was chilly, and I saw that his lordship wore a heavy woollen cardigan over another jumper. I followed him over threadbare carpeting and into the room where I could tell he lived, the library. We *did* have something in common beyond a mutual listing in the electoral roll of Christ Church Chenies: I lived in my library as well.

"Scotch. Neat," he said, deciding my drink.

"Thanks very much," I said, setting down my briefcase. I decided to leave my coat on.

"Ever seen a polyglot Bible?" He crossed to the bookshelves with his own drink.

"Not in the flesh," I said. "Only facsimiles in—"

"Look at this," he interrupted, not caring one jot *what* I'd seen. What he was passing into my hands stunned me. I put down my tumbler of whisky and took from him one of the great treasures of printing, one of the eight volumes of the *Biblia Sacra* printed by Christophe Plantin of Antwerp from 1569 to 1572. There on the same page were the Hebrew, Chaldaic, Aramaic, Greek, and Latin languages in one of the most beautiful specimens of ecclesiastical literature ever printed.

"Good heavens, m'lord," I breathed. "I never knew you collected."

"Value my privacy."

No sooner had I begun to enjoy the smooth vellum in my hands than he brought over another volume and abruptly removed the Plantin. I felt my eyes widen. This was one of the most coveted books in the world: the Doves Bible. It had been printed by the founder of Doves Press, a man named Cobden-Sanderson. His reputation as one of the finest printers and binders lives on. The Doves Bible was printed in five large quarto volumes, published during the years 1903 to 1905. Quickly, before Lord Chenies could take it from me, I turned to the first chapter of Genesis. There it was, the trademark of Cobden-Sanderson's printing genius: a huge IN THE BEGINNING, stretching across the entire page, with the red initial capital *I* stretching right down to the bottom of the page. Nothing so profoundly elegant had been printed before or since.

In awe of the treasures this gruff lord of the manor possessed, I sat mutely, appreciating the parade of typographic and publishing history he passed through my hands. One of the most astonishing things about his collection was its indication of a love for fine printing. He had some of the finest print specimens in the world. There were *The Four Gospels* from The Golden Cockerel Press in 1931; the Ashendene Dante, 1909; and, most incredible of all, the *Mainz Psalter* by Fust and Schöffer—the audacious pair who'd snatched Gutenberg's press from him as repayment for debt.

Dazed, I watched Lord Chenies replace the volumes on his shelves. I thought I heard him say, "Kept the flame burning for another generation," as he slid them into place. Then I understood, and for a moment even felt a pang of affection for the man. These books—and keeping them carefully preserved—were the elderly lord's way of preserving the faith. As lord of the manor, perhaps he still felt a certain responsibility in that respect—though all that had changed since his boyhood.

But then I felt my stomach twist as he began to pace before his bookshelves, systematically reviling all of the foreigners whose names graced his shelves. "Bloody Krauts," he said, referring to Fust and Schöffer, and their famous associate, Gutenberg. "To think they printed the first Bible. And the blasted Frogs . . . between them, they're plotting to take over the whole of Britain. Damn near succeeding, too, with this EU fiasco. Fought this war fifty years ago; here we are again. Making Roman Catholicism the pan-European religion, too . . . fought that war *five hundred* years ago. . . . And England doesn't even know there's a war on."

Mentally I plugged my ears, not wanting to hear it. But he went on and on, until finally he got round to the Americans. "Bleeding Yanks . . ."

"My lord, you know I'm half Yank myself." *So were Winston Churchill and Harold Macmillan,* I added privately. "But I'll still publish your book if you'll let me."

He looked at me, scowled. "Yes, remember now . . . pater rather stepped out of line there, what?"

I prided myself on not revealing my emotions. Calmly I reached for my briefcase, opened it on my lap, and took out contracts and a pen. I placed them next to my untouched drink on the table, and his lordship signed them. I put my name to them as he finished, leaving one copy with him. Reaching for the thin manuscript box he'd brought to the table, I placed it and the other contracts in my briefcase.

"Specifications for the book in there," his lordship barked. "None of this soy ink, now, and weed paper. One reason Malcolm lost my contract; didn't comply with instructions."

"Thank you," I said, civilly enough, and stood.

"All right, young man. Long line of blue-blooded Plumtrees before you," Chenies said, walking me to his door. "Touch of Colonial blood won't do too much damage. Would've helped if your father had managed a title, though." *Slam.*

I should have torn up the contracts there and then.

As I pulled into the driveway of the Orchard, my beloved home in the Hertfordshire countryside, hedgerow vigilantes swarmed over my rows of greenery. Nearly every day now I found a crowd surveying my medieval hedges. Wendy Dedham and her colleagues trained their recruits to spot really ancient hedges in order to save the historic shrubs, along with their dependent wildlife.

My rows of shrubs were particularly precious to the hedge folk for two reasons: they marked the Hertfordshire-Buckinghamshire county boundary and were therefore historic; and they contained more than seven species of shrub—hazel, elm, hawthorn, dog rose, maple, and damson plum among them—which made them medieval. Both classifications protected them under recently enacted legislation.

A gaggle of two dozen or so near-frozen locals looked up as my car approached. It was nearly dark, and with the sun, the mildness and warmth had gone out of the day. I marvelled at their enthusiasm. Stopping the car at the entrance to the drive, I climbed out and went to have a word. "Evening, Wendy," I said. "Quite an assembly today."

Wendy Dedham looked up at me, shining with righteous enthusiasm in her headscarf, long print skirt, and pea-green wellies. "Yes, thanks, Alex, isn't it? Hedges in Transition is going from strength to strength. Fifty members now, in Chorleywood alone! And we've nearly the entire lot of protected hedges in the town plotted on our maps, and registered."

"Remarkable."

"It's really very good of you to let us trespass on your property like this—it's most useful to be able to show the new recruits all seven species here. You can't imagine some of the rudeness we've encountered from other landowners. I hope you don't mind."

"Delighted to be of help. I never could have imagined our hedges would be the source of such excitement."

Wendy giggled and waved as I went back to my car and zoomed off up the drive.

All the same, I was secretly relieved that I didn't have to entertain them all. When they came on Saturdays, I brought out the vacuum flasks of coffee and my biscuit tin. If I didn't watch out, I'd soon be as reclusive as Lord Chenies. I scrambled a few eggs and threw in some ham, onion, and cheese. Picking up the phone, I placed a quick call to my brother as I sat at the table.

"Max. It's Alex." Max used to write full-time for the *Watch*, the paper favoured by Labourites, but he'd left that frenetic world. Now he enjoyed a life of sobriety, herb tea, marriage, and rare-book dealing. When something in current events interested him, however, Max enjoyed keeping his hand in with a bit of freelance copy.

Unfortunately, his brother—yours truly—was all too often the one *making* news.

"Hullo! What's up?" I told him about my little effort for the prime minister's re-election. Max asked a few questions and said he'd enjoy putting the story together. "Thanks, Alex—I'll let you know when I get it written."

I'd fulfilled my obligation to let Ferris-Browne know that we were on. Placing Lord Chenies's manuscript in front of me, I ate with my right hand and turned pages with the left. The first chapter was all too familiar; but as I moved through the novel, I saw that it had been judged unfairly. Yes, the fatal "wilding"—a horrible American term for a group attack mainly for the attackers' pleasure—committed against a foreigner and a poor homeless London urchin had been unforgivable. It was tragic that this form of violence had travelled across the Atlantic; despicable that the word "wilding" had been introduced into our vocabulary. But the rest of the book was a portrait of an aristocratic family losing everything it had.

When the fictional family's patriarch died, his extended family was forced to sell the manor house, stables, sterling, ancestral paintings, everything—to pay crippling estate taxes. The family's youngest teenage boy could not understand this, and his father made the mistake of lamenting that they were losing everything to support a lot of undeserving people on the dole who'd never worked a day in their lives. The boy heard this, and in desperation lashed out against the people he, in an adolescent fog of emotion, held responsible.

The story of the tax- or otherwise-motivated destruction of the wealth and property of England's richest families was an old one; Lord Chenies had made the mistake of trying to tell it in a year of unprecedented friction between Liberal and Conservative, thanks to the EU debate. And with the wilding in the first chapter he'd whipped people's emotions into a frenzy. Good artistry, I thought; bad judgement.

As I patted the manuscript back into a fat pile and looped elastic bands round it, I reflected that I wasn't quite so ashamed to be publishing *Cleansing* now that I knew the full story. Only after reading the entire novel had I come to realise that the title referred to government policies cleansing Britain of its upper class, and not to cleansing Britain of foreigners.

I just hoped the rest of Great Britain would be open-minded enough to read the book and come to the same conclusion.

CHAPTER TWO

———◆———

Learning hath gained most by those books by which the printers have lost.

THOMAS FULLER, *Of Books*

ONE WEEK LATER, I AWOKE WITH A SENSE OF ANTICIPA-
tion and gritty eyes. Seven o'clock . . .

Anticipation finally triumphed over fatigue, and I got
myself moving downstairs. Throwing open the front
door, I found that the Davies boy had flung my copy of
the *Tempus* into the lamp above the door. Shards of expensive handblown glass littered the granite step. Last week
the bird's nest; this week the lamp.

Muttering, I plucked the newspaper out of the broken
glass, careful not to step in it with my bare feet. There it
was on page three: a brief article proclaimed to the world
that Plumtree Press was publishing *Cleansing*, the eleventh
novel by literary lion Nigel Charford-Cheney, Lord Chenies. Max had finally got the article written a week after
I'd told him about it—never the promptest, our Max—
but I was grateful he'd got the job done. He told me he expected it to run in the *Watch* this morning, but I'd hardly
hoped to see it scooped by the *Tempus* on the same day. I
wondered how they obtained their nuggets of news from

competing papers. Moles? Bugged phone lines? Powerful remote cameras? The stuff of James Bond again.

While I got the all-important coffee brewing, I reflected with satisfaction that Guy Ferris-Browne would see the article and know that our little project was off the ground. Lord Chenies would see it, too, and be impressed with the publicity he was getting . . . I hoped.

Coffee in hand, I shuffled off toward the shower. The newly hired editor of Plumtree Press Trade Editions, Nicola Beauchamp, was to start today. I didn't want to be late.

I was halfway up the stairs when Ian blew in the door wearing his jogging clothes, looking flushed and full of high spirits. He saw me and lifted a hand in greeting. It was a comfort to have Ian Higginbotham, my surrogate father and head academic editor, staying with me temporarily. His home near Bedford Square was undergoing some much-needed structural repairs, which he ascribed to the continual thundering of traffic down nearby Gower Street.

Ian, a gaunt, perpetually tanned man past his seventieth year, began his post-run push-ups. I loved Ian as I'd loved my father. I well knew why he and my father had been friends for life, and why my father had trusted Ian with running the day-to-day operations of Plumtree Press so many years ago.

As I sipped my coffee, I watched him do fifty push-ups and wondered what Ian would have done if Graeme Abercrombie had asked him to publish *Cleansing*. Ian was a man who never denied that there was a difference between right and wrong. He further knew that doing the right thing often entailed a significant cost. For Ian this way of life embraced business issues as well as personal ones, which made him a hero in my eyes.

He had suffered immense losses over the years, including the death of his wife mere years after their marriage, decades of separation from his daughter, and the loss of his best friend—my father. Yet he'd been the rock upon which Plumtree Press prevailed, especially since my father's death. He'd kept the Press ticking over profitably since then, but he'd let me feel that the success and growth of the business was entirely my doing.

One of the happier surprises to manifest itself in recent years was Ian's relationship to my fiancée, Sarah Townsend. Through circumstances too complicated and harrowing to repeat, I'd learned two years ago that Ian was Sarah's grandfather. The daughter Ian thought he'd lost to the blitz had actually been sent to America with a boatload of child refugees, and safely adopted by an American family in Massachusetts. Ian's daughter, Elizabeth, was Sarah's mother. So Ian was family to both Sarah and me. We'd shared many a late-night Indian takeaway at the Press—always vegetarian for him—with endless conversations on ethical, moral, religious, and a multitude of other topics.

I'd also learned that he was almost certainly the anonymous, unsolicited author who had brought my newborn trade division its first two national best-sellers.

But Ian was more than these things: he was my conscience.

"Good run?" I asked.

"Wonderful," he panted. "Makes the whole day worthwhile."

"We're in the paper," I said, nodding toward the kitchen. I'd purposely kept from him news of my arrangement with Ferris-Browne and the PM; I still felt slightly uncomfortable about it all.

"Oh?"

I anticipated a look of wonder on his face when I told him I'd had lunch with the prime minister and Ferris-Browne. Instead I got concern.

"Why?" he asked, mopping his face with the towel round his neck, frowning.

The frown irritated me. I suppose I'd wanted him to

fall over himself with excitement and delight on my behalf.

Ian would have to be the exception to the rule; I needed to tell him exactly why I was publishing Lord Chenies's novel. "They want me to publish *Cleansing*. They want it to sway public opinion away from Dexter Moore. The arrangement is absolutely confidential, of course."

Ian was a master at keeping his feelings to himself. "Do you want it on your trade list?"

"No. But I've read the entire manuscript; it's not at all the hate-crimes book the first chapter would indicate. It's more about the decline of the upper class than about galvanising hatred against foreigners. . . . Besides, I do want to help Graeme Abercrombie hang on against Dexter Moore." I watched him for a response but got only a level gaze; his piercing blue laser-beam eyes finally forced me to blink.

Carrying on shamelessly with my rationalisation, I said, "There's the business angle, too: our balance sheet can certainly use a best-seller. As a publishing decision, it's sound. And you must admit, Ian, whatever his politics, Nigel Charford-Cheney will move us into a completely different literary stratum."

Ian remained silent. That was his technique. I used to think he did it to frustrate me, but now I knew that he resolutely refused to give unsolicited advice. If I asked him what he thought, he'd tell me.

Did I want to know?

I bit the bullet. "Do you think I made a mistake?"

"Politics and literature are bad bedfellows, Alex. Things get very messy indeed in politics, though I do admire Graeme Abercrombie. Your father thought very highly of him, you know, worked with him quite closely. He's a personal friend of mine as well. Still, you know what things are like at the moment, politically. I hate to see you embroiled in it."

That was it; no reprimands, no "I-wish-you'd-asked-me's."

"Off to the shower?" he asked.

"Mmm. Nicola starts today; don't want to be late."

"Oh, right," he said, remembering. "By the way, would you like to come to my book group meeting tonight at the Athenaeum? It's excellent company, and you should come sometime—you'd enjoy it."

"I'd like to, Ian, but I've that *Talkabout* interview on TV tonight. Thanks anyway." Ian was forever inviting me to join his book group, which met at one of London's most exclusive clubs, but I never seemed to have the time.

"Maybe next month," he said good-naturedly, ambling off toward the kitchen. "I'm glad Nicola's coming on board. You certainly found a winner there."

And so I had, I thought later that day, as Nicola and I walked back from Amanda's Print Shop. I couldn't help but be troubled by what we'd just learned at Amanda's: the printer claimed she'd sent proofs of *Cleansing* three days earlier. But I'd never received them at the Press. Nicola and I had waited while Amanda asked Bruce to have copies made of the originals—only to discover that her *original* set of *Cleansing* proofs had somehow gone astray, too. "I'll have to run new ones and send them over this afternoon," she'd sighed.

I tried to brush off the feeling of disaster that came with every discussion of *Cleansing*. Poor Nicola—it wasn't fair for her to be saddled with a book like this, right from the start.

"All right," I teased her now as we strolled down Clerkenwell Green. "Here's one that might stump you. What, I ask you, is the literary significance of the Farringdon Road bookstalls?"

It was a deceptively balmy March day, and I'd suggested we stop at the Farringdon Road book carts on our way back to Bloomsbury. There was no telling what rare treasure of an old book might wait for us in that ramshackle collection—if there was a cart there today. The book carts had almost become a thing of the past, but if you were lucky you could sometimes find one.

Nicola smiled at me, brown eyes narrowed, ever in control. Her French knot of glossy dark hair only accentuated the impression. Since I'd interviewed her for the job a month ago, I'd been stunned not only by her knowledge of literature but by her poise.

"Alex. Surely you don't think I'd apply for a job in Bedford Square—let alone with the leading publisher of literary anthologies—without having read my Dickens?"

Nicola was twenty-eight, ex-editor of a literary magazine, and never caught off guard. I was thirty-four, a book publisher, her employer—and all too frequently caught off guard. I was incredibly fortunate to have hired her; from our first meeting it was clear that she was the product of the best of families and schools. Her discretion and tact were exceeded only by the Queen's.

"Oliver Twist was set up by the Artful Dodger," Nicola went on, "who had stolen the wallet of a Mr. Brownlow as he browsed in the Farrington Road bookstalls. Clerkenwell was the site of Fagin's den, as I recall."

"Bravo!" I was going to have trouble keeping up with her. "Dickens would never recognise the street now. I read the other day that houses here go for more than three hundred thousand pounds—evidently it's the latest yuppie haunt."

Clerkenwell had, indeed, a varied and colourful past. It had enjoyed centuries of ecclesiastical splendour as the home of the Order of the Hospital of St. James of Jerusalem, a monastic order established in 1113. The Knights of St. James, or the Knights Hospitaller, crusaded in the Holy Land with the Knights Templar. The priory's clerks held plays at the Order's well, and soon the area became known as Clerkenwell. But in the nineteenth century the area slid into infamy as the home of London's worst thieves, jails, and slums. Over the last decade it had enjoyed one of those renewals that sometimes take a neighbourhood by surprise, and now housed trendy, pricey shops. The Clerkenwell Neighbourhood Association had provided grants to artisans like Amanda to repopulate the area with the arts and crafts of its past; it had once been a printing and publishing centre, and a number of magazines and newspapers still had their offices there.

As we arrived at the huge wooden book cart, which had undoubtedly been drawn into Farringdon Road by horsepower at some point in its history, I couldn't help but notice the way Nicola caught the eye of every passing male. Journalists walking from the nearby *Watch* newspaper offices to the Farringdon tube station couldn't resist a glance at the well-sculpted leg muscles rising out of her high heels, and then did a double take to absorb fully the wonder of her upper half, which was loosely cloaked in an expensive-looking taupe linen suit. I wondered how they'd react if they knew that her appearance was excelled only by her mind.

Nicola delicately touched the spines of several books on the cart, then plucked one out. *"Riceyman Steps!"* she exclaimed. "By Arnold Bennett. I haven't seen this about anywhere recently." I looked at her, my own rare find for Plumtree Press, and saw the intent, wistful faces of men passing behind her on the pavement as she spoke.

Nicola exclaimed, "This novel was set here in Clerkenwell, you know—1928."

"'No moss on you." I laughed, shaking my head. "I thought Plumtree Press employees were the only people who'd heard of *Riceyman Steps.*"

She looked at me curiously. "Why's that?"

"Nicola, you must admit it's one of the world's more obscure novels. The only reason I've ever heard of it is that we were asked to publish several commemorative editions of Clerkenwell-based works—*Riceyman Steps* being one of them—in honour of the Clerkenwell Neighbourhood Association Fête next month. The books are already in the shops; they're doing a world of good for Clerkenwell. Didn't I tell you about the boxed set?"

She shook her head.

"*Riceyman Steps, Oliver Twist,* and *William Morris: Writings from Clerkenwell.*"

Nicola's face lit up. "Really? But what does William Morris have to do with Clerkenwell? He was a printer, I know, and designer, but—"

"Aha! Finally, something you don't know. You can't imagine my relief." I pointed up the road behind us. "Just up there, across from Amanda's Print Shop, is the Marx Memorial Library. But before its incarnation as a library, it was the first Socialist publishing house—founded by William Morris. He published *Commonweal* there, the newsletter of the Socialist Party."

She raised her eyebrows, and with a "Well, well," turned her bright gaze away from me, back to the book. "I'll buy it," she said, flipping open the weathered cover to check for a pencilled price inside. "Just for the privilege of reading it from yellowed paper."

"I'll give you a boxed set, too, when we get back to the Press. Amanda did a fine job on it."

Nicola's smile of thanks was lighting up the vicinity when I was startled by the pounding of running feet on the pavement behind us. I wheeled at the same instant that a winded young black man, who was looking over his shoulder, crashed into Nicola and me. *Riceyman Steps* flew into the carbon monoxide cloud over Farringdon Road, and my tailbone slammed into the base of the book cart.

For the next few moments I seemed to see through a

lens that translated events into slow motion. I caught a glimpse of the boy's dreadlocks as he fell; saw him grasp the strap of Nicola's shoulder bag and hang from it, desperate to recover his balance. Nicola, off-balance from his impact, tumbled over backwards, graceful arms flailing. I heard her head *thunk* ominously into the edge of the book cart.

The boy crouched next to me for a fraction of a second. He cast a panicked glance in the direction he'd come. Breathing hard, he looked up at me. His eyes were blank with terror.

The next moment he scrambled under the book cart, then disappeared into the chockablock traffic on Farringdon Road.

The world miraculously emerged from behind the slow-motion lens and returned to normal speed.

"Hey!" I called angrily, catching a glimpse of the boy's fleeing form as he darted between the cars. As the shout resounded, people turned to look.

Nicola. Momentarily torn between helping her and chasing after the boy, who was already halfway across the busy road, I recalled the thud of her head against the cart and opted for Nicola. But I stopped short again as a pack of half a dozen urchins raced past, issuing catcalls and obviously chasing the terror-stricken boy. As their leering faces flew past, one caught my eye. He looked familiar—a blond, blue-eyed version of an adult I knew. By this time their quarry was making a getaway up Clerkenwell Road opposite us, having somehow made it alive through the onrushing cars.

"Nicola!"

Her face was in shadow beneath the cart. I put one hand under each well-tailored arm, gently lifting her up and out from underneath the cart, into a standing position.

"Are you hurt?"

"No, I'm fine," she murmured softly. Still, I kept an

arm around her; she looked exceedingly pale. The next moment her legs buckled and she sagged. "Sorry, sorry," she said weakly, as I supported her, as if the spirit were willing but not so the flesh. "I . . . " To my horror, she went limp.

"Dear God," I breathed, gently letting her down onto the pavement. I rolled up my jacket and shoved it under her head as a makeshift pillow, pulled out my cell phone and punched 999. The answer was immediate. "I need an ambulance in Farringdon Road, Clerkenwell, just north of the *Watch* newspaper offices."

Once again I'd endangered someone near me. It seemed to happen all too often as I went about my business at the Press—not at all what I'd expected when I agreed to run my father's sedate academic publishing business.

By this time the great British public was reacting to the disturbance—in an orderly manner, of course. The bookstand owner came at a run. Someone had flagged down a police car and was directing constables up Clerkenwell Road after the boys. I saw someone with a notepad approach, his step quickening as he drew near. Of course. It was nearly noon. Journalists employed by the *Watch* just up Farringdon Road were on their way to the City Pride for an early liquid lunch.

Another police constable knelt next to me, studying Nicola's inert form. Reaching for his radio, he said, "I'll get an ambulance, shall I?"

"I've done it. Thanks."

"What happened here?" the constable asked. Indignant bystanders related the story to both the policeman and the journalist. They told the story with a twist, claiming that the first boy had attacked Nicola for her handbag—they'd seen him clinging to it—and then run off.

A bystander pointed at me. "He—yeah, the one in the

white shirt—he yelled, and the bloke scarpered. But by that time a pack of boys chased after him, up there." More fingers, pointing up Clerkenwell Road opposite.

The constable radioed this information to his colleagues. Nicola's eyes fluttered, then opened. She blinked, then seemed to grasp what had happened.

"It's all right," I assured her. "Don't worry. You got quite a bang on the head." Even as I said it, I was aware that the bystanders had told the wrong story; the young black boy hadn't attacked Nicola. In fact, his grab at her handbag hadn't been deliberate.

I brushed a wisp of hair off my new employee's pallid face. The journalist chose that moment to approach; I felt myself stiffen. The Fourth Estate had proved to be far from friendly in the past.

"If I could have your name please—I just need you to answer a few questions for me."

The young journalist was trying the oldest trick in the book. He wanted to establish himself as an official on the scene, to make me think he deserved my cooperation. But I knew better. Max had been with this journalist's paper for years. He'd told me all the tricks.

"None of your business," I mumbled, wishing—all the while doubting—that he'd take the cue and bugger off.

"Pardon me?"

As he bent down to get a closer look at Nicola, I let my irritation get the better of me. How *dare* he capitalise on her injury? I stood abruptly and—how frightfully clumsy of me—knocked him right over.

"Oy!" he exclaimed, in high dudgeon. "Mind who you're . . . " Picking himself up, he began to dust himself off, then caught my eye. I was not effusive with my apologies. He stopped and glared at me.

"You'll be sorry for that," he said quietly, forefinger in my face. The threat of unflattering journalistic coverage went unspoken as he stalked off to find more cooperative witnesses.

Some time later, as the paramedics urged an ambulatory but embarrassed Nicola into the ambulance with them "just for a check," I heard my name spoken. I turned to see a bystander speaking to the sneering journalist. The writer caught my eye again and held it as he smirked. "Alex Plumtree. Right. Heard of him, have you?"

Sighing, I turned away. My face had been in the papers too many times since I'd been with Plumtree Press. I couldn't seem to avoid it. First it was success over an unsolicited anonymous manuscript that made the Press, and me, news. Then a Plumtree Press author uncovered a shocking secret about one of Britain's most revered novelists. Suffice to say that it's been one thing after another.

At least this time they had nothing bad to say about me, justified or not.

But there I was wrong.

If I thought the afternoon was eventful, it was a doddle compared to the evening.

Having seen a mildly concussed Nicola safely home to Sloane Square by taxi, I asked the driver to take me to the BBC Studio at White City in West London. Our publicist, informed last week of our contract with the famous Lord Chenies, had promptly got him on one of the early-evening chat shows. She'd rung me after receiving a firm *"No public appearances!"* from the grumpy aristocrat. Actually, I knew about his lordship's reclusiveness; it was well known in the book world that he never appeared at signings or spoke in public. "Will you do it, Alex?" she begged. "It's the *top show—Talkabout*, with Mimi Reed."

I'd agreed, knowing full well what would happen. I might be publicly skewered for publishing the book, but at least it would give me a chance to attract more attention for the PM's purposes, and also to tell the truth about the book—the *real* cleansing to which its title referred. I began to hope that I might have my cake and eat it.

Mimi, BBC Two's engaging host, had provided scant information on the upcoming evening. All I knew was that she'd invited five of us for an intimate little tête-à-tête on her prime-time programme. In a set-up certain to draw blood, I would be facing the distraught parents of two children killed during a wilding crime—the bizarre and disturbing form of violence that had drifted across the Atlantic last year. I decided Lord Chenies was frightfully clever not to make public appearances. Perhaps someday I'd adopt that rule myself.

At times a still small voice said from within: this is *fiction. Art.* Doesn't everyone have the right to produce a work of art? I remembered a case in America, in which an artist funded by the National Endowment for the Arts exhibited an image of someone urinating on Jesus Christ. It was displayed in a prominent gallery. It was art; it was therefore *sacred*—more sacred to the visual arts community, evidently, than was its subject.

Both sets of parents refused to acknowledge my presence in the studio as the make-up people crawled over us, blotting powder on our faces. "Three, two, one," a cameraman said from behind his gear, then pointed at Mimi with a flourish.

"Good evening, and welcome to *Talkabout*." Our host had an engaging habit of crossing her long legs and leaning toward the camera as she uttered her opening greeting. A slight overbite gave her a homegrown look. She wore a silk blouse the colour of autumn wheat, which blended perfectly with her shiny, blunt-cut hair of precisely the same shade. Only someone with strong good looks could get away with such a subtle colour scheme.

"Tonight I have with me Alex Plumtree, publisher of Nigel Charford-Cheney's controversial new novel,

Cleansing." I nodded at her civilly but seriously. I knew what was coming.

". . . and the parents of the two teenagers killed last year in the famous *U* case, Mr. and Mrs. Gupta and Mr. and Mrs. Finch." Here Mimi looked with limpid eyes first at the parents, then into the camera. She dropped her voice. "Few of us will ever forget the night on which two boys from one of Britain's finest public schools murdered Nicky Finch and Rajahandra Gupta for the sole reason that they were not *U*, or upper-class." Mimi closed her eyes and shook her head to express her revulsion at the thought.

Mr. and Mrs. Gupta looked dangerously impassive, while the Finches held hands as if their lives depended on it. Mrs. Finch's lower lip quivered ominously.

"Alex," Mimi said, turning suddenly toward me. "How do you feel about publishing a book that condones the supposed 'cleansing' of foreigners and lower classes from England's population?"

Mimi had no choice but to engineer a confrontation; it was exactly what I'd have done in her position. Which, I thought, would be a good deal less traumatic than mine at the moment. I'd carefully prepared my answer to her question. I certainly couldn't tell her that I was publishing *Cleansing* as a favour to the nation's two most powerful men.

"Mimi, first I want to say that I am repelled and outraged by the *U* wilding." The Guptas and the Finches steadfastly refused to look at me. "The thought that this sort of violence has come to our country is appalling, and I agree with the Home secretary that the severest of punishments must be administered to prevent further violent crime."

The set was hushed. Even the cameramen seemed to hold their breath at the tension in the air. Mimi gave me her most cynical look.

Gently, firmly, I continued. "At the same time, unless

we are to introduce censorship and resort to book-burning, we must allow people to write and to be published. The decline in the fortunes of England's upper classes in the late twentieth century is not an invalid background for fiction—and I would emphasise that this is fiction."

The Guptas turned angry stares at me, as if I'd flipped a switch. Here we go, I thought.

"What's more, I see Lord Chenies's book as the strongest possible indictment of the U wilding and the hatred that inspired it. Far from condoning such behaviour, *Cleansing* is a tragic, ironic exposé—the strongest possible criticism. If you read the novel, you'll find that Lord Chenies is discussing the cleansing of the wealthy *upper class* from Britain, and not the racial cleansing the public has inferred from only Chapter One."

What I didn't share with the audience was that the author, his lordship, Nigel Obnoxious Charford-Cheney, did not share my attitude. I now knew for a fact that he despised all but the upper crust of England's society and secretly wished that he personally could do away with the rest.

"You—*you*, in your bespoke suit"—Mr. Gupta sneered at my grey woollen jacket—"are going to make money off my son's death. And you are giving this monster Charford-Cheney a voice!"

His heavily accented English took considerable effort to follow, but I understood him all too well. Gupta leaned forward in his chair threateningly, stabbing a finger at me. "How *dare* you pretend this book was written as an exposé? You know that man would have killed my son himself, if he could have."

Tears coursed down his wife's cheeks, dripping from her face onto her brown sari. The studio monitors revealed that the camera had zoomed in on her. She ignored the thoughtfully placed box of tissues at her elbow.

In her best TV anchor-woman style, Mimi restated Mr. Gupta's comments for those in the audience who hadn't been able to cut through the accent. "So you feel, Mr. Gupta, that *Cleansing* isn't ironic at all—that it is not only exploiting your son's death but *encouraging* race and class hatred?"

Gupta nodded bitterly, aware and resentful of the fact that she had to translate for him. Mimi turned to the Finches. I could see the pleasure beneath her earnest expression. This interview was igniting just as she had hoped.

"Mrs. Finch? Mr. Finch? How do you feel about this?"

"I'll tell you 'ow I feel." Mr. Finch's London accent was as strong as Mr. Gupta's Indian one. His "I think" came out as "oy fink." "I think some of us as keeps gettin' trod on ought to rise up and tread on them for a change." When he said "them"—or, rather, "vem"—he bent his head sharply and obliquely in my direction.

Marvellous, I thought. I had accepted the fact that I was that evening's sacrifice to the gods of chat-show entertainment. But now I was to be the victim of a revenge wilding, in Studio Number Two at the BBC.

Mrs. Finch gripped her husband's hand more tightly and gave him a worried look, as if she'd heard this before and wished he hadn't said it on the telly.

At that inopportune moment someone passed Mimi a slip of paper. I knew this was for the viewers' benefit—the "you're witnessing fast-breaking news" effect—because she had an earpiece they could jolly well have used to breathe a word or two into her cunning ear. A few moments before, I'd seen some emotion pass over her face—thirst for blood, I'd be willing to wager. What were her producers telling her through that twisty cord they'd hidden so discreetly in her glossy hair?

"We've just received word," Mimi announced, doing her best to look discomfited, "there's been another wilding this evening." To my horror, she turned to me with the thrill of the hunt in her eyes. "Alex Plumtree. You were the

last person known to see this boy—Mmbasi Kumba—
alive, on Farringdon Road. You accused him of assault,
and . . ."

Her voice faded out as I grasped the import of her
words. But it couldn't be. The boy with the terrified eyes
who'd run into us so innocently at the book cart—he was
dead?

I remembered the crowd of boys pursuing him—
remembered their fair skin and hair against his darkness—and that terrible blind panic in his eyes. How could
I have been so stupid? How could I have let him run to his
death?

What were the odds that *I*, the publisher of a controversial novel including wildings, should have been the last
to see this boy alive before he was dead from the same
crime committed in the novel?

"Alex?" Mimi's eyes were hawklike. Three of the four
parents stared at me with incredulity and utter hate; Mr.
Finch looked as if he'd expected just this sort of thing to
happen, his head bobbing up and down as if Mimi had
just proved his point.

I realised that she had been prompting me for a response, as I sat stunned by the disastrous turn of events.

"Yes," I said. "And no." I hoped and prayed that I
would get it right. "I did see a boy who might have been
Mmbasi Kumba this afternoon. I was looking at a book in
Farringdon Road, at a book cart—" I hesitated here as the
similarity to *Oliver Twist* struck me.

Not again, I thought. More often than I liked, I found
myself living out bits of classic literature—always with disastrous consequences. I've come to think of it as a cosmic
joke on me as a book publisher—one that could only have
been engineered by the Senior Editor in the Sky.

"He ran into me—us—and was obviously on the
run," I continued. "Of course, I didn't know why. He
looked frightened. A journalist at the scene was trying to

make it look as if the boy had robbed my employee, but he'd merely fallen against her handbag and accidentally knocked her over.

"The last I knew," I continued, "a group of boys had chased this boy up Clerkenwell Road, toward Hatton Garden, and the police were searching in that direction. I told the police what had happened, that he hadn't stolen anything after all."

"Did you set the boys on him?" Mimi's eyes shone.

"*Set* them . . . ?" Seething with rage, I struggled for calm. "Mimi, I just told you. I was looking at books when he literally *ran into us.* The other boys ran past *after* he knocked down my associate. I'd never seen them, or Mmbasi Kumba, before in my life." As I said it, I was aware that I lied; I had recognised the one blond, blue-eyed boy, though I couldn't place him.

"Right." With a sceptical glance at the camera, Mimi managed to sound as if she and the rest of Britain had a secret. They knew the real truth: I had incited a wilding.

There was very little time to set the record straight, I sensed, before events took on a life of their own. Inspiration came to me in the next instant: put the onus of responsibility on her.

I said, "Mimi, you're a responsible journalist. Why don't you read us the police report?"

Her eyes widened. Before she could quite recover, I seized the opportunity to continue. "You wouldn't put something like this on television without checking the *facts* first."

Her nod to me was a study of condescension. Her advisors on the other end of the earpiece had her moving in the right direction. I should have known better than to think I could outwit a seasoned performer—and her staff of spin doctors and barristers.

"Of course, attempting to discredit me probably seems your best defence." Mimi smiled a superior smile, secure in the knowledge that the BBC's legal experts, experienced in this sort of thing, were better than mine. "But, Alex, you must admit it seems rather odd that you should have been involved in the Clerkenwell wilding, given the book you're publishing."

There it was, the sound bite. She'd made history, given it the name I would hear for years to come: the Clerkenwell wilding.

"Of all the people Mmbasi Kumba could have *run into*"—she made the words sound wildly improbable—"it was you. The publisher of *Cleansing*."

She let the Finches and the Guptas have another go at me, then, mercifully, was out of time. Fully aware that she'd done me an injustice, Mimi pretended to be very busy preparing for her next segment. Her producer and director and their assistants closed ranks round her, and she steadfastly refused to look at me as I stood to leave. The parents were surrounded by studio personnel offering them hospitality and sympathy, and I found my way out of the studio alone, a living embodiment of the word "pariah."

CHAPTER THREE

———◦§§§◦———

The stupendous Fourth Estate, whose wide world-embracing influences what eye can take in?

THOMAS CARLYLE, ON *Boswell's Life of Johnson*

INDULGING IN A RARE BATH OF SELF-PITY, I WANDERED out of the studio and down the hallway to the exit. Oddly enough, I felt I deserved the parents' hatred. I *did* feel guilty about publishing Nigel Charford-Cheney's book, and now I felt responsible for the Kumba boy's death as well. What quirk of fate had put me in his path that day?

Lost in thought, I didn't notice an acquaintance approaching until we were practically on top of one another. "Hullo, Plumtree," he said cheerfully, oblivious to the hell I'd just endured. I looked up, startled, and saw that it was Richard Hotchkiss, road construction baron, London Water Board president, and fellow Old Boy from Merchant Taylors School. With horror it occurred to me that if Mimi's camera people caught me with Hotchkiss, I'd be mincemeat, for the illustrious Hotchkiss just happened to be head of the Chorleywood Conservative Association.

"What're you doing here?" he asked. "Your hedges again?" Hotchkiss beamed at me, the quintessence of success. His good-looking face fairly shone with it, greatly enhanced by vivid hazel eyes and a positively presidential navy-blue suit. He radiated authority, wealth, and power. I remembered that power well from the days when I'd dated his daughter, Helena. Fear was an emotion I'd had to wrestle with every time I'd fetched Helena for a date.

I reminded myself that I was now an adult and every bit this man's equal. I was also well aware that Hotchkiss, as head of the Chorleywood Conservative Association, knew Lord Chenies well. I couldn't bear to re-air the whole issue so recently after my crucifixion by Mimi.

With an effort, I remembered that Hotchkiss had asked me a question. What was I doing there?

"If only it *were* the hedgerow vigilantes again—I don't mind them." It was Hotchkiss's daughter who had made hedges the battle cry of the politically and environmentally correct. As a prominent pharmaceuticals entrepreneur, she'd become an outspoken advocate for national environmental causes. Helena Hotchkiss was also politically correct in that her medicines came directly from the long-neglected plants of the rain forest. Ten percent of all Helena's Nature's Chemist corporate profits went toward saving that beleaguered habitat.

"No, I'm afraid it's Lord Chenies's novel. It's all . . . a bit awkward." I hoped he'd take the hint and not pursue the subject.

"Ah, yes. I read in the paper that you're publishing his next best-seller. That's our Nigel, stirring the pot again." To my surprise, Hotchkiss laughed. "Well, I'm here on a rather inconvenient little errand myself." He shot his left cuff with power and grace and glanced at his watch. "The London Water Company. You know." He wrinkled his nose.

"Ah. Yes, I see." As the Guptas and Finches marched down the hall toward us like enemy troops, I flattened myself against the wall. As it happened, three of the four parents passed with a pointed lack of acknowledgement. Finch alone shot me a look that could kill.

Hotchkiss widened his eyes at me briefly, in acknowl-edgement of their undisguised hatred, and I realised that he'd experienced just the same thing in his own way. Hotchkiss was in the hot-seat, too, politically. Britain had, in fact, endured something of a water crisis over the last couple of years. Hotchkiss, as a vocal member of the board of London Water, had turned out to be their spokesman and had dealt with much of the public's wrath.

The fracas was about a water shortage. The public perception was that London Water was pumping the stuff fast and furiously, despite the shortage, all the while charging an arm and a leg for it. But they never invested in the infrastructure to avoid future shortfalls. And there was no ignoring the massive profits of London Water and its sister companies. It was yet another issue Labour and the Socialists could point to and say, "See, the Tories were wrong to privatise our public industries."

"Well, I'd best be off to meet the lions." He smiled again, in remarkably good spirits, I thought, considering what he was about to face. Maybe one grew accustomed to public humiliation. "See you at the County Boundary Committee meeting—Wednesday night, right?"

"Right—yes," I said. Quite honestly, I'd forgotten all about it.

"Illegitimi non carborundum," Hotchkiss murmured in my ear before departing.

His conspiratorial air—as if he and I were in it against "them"—was startling. Perhaps he was more than the moderate Conservative I'd taken him for, and was of one mind with Nigel Charford-Cheney. Perhaps he thought I was a flaming ultra-Conservative, like my author. . . .

The possibility was too awful to contemplate. I checked my watch—seven o'clock—and trudged outside for a taxi. I had yet to retrieve my car from its parking place on Bedford Square. Had I not been an object of national hatred, someone at the BBC might have been willing to phone for a taxi on my behalf. Mimi had not offered so much as a thank-you for the sacrifice of my reputation on her show, let alone offered to help with such minor inconveniences as transport.

Two taxis sped past my outstretched arm without slowing. They, too, must have seen *Talkabout*, I thought. Did they all have dash-mounted televisions in the new taxis? I told myself it was my imagination as a third, then a fourth available vehicle cruised past.

I'd become almost paranoid when one finally stopped, switching off his yellow light. I slumped into the back seat. "Bedford Square, please. Number 52." Just saying the words brought comfort. Even in bleakest March, in the midst of embarrassment on BBC Two, I loved our offices on the edge of Bloomsbury. They were newly expanded and remodelled, in the traditional square of book publishers in the West End.

In Bedford Square literary associations rustled in the breeze, and the ghosts of writers and publishers lurked on the steps of every Georgian terraced house. My troubles, I consoled myself, were surely no worse than those of my predecessors. Somehow life went on, and great literature endured. I drew further comfort from the thought that I would stop briefly at home, then proceed to Chez Lisette for dinner.

Afterwards I could return home for the ultimate gratification: a late-night phone call to Sarah. The thought of Sarah instantly dispelled my weariness and discouragement. My gorgeous American fiancée would be having a bath in a ski house somewhere at Verbier. Sarah would pick up the phone, and I would be able to enjoy the entire conversation knowing that she was stark naked, with the possible exception of a few bubbles clinging to her scented skin.

I'd first met Sarah while attending Dartmouth College in the States. Sarah and I had both rowed with the crew, but I'd met her through my best friend, Peter. Later I'd stood as his best man while he married Sarah; barely a year later I'd stood next to her at his funeral. It had been roughly ten years since Peter had died, and it had taken me that long to slowly, gently persuade Sarah to marry again. I'd had a massive advantage in that she'd come to London to work for an international investment bank, and I'd arranged for her to row at my club near Henley and spend the odd friendly afternoon or evening out. George, Lisette's husband, had been my willing accomplice; he was always with me at the club and served as a sort of chaperone, oiling the wheels, as it were. His presence had made Sarah feel that there was nothing remotely romantic about seeing me; therefore I was safe. My plan had worked, though it began to look as if George, for all his efforts, wouldn't even be at our wedding.

But the thought of my best friend's voluntary absence from our lives couldn't ruin the joy of anticipating marriage to Sarah. Just six months until the wedding, I told myself. And in a week or so, she'd be back from Switzerland, away from Jean-Claude; she would listen to my troubles and hold me, wordlessly reassuring me that everything would be all right. *You've waited a decade for her, Alex. You can hang on now.*

The taxi disgorged me in the square outside the handsome door to number 52. I gave the driver a large tip, feeling he'd rescued me from a very unhealthy episode, and he rewarded me with a smile. Turning toward the building, I looked up from the kerb and saw something move at an upstairs window. Lisette, no doubt.

I put my key in the old brass lock and turned, then pushed the heavy door open. The delightful smells of the old place met me—floor polish and paper—now enhanced by new-carpeting scent from last year's redecoration.

" 'Allo, you," Lisette said as I appeared in the doorway

to her office. Briskly, she turned off her desk lamp and stood, ready to go. She took one look at my face, now illuminated only by the wall sconces, and exclaimed, "Oh, *mon Dieu*! What now?"

"You're not going to believe it," I sighed, hardly knowing where to begin. Should I tell her about Nicola and the book cart? The horrors of the interview? My inadvertent association with the wilding in Clerkenwell? Or all three?

"Nigel Bleeding Charford-Cheney," she guessed, gathering handbag and briefcase. "Am I right?"

"Mmm." I turned my head, hearing a noise down the hallway we'd just abandoned. Normally everyone had gone home by seven but Lisette and me. "Go ahead, Lisette. I'll be down straightaway."

She took the delay in good humour, having perceived that I'd had a rough time at the BBC. She continued stoically down the stairs as I dashed back up to see who was working so late.

A desk lamp glowed as I rounded the corner into Rachel Sigridsson's office, and I felt a rush of trepidation as I peered inside. Rachel hunched over a monumental stack of manuscript pages, her back to me, watched over by the innocent-looking white seal on her Greenpeace poster. Her razor-sharp pencil audibly scratched precise notations in the margins. On her filing cabinet, a tall stack of Hedgerow Action Kits maintained a precarious balance.

Rachel hadn't spoken to me since I'd agreed to publish *Cleansing*. It was painful to me that such a loyal and goodhearted employee of three decades now regarded me with contempt. When I thought of her unswerving loyalty to my father and Ian, which until now had been transferred magically to me, I wondered if perhaps she believed that the line of *respectable* Plumtrees had come to an end. It could be that the publication of *Cleansing* was beyond the pale for her, and decades of dedication would die with its publication.

"Evening, Rachel," I offered quietly.

She looked in my direction without meeting my eyes, nodded, and returned to her work. Once again I found myself looking at her grey chignon and broad back.

"Rachel. I feel uncomfortable with this . . . this issue between us."

She wheeled in her chair. "*You* feel uncomfortable? With all due respect, *sir*"—she spat the words with anything but respect—"how do you think *I* feel? Here I am, a charter member of Hedges in Transition, with thirty years of service to a firm that is now publishing Lord Chenies's hate-crime novel. That man pulled up his hedges just to spit in our faces. I'd like to know how *his lordship* can be so sorry about the passing of the aristocracy, when he feels no regret whatsoever about a far greater national treasure: the *hedges*. Our countryside is losing its heart and soul, with people like him pulling up hedges right and left—all we'll have soon are oceans of housing estates and a great desert of erosion, like Oklahoma in the Steinbeck novel. And speaking of *The Grapes of Wrath*," she said, warming to her subject, "my friends are furious with me. No one would even sit *next* to me last night at the Finsbury HIT meeting. I'm being ostracised. There could be no more repugnant piece of literature in the nation, and I'm helping to publish it. I'm ashamed."

It was the most Rachel had ever said at once in the four years I'd worked with her. I refrained from pointing out that, knowing her views, I myself had line-edited *Cleansing* and hired a freelance copy-editor to save her from that odious duty. Truth be told, I hadn't relished asking her to do the job only to be refused.

"I'm sorry, Rachel—"

At that moment there was an urgent and highly unusual summons from Lisette. *"Alex!"* she bellowed.

"Excuse me," I murmured, hurrying out into the hall-way. Saved by the bell, I thought. I'd have to give some thought to making peace with my senior editor.

"Alex—'urry up!" Something was wrong: Lisette could handle virtually any situation without help from me, so I took the stairs three at a time. I heard Rachel in her immensely sensible shoes plodding heavily down the hall behind me. My heart sank. From the bottom of the stairs I could see the swarm of newshounds, fully equipped with video and still cameras, recorders, and old-fashioned notepads, mounting the steps to our front door.

"Good Lord," I murmured, turning to meet Lisette's upturned face. I had to fill her in, and quickly. "They're here because there's been another wilding, Lisette. A boy accidentally ran into Nicola and me while we were standing at a book cart in Farringdon Road this afternoon. A crowd of boys dashed after him, but I had no idea they were going to *kill* him."

Lisette looked aghast. I was aware of Rachel listening from above.

"And in the middle of the *Talkabout* interview about *Cleansing*, Mimi Reed pulled out a slip of paper and announced that I'd just been implicated in 'the Clerkenwell Wilding,' that I was the last person to see this boy alive."

"Oh, *no*," Lisette breathed.

"These blasted hack journalists don't even *care* what *really* happened. They've got it all back-to-front."

I regarded them through the door's sidelights, then turned back to Lisette. A tear had fallen onto her cheek. Without thinking, I wiped it away, and said gently, "I'm sorry, Lisette. There's nothing for it but to brave them, lock ourselves in the car, and get home. You needn't say a word to them, okay?"

She nodded, sniffing. I pulled the door open, and we dashed out into the shouting, flashing melee.

I held Lisette's hand and pulled her behind me in the

dark, marvelling as ever at the speeds she could reach on her spiky heels, acutely aware that it didn't look right for me to be holding the hand of a married woman, with whom I worked very closely. But I couldn't let the crowd separate us. Doggedly we made for the car, pushing forward as if through molasses. Two dozen people pummelled us with questions while doing their damnedest to delay us.

"Mr. Plumtree! Did you have Kumba killed for assaulting you?"

"What was your role in the Clerkenwell Wilding?"

"What were you doing in Clerkenwell this afternoon?"

"Don't you think another wilding was a bit over the top for a publicity stunt?"

"Are you going to withdraw *Cleansing*?"

It seemed to take at least twenty minutes, but could have been as few as five. We were a bare seven feet from the car through sheer heads-down persistence, when I saw him.

It was the journalist whom I had unwisely confronted at the book cart. He had orchestrated this; I knew by the look of pride on his soft young face. He'd had his chance for a big story. For once he'd been at the right place at the right time. Now that his story had been filed at the *Watch*, he was whipping the rest of the media into a frenzy over my once good name—out of revenge.

"I told you you'd be sorry," he shouted, smiling nastily despite the fact that he'd been squashed against my car. He was now the one impediment between me and the car door. "You shouldn't have pushed me, Plumtree."

Struggling with the desire to knock him halfway to Sunday, I said quietly, keeping emotion out of my voice, "Would you kindly step aside."

He met my gaze for a moment, his mocking smile fading, then stepped ever so slightly backwards.

Immediately I jabbed my remote unlock button and

reached for the driver's side door, yanking it open. I half-shoved Lisette into the front seat. She hurriedly gathered up her sueded silk skirt, crawled over to the passenger side, and locked her door. I climbed in after her, furiously punching the central door-lock button.

Someone pounded angrily on my window. I started the car, revved the engine to warn the journalists of our imminent and speedy departure, then accelerated round the curve, leaving a bit of rubber on the road as a souvenir. Indignant shouts followed us, including a furious "Effing maniac! He'd kill us all!"

I shuddered to think what I'd read in the paper the next day.

Safely in the car, I took one fleeting look back at the building through the rearview mirror. Aware of a presence in Lisette's office window, I did a double take.

It was unmistakably Rachel Sigridsson.

There was fury in Lisette's pouting lips and furrowed brow. Good, I thought. I needn't worry about her if she's angry.

"Not the best of times for you, is it, Alex?" Lisette always thought of others, even when she was in the midst of crisis.

"Nor for you," I said, keeping my eyes on the road. Suddenly I was acutely aware of the strength of the emotional intimacy between us. There was nothing at all physical about it, but we *were* very familiar. Was I supposed to feel this close to my best friend's wife? *Estranged* wife?

Perhaps she sensed it, too. We travelled in silence most of the way, and I bypassed the turning for my home, making straight for hers. The Stonehams had named their new home—one hundred fifty years old but new to them—Chez Lisette. On the way through her historical, almost entirely listed neighbourhood of Heronsgate we passed the Hotchkiss house, just three doors from the Stonehams'. Being listed meant that few alterations would be allowed, and those that were would have to be completed using original materials.

Lisette and George's was a huge pile that had been built at some point over one of the original cottages. It was half-timbered. In summer the brown wood and white stucco of their home was lost in a sea of pink mallow and climbing roses. The house would have served admirably as the cover photo for a book entitled *Charming Houses of Britain*.

Pulling up into the long drive with the crunch of gravel under the wheels, I relaxed. At least here there were no screaming hordes of journalists. Even Mimi Reed couldn't enter our homes unless we invited her in via the television. The boys ran screaming up to us, Swedish nanny close behind, and jumped on me as you would expect two boys to greet their—um, father—after a long day at the office.

I caught a flicker of disquiet in the glance Lisette threw my way as she watched me carry the boys, one over each shoulder, like sacks of potatoes into her kitchen.

Had the sight of her boys made her, like me, think of Mmbasi Kumba, and the mother to whom he would never again come home at the end of the day? Or did she share my vague feeling of a gathering storm, and my uneasiness at its growing threat?

Weary, I meandered home from Lisette's along the Chorleywood lanes, and turned into the drive of the Orchard. As I pulled the car into the garage I saw Ian open the door. He stood watching my arrival, framed in the kitchen doorway.

"Evening, Ian."

"And *what* an evening," he said quietly, ushering me in. "I'm sorry, Alex. I'm afraid you're under siege again. I've turned the ringer off the phone, and the volume down on the answering machine."

I nodded. "You saw *Talkabout*, then."

"Mmm. Recorded it while I met with the book club." He frowned. "I'm a bit surprised at Mimi. Would have expected more objectivity from her. Makes me wonder who's behind it all. Tea?"

"Please," I said gratefully, following him into the kitchen. He flipped the switch on the electric kettle, and the immediate hiss of the coils heating was comfortingly familiar. Wildings might come and go, I thought, but there would always be an England. And tea.

I sank into a chair, frowning. "Who specifically are you thinking might be 'behind it all,' as you say?"

"Well." He stuffed Twinings teabags into our old blue-and-white-striped teapot. "Guy Ferris-Browne, the MP who asked you to publish Charford-Cheney's book, has probably asked others besides you to help the PM survive this election. Mimi or her boss or even the BBC bigwigs may have received a call similar to yours." He went to the fridge in search of the pint-sized milk bottle with the gold top. "In fact, I'd say it's extremely likely. There's quite a lot at stake."

I rested my elbows on the pine surface of the trestle table, worn smooth by decades of similar family chats conducted over tea. "Sorry, you've lost me. What does the PM stand to gain from Mimi making *me* an accomplice to the Clerkenwell Wilding?"

"My dear boy," he said patiently, "you are trusting to a fault. I hate to remind you of the baser instincts of human nature, particularly in politics, but it is entirely possible that Ferris-Browne is using you. In a particularly odious way, I might add."

He must have seen the distress on my face, though with anyone but Ian and Sarah I pride myself on being inscrutable. I could think of nothing to say. If I had already been through the difficulty of attempting to publish *Cleansing* and now found out it was all a bad joke on me, I wasn't sure what I'd do.

But I did see his point. With *Cleansing* published, and yours truly taking a drubbing from the press for being involved with a wilding, Ferris-Browne or the prime minister could point to it all and say, "See how out of hand this xenophobic nationalism is getting? We're already down that path to the extent that this book, and this book publisher, are involved in *wildings*. Think how much worse it will get if you elect someone from the Far Right!"

But my father had trusted Graeme Abercrombie. Ian trusted him, too. As a result, I had supreme confidence in the PM myself. Ferris-Browne, on the other hand, represented more of a grey area. It was true that the man was bent on submerging England into the Economic and Monetary Union at the earliest possible date, come hell or high water. Did he want it so badly that perhaps he'd lost a few scruples along the way? Had it been a mistake for me to trust him?

I felt a sudden frisson of fear. How could the prime minister, or Guy Ferris-Browne, have known that I'd be anywhere *near* a wilding in Clerkenwell? Perhaps they knew someone who had heard about it from my journalist friend at the book cart, and had learned in time for them to get to Mimi on *Talkabout*. Perhaps the obnoxious young journalist was a mole for Ferris-Browne. Or—and this was the possibility that really made my blood run cold—perhaps one of them had *paid* Mmbasi Kumba to run into me but hadn't told him what would happen to him afterwards. . . .

Ian was watching me. I finally lifted my eyes to meet his, and in the silence the kettle clicked off. He picked up the kettle and poured boiling water over the tea bags, then plonked the lid down on the pot.

"I'd almost like to find a reason not to publish the damned book." Not for the first time, it occurred to me that if I had listened to Ian, I'd lead a far less anguished life. Hadn't he urged caution when he'd heard I was publishing *Cleansing* for political reasons?

He crossed to the table, carrying the pot in one hand and two milked mugs in the other. His silence said more than any words. *Right from wrong,* it said. *Do the right thing, Alex.* But what *was* right in this case? Keeping my promise to the PM? Or refusing to publish the book?

It was only after he'd pulled out a chair and sat down that he spoke. "How's the latest set of proofs coming?"

I groaned. Ian knew that the first set of proofs had gone astray, and he'd just reminded me that the next set hadn't appeared as promised by the end of the day. "The replacements haven't arrived yet. If it weren't for the contract, I'd skip the special edition altogether and just release the trade edition printed in Hong Kong." I couldn't imagine why I had agreed to Ferris-Browne's suggestion of a special first edition to be released first, two weeks before the official trade version. I suppose I hadn't thought it would be much of a problem, and he'd been so persuasive.

Ian's mere presence was enough to make me feel keenly the irresponsibility of disregarding the contract and killing the special edition. Working with Amanda was very different from our usual production process, and more difficult for us. She was a small fine-art printer, and we were used to sending our books to the big boys in Asia—the huge professional printers with customers round the globe, whose presses never stopped.

To make matters worse, in the week after the contracts were signed, your friend and mine Lord Chenies had his solicitor draw up a further addendum that specified still more detailed conditions for production of the special edition. Now it had to be printed using the Caslon typeface—heaven forbid that Chenies's prose should be desecrated by anything less than a purely English font, I thought cynically. The more attractive (in my opinion) Garamond typeface, created by a Frenchman, would never do—nor would Bodoni, which had been conceived by an Italian. Unthinkable.

We were also now required to use extra-thick coated paper for artwork and, as Amanda had laughingly predicted, paper with as much wood content as was possible. I'd suggested rag, which is both environmentally sound and much prized by bibliophiles, but Lord Chenies wouldn't budge. The oil-based ink was even to be specially mixed using a formula designed by William Morris, one of the finest publishers ever to grace England's soil.

All of that didn't even take into account the casing, or cover, which was to be done in almost unheard-of luxury, in leather. Not the highest quality morocco leather, granted, but leather nonetheless. At least we wouldn't be losing our shirts on the job: each book would bring in one hundred pounds, and after royalties, printing, and contributions to the Clerkenwell Neighbourhood Association we would keep twenty percent of that.

Elbow on the table, I supported the weight of my now-aching head on a fist. "If I don't publish the book at all, in any form, I break a promise to the prime minister. If I do, and if Ferris-Browne is using me, God only knows what'll happen next."

Ian lifted the teapot, gave it a swirl, and poured. Once again his silence was eloquent.

"I know," I said. "I know."

Half an hour later I was on the phone to Sarah in Switzerland. "Hello, gorgeous," I began, "how's my very own skiing film star?"

She laughed. "You make it sound so glamorous. If you could only see how many times I had to go down the same slope to give them exactly what they need. Today they got quite cross with me."

"I don't believe it. Promise me you'll be careful on those pistes." I didn't even like to *think* about the slopes she skied. I myself usually kept to the groomed tracks, whereas she skied literally in the trees and on horrifically icy, rutted racecourses.

"Alex, you know I'm being careful. They're not pleased at my wearing the helmet for the actual takes, but I told them to find someone else if it bothered them that much."

How I loved her. Her bold and courageous spirit, her athleticism, her voice—everything. "And did they?"

"No. But enough of that. Aside from Jean-Claude, these people are a little crazy. And you know Verbier . . . there are some wild partiers here." I tried to put the combination of Sarah, Jean-Claude, and wild parties out of my mind. I heard splashing and smiled. She *was* in the bath. "So what's going on over there?"

"You don't want to know, Sarah. Another wilding, I'm afraid."

"Alex, that's awful." I could picture the little wrinkle between her eyebrows. "What's happened to people? Is this all over Dexter Moore's rise? Or is it the European Union business?"

"A little of both, I think. Still, we're holding together." A pause. "I gather you're neck-deep in bubbles?"

"Mmm-hmm. And it feels wonderful. It was really cold out there today. I hope it's nicer by the time you get here. I'll see you in . . . less than two weeks now."

"Two hundred and fifty-two hours, to be exact."

She laughed. "Promise you'll still be like this on our twenty-year anniversary."

"Right. I promise. So . . . the wedding's still on?"

I received the usual cheerful assurance that it was very much on indeed. We chatted on for a bit, and I sighed as we rang off. August twenty-ninth couldn't come soon enough.

CHAPTER FOUR

———◆———

*We have legalised confiscation, consecrated sacrilege,
and condoned high treason.*

BENJAMIN DISRAELI

IT WAS A TUESDAY THAT WILL LIVE ON IN MY MEMORY FOR
some time.

The first extraordinary event of the day took place at
the end of my own driveway. As I pulled out into Old
Shire Lane, I was surprised to see my hedge-obsessed
friends from HIT waiting in what looked like an angry
knot. They stared at me with hostility as I approached.
Good Lord. *What now?* I thought, and rolled down my
window.

"Morning," I began, pulling alongside them.

Wendy Dedham stepped to the fore. "How *could* you
do this?" she demanded, her eyes tearing up. "We thought
you were on *our* side." She shook with emotion.

"What on earth do you mean? The hedges?" I asked,
confused. "Of course I'm on your side."

"No you're *not*," Wendy spat, hurt. "You've become
one of them. Like Lord Chenies. Next thing we know
you'll be ripping out your hedges as well, and damn the
restrictions." The group behind her glared at me.

"Wendy, I really don't know what you're talking about." Incredulous, I grasped at a straw. "Do you mean that because I'm publishing Lord Chenies's book, you think I share his views on hedges, and the environment in general?"

But she didn't seem to have heard what I said. Her angry stare was almost frightening. She'd always been such a mild person, so grateful for the use of my hedges to train her new recruits.

"We'd never have expected this of *you*. I—really, Alex, I can't tell you how disappointed I am."

I tried to explain that my publishing *Cleansing* had nothing whatsoever to do with my hedges. After several attempts, I came to a painful realisation: the hedge folk were absolutely convinced—nothing I said could persuade them otherwise—that because I had aligned myself in a business capacity with Lord Chenies, one of *them* (Dexter Moore's people), I was utterly opposed to saving hedges. I was automatically classified an anti-environmentalist and a follower of Moore's. Stunned, because I'd known most of the people in the lane all my life, I tried for several minutes more to set the record straight.

But in the end I drove off, feeling much misunderstood, not to mention maligned. I glanced in my rear-view mirror only to see them muttering amongst themselves as they watched me go.

When Lisette and I—Ian preferred to take the train—arrived at Plumtree Press at eight-thirty, we were surprised to find the door unlocked.

We were even more surprised to find three men in my office, wearing dark blue overalls emblazoned with "Best Communications" in red. One was actually sitting on my desk, fiddling with something on the bottom of my telephone. Another was on hands and knees, doing something with a screwdriver at the jack in the wall. A third was opening a box with a picture of a shiny black console on it—a miniature push-button switchboard, evidently.

I cleared my throat in the doorway, and they looked up, surprised. The one working with the phone coolly turned it over and put it down on the desk.

"Good morning," I said. "I wasn't aware that we were having any work done on the phones."

Lisette said, a bit hesitantly, "Well—we are 'aving the voice mail system installed. But you are 'ere quite early, I think."

Silence.

One of the overalled men lifted a shiny black box covered with soft grey buttons from its cushion of polystyrene. The one sitting on my desk threw a frosty smile in our direction. "Yes, I hope that's all right. We had a busy day stacking up, and we'd promised to get you set up today. We rang"—here he pulled a small notebook out of his pocket and flipped through the pages—"yes, here it is. We told your assistant, Shuna, we'd come first thing this morning. She said it was fine." He shrugged. "You don't mind, do you?"

I looked at Lisette, who raised her eyebrows at me. Her features revealed that she was thinking the same thing I was: English tradespeople were certainly becoming more eager to work. Normally you had to beg, borrow, or steal to get a telephone person in for anything—and they never came before ten. Still, this was the nineties. Perhaps these men were on some sort of Thatcherite profit-sharing scheme. The more work they did, the more money they got—that sort of thing. I couldn't put a finger on why their unexpected appearance was so irritating to me: after all, they'd rung the office and got permission to come.

"No. Of course not," I told them. "Just surprised."

Lisette gave a single, eloquent Gallic shrug, as if to say, *And I thought I had come to understand the English,* and left.

I stepped inside my office and hung up my coat. "How did you get into the building?"

"Gent by the name of Derek let us in," said the one on my desk.

"Ah," I said. Derek, our mail clerk, came quite early and also left early, which was fine with me. Normally, though, he left the front door locked until I arrived and opened it nearer to business hours—a relaxed nine o'clock or so.

"Well, tell me what I've got here," I said, and sat down behind my desk, bracing myself for the complexities of a new system.

Had I known what I was *really* getting, I'd have rung the police.

The phone men had only just departed when my new-fangled contraption rang.

"Alex Plumtree."

"Alex! It's Amanda. I've just got in this morning, and—well, you know those proofs I sent to you yesterday?"

Oh, no, I thought. Here we go again. Either the couriers from Clerkenwell were extremely and chronically inept or someone really was sabotaging the printing of this book. I knew which option I thought more likely.

"We didn't receive any proofs yesterday, Amanda."

She hissed an expletive. "They're worthless anyway. Someone's come in and dumped all my galley trays— pied, as we say. You should see this place, Alex. Type everywhere."

"Have you rung the police?"

"No. And I'm not going to."

"Amanda, someone broke into your shop. What if you'd been there? What if they'd attacked you? I don't need to tell you that this book has enemies. I'm getting worried about you—and all of us."

"Alex, this neighbourhood is only just turning round its reputation. The Neighbourhood Association's been very good to me. I don't want to make it look as if I've caused a crime wave in Clerkenwell. Besides, Bruce is here with me. Aren't you, Bruce?"

"Yeah!" I heard in the background. "But I still think she should ring the police!" he shouted.

"Don't mind him." Amanda sighed. "We're going to start tidying up here."

"Nicola and I will stop over later, all right? We've got to find a way to get this book in production and keep everyone safe."

"Right. See you later, then." *Click.*

I'd no sooner hung up the phone than Nicola popped into my office. "Have a minute?" she asked.

"Of course. Sit down." I waved her to the comfortable sofa against the wall. "How's the head?"

She brushed off my concern. "I'm fine. And the bump has excellent camouflage." She touched a hand to her burgeoning mane of thick, dark hair and hesitated. Her brown eyes regarded me seriously. "Alex. I've seen the papers. I'm so sorry this has turned into a disaster for you. And the strangest thing occurred to me. . . ."

"What?"

"Well, I couldn't help but think . . . what happened yesterday was remarkably like that bit in *Oliver Twist*, you know, when Oliver is—"

"Yes, strange, isn't it?" Yet another link in the psychic bond between Nicola and me, I thought. Incredible luck to have found her to run the trade division. I decided not to tell her that in the past such reenactments of literature had proved—to use her own word—disastrous.

"Well, anyway," she said, "I think you and I understand each other quite well, but I did want to ask . . . do you think you might refrain from publicising my stint under the book cart yesterday?"

I did in fact understand her perfectly. And she didn't know me very well yet if she thought I'd embarrass her by spreading word of her wobbliness after being unexpectedly bashed on the head.

"I won't breathe a word. You were right. We understand each other."

Her lush red lips curved in a smile, and she made for the door. "I thought so."

"Nicola, there's just one more thing."

She turned back, questioning.

"This morning Amanda found her trays of type, all locked up for printing, dumped out. And we never got the second set of proofs she ran for us yesterday. I'm afraid we have to face the fact that someone's sabotaging *Cleansing*."

"I see," she said, her face stony. "Not that we should be surprised, I suppose. Who, do you think?"

"Could be anyone—enough people have reasons."

She nodded, still without emotion.

"We'll go over after the editorial meeting, see what can be done. Meeting's at ten o'clock," I said, by way of reminder. It would be Nicola's first editorial meeting with Plumtree Press.

"Righto." She turned and went out.

I looked after her, impressed with her reaction to crisis. And it was beginning to look as if she'd need every bit of her sangfroid.

Lisette had arranged the usual party atmosphere for our Tuesday morning editorial meeting. When I entered the bright, airy room that housed the desks of Lisette and our editorial assistant, Shuna, the scent of coffee and the sound of laughter greeted me.

A semicircle of chairs ranged round the fireplace, its painted metal fire screen hiding what remained of last winter's ashes. Lisette had placed that week's bouquet of flowers—red tulips—on the mantelpiece. I couldn't help but observe that, despite the unpleasant events of the previous evening, this was a happy place.

With the exception of Rachel Sigridsson, who sat morosely to one side, the circle of smiling faces included our full cast of editorial characters (and characters they were, I thought): Timothy Haycroft, senior academic editor; Lisette, deputy managing director; Shuna, editorial assistant; Ian, head of the academic division; and Nicola, our new trade division editor.

Everyone was looking at Nicola's once-black jumper, now covered with white confectioner's sugar, and laughing helplessly. From what I could deduce, it seemed that Timothy Haycroft had liberally dusted Nicola by snorting with laughter while biting into his almond croissant.

"It's all your fault, Lisette," he was saying, a white dot of sugar on the tip of his nose. He was red to the roots of his hair, but that wouldn't deprive Timothy of his native wit. "No one should tell *that* sort of joke, *this* early in the morning. The brain can't cope."

He broke off to pick up a serviette and begin to dust the sugar off Nicola, but soon realised that he couldn't do the job properly without intruding on forbidden and unavoidable physical features. Redder and more flustered than ever, he blurted, "Sorry, sorry." He finally resorted to passing Nicola several serviettes and sitting down again.

"Morning, everyone," I mumbled, taking the one empty seat. "Ah, Timothy! Well-acquainted with Nicola already, I see."

"Yes, thank you very much, Alex," Timothy replied. I could tell he wanted to make some quip that would give me as good as I'd given, but he stopped short of making a joke about my new career in wildings.

I knew they were all aware of the contents of the morning paper, which had indeed been as awful as I'd feared. PUBLISHER OF WILDING BOOK CONNECTED WITH

CLERKENWELL MURDER, one of the kinder headlines had screamed.

Instead, Timothy said, "And have you managed to—er—*clean* up the *Cleansing* proofs yet?"

There were assorted moans from all six of us at Timothy's usual foray into lexical humour. From all of us, that is, except Rachel. She stared at the floor, resolutely abstaining from coffee and pastries, lest she appear to be joining the party.

"Ha ha ha," I said, and lifted my coffee cup to my lips for a quick slug. "I think it only proper that I forward that enquiry to the editor responsible. Nicola?"

As I pronounced her name, Nicola had just sunk her teeth into an apple turnover. Poised as she was, her eyes widened at the prospect of being unable to speak on the occasion of her first editorial report. Hurriedly, she put down the turnover and chewed rapidly.

I will admit to getting some pleasure out of seeing her even slightly off-balance, so composed and dignified had she been at every turn. Even now she somehow managed to make me feel that I'd been out of line, sending a question her way when she was indisposed.

Seeing her plight, I filled a moment or two explaining to the group that Nicola and I had been to see Amanda the day before. My statement was met with grave nods; all were thinking it was because of that visit I had become involved in yet another mess—that is, in addition to publishing the Charford-Cheney book.

"Yes," Nicola finally began, licking her lips to rid them of unsightly crumbs. "Somehow not one but two sets of proofs have now gone astray between Amanda's shop and here, and evidently this morning she found all her galley trays, ready and waiting to print the book, dumped on the floor. Alex and I will meet with her today to see how we can help." She shrugged and smiled ruefully. "What else could possibly go wrong with this book?"

"Touch wood." Lisette's eyes grew mischievous. "You know, Nicola, we always give the worst jobs to the newest employees. Just to break them in."

There were smiles all round. Nicola said gamely, "Well, I've always said it's best to dive right in." She shot me a quick look, and we had a moment of private mirth at her little joke. Diving under book carts, propelled by strange men crashing into her, had probably not been her idea of working for a book publisher.

"All right. Whose go is it this morning?" We took it in turns to lead the editorial meetings, to give everyone a chance to practise management skills.

"Mine," Rachel said humourlessly. "I'll begin, if we've finished wasting time." She paused, allowing us to feel the full weight of her disapproval. "The MacDougal manuscript is—"

Lisette interrupted in her inoffensive way, smiling. "Come on, Rachel, move into the circle. I will 'ave a stiff neck, turning round to look at you all morning." She stood to help Rachel move her chair, and the older woman didn't dare refuse. Lisette and Shuna moved their chairs apart to make room for her, and Rachel settled her amorphous bulk and customary sheaf of papers in the circle.

"All right. *If* I may continue . . ." As Rachel began to report on *The Storms of Time*, a troublesome novel we'd taken on last year in another mistaken act of goodwill, my thoughts wandered. I'd never seen her so contentious. She might be less hostile if I told her why I was publishing *Cleansing*, but the more people I told, the bigger the risk became that one of them would let it slip. And I had promised to keep it secret—telling Ian had already pushed at the edges of that promise.

"That's it for me," Rachel finished, balancing her papers on her lap and purposefully folding her arms akimbo. "Timothy."

"Mmm?" Timothy looked surprised at being called upon next. "Oh, yes. Well, Ian and I have been sharing the editorial work on the new Modern anthology with historical notes. So far, all the author biographies and commentaries have been on time, so that's well in hand, on schedule for September, as we'd hoped. The trip to Devon to see Theodore Barnes paid off; he's agreed to do the Kipling survey. We're looking at a minimum of two years on that one, I think, though I'm putting eighteen months in the contract. So—good heavens—that'll be on the list for 2001. Otherwise, everything's the same as last week." Looking satisfied, he gazed round the circle at us. "Oh, yes. Nearly forgot. I'm going to be at that poets conference at Durham from tomorrow through Friday. See if I can recruit an ambitious young professor to write something fascinating for us."

"Ian?" There was still a touch of respect in Rachel's voice when she pronounced his name.

He acknowledged her with a nod and told us that he'd been pleased to sign a professor from Oxford whose speciality was Victorian authors, especially Dickens.

Nicola shot me a glance that might have said, *Not Dickens again!* I widened my eyes at her briefly, and we turned our attention back to Ian.

Ian reported he had also met with a professor from Columbia University who had an idea for a volume entitled *Great American Novels*, which Ian thought sounded promising for our growing American market, and might be of interest domestically as well.

"And I'm attending the environmental summit in Verbier next week; I'll take a few days to ski with Sarah after. I'll be back Monday week. That's my news," he said with a shrug.

"Mr. Plumtree." I had entreated Rachel for three years

now to use my Christian name, but she stuck doggedly to
formality. Now my last name sounded like an insult.

"Unfortunately you all know from the morning papers what's on my plate this week: more *Cleansing* absur-
dity. And if I can manage to get five minutes' respite from
the press, I'll be talking to the bank about financing the
acquisition of that new imprint. I had also planned to set
some plans in motion this week for the bibliophile's subscription book club, though there's no urgency there. And
I still hope to spend some time next week skiing with Ian
and Sarah; I'll be back a week from Monday too."

An unmistakable "hmmph" arose from Rachel's quarter. She thought the worst of me these days: a weekend in
Switzerland was an unseemly romp with my fiancée. Going out to lunch with a female member of the staff, if
Rachel heard about it, was also hmmph-worthy—though
she'd enjoyed her share of lunches out on my shout over
the last three years. Driving home nightly with Lisette was
perceived as another sin. These innocent activities were
seen—and judged—in the worst possible light.

"Otherwise, there's—" I stopped short as the eyes on
the opposite side of the semicircle shifted to the doorway
behind me. Turning to look, I saw Dee, our receptionist,
knocking perfunctorily on the doorjamb.

"Urgent letter, Mr. P.—bloke made me promise I'd get
it to you straightaway." She strutted into the room in her
usual attire: militant black boots, short black leather skirt,
and stretchy knit black top. Dee looked out of place up
here in the rarefied atmosphere of the editorial offices. She
was much more comfortable on the street level in reception. She was a natural at dealing with people who walked
in, and at flirting with any male on the other end of the
phone line. I sensed concern behind her casual manner as
she handed me the letter, her fingernails varnished in
black.

"Thanks, Dee," I said, ripping open the envelope. My spirits sank as I scanned the page.

Dear sir,

You are hereby informed that Mr. and Mrs. Malcolm Charford-Cheney of Serials, Ltd., 12 Chenies Street, London WC1, are bringing suit against you in the amount of one million pounds sterling for the unlawful publication of the novel *Cleansing*, written by Malcolm's father, Nigel Charford-Cheney, as it is still under contract to them for serial publication.

Yours sincerely,
Littie, Gate & Harris, Solicitors

"Great. Just great." I groaned and passed the letter to Ian. "We're being sued, everyone—guess which book, and which son."

Timothy moaned. Lisette shot up ramrod straight in her chair and said with passion, "But 'ow can 'e sue *you*? I thought Charford-Cheney said 'e cancelled 'is contract with 'is son, because they did not get Chapter Two out by the deadline agreed. And they didn't comply with 'is bloody paper and design requests!"

Lisette's language sometimes left something to be desired, but in this case I couldn't blame her. Beside her, Rachel's lips were curving up into a nasty smile. She was pleased, and that was disturbing. The woman actually wished me ill.

True to his character, Timothy said, "Look on the bright side, Alex. Maybe this lets you out of publishing the damned thing."

I had to admit he had a point. Perhaps this was the lawsuit from heaven. If we withdrew the book, the young

Charford-Cheneys could withdraw their suit, and we would have an inviolable reason to renege on the contract. We had some costs sunk into the project, it was true, but I'd gladly swallow them for the pleasure of *not* publishing *Cleansing*.

But a boy had *died* over this. I felt increasingly certain that the wilding had been arranged by some political group—if not Ferris-Browne, someone equally desperate to achieve his ends at any cost. And if it was Ferris-Browne, he knew *I* knew. Not only could I not let the boy's death go unpunished but I wouldn't be safe until the person who'd organised it was brought to justice.

Once again, Ian's silence was deafening.

"In retrospect, I should have had our solicitor investigate his previous contract. *Damn.*" I hit the arm of my chair with a fist and stood. "I'm going to have a word with Neville Greenslade. Nicola, it's to be baptism by fire for you."

She looked ready to take on whatever was in store for her, rising to her feet with the usual grace.

"Sorry," I said to the remainder of the group. "Carry on—I'll catch up later." Lisette nodded; I knew she'd fill me in. Nicola and I went to my office, where I dialled our solicitor's phone number on my new black box.

"Alex! Are you all right? What's all this about the wilding?" Our old family friend Neville Greenslade had handled the Press's legal affairs—and the Plumtree family's—for thirty-five years. And of course he read the headlines.

"A misunderstanding—but one that sells papers. I've a mind to take your advice, Neville."

"Ready when you are." Neville chuckled. He'd advised me more than once in the past to take legal action against my journalistic enemies. "Is that why you're phoning? Libel? Slander?"

"Tempting. But no, unfortunately, *I'm* the one being sued today. It seems Charford-Cheney still has a contract to publish *Cleansing* with his son and daughter-in-law, the serial publishers. They claim I'm publishing it with an invalid contract. It seems I'm the flavour of the month."

"Hmm. Better come for a chat." I heard him consulting his secretary in the background. "Marie tells me we've had a cancellation. Two o'clock suit you?"

It was ten forty-five. "Perfect. Thanks, Neville. I'll be bringing Nicola Beauchamp, our new editor. *Cleansing* is officially hers."

We rang off. "I'll just ring Amanda," I murmured to Nicola, shaking my head. I let it ring repeatedly, but to no avail; Amanda didn't have a messaging service or an answering machine.

"That's odd," I told Nicola, who sat perched on the corner of my desk, taking it all in. "No answer. She's *always* there. Then again, there was the day I walked into her shop and was nearly deafened by Mahler at top volume. And sometimes she wears earplugs when she's running a particularly noisy machine."

But privately I wondered where Bruce, her printer's devil, was. Whenever Amanda left the shop, he was in charge. A prickly feeling crept up the back of my neck as it occurred to me that the pied trays the night before might have been only the first instalment of punishment for the printer of *Cleansing*. I considered ringing the police, but decided intuition wasn't enough for them to go on.

Trying to hide my concern, I finally hung up the phone and stood. "Let's pop round to see her now, Nicola." Surely if I went to Clerkenwell again, it was unlikely to result in another wilding.

Wasn't it?

"I'll get my coat," she said, and returned with it in less time than it took me to get mine off the rack in the corner. As we passed Lisette's office I stuck my head in. The semicircle was still assembled, and Lisette was holding forth.

"We're just going round to see Amanda," I said. "Then the solicitor at two."

"Right," said Lisette.

"Hmmph," said Rachel.

"Mind your backs," said Timothy.

Old leaves and dirt blew in a frenzy around us, and as if by mutual agreement, we hunkered down into raised collars and didn't speak until we'd reached the shelter of the Tottenham Court Road station. Though I had spent less than eight hours in her presence, I knew that Nicola had something on her mind. It wasn't long before she gave voice to it.

"Whew!" she said. "It's an ill wind that . . . oops. Sorry." She caught the unfortunate quote too late.

"No, please. If we don't laugh, we'll cry."

"Alex, if you don't mind my asking—" She stopped in front of the ticket machine and turned to face me. "Why are you *really* publishing *Cleansing*?"

Her meaning was all too clear. Charford-Cheney's novel wasn't Plumtree Press's usual fare. It was political; it was controversial; it wasn't even related to literature, aside from its author's literary pedigree.

Was it necessary to tell her? She was going to be up to her neck in this book soon, almost as deep as I was—if we didn't abandon it entirely.

I put my money in the ticket machine, tapped in my destination, and a stub of printed paper popped out. I repeated the procedure and out came another.

"All right," I said, glancing round as I handed her a ticket. "Something tells me you're good at keeping secrets." It was reasonable and necessary for the book's editor to know, I thought.

I sighed and told her about the request from the PM's behind-the-scenes man, though I didn't reveal Ferris-Browne's identity.

She fed her ticket to the machine at the gate and walked through the little barrier next to me when it opened, retrieving her ticket as the machine spat it out again. She seemed lost in thought—hardly surprising under the circumstances.

"I think I understand," Nicola said slowly, trotting gamely down the stairs next to me. "The government insider who asked you to publish *Cleansing* is expecting it to turn the tide in Abercrombie's favour, away from Dexter Moore and isolationism."

I nodded.

"I wonder . . . how can he be so sure?" she asked, frowning as we sat to wait for the next train. The platform was so quiet that I looked around to see who might hear us. But we were alone. "What if the publication of *Cleansing* does more harm than good to the prime minister's cause? Couldn't it actually *attract* followers to the Right for nationalistic reasons?"

"I asked exactly the same question, Nicola. The PM's man said it was his business to manage public opinion, and he'd already done preliminary polls to check the reaction to Chapter One from Serials, Ltd. He was confident it would work if I would only cooperate."

The whine of a train came down the rails. A breeze stirred down the tunnel, bringing the characteristic aroma that was the Underground: brake dust and damp.

"Does it make a difference to you?" I asked. "Was it wrong of me to ask you to work on this book, when you didn't know the full story?"

"No, Alex. It makes no difference." She stood as the train sped into the platform area. "I learned at an early age that *everything* comes down to politics."

So much bitterness came through her words that I found myself wondering exactly how much she *did* know about politics . . . and what else I *didn't* know about her.

CHAPTER FIVE

———◦⎯◦———

Finality is not the language of politics.

BENJAMIN DISRAELI

WE TURNED LEFT UP COWCROSS STREET, THE WIND whipping our faces like fine-gauge sandpaper. Grit flew round us in a storm of filth, thanks in large part to Richard Hotchkiss's construction project down the road.

"You'll be glad to get away at the weekend." Nicola spoke loudly, to be heard over the wind.

I shouted back, "Yes. Timing could be better, though."

"Well, perhaps it's best that you disappear for a bit—even a couple of days."

I didn't respond. Not only was I thinking about how much her statement made me feel like a criminal, but any words I'd spoken would have been drowned out by the grumbling and beeping of Hotchkiss's earthmovers as we walked toward Amanda's.

Privately—and unreasonably, I knew—I cursed Hotchkiss's construction project. Their industriousness, down in the depths below Farringdon Road, even made me wonder about the safety of the tube station. I couldn't help but think of the subterranean river Fleet directly beneath the construction area. How could even an expert like Hotchkiss, with all his engineers, figure out how to build a road on top of an underground river and a network of tube tunnels? It made me feel distinctly vulnerable, like riding the lift to the fiftieth floor of a skyscraper and feeling it sway in the wind.

When at last we crossed the euphemistically named Clerkenwell Green, I longed for a shower and a bottle of contact lens solution. I had recently visited the eye doctor, who announced that he now had the technology to fit even someone with my eyes for contacts. Unfortunately, he'd also diagnosed a degenerative condition that could render my already abysmal eyesight much worse—and eventually eliminate it altogether. I tried to put it out of my mind and blinked as I peered through the glass in Amanda's door. No one. I tried the knob as the wind did its best to blow us into the building. The door opened, and we stumbled in with relief.

"Good Lord," said Nicola, shaking herself. "A blizzard of dirt."

Small bits of it hit the glass behind us as the scent of Amanda's domain hit me in a familiar wave. I led the way through the tightly packed entry to the shop, between Amanda's treasure trove of printer's cabinets. Not a single piece of type on the floor anywhere; she'd been busy cleaning up.

"Where on earth are those two?" I asked, puzzled. "Normally she won't even leave for lunch; it's only just elevenses time. And look—she's left the light on." Even Nicola raised her eyebrows at that. In her brief association with the printer, she'd already learned that Amanda was ultra-frugal, to the point of saving paper shavings to press into fire kindling. She'd trained Bruce to practise the same small economies that she claimed made all the difference between solvency and unemployment.

Nicola wandered toward Amanda's desk, while I went to her large hanging progress board on the back wall. Its shiny write-on surface would reveal where *Cleansing* stood in her lineup of jobs. A column labelled "Proofs" had been ticked in bold black marker twice, with yesterday's date written next to the last tick, and an exclamation mark.

"Alex . . . look at this," Nicola said hesitantly.

I joined her at the oak library table that served as Amanda's desk. On top of neatly stacked piles of paper, each with a sticky label stating the name of the project, a mug of tea had spilled. The bag on the bottom of the cup, which had probably smelt pleasantly of camomile, now reeked of rancid weed. No attempt had been made to clean up the spill, and tea had dripped into a puddle on the floor. But the mug had been righted and set at the edge of the table.

"Oh, no," Nicola breathed, her eyes focussed on her hand. It was smudged with something dark and red.

With the same sense of horrified responsibility I'd felt at seeing Nicola under the book cart, I first stared at the stain on her hand, then followed her gaze to Amanda's straight-backed hardwood chair. I walked round to see the back of the chair. There wasn't much of the stuff, but it certainly did appear to be blood.

She had probably cut herself on some everyday printing hazard, I told myself, and then upset the tea as she went for plasters. Bruce might have gone with her to have the injury looked after.

But in my heart of hearts I knew that this was far worse than that. Amanda would have sent Bruce for plasters and kept working if it had been humanly possible. On a hunch, I leaned over and opened the freezer of the tiny fridge under a counter against the wall. Amanda's wallet was there behind the ice-cube tray, as usual.

The door flew open. The wind moaned eerily as an elderly man blew in and struggled to close the door behind him. "Hullo!" he chirped, registering surprise at seeing us instead of Amanda at her desk. "I nearly took flight!" He had the wizened, shrunken look of the elderly, but the sparkling eyes of a much younger man. Snow-white hair peeked out from under his woolen cap. "Where's Amanda?" he asked, glancing round the small office. He checked his watch, as if confirming this was the time she'd agreed to meet with him. "Something wrong?"

"I hope not." I tried to smile reassuringly. "We're customers, too. We're a bit surprised to find her gone, as well."

He took this in, then decided introductions were in order. "I'm Robert Lovegren. Order of St. James. I manage the shop next door to St. James's Gate, and see to the reprinting of the materials." He smiled benevolently. "I also look after Amanda a bit, to be honest," he added, as if in confidence. "There were times when this wouldn't have been any place for a lady to keep shop alone, Bruce or no Bruce."

"No, I suppose not," I acknowledged. "I'm Alex Plumtree; this is Nicola Beauchamp. Amanda's printing a book for us at Plumtree Press."

Lovegren's eyes lit up. "Yes, I've heard all about you." He stuck out his hand, as if he were actually pleased to meet me. I couldn't imagine why, in view of the morning papers. "Yes, you're publishing that book by Lord Chenies, about the wilding. Amanda told me all about it."

The awkward moment arrived when we realised we didn't have much more to say.

"Well. You don't know where she is, then," Lovegren said. "I'll just leave this job for her." He was quite cheerful until he walked round and saw the spill on her desk. "Oh, now that's not like Amanda." He shook his head as he viewed the carnage of tea and paper. "Not at all like her."

"We're a bit worried too. And it looks as if she might

have cut herself, or worse. We don't actually *know* something's wrong; otherwise I'd ring the police." I thought for a moment. "I've no idea where to begin looking for her."

"Mmm." Lovegren put his papers on a clean corner of her desk and patted them a couple of times. Then he pulled out his handkerchief and sopped up the remaining tea on the table's surface. "I know where to look for her. As I said, I try to look after her a bit."

"Let me come with you," I said, battening down my coat again. "Nicola, you can go back to the office—no sense in both of us charging round Clerkenwell."

"No, no," Lovegren said. "I know Amanda. I'll find her. Don't you worry. I'll ring you later, if you like." He sounded confident as he balled up the tea-stained handkerchief in his hand and prepared to leave.

"Alex, we have the meeting with Neville, don't forget," Nicola said. "In an hour and a half."

"You're right." I was torn. It didn't seem right to simply leave, when something serious might have happened to Amanda. On the other hand, what could we do? It didn't seem appropriate to ring the police, yet. . . . Reluctantly, after further assurances from Lovegren, we began to follow him out the door.

He had gone when I turned back to see Nicola staring up at the Morris quotes, the ones on the front wall of the shop. "Alex," she said softly. "Look . . ."

I had to read for a moment before I saw what she meant. Several of the lines of Morris quotes on that wall had been changed. More specifically, they had been augmented with a noticeable lack of artistry in black spray paint. The vandal had been a fan of Morris's more political writings, and had sprayed erratically, "I LOOK AT IT AS A MISTAKE TO GO IN FOR A POLICY OF RIOT . . . THE SOCIALISTS WILL ONE DAY HAVE TO FIGHT SERIOUSLY."

Once again, one of the books I'd published that year had come to life. The paper that the spray-painted quote had been taken from was one published in our Clerkenwell Fête boxed trio: *William Morris: Writings from Clerkenwell.* First Dickens, now Morris. What was left? Arnold Bennett's *Riceyman Steps.*

"I've a bad feeling about this," I said, and began to usher Nicola out of Amanda's domain. "No doubt the vandals who trashed her shop last night did it. Let's get out of here." Just as I was about to open the door and brave the wind, the telephone rang. Nicola went back to pick it up.

"Amanda's Print Shop." How like her to answer professionally, in case it was one of Amanda's clients ringing. I thought it odd that she said nothing further, but listened for several moments. Then she put the receiver down hesitantly.

"That was strange," she said. "What on *earth* . . ."

"Why? Who was it?"

She frowned. "I don't know; a man with an accent—Italian, I think—said he was Bodoni. He sounded like a friend, but . . . the things he said . . ."

The call had clearly upset Nicola. I went back to the desk where she stood rubbing her arms as if chilled. "Tell me what he said."

"This Bodoni said that Jenson has it in for me—he meant for Amanda, of course. He said she should leave the country, and that Goudy would have her."

"Bodoni . . . " I felt a strange urge to laugh. "Do you realise—those are all names of typefaces?"

"No . . ."

"We'll tell Amanda, immediately she turns up." What I *hadn't* said hung in the air like an echo: *if* she turns up. I scrawled a note and left it on her desk, asking her to ring me at any hour, at home or at the Press.

My eyes strayed briefly to the words on the wall. I made a decision. "We'll have to get something to eat before we see Neville. I'll show you a bit of Clerkenwell—the Bleeding Heart Wine Bar is just up the road."

We fought our way back out of the shop, into the frenzied windstorm, finally taking refuge in the walled red-brick Bleeding Heart Yard. I'd chosen the Bleeding Heart because it was too nice for the rabble of journalists who preferred to drink their lunch at the pub. Here I might run into a managing editor or two, or even a publisher, but probably not the obnoxious journalist who'd plagued us at the book cart. I'd learned with the morning paper that his name was Lloyd Branscomb.

"Mmm, nice," Nicola said, and stood for a moment blinking as we finally emerged into the subterranean wine bar. Brick walls rose from a raw wooden floor, and the only light came from votive candles on the tables. It felt a bit like retiring into a capacious womb—all comfort and darkness, with a bit of pulsating French music in the background. Editorial bigwigs from all sorts of publications dined here—mostly drank, actually. You could practically *feel* news being made.

And news was *made*, after all, not merely reported. What was a story without its spin? As a slender waitress with flowing blond hair and a French accent escorted us to a table for two, I heard a middle-aged man say to a younger colleague, "Better have him slant it a bit more toward its effect on Abercrombie's chances—you don't want to be namby-pamby." And there you had it, I thought. These people didn't merely report the news, they *shaped* it—packaged sound bites for easiest consumption, like Smarties.

"Something to drink?" the waitress asked as we sat, shedding our coats.

"Glass of wine?"

"Sounds good," Nicola said gratefully.

"Two glasses of your burgundy, please." The waitress nodded briskly, depositing two beautifully handwritten menus, and was gone.

Nicola came to a decision quickly on her choice of food, almost immediately replacing the menu on the table. "What do you think our chances are of winning the lawsuit?"

"It's hard for me to believe that the Charford-Cheneys have a case, as we do have a legal contract with Lord Chenies. But suits seem a black art to me—the outcome is so rarely what I would predict. This is our first—as far as I know—at the Press."

She nodded. "Did you suspect *Cleansing* would develop into a controversy like this?"

"No. Never. In retrospect, I should have known."

The waitress set down our wineglasses and disappeared again. I saw an older man move his newspaper slightly. Had he been watching me? I decided it was my imagination, and turned back to Nicola.

She took a sip of the dark wine, but her eyes never left mine over the rim of the glass. To my surprise, she said without preamble, "It was Guy Ferris-Browne, wasn't it? The PM's man who got you into this?"

Stunned, I stared at her. The little candle flickered, one moment illuminating her face, the next casting shadows over it. She was right again.

"Yes," I said softly. "But how on earth did you know?"

She looked down, toying with the pepper shaker. "Oh, Reg and his cohorts. You begin to recognise the styles of certain people."

I'd never asked about the specifics of her fiancé's work, and Nicola hadn't been forthcoming with the information. She'd mentioned in the interviews of weeks past that Reg, who was Someone in the City, was deeply involved politically. I had the impression Reg D'Arcy was on the Conservative side, because Nicola had mentioned that he was an authority on the economic disadvantages of the EU. She'd passed along the little-known but stunning bit of information that each year, just to stay in the EU, Britain handed over 4 billion pounds to Brussels. Moreover, to achieve Economic and Monetary Union, Britain would have to place a percentage of its reserve gold bullion in the coffers of the recently established European Central Bank. This esteemed institution had just announced that it would not publish minutes of its meetings for a minimum of sixteen years . . . which did make one wonder.

"Does this present you with a problem, Nicola?" She knew I was asking whether she'd need to tell Reg, an action that would compromise her position at the Press.

She shook her head and picked up her wineglass again, her expression one of such world-weariness that she suddenly looked years older. I'd seen that expression before, I thought as I watched her downcast eyes, when she told me she'd learned at an early age that everything came down to politics.

There were unplumbed depths here, I could see. And I wanted to plumb them—in a brotherly way, of course.

The waitress delivered fettuccine for Nicola; I tucked into a vegetarian lasagna. The warm baguette with sweet butter would have been a worthy main course in itself, and the salad vinaigrette, after the meal, was better than any pudding. We ate in companionable silence, not lingering, more than a bit subdued.

I sensed that she shared my discomfort about Amanda's odd disappearance, especially as it followed the print shop break-in last night and Mmbasi Kumba's death, not to mention the lawsuit and our difficulties with the printing of *Cleansing*. My only remaining dilemma was why Nicola didn't quit her job immediately, under the circumstances— particularly in view of her fiancé's position. It had to be awkward for her.

"Nearly time, isn't it?" she asked, glancing at her watch. It was refreshing to see someone who took responsibility even when the boss was around. I nodded in answer, wondering if she'd caught me checking my watch as well. I liked to think I had the unobtrusive checking of timepieces down to an art, because I thought it rude—

like looking past a person's head at a party for someone more important to talk to.

As I stood to don my coat, my eyes roamed to the gentleman in the corner. Now I found him concentrating studiously on a framed print next to him on the wall, something he'd already had nearly an hour to memorise, if he'd wished. Had he followed us into the pub or been seated before us? I couldn't remember.

We climbed the restaurant's wooden steps up to street level and allowed ourselves to be blown right over to Farringdon Road, where we hailed a taxi. "Lincoln's Inn Fields, please," I said to the driver. As he drove on, we passed the spot where the boys had crossed Farringdon Road to chase Mmbasi Kumba up Clerkenwell Road. Suddenly, out of nowhere, the face of the boy I'd recognised came back to me. My stomach knotted as I recalled where I'd seen him before: he was a miniature of the PM's bodyguard, the blond giant with the white eyebrows.

"What?" Nicola asked, tensing. "What is it?"

"I've just remembered where I saw one of the boys who chased Mmbasi Kumba in the wilding."

"You *knew* one of them?"

"No, not exactly knew, but I'd seen him. Not really even him, but his father. He was the PM's bodyguard, I think."

She looked shocked; she understood the significance of my recollection. The prime minister was linked to the wilding. Ferris-Browne? Perhaps he'd set it all up without the prime minister's knowledge. But I wanted to believe that my father's friend was innocent.

"Alex, do you think they planned to kill that boy?"

"I don't know, Nicola; I just don't know. The wilding might have been planned—to include me—but the murder could've been an accident." We rode in silence as the driver ferried us to Neville's. The implications of this were stunning. We were not safe.

Dear God, what had happened to Amanda?

After another brief, blustery interlude we found ourselves cosseted in the law offices of Neville Greenslade.
The plush prosperity of his premises seemed surreal; after
all, we'd just been discussing murder arranged by the
highest office in the land.

We were offered coffees, which we accepted, and it
wasn't long before Neville stepped out to greet us. Greenslade resembled no one so much as Desmond Llewelyn,
"Q" in the James Bond films. Like all my father's friends,
with the exception of Ian, Neville was beginning to look
smaller as he aged. As he stuck out a liver-spotted hand, I
reflected that I prized his wisdom and experience
greatly—not to mention his kindness. Perhaps he could
help me . . . with all my problems.

"Alex. Good to see you again." Shaking my hand, he
turned his gaze to Nicola. "Neville Greenslade," he said.
"A pleasure."

"Nicola Beauchamp, our new trade editor," I said,
completing the introductions. Nicola was able to turn her
smile on him at half wattage, and I could see that she had
the usual effect. A sort of warmth suffused Neville, the
warmth an older man would feel toward a beautiful
young creature who reminded him of his daughters, now
older than Nicola. His gaze also held a touch of sadness
for the hard blows that life would inevitably deal her and
the resulting bitterness that was sure to ensue.

"Delighted to meet you," she said, offering her hand.
"I understand you're going to extricate us from a nasty little mess."

"Indeed I'll try," he replied. With some difficulty
Neville turned his gaze from Nicola's magical features and
ushered us into a conference room. "Well now," he said,
rubbing his hands together as we settled into heavy
wooden chairs around a polished oval of cherry wood.
"I'm not exactly sure why the young Charford-Cheneys
are trying this on. Unless I'm mistaken, they're angry and

want you to know it." He sighed. "I've looked over your contract with Lord Chenies, Alex, and I see that we're protected by the usual clause stating that the author has no existing binding relationship for the work under contract with any other party." His mouth curved in a bitter little smile. "Perhaps they're in need of a bit of cash and hope you'll settle for enough to pay off their debts."

"Mmm, that's a possibility," I admitted. "I think they were a bit optimistic about the viability of a publishing house that produces solely serial works." I also happened to know that they had a frighteningly expensive house in Belgravia, not to mention a country estate. No doubt they expected to inherit the family fortune belonging to Lord Chenies, but as with many members of the English aristocracy, their tastes far exceeded their income. I wouldn't have been surprised to learn that they were seriously overextended.

Nicola was frowning. "But wouldn't they know that what Mr. Greenslade's just said is true? Why would they go to the expense of a suit if they know they don't stand a chance? Surely you don't even have to settle if the suit is thrown out."

Neville nodded. "Yes, I think they do know. But you see, Nicola, sometimes businesses use lawsuits as a sort of warning—nothing more than an expression of anger. It's quite possible," he said thoughtfully, "that they want something from you and will withdraw the suit if they get it. No telling what lengths—or should I say depths—some people will go to in order to get what they want."

"Perhaps they do want money," I said. "Or they might actually think I would still give the book back to them— let them publish it serially." I shook my head. "They're badly mistaken, if they think I've gone through all this just to hand the book over. Not to say that I wouldn't be much happier if I'd never heard of it." There was silence round the table; I doubt I was the only one remembering the painful *Talkabout* programme.

"Neville," I said, with a glance at Nicola, "I think you need to know another pertinent fact about the publication of *Cleansing*. It's absolutely confidential, of course."

He nodded and leaned over the table toward me, utterly intent on what I was about to say. "I'm publishing *Cleansing* as a political favour to the prime minster, through someone close to him who's doing his best to keep him in office. Otherwise I wouldn't have touched it with a barge pole."

"Ah, yes. I see. Well, that does change things a bit," Neville murmured uncomfortably.

"There's—um—still a bit more, I'm sorry to say." I rubbed my forehead. "I have reason to believe that the Clerkenwell Wilding was arranged, and arranged to involve *me*. I know that sounds absurd, but believe me, I would prefer to think otherwise. On the way here, I realised that I'd recognised one of the boys in the wilding. I could be wrong, of course, but just the day before the wilding I was in the PM's office, and the boy's adult double was there. He was even taller than I am, at least six feet five, and had white eyebrows.

"So, although you know that I trust the PM," I said to Neville's knowing look, "I fear that his minions are rather using me."

Something flickered in Nicola's eyes, and I was fairly certain she'd concluded that it was Ferris-Browne who'd set me up. But the emotion I saw was not what I'd expected, not a thrill of victory at guessing the truth, but more like shame—or guilt. I tucked the information away for what it was worth.

"I'm not exactly certain how involving me in a wilding helps them," I continued, "except that they can make Lord Chenies, and by association Dexter Moore, appear even less desirable. After all, they asked me to publish the book so people would hate it. But being linked to wildings was never discussed when I agreed to publish the book. As I say, I doubt that the PM himself knows about the attempt to disgrace *me* along with the novel."

"Nastier and nastier." Neville tapped his Montblanc pen on a legal pad as he stared at it. I could see his mind was racing.

Nicola had withdrawn into herself, her shoulders slumped as if this latest revelation had hit her a bit hard. But as I watched, she seemed to recover herself. She sat up and straightened her shoulders. "I think we need to send a signal that this sort of abuse won't be tolerated." Her eyes met mine. "Don't you think?" She turned to Neville. "What can you do in a situation like this—legally?"

"Well." Neville looked cheered at her line of thought. "If you want to send an equally strong message to Malcolm and Hillary Charford-Cheney, I'll draft a letter that will send the pair of them whining into a corner, tails between their legs." He smiled at us. "As far as the PM's henchmen go"—out of the corner of my eye I saw muscles tighten in Nicola's jaw at Neville's use of the word—"we're dealing with an entirely different sort of person."

He paused delicately, pursing his lips. "Naturally, I can't advise you to do anything illegal . . . " Another pause as his tongue explored his cheek. "But perhaps you know something about this—er, friend of the prime minister's that he would prefer to keep a secret."

To my surprise, Nicola abruptly said, "Let me look into it. I know what to do." Her eyes were steely. She looked down and plucked a bit of fluff from her skirt, as if she dealt with the PM's inner circle every day. Perhaps she did, through her fiancé, Reg.

Neville seemed to find nothing odd about Nicola's of- fer. It wasn't that I was surprised that she *could* take care of it—I don't think anything about her would have surprised me. She exuded capability and *savoir faire*. Somehow her youth only added to this aura of infallibility. I suppose it was difficult for me to believe that she would willingly offer herself up for that sort of ordeal.

"That's an excellent idea, Nicola," he said, and I thought I saw a look pass between them. Did he know something I didn't?

Suddenly I found it a bit overwhelming that I had an employee with such political know-how. What other surprises did Nicola hold for me in the days to come?

Clearing his throat politely, Neville said with a bit too much bluster, "I'll draft that letter then, shall I?"

"Yes, do," I said, and stood. I looked at Nicola. "I can hardly wait to see what happens next."

She looked grim as we walked, by mutual agreement, back to Bedford Square. The wind had died down to intermittent gusts, and the sun was shining. The occasional black-bottomed cloud raced across the sun, momentarily darkening our surroundings, which matched our mood nicely.

We walked down Holborn past Bloomsbury Square Gardens. Tramps rested in hazy stupors on benches in the garden; red buses thundered down Gower Street. Usually this scene restored my sense of perspective, but not today. Murders, betrayals, mysterious disappearances, threatened legal actions, and verbal beatings by the press took their toll on a blustery spring day. And now my trade editor was going to "look into" a man who had probably arranged a murder?

"Nicola, I don't think it's safe for you to go poking round Ferris-Browne. If he arranged a murder—and maybe Amanda's disappearance—there's no telling what he might do to you."

She stopped in her tracks, turning on me almost angrily. "You're going to have to believe me, Alex: I know what I'm doing. I'm just going to get some information. Tonight, in fact."

Somewhat taken aback by her tone, I turned up

Bloomsbury Street. It was impossible not to notice the handsome yet unobtrusive new structure that joined the original Plumtree Press building to the building behind; it had been a hotel until we'd annexed it last year. So much had gone right—until the *Cleansing* fiasco.

"The more I think about it, I can't understand why I didn't take a warning from the two sets of missing proofs." The roar of traffic was so loud I had to shout. "As Amanda herself said, too many people hate this book." I shook my head at the irony. "Which is exactly why I'm publishing it."

A huge lorry belched diesel exhaust in my face as if to add insult to injury. Waving the thick smoke away as we continued down the pavement, I lamented, "Only Lord Chenies himself likes the novel, and Malcolm and Hillary— for financial reasons. And Richard Hotchkiss."

Nicola raised her eyebrows. "The road construction baron? King of the Clerkenwell dust devils, and London Water Wizard? How do you know he likes the book?"

"Hotchkiss is a sort of neighbour of mine—I'm involved in some local Chorleywood doings with him about the exact location of the Buckinghamshire-Hertfordshire county boundary. There are water rights involved, and hedges. *My* hedges, in fact." There had been another story in the *Tempus* just that morning, in which Helena Hotchkiss of HIT had been quoted as saying that the Herts-Bucks boundary vote was vital because of scores of miles of ancient hedges along the existing boundary. If they were suddenly no longer on the county line, they wouldn't be protected under law. Hedges delineating county or parish boundaries were even more sacred to conservationists than the seven-species type.

"I ran into Hotchkiss after my interview with Mimi the other night," I continued. He's an old friend of Lord Chenies's and happens to be head of the Chorleywood Conservative Association. He made rather encouraging noises where Nigel's book was concerned."

"Ah."

There were no press vultures hanging about the entrance to the Press, so we mounted the steps with impunity. I paused just outside the door, my hand on the well-buffed brass door handle.

"Nicola," I said. "About what we discussed at Neville's office. I'm worried that you—"

"Don't worry about it, Alex," she broke in. The words were toneless, nonchalant. "Really. Just leave it with me." She strode past me into the comforting dark of the Press foyer. It was three-thirty, and as the door closed behind me I felt an ominous quiet in the building. It was totally out of keeping with the maelstrom of activity outside, not to mention the volatile political atmosphere. Normally the Press seemed a refuge from the petty wrongs of the world, but at that moment it seemed a fortress poised to fall.

I might have been wrong, but I felt certain that Nicola knew what I was thinking. We had that rare understanding that sometimes exists, inexplicably, between two people.

"Come on," she said. "We've work to do," and she led me into Dee's domain with a hardened, resigned little smile that managed to work sympathy into the mix.

Dee looked up at us perkily as she turned her romance novel over on the desk, still conveniently open to the page. "Wotcher!" Though she could produce a lovely receptionist's accent, Dee was a Londoner at heart.

"Wotcher," I said in return, by way of greeting. "Anything interesting while we were gone?"

"Na," she said airily. "Only the post." She indicated a pile of letters and miscellaneous publications she'd already sorted by department. "You can take yours up, if you want. Derek's not picked it up yet." She hesitated. "This new voice mail's going to do me out of a job, though, i'n it? I still reach for the handset every time, out of habit, like. Your phone rang a few times, but it's none of my worry now, is it?"

Clearly Dee felt that some of her power had been usurped by the all-singing, all-dancing phone system. Before we'd got the new set-up, she'd known everything that went on in all of our lives, every last phone call, from creditors to lovers.

"Don't worry, Dee," I said, picking up the upstairs-bound piles of post. "We couldn't do without you." Glancing through the letters, I made a mental note to think about how I could expand her duties. She could certainly handle more than reception.

"Oh, I nearly forgot. Mrs. Khasnouri rang. She won't be coming for her literacy tutoring today."

"Is she ill?" My pupil, our accountant's grandmother, was elderly. I worried about her making the trip in to central London every week from Watford, but she insisted on fitting in with my normal workday. And I had a passion for teaching adults who couldn't read—it was yet another tradition passed on by my father.

"Er, no. She—ooh, I hate to say this, Mr. P, but I suppose you'd better know. She said to tell you she didn't associate with people who endorsed wildings." Dee cringed, knowing how those words would sting. "I'm sorry."

This was a devastating blow. Mrs. Khasnouri was a sweet, kind woman whom I felt privileged to help. She was progressing very well and seemed to enjoy our weekly sessions together. I certainly did. Now this lovely lady wanted nothing to do with me.

After giving me a sympathetic look, Dee glanced at her master console. "You've got three other messages," she said, her "three" coming out as "free," "and Nicola, you've got one." Her gaze left Nicola immediately, and I sensed that she was somewhat intimidated by this woman who was so different from her, yet the same age.

"Thanks," Nicola replied easily. "Is that any good?"

"Wot, this?" Dee held up the bodice-ripper, its cover illustrating the origins of the genre nickname perfectly. "Yeah, all right. 'Bout what you expect." She crinkled her nose and reddened slightly. "You know."

Nicola nodded. "Let me guess: it's like her last one, *Love's Lost Years,* but with different characters in a different city, right?"

"That's it!" Dee laughed. "How'd you know?"

"Well, I have to keep up on all sorts of literature, don't I?"

Dee was impressed. She'd have something to joke about with Nicola from now on. I was impressed, too, and wondered for the umpteenth time what other surprises lay beneath that smooth veneer.

CHAPTER SIX

I tell you naught for your comfort,
Yea, naught for your desire,
Save that the sky grows darker yet
And the sea rises higher.

G. K. CHESTERTON,
The Ballad of the White Horse

IT MAY NOT HAVE BEEN QUITE CRICKET TO FOLLOW Nicola that evening. But for once I wasn't taking Lisette home, as she'd had to take her own car to drive to one of the boys' football games. And I was extremely curious to see what my new employee had planned—not to mention concerned. I suppose I hoped she might have a quiet drink with her fiancé, Reg D'Arcy, to gather information. But she had something completely different in mind.

She set out on foot and caught a taxi in Tottenham Court Road. I was lucky and nobbled one myself, just moments after her.

"See that taxi up there?" I leaned over the seat toward the driver and pointed up ahead about eight cars in the chockablock traffic.

He nodded.

"If you could follow him, I'd be grateful. And I—er—don't want them to know we're following." I extended a ten-pound note toward the steering wheel.

"Absolutely," he said without hesitation, deftly sliding the money down and out of sight. "Thank you, sir."

We wove through the crowded side streets of London, always far enough behind Nicola's taxi that I felt sure she wouldn't notice us. Her driver took a consistently southern route, moving parallel to Charing Cross Road, down through Soho, and finally my suspicions were confirmed. Her taxi carried on straight past the government offices to the Palace of Westminster, commonly known as the Houses of Parliament.

Was she speeding directly to Ferris-Browne? That would imply a much closer relationship than I had imagined. Or was her fiancé here for some reason? Perhaps she was visiting someone else entirely.

My driver cooperatively pulled to one side and effectively hid, the nose of the car pointing away from the Palace of Westminster and Nicola's taxi. Waves of traffic flowed around us. "Perfect," I said. "Thanks."

"Any time, Guv."

"I'm just going to watch here for a moment, if that's all right. No need to turn off the meter."

"Right you are." He settled in his seat, took down a small notebook from the visor, and began to write with a stubby pencil.

As I watched Nicola advance toward the imposing hub of British government, none other than Guy Ferris-Browne emerged from the massive visitors' doors. He stopped dead in his tracks when he saw her. Even from a distance, I could tell that the man was badly shocked. For a moment I thought he was going to embrace her, moving toward her with his arms extended, but she rebuffed him.

Standing a good two feet away from the man, she said something vehemently—I could tell by how still she held herself—then turned abruptly to go inside the building. Ferris-Browne followed, looking stunned.

He wasn't the only one.

When they disappeared, I asked the driver to take me back to Bedford Square.

He nodded, turned the vehicle around at the earliest opportunity, and wended his way back north to Bloomsbury. I tipped him handsomely as he came to a stop in front of the Press, and climbed out, feeling very weary. It was six-thirty. I would just have time to get home and change before dining with Martyn Blakely—my old Merchant Taylors school friend, now back as the newly appointed vicar of Christ Church Chenies—in an hour.

That would be a bright spot, I decided. But first I wanted to check on Amanda. The Press had been locked up for the night—even Rachel had left, evidently—so I unlocked the door and hurried in to Dee's phone. There was no answer at Amanda's. Then I had the bright idea that Lovegren might have called and left a message. I checked my voice mail and found the he had indeed rung. *"Yes, Alex. This is Robert Lovegren, with the Order of St. James. Please give me a ring at Amanda's flat at your earliest convenience. That's—"* I quickly punched in the numbers and waited.

"Yes?" It was Lovegren, sounding guarded.

"Robert, it's Alex Plumtree. Have you found her?"

He paused before answering, which didn't bode well. I felt my skin prickling, the harbinger of bad news. "I'm afraid so." I had the impression he was composing himself to get the words out. I waited, my dread growing with each moment. "The good news is that our girl's all right. A bit shaken, but still with us."

"What is it, Robert? What's happened?"

"I don't know if you've met Anthony Simino, one of the leaders of the Clerkenwell Neighbourhood Association."

"Yes," I confirmed, practically holding my breath. I'd met Simino with Amanda in the Clerkenwell Neighbourhood Association offices three months ago.

"Well, Simino, when he's not selling property, conducts

tours of Clerkenwell's notable spots—such as the House of Detention." The House of Detention had been one of the worst of the hellish prisons in London—dark, damp, entirely subterranean. It was one of Clerkenwell's more dubious claims to fame, but recently it had become a popular tourist attraction with Americans. "He found Amanda down there, chained to the wall in the dark—with those tapes of prisoners moaning and groaning playing at full volume."

"Good Lord!" I exclaimed. "What on earth—"

"Clearly someone wanted to frighten her—they didn't do any physical harm. The really awful thing is that the House of Detention isn't even *open* on Tuesdays, normally. Simino was down there today only because a group of Americans had booked with him specially, just for today. Otherwise Amanda would have been there all night."

Feeling utterly responsible, I blurted, "I—I don't know what to say. Is she really all right? Was she hurt?"

"Not beyond the shock of it all. She claims she'll be back at the print shop tomorrow, running proofs. She wanted to talk to you, but I've called in a doctor, a friend of mine. He's made her take something. She's sleeping now." I could hear by the way his voice grew faint at the end that he'd turned away from the phone to look at her, or toward the room in which she slept.

"Robert, I—I know I'm partly to blame for this. I'm coming right over."

"Alex—wait. The doctor said she needs sleep. You can come see her if you want, but he said she mustn't be disturbed."

"I see." I thought for a moment. "It's this blasted Chenies novel, of course, causing all the trouble. Would you please tell Amanda to forget about the special edition for a few days and recuperate? I'll come round to see her tomorrow. And please tell her I'm terribly sorry."

"I'll tell her, Alex. But you know Amanda. I doubt anyone will keep her out of that shop tomorrow."

"Did she say *who* did this? Or why?"

"Only this: she claims someone came through the cellar door—*her cellar door*, mind you—and put something over her head. She fought the man, whoever he was, and thinks she managed to scratch him." Perhaps that explained the blood on the back of her chair. I imagined the sheer terror Amanda must have felt when someone grabbed her from behind—someone from the depths of her own building.

I fought off a shiver. "It's more than disturbing. It's . . . sick." My inadequate words hung in the air. "You've phoned the police, of course?"

Lovegren sighed. "My first thought, too, Alex. She won't let me."

"Why on earth *not*?" I was incredulous. "But she *must*! There could be samples of the attacker's skin under her fingernails, fibres on her clothing—"

"Alex," he interrupted gently, "I know. But even after all she's been through, she's *still* more worried about Clerkenwell's reputation than she is about herself. She said there used to be a problem with crime, and now, with the wilding there . . ."

He let the sentence drift off. With the wilding associated with me, the otherwise gentrified Clerkenwell had become suspect again.

"Ah," I said.

"And considering that she gets her grant money from the Neighbourhood Association, she doesn't want to give the area a bad name. People can ring the police for a record of crime in a given area, you know. Believe me, I argued with her about it, but she was already so distraught, and felt so strongly, that in the end I let it go for the moment."

"Yes. I see." There was an awkward silence. "Robert, there's something I need to tell you. The phone rang at the shop just after we talked to you. It seemed to be almost a threat. Now I feel an idiot for not doing something about it—Whoever it was obviously thought Nicola was Amanda, and said his name was Bodoni."

Lovegren was oddly silent.

"He said that someone named Jenson was coming after Amanda, something to that effect. I suppose Jenson—whoever he is—might be responsible for what happened."

"Anything else?" The old man sounded upset.

"Just that this bloke Bodoni, who had an Italian accent, according to Nicola, said that Goudy was willing to have Amanda stay with him."

I heard his breath down the line.

"I know just enough to be dangerous, Robert—but I believe those are all names of typefaces. And now I think of it, they're all from different countries. Bodoni was Italian, Jenson was French, and Goudy was American, if I'm not mistaken." My father's lessons in the barn had stuck with me, after all. I remembered more than I had realised.

"Very good, Alex," he said quietly. "Didn't know you were a printer."

"I'm not, really—but do you know what this is all about? Who these people are?"

"I'll tell Amanda. I think that's really all we can do."

I noticed that he hadn't really answered my question—only deflected it. Somehow I felt he knew more about this than I did. But he seemed eager to get off the line, and after explaining that he'd arranged for one of the St. James's ambulance nurses to stay the night with Amanda, he rang off.

Suddenly the dark, quiet Press felt very ominous indeed.

As I replaced the phone, all I wanted to do was sit there in the dark, in temporary escape from the parade of horrors I seemed to have stumbled into. First Mmbasi Kumba and Nicola's injury; then the proofs, the tampering with Amanda's galley trays, the lawsuit, Amanda and her mysterious Italian caller, Nicola's obvious familiarity with Ferris-Browne; and now Amanda's violent abduction.

Martyn was expecting me in half an hour. How could I hope to be a dinner guest with the world caving in around me? I picked up the phone to cancel, but before the vicarage phone rang, I changed my mind and hung up again. Little would be achieved sitting at Amanda's bedside watching her sleep, or brooding somewhere alone. I locked up the Press and headed for my dark green Volkswagen Golf parked outside, sporting its precious Bedford Square parking disc on the windscreen. I found myself slipping into a foul temper as I climbed in. Amanda's disaster and Nicola's betrayal combined to make me feel that everything was tumbling out of control.

"Damn!" I hit the steering wheel as I accelerated out into the road, earning several hoots from irritated motorists. This was getting more serious by the moment. I would have to take action to keep others from being hurt—or even killed. Right there and then, as a preliminary step, I rang my security firm friends in Ealing on the cell phone and had them post security guards round the clock at Amanda's flat, the print shop, and the Press. As an afterthought, I asked that the guards check daily for bugs in the telephones at each place. I considered placing a guard at the Orchard as well, but decided Ian and I could take care of ourselves.

The drive home was a nightmare of fevered thinking

and rush-hour congestion. There'd been an accident on the motorway, and traffic dragged to a halt for a full ten minutes. My mind ran over the same questions again and again. Who was sabotaging the printing of the special edition? Random *Cleansing*-haters? Liberal or social activists? Ferris-Browne, executing some unfathomable master plan? But why? It was no secret that the trade edition was to be released a mere two weeks after the special edition: Max had put it in his article. With tens of thousands of copies of the paperback hitting the market, why try to stop a special edition?

The only reasonable answer seemed to be the type of irrational hatred shown by my local HIT squad that morning. Emotions were running so high that normally reasonable, civilised people were acting irrationally. Perhaps in the same way that the neo-Nazis who gathered under Dexter Moore's flag had their own élite terrorist group, G18, the Socialists had theirs. I just hadn't heard of them until now. Or the father of Nicky Finch, last year's first wilding victim, was out to get the book and, disturbingly, perhaps Amanda and me, for being associated with it. These were not acts of rational people. It was not a rational time.

As I waited impatiently for the traffic blockage to clear, my thoughts drifted back to Nicola. Now that I knew she was intimately acquainted with Guy Ferris-Browne (who happened to be old enough to be her father), and had seen her odd authority over him, I knew I was in deep waters with her. Could she be trusted? Was she working with the man? Had she only got the job as head of my trade division, with perfect timing to coincide with the publication of Charford-Cheney's book, to further set me up and guarantee a black eye for Plumtree Press? I had even *told* her that I suspected foul play on the proofs. It was so embarrassing. I'd never thought to sus-

pect that Nicola could be involved. . . . Now that I'd
bared my soul to her about my suspicions that Ferris-
Browne was using me, she could go straight back to him
with the news. No doubt they'd covered that in the first
ten minutes.

I was going to be still later to Martyn's, caught in this
paralytic traffic. . . . My friend had invited me to dine with
him in the vicarage to say thanks for helping him move in
on the previous Saturday. Martyn and I had picked up
right where we'd left off sixteen years ago—I hadn't seen
him since before University. I felt fortunate to be able to
reclaim an old friendship.

When at last I got home, feeling overwhelmingly de-
feated by traffic, kidnappers, and employee betrayals, I
found a note on the kitchen worktop: *Cheers, off to Verbier
for the European Environmental Summit. See you there Friday night. Ian.* I'd almost forgot about the summit and
Ian's departure. British horticultural and environmental
experts were particularly in demand at the summit this
year because of the hedges preservation frenzy and HIT's
fine example of grassroots activism. It was also a hot
year for the Euro-Enviro Summit, because the EU's environmental policy was really getting off the ground, with
punishingly stringent regulations on everything from car
exhaust to water consumption.

Ian wasn't the only local attending the Summit; I'd
read in the newspaper that Helena Hotchkiss was a guest
of honour. Officially, the summit would start on Monday
and fitted in perfectly with Sarah's and my plan to meet
for a ski holiday with Ian.

I shook my head in amazement as I tossed the
note in the rubbish bin. Ian was a mass of contradictions
that never failed to fascinate. He was an outspoken environmentalist, a rare non-Labour, non–Socialist in the
ranks of the environmentalists. In fact, Ian was a bit

offbeat politically—he'd joined the successor to Sir John Silversmith's anti-EU Reform Party, now a political pressure group called the Campaign for an Independent Britain, or CIB. No doubt he was also one of the few septuagenarians who would negotiate the super-expert, off-piste slopes at the ski resort—on the metal Volant skis Sarah had given him for Christmas.

As I crossed from the kitchen to the staircase, I enjoyed the quiet darkness of my peaceful old house. There was a distinctive scent about the place: a cross between the smell of toast and the scent of old books. Not exactly musty, but infinitely cosy and comfortable. I trudged up the creaky stairs and exchanged work clothes for baggy corduroy trousers, polo shirt, and sweater, then wandered down again, much subdued. As I passed through the kitchen I decided to ring Martyn and let him know that I was just leaving. I doubted that he had a soufflé timed for my arrival, or indeed anything more than a defrosted microwaveable hamburger, but it would take me several minutes to drive to Chenies.

But as I lifted the wall-hung receiver I saw something that made me stop cold. A bright bit of red-clad copper wire sat on the worktop, just behind the toaster. The wire hadn't been there that morning. No one had been in the house but Ian. I couldn't think what might have spurred him on to a sudden burst of household wiring, even if he'd found time before leaving for Heathrow.

Then I remembered the telecom blokes who'd appeared so unexpectedly in my office, and I slowly hung up the phone. I plucked the cell phone out of my pocket and amended my instructions to the security company: check the Orchard phones for bugs daily as well.

I drove to Martyn's feeling that the sky was falling—again.

◆   ◆   ◆

"Plumtree! You came after all. I thought maybe you had doubts after seeing the mess this place was in at the . . . weekend." Martyn stopped, still standing in the doorway, and studied me. My face must have shown more than I willed it to. In a way, I suppose I wanted to share my troubles with an old friend.

His tone changed and he ushered me inside, taking the bottle of wine from my hand. "Sorry about all the fuss on *Talkabout* last night, Alex. It can't be easy."

"Thanks, Martyn. There've been a few more ripples in the water, I'm afraid, since then."

"Oh, no." He looked at me with concern.

"The wilding seems to have been only the beginning—not just for me but for my printer, my new editor . . ."

"And now you've come *here*?"

Martyn had coaxed a smile out of me, and I had to admit to feeling the better for it. Over wine by the fire I told all—with the exception of my little deal with Ferris-Browne and the prime minister. He listened with the practised attentiveness of a clergyman.

"You really have had the week from hell," he said sympathetically when I'd concluded. "I'll put in a good word for you."

"I'd appreciate that, yes, Martyn. I trust you're on good terms with Him?"

"For the most part, yes." He winked. "And I seriously hope He's been on my side tonight, as I'm attempting poached salmon for the first time. It'd be a shame if in addition to everything else you came down with ptomaine poisoning."

With that we ventured into the kitchen, which was also a throwback to some time between the late 1700s and Queen Victoria's reign. The Aga cooker may well have been the better part of a hundred years old. But it was all neat as a pin, and very comfortable—the corners of the old table in the center of the room were nicely smoothed from centuries of use, and the floor, which at some stage had been covered in oiled cork squares, was soft and polished.

"I see Emily's been in." Emily was the woman who'd cleaned the Orchard ever since I could remember. She'd always done the vicarage as well.

"Yes, amazing, isn't she?" Martyn smiled at me over his shoulder as he poked a boiling pot of new potatoes with a fork. "Definitely one of the perks of this job." He put the lid back on the pot, set down the fork, and slid an oven mitt over one hand as he opened one of the Aga's doors. "I picked up some bhajis from the new Indian take-away. It's going to be an eclectic meal." Lifting out a warmed plate of the small cakes of fried vegetables, he motioned for me to follow.

"The best kind," I said, following him out of the kitchen and bearing our wineglasses to the tiny dining area. We pulled out Victorian oak chairs topped with carved crowns, and Martyn said a brief and humorous blessing having to do with my continued survival. After the first bite of bhaji I said, "So tell me. How does it feel to be vicar of Christ Church Chenies?"

"Well, I can tell you, it's quite interesting having two Lords." He smiled wryly as he chewed, and tossed his head in the direction of Chenies Manor. "There's no question, his lordship's very good to the church, and to me, for that matter. But he's definitely under the impression that I work for *him*."

"Really?" It seemed that Charford-Cheney's authoritarianism knew no bounds. "How do you mean?"

"Oh, he popped over last night and let me know that he expects me to continue doing Wednesday morning matins for him and a few old fellows who live hereabouts. It's not that I mind—I'm happy to see faith survive in any form. But it really is a custom service for him."

"Hmm," I said. "Your occupation certainly entails different problems from mine." I could hear the envy in my own voice. Greener grass, I thought.

"Yes. And in presenting a welcoming gift, the first of those I've ever received in my total of three placements, he let me know in no uncertain terms that there were to be no 'happy-clappy,' toe-tapping tunes in *his* church."

He bit into another bhaji with relish. The dining room was filled with the scent of exotic Indian spices. "Mmm—I don't mind that at all, because I'm not a happy-clappy fan myself. Give me 'Jerusalem' and the 1662 service any day. More reverent, I think. It's just that he really did say '*his* church.'"

"I suppose when you grow up just through the gate from the church, and are told you're responsible for it, in a sense, you could feel that it was yours. Extraordinary perspective, though, isn't it?" I shook my head and grimaced. "I can imagine what his lordship's anti-Conservative critics would think of that. No wonder they want the royals out, the whole structure demolished."

"I don't know," Martyn ventured, a bit hesitantly. "I'm not so sure that it isn't better for some people—especially those with sufficient resources—to feel some responsibility. From my perspective, a bit of that is a good thing. Most people these days don't realise that I'm not supposed to *be* the church, just the leader. Frankly, most people think it's my job to run the whole thing for them, and provide entertainment on Sunday mornings. I suppose I shouldn't complain about his lordship. At least he's involved."

From there our discussion drifted to Sarah's and my wedding that summer, at which Martyn had agreed to officiate. He told me tales about weddings he'd performed in the past—both good and bad. From there our discussion drifted to the past, and the girlfriend Martyn had left behind because she didn't want to leave her home village—even for him. It had nearly broken him, he admitted over the baklava, and he was just now feeling himself again, though it had happened three years ago.

"I'm sorry," I told him. "I never knew you'd been that serious."

"Well. It's over now." He stood to clear our plates. "I have an idea. You like old books, don't you?"

What a question.

"I thought," he continued, "we might take our coffees upstairs—I think you'll appreciate some of the relics up there. I don't think the attic's been touched in centuries." With enthusiasm I picked up my coffee and, after adding cream, went with him as he opened a door off the kitchen. "I admit, I do have an ulterior motive," he said mischievously.

"Oh? What's that?"

"Well, I have an idea that it would be nice to have a home study. All the rooms downstairs are already decorated for a purpose—and I'd like to have a place that's mine to use. Just room for a desk, a filing cabinet—you know. For that novel I've always meant to write. A grubby little study that no one will ever see but me. I'd never have to tidy it up." Martyn's eyes shone. "So I wondered if you'd be willing to help me move a few things to one side. I could do it myself, of course, but when you see it, you might understand why I need a bit of moral support."

I was curious as to what we'd find as we climbed the narrow staircase, our passage illuminated by a single naked bulb on the wall. It was steep, and I had to concentrate to keep from tripping on the tiny wooden steps.

"I have a distinct sense of snooping into someone else's business," I said. "I never could have dreamed of entering the attic while your predecessor lived here."

"I doubt he was ever in it," Martyn replied. "Too difficult a climb."

"I suppose. I also had the feeling that he and his wife never really felt this was their home."

"Yes. No doubt Charford-Cheney pointed out to them that it's still technically part of the Cheney estate, and has never been formally given to the Church. They were probably glad when they could retire to a home of their own."

"Probably," I said, careful not to go on too much about Martyn's predecessor. He'd already told me that everyone had praised Michael to the point that he didn't see how he could ever take his place. That was one part of Martyn's job I didn't envy, because I knew what it felt like. It had been hard enough trying to take my father's place at the head of Plumtree Press. I wanted to tell Martyn not to try. He wasn't taking someone else's place; he was creating a new one.

At the top of the stairs, I heard the click of a light switch being flipped, and yet another naked bulb illuminated a remarkable sight. I gave a long, low whistle as I looked over stack after stack of books—many of which appeared to be entire hymnal collections—standing like waist-high pillars in the narrow room. Interspersed among them were oceans of roughly stacked papers—pew sheets and other congregational memorabilia from many, many years gone by.

"Let's hope the vicarage never catches fire," I said. "I can certainly see why you need a bit of moral support. This is incredible."

"Isn't it. Some real treasures in here, I expect."

"Um—Martyn."

"What?" He looked at me with delight.

"We're not going to try to organise all this tonight, are we?"

He guffawed and practically spilt his coffee as he put it down on top of a pillar of hymnals. "I certainly hope not.

I think the mere weight of history would crush us, if not the hymnals. No. But if you're willing, we might shift the things by that little window to that side over there."

I nodded. "I'm surprised the floor can stand the weight. Eureka! Look at these—the songbooks we used when I was a child." I picked one up and leafed through it, smelling its lovely mustiness, shaking my head. "Sometimes I wish things would never change."

"I know what you mean," Martyn said, serious again, and I had the feeling he was thinking about his girlfriend. He stepped carefully over one pile of papers, then another, until he reached a chair placed against the wall. There was a shoe box on its seat, which he picked up. "Photographs," he said. "You're not going to believe these. I should put them into an album, for the parish to enjoy."

"Good idea. Do you have an actual plan of where you want things, or do you just want to move things away from that side of the room?"

He shrugged. "It can't be any more of a mess than it is now. Let's just shift things from here to there."

As I walked toward the area he planned to reclaim, I saw why the idea of a study up here appealed to Martyn. Not only was it a place he could claim for himself in this house full of other people's history, but this little corner was a charming nook. The roof sloped on both sides of the gable, so that there was a perfect triangular space for a desk and perhaps a filing cabinet against the wall. The wall was decorated with a small fan window in the centre, presumably an addition in the eighteenth or nineteenth century, so that Martyn could look out onto the church. And the church was a lovely sight, I thought, though now only darkness was visible through the one corner of window not obscured by hymnals.

We set to work. "Wouldn't you think these could have been put to use somewhere?" I picked up a stack of books, aware that I sounded like a grousing parishioner. "I mean, doesn't the C. of E. have a program to re-use these things, or at least recycle them?"

"Ah," Martyn shuffled to the far side of the room with a heavy load of volumes. "That's where our friend Lord Chenies comes in."

"Oh, really? How's that?" I knelt and picked up a formless heap of papers off the floorboards, fully expecting a rodent to come eek-eeking out of the mess. Perfect nesting material.

"Well, with his instructions to each vicar before me, I presume, not to adopt any of the newer songbooks as they came along, by the time these were ready for retirement they were utterly obsolete. I doubt anyone wanted them. Some of these go way back. . . . Look at this one. Eighteen-twenty. How much would you like to bet this particular book was used for one hundred years?"

"I see what you mean." I passed him with my load, and set it down gently on top of a recently moved stack. We worked in contentment for some time until Martyn announced, "We're making good progress. How about some more coffee?"

"Great," I said, from behind another load of books—I was working on a set of dark green ones this time—older than the burgundy ones that had been closer to the top of the stairway. We were really getting into the distant past, now. "You know, I'd quite forgotten my own problems there for a bit." I grunted as I set down my load.

"Excellent," Martyn said. "I'll bring the Rémy Martin, too."

"Splendid idea." I found myself amused that Martyn had put me to work after what he had called a thank-you dinner for helping him move in. Martyn always had shown a streak of what might be called extreme practicality—if he needed help, he asked for it. If something or someone could be put to use in his favour, he used it—or him. I didn't mind, because I would do virtually anything for a real friend, although as I approached middle age I had learned painfully that some of the people I'd thought of as friends fell far short of the distinction.

The cramped attic had a ceiling height of just over six feet. More than enough room for the mice, and Martyn, for that matter, but not very comfortable for overgrown Plumtrees. My hands were covered with dust, and I brushed them together in an effort to get some of it off.

As I went toward the next pile of books to be moved—King James Bibles this time—I thought I saw something scurry into a nearby ocean of papers. Great. Just what I was hoping for—battle with a mouse. But at least this pillar was next to the wall; we had nearly finished. I lifted twelve of the Bibles off the top, relieved that only four more pillars remained. As I did, I saw that there was a different sort of book—a very large, thick one—wedged between the rear two stacks and the wall. As I traipsed across the floor yet again, I thought that it looked almost as if the book had been hidden. I made a mental note to look at it after moving the other books, and heard Martyn mounting the steps.

"All right?" he asked, pleased, I could tell, with the new look of the attic. It was still a mess, but now nearly a quarter of it was cleared of debris and actually looked like a room.

"Will you put your desk just under the window?" I asked, stopping for a moment.

"Yes—exactly what I thought." He put down the tray he'd used to carry the coffee pot, cream jug, brandy bottle, and glasses and headed over to the wall for another pile of books. "These Bibles," he said, opening the cover of one. "Eighteen hundred." He read from the page with a sense of awe. "Your brother will be wanting to see these, I shouldn't wonder."

I didn't want to disappoint him, but my brother the

antiquarian book dealer wouldn't be interested in these books. Since coming into the amazing library of the rare book dealer Armand Beasley, Max was spoiled. He was into one-offs, extremely early and rare editions, particularly incunabula. But I had to admit, there would be people who'd want to get their hands on those books.

"I spotted something interesting," I said, reaching behind the two remaining stacks of the pillar to lift out the heavy old volume with both hands. Martyn came to stand next to me. When I saw what I held in my hands, I was speechless.

This was a book Max would die for, but Martyn's parishioners, I thought, would die for it first.

"Good heavens," he said.

The volume was huge—roughly two feet tall by one-and-a-half wide, and was covered in leather stretched over boards. Its binding was one used from the year twelve hundred on, leather thongs holding the spine to the boards. Stamped in gold leaf on the cover was the following:

Parish Book
Christ Church Cheneys
Gloria in Excelsis Deo

"Wow," I said, finally.

"Come on, let's have a look at it." Martyn urged me to sit down on the dusty floor with him. I could tell that he, like me, felt awe for the ancient book. He saw at the same time I did that we couldn't put it on the filthy floor, and looked round for something to lay down first. Pulling off his sweater, he made a little nest for the volume, and I set it down.

I let him open the heavy cover, and we gazed in wonder at the vellum inside. The first page repeated the information on the cover, and as he delicately turned each page we saw that a section in the front listed all the vicars who had ever presided over Christ Church Chenies, starting in 1343 and running up to 1966.

"Why would someone have hidden this away up here?" he asked.

"Good question. And it did look as if it had been hidden, if you ask me."

"Hmm." Martyn turned the pages slowly, reverently. I was glad to see that he realised the paper might be brittle, and treated it with great respect. Interestingly, the vellum gave way to cotton rag in the late sixteenth century, and rag gave way to wood pulp paper around 1850. Only the latter was severely yellowed and brittle. "Look at this," he said. "Here's a Blakely . . . born 1694 to Emma and Gabriel Blakely." He laughed, thrilled. "This is amazing." We skimmed each page for names we recognised, and found a surprising number of families listed who still lived in the area.

Including mine. "Look at this!" I exclaimed. "My great-great-great-grandfather, Eleazar Plumtree, born in 1814." I stared at the entry for a moment. "Mind if I skip ahead to my parents, and my birth?"

"Be my guest," Martyn said. "This is going to help my standing with the parishioners. I might not be Michael, but I am in the parish record book! What's more, I've *found* the parish record book!"

I shared his excitement as I turned forward to the 1940s, but didn't point out to him that it was *I* who had actually found the parish record book. At least I knew to expect this kind of behaviour from Martyn. I was happy to be of use to him.

"Now you and Sarah can be listed in this book. Lovely, isn't it?" As usual, Martyn also found a way to point out that by helping him, I had also done myself a favour.

"Here we are," I said slowly, having found the entry I'd sought: "Maximilian Plumtree and Alexandra Packard-

Lodge, united in holy matrimony on February 15, 1946."
I turned the pages until I came to the births for 1965.
"And here you and I are," I said, chuckling. "Alexander
Christian Lodge Plumtree, born April 18, 1965. And
Martyn Joseph Simon Blakely, May 21, 1965."

Satisfied that we were official, I thought of something
else I could look up, just for the thrill of it. "My father's
birth," I said, gently turning the pages back, "would've
been 1925 or thereabouts. . . ." I began to turn the pages
back and, on the way, found Nigel Charford-Cheney in
1926. "Look at this." I pointed to a small, beautifully inscribed *A* in the margin. "Wonder what that means?"

"I've no idea," Martyn said. "I've never seen a nota-
tion like that before in a parish record book. Have you?"

I shook my head. Time stood still as we skimmed
through the book to the end, the year after our birth. At
the rear of the book was a sheaf of papers, evidently items
that successive vicars had tucked inside the back cover to
preserve for the future. There was a pew sheet recording
the visit of a bishop, a number of wedding programmes, the
forms of service for the dedication of a new window, programmes for the installation of a number of vicars, and a
large envelope bearing the words, "Pertaining to The
Birth of Nigel Charford-Cheney—To Be Opened by the
Vicar Only."

Martyn lifted out the envelope delicately. It was
brown paper, darkened with age, and the inscription had
the calligraphic look of a fine old fountain pen. He turned
it over, and we saw that its backside bore an official-looking
burgundy wax seal, stamped with the Cheney coat of arms.
"Well, it's addressed to *me* now," he said. "Good Lord.
Cheney family secrets in my humble hands. Why do you
suppose it's not been opened before?"

"No idea. Maybe it's kept the curse of Chenies Manor
dormant all these years. Are you sure you want to open it?"

Grinning, Martyn said, "Very funny, Plumtree." He

eyed it for another moment. Then he shrugged, cast a glance at me, stuck his finger under the flap, and ripped the envelope open. He reached in the open end and pulled out a single sheet of fine, soft white paper, A4 size. We read it silently:

> Let this document bear witness that Nigel Charford-Cheney is legally, by adoption, a member of the Charford-Cheney family, and is legal heir to all Cheney lands and moneys. Should the matter arise for purposes of marriage and records of heredity, let this document state that the child was born to the Simino family of Clerkenwell and was readily and willingly given up for adoption by Maria Simino through the Order of St. James, Clerkenwell, London EC1. For obvious reasons, this is a matter of the utmost confidentiality and is entrusted solely to the vicar of Christ Church Chenies.

Oops, I thought, I wasn't meant to see this. I tore my eyes from the paper as Martyn read the document again, in stunned silence. Wouldn't Ferris-Browne love to see this! It would be the final weapon he'd need to take Lord Chenies down via public humiliation. It wasn't that being adopted was a humiliation; not in the least. It was the irony of *Lord Chenies* being adopted. All of the man's repugnant theories about inbred inferiority, stated all too clearly in the first chapter of *Cleansing*, rested on the idea that nobility is passed at birth to children of the upper class. The author was known for using phrases such as "We who have the blood of old England coursing through our veins," which left no doubt that he believed himself to be an aristocrat by birth.

The second shocker in the letter was the mention of the Simino family of Clerkenwell. Were Anthony Simino and Nigel Charford-Cheney related? They were certainly of a similar enough age to be brothers or cousins. I struggled to remember Simino's features; I'd met him only once. No, I couldn't recall any physical resemblance.

"He doesn't know," Martyn said softly. "Dear God, he doesn't know. Alex, it was a mistake for me to let you see this. You'll have to promise absolute secrecy."

"Of course."

At that moment we realised the awful responsibility we had shouldered upon opening that envelope. I also realised that I wouldn't want Martyn's job, with its intricacies of highly sensitive personal information, for anything. Book publishing, even with all the problems at Plumtree Press at the moment, looked like a walkover in comparison.

We had indeed unleashed a curse on Chenies that night. The old place, and its occupants, would never be the same again.

CHAPTER SEVEN

———————

Democrats object to men being disqualified by the accident of birth; tradition objects to their being disqualified by the accident of death.

G. K. CHESTERTON, *Orthodoxy*

MARTYN LED THE WAY INTO THE SITTING ROOM, TURNED on a lamp on the dark oak table between the two most comfortable chairs, deposited our brandies on the table, and sat. I placed the massive book reverently on the table. We sipped silently for quite some time before I said, "I don't think you should tell him."

Martyn didn't so much shake his head as incline it sceptically. "I don't know, Alex. He has the right to know his own background."

"Perhaps. But is it the *kindest* thing to tell him?"

He looked at me askance. "I must say, you're living up to your father's standards, Plumtree. After all the trouble his lordship has caused you, you're still worried about being kind to him? It's incredible. But I'm afraid I have no choice; even if the truth isn't kind, he deserves to know it. It's the *right* thing to do."

I'd forgotten that Martyn saw things in absolutes. The world was black and white to him, whereas to me it seemed shaded in every possible hue of grey. Perhaps that was how he stayed sane amidst the multitude of ethical and moral issues that confronted him and his parishioners every day.

"Martyn, it'll kill him."

He looked at me defiantly. "If I've learned one thing in my years in the ministry, Alex, it's that I can't play God. I don't have the right to decide *for* Lord Chenies whether he knows his own parentage or not. I can't hide the facts from him." He gazed at the brandy in his glass, swirling it gently. "In fact, I feel absolutely obliged to pass the information along. It's his, by rights. And it's his own business how he reacts to it."

I felt the blood rise to my cheeks. "Look, Martyn. The man has built his life on who he *thinks* he is. I would've thought that a decade of ministering to troubled souls might have taught you the opposite—that you're obliged to do the *kindest* thing, not the most obvious."

I groped for the words I needed. "You know better than I do that the ethics of your faith and the ethics of the world are two very different things. Something could be perfectly right from a legal, even moral, point of view that would still be wrong for you in your position."

"Agreed." He met my eyes. "But I'm telling you, in this case, Alex, I feel the *proper* thing to do is to inform him. The man has a right to know."

With an effort I maintained self-control, stood, and said, "Well, it doesn't look as if we're going to agree. I'll start on the washing-up."

Martyn didn't protest, and followed me to the kitchen, bringing his brandy. I washed and he dried—the vicarage hadn't splurged on a dishwasher—passing pots and plates in absolute silence. It would have been painfully awkward had we not known each other so well. We were too valuable to each other to allow anything to ruin our easy friendship.

Still, it was uncomfortable when I said good night at

the door and Martyn waved a distracted good-bye. At my car, on impulse, I turned. Martyn remained in the doorway, his gaze drifting toward the gates of the manor house. A single light shone in an upstairs window, presumably his lordship reading something before retiring to spur him to greater heights of hatred. I was becoming less charitable by the moment, I realised with distress.

"Martyn."

He started, as if surprised that I was still there.

"Could you at least wait for a few days before you do anything? Think it over?"

He didn't answer immediately. At last he nodded and said grudgingly, "All right, Alex. All right."

As I drove away, he still stood there, the door open behind him, the light from the lamps inside framing his small figure. I was much disturbed by the details of Nigel Charford-Cheney's birth. I had no business knowing them. Moreover, the thought of Martyn actually telling Lord Chenies that he had come from a family of lower-class immigrants of exactly the sort he blamed for cleansing the nation of the aristocratic old families was abhorrent.

"It'd kill him," I said aloud, shaking my head as I barrelled down the narrow lane towards home. What a mess he was in, and what a mess I was in because of him. The nation detested me, Ferris-Browne had evidently turned nasty on me, and who knew what the implications might be for Plumtree Press? Boycotts, bombings . . . my imagination ran wild.

But the spring night was deceptively peaceful, and no matter how bad things got, I drew immense comfort from living in this semirural corner of the world. I told myself that *Cleansing* and all the furore over the European Union and hedges would pass one day, and this single-track lane would remain—as it had for at least a thousand years. This place was real, permanent, whereas my current problems—

well, actually they might be permanent as the *grave*, if I wasn't careful. But I had to find a way through this safely, for myself and everyone else. Sarah had agreed to marry me. I wouldn't miss a lifetime with her.

I'd told myself the same things many times, in similarly dismal circumstances. As long as I survived, I could sell the publishing business at some point. I could get out of the public eye for good, do nothing more than gardening at the Orchard, play the occasional round of golf at Moor Park, and read every book ever published.

I knew I'd never do it, but having acknowledged the next-to-worst case seemed tonight to serve as a bit of bedrock. After putting the car away in the garage, I wasn't ready to go in to bed. Instead I walked the perimeter of my property, something I did when the going got rough. It was a bit like an animal stalking his territory, but tonight I needed the comfort.

At the very back of the garden, by the tall pines, I heard something—someone?—shuffle off into the wood. Surely there weren't HIT members with night-vision scopes working round the clock. . . . But for my awful night vision and the almost non-existent moon, I might have seen who or what it was. Instead, the invisible creature—or person—served as a sort of warning. As it fled through the underbrush, it seemed to whisper, *"You are not alone. You are not safe."*

On an impulse I walked on to the barn at the far end of the property. It had been a year since I last peered in through the rough plank door; I hadn't actually gone inside in more than five years. As I paced the stepping-stone path, a sudden dramatic sinking feeling of such intensity overtook me that I stopped dead in my tracks. As I stood there, perfectly upright, I had an impression of tumbling, head over heels, and heard a long, desperate scream—in my mind.

This had happened to me once before, four years ago: I had awakened in the middle of the night on the yacht that was my home at the time, hearing the echo of what I assumed to be thunder. The next day, I was informed that my parents had been killed at the exact moment of my awakening, when the propane tank on their forty-foot yacht had exploded.

I fought down fear and took the last few steps to the barn door. *If anything's happened to Sarah . . .* The thought was unbearable. To have loved her for so long, and to be so close to marrying her at last . . .

I lifted the latch and pulled the door toward me, catching a whiff of the smells of Amanda's Print Shop as I groped for the light switch. Miraculously, a naked bulb hanging from one of the rafters glowed to life, revealing the work of small animals and insects among my father's printing things. A comfortable-looking nest made of bits of straw adorned the bed of the platen press, and the rafters of the barn were strung with spiderwebs the way Regent Street dripped with fairy lights at Christmas.

I stepped inside and latched the door. A feeling of closeness to my father came over me, as if he were actually there. Perhaps the episode on the stepping stones outside had been a memory of that other dream I'd had four years ago; perhaps visiting the barn had brought it on. I still missed my father; still didn't want to believe that he and my mother were gone forever.

I trudged past the press and the work-table next to it, which was heavily loaded with little jars of ink and containers of white gas for use as a solvent, to my father's "gallery." Along one wall, my father had pinned up a series of broadsheets—single, large pieces of heavy paper printed as experiments or for displaying a typeface. The printed sheets of paper were the only decoration in the rustic place.

I stepped over to an eye-catching invitation to the yearly garden party hosted by my parents, printed in a riot of colour. He'd had a photo-engraved plate made of the house, and the image of the house stood in the center of the ten-by-fourteen-inch sheet of paper, surrounded by words printed in various hues of green and blue:

> I have a garden of my own
> But so with roses overgrown
> and lilies, that you would it guess
> to be a little wilderness

ANDREW MARVELL

At the bottom of the sheet the actual invitation had been issued, with roses and lilies encircling the small print: *Join us for a garden party, Saturday, 20 July, four o'clock, Maximilian and Alexandra Plumtree.*

Suddenly I felt a keen desire to know what my father had been working on during his last visit here. Moving across the dusty concrete floor, I swept the empty nest off the bed of the handpress and studied the framework that held the bits of type in place. Called the chase, this metal square housed not only letters, which were of course backwards as I looked at them, but also "furniture"—little bits of metal used to fill in the space not consumed by letters and words.

The words I saw in the chase made the breath catch in my throat. WELCOME, ALEX. It was almost as if my father had set the type for tonight, for my return to the barn. I took in the hugely exaggerated size of the *W* and the *A*. It was playfully done. . . .

Be reasonable, I told myself. My father probably had a good cause to print that message four years ago. No doubt he was planning to post it on the front door when I returned home for Christmas. Yes, surely that was it. How thoughtful of him to have planned it as early as August. I shook my head and turned away from the platen press and its startling greeting, thinking that when the *Cleansing* mess settled down I'd quite like to have a go at printing something myself. With one last fond look I switched off the light, latched the door, and walked slowly back to the house.

I discovered I'd left the library door unlocked during the ill-fated dinner at Martyn's. Or had someone been here . . . ?

Summoning my nerve, I searched from one end of the house to the other. No lurking murderers anywhere. Reminding myself to be more careful about such things, I made sure all the doors were securely fastened before climbing the stairs to the bedroom.

The next morning, things didn't improve. The instant I awoke to find sunlight in my face, I was haunted by the thought of Amanda in the House of Detention, by the parish book, and by the memory of the words in the chase. I dragged myself out of bed, wishing the birds wouldn't sing quite so beautifully, and trekked downstairs to start the coffee in my boxer shorts. I saw the telephone as I entered the kitchen, and felt the presence of the bug as if it were an unwelcome guest in my home. As indeed it was.

When the first few drops had dribbled down into the pot, I padded to the front door and opened it. This morning the paperboy had thrown my *Tempus* into the bay-laurel at the side of the door, breaking two branches. I snatched the paper out of the greenery, unmollified by the delicate herbal scent that wafted into the air. I sensed it would be another difficult day.

Before opening the paper I fortified myself with several sips from a cup of extra-stiff French Roast, augmented with full-cream milk. Nevertheless, the thirty-point leading headline that stared up at me was a stunner. "Wilding Rocks City: Four Injured." I read on, dreading and yet greedily consuming each word:

London——In an attack that police think may be linked to the Clerkenwell wilding of two days ago, four cleaning personnel were beaten last night around 2:00 A.M. at the Printer's Society in Paternoster Square. The victims were found by an all-night security guard who heard the scuffle. The guard, whose identity is being protected for his own safety, heard what he described as "three young people with Oxbridge accents" shouting racial epithets and warnings for foreigners to leave the country.

Police Detective Sergeant Melvin Wickham said, "We believe this is linked to a similar crime that took place on Monday in Clerkenwell, in which an African immigrant was killed. Our sources report that the emotions of ultra-Conservatives are running high, due to the impending election and talk of Economic and Monetary Union with the EU. I would ask everyone to remain calm and exercise self-restraint."

Some feel that the recent wilding uprisings have been prompted by news of the imminent publication of a novel that appears to advocate removing foreigners and poverty-stricken people from the country. The father-of-chapel of the Clerkenwell National Union of Pressworkers (NUP), Nick Ramsey, said, "It's sickmaking. A book like that gives all the neo-Nazi nutters an excuse to be violent. I'm warning them, they'd better watch themselves, or the whole country's going to be in a state of riot." The NUP is known for its Socialist activism, and last week demonstrated for faster and more enthusiastic movement toward EMU.

MP Guy Ferris-Browne, Minister for the Environment and pro-European spokesman, issued a statement immediately after the wilding: "We must not allow xenophobes to ruin our future in the European Union. Britain stands at the edge of a glorious future in a borderless, united, environmentally sound Europe. No one is suggesting that we do away with Great Britain, but surely the union of so many countries—countries that have been at war with one another in the past—can only lead to greater good for us all."

I'd read enough. The spin of the article certainly made Ferris-Browne look like a hero, and those of us associated with *Cleansing* seem like murderers. Feeling ill, I abandoned any thought of breakfast and headed for the shower. Even the pumice soap I kept to remove evidence of oil changes on the Golf wouldn't cleanse me of the responsibility I felt not only for wildings, murders, and abductions, but the uproar of an entire nation.

What to do? I rubbed shampoo into my hair viciously with my fingernails. Should I make a public statement, exposing what I believed to be Ferris-Browne's deception, and declining to publish the book? Or did I owe it to the prime minister to keep my promise and publish it anyway? There in the shower, I finally realised that I *wanted* to suspect Ferris-Browne, because I hated the thought that the prime minister might be responsible for Mmbasi Kumba's murder, and who knew what else.

It was time to contact the deputy prime minister, and damn his precious confidentiality. Far too many people had suffered already for the sake of his little experiment in manipulating public opinion.

Then again, perhaps I should continue with publication and see where it led. It would be risky, not just for me but for everyone. But that way I might at least expose the rat in the woodpile.

I agonised my way to the car and made the brief trip to Heronsgate. Lisette's normally vivacious face looked grey and pinched as she stepped out of the side door, bearing her bulging shoulder-strap briefcase and the ever-present car coffee cup.

"Alex, I am so sorry," she said, gathering up her full white skirt before plopping into the passenger's seat. A wave of the delicate and expensive scent she preferred swept over me. I knew she'd already read the *Tempus*, somehow managing to glance over the front page while preparing the boys for school. She closed the door, and both of us put on smiles and waved to the boys and the nanny in the window.

"Not exactly what we'd hoped for, is it? Plumtree Press single-handedly plunging the nation into crime and riot," I said, as we drove away.

She gave a contemptuous snort. "Not Plumtree Press, Alex. It's these crazy people. The politics—they make them lose their minds. As if attacking anyone is going to 'elp." Shaking her head, she asked, "Did you know that all of this was the work of a political idealist? Another failed idea?"

"What was?" She'd lost me.

" 'Eronsgate." Heronsgate was a small network of narrow old streets in rolling Hertfordshire countryside, lined with tall hedges and decorated equally with mansions and small semidetached cottages in traditional pastel colours.

"It was all organised by the Chartists—they rioted in Clerkenwell too, by the way," she said. "They were utopians. Just like William Morris, in fact, except 'e came a bit later. Anyway, the 'ead utopian, someone named Feargus O'Connor, decided all the poor northern industrial workers would be better off as gentleman-farmers, living 'ere in the countryside.

"So 'e built all these cottages—see that little symbol on the chimney?" She pointed to one of the little cottages we were just passing, and I ducked my head to look out the window at the notched square design on the chimney.

"That's the Chartist symbol," she went on, as I turned out of Heronsgate onto Long Lane, heading for the motorway. "O'Connor 'eld a lottery, and more than eighty families came to 'Ertfordshire to start a new and perfect life in the 'land of liberty, peace and plenty,' as O'Connor called it. But guess what? The northern textile workers were not 'appy with their new lives. And the plots of land weren't big enough for them to make a living on. So they moved back north. Experiment failed." She threw her hands up in a gesture that expressed the futility of it all.

At that moment, as if to illustrate the irony of O'Connor's experiment, we passed the local pub called Land of Liberty, Peace and Plenty.

"He'd have done a lot less harm if he'd kept his ideas to himself. People like O'Connor must think they're frightfully important to make the rest of the world suffer for their beliefs."

Lisette harrumphed and settled in her seat. Then she said quietly, "George rang last night."

I didn't miss the link with our former topic of conversation. George was making his family suffer for whatever crisis he was enduring personally. I had to admit that it was difficult to forgive my good friend for his selfishness in traipsing off with the medical equivalent of the Peace Corps. I saw the pain on Lisette's face daily, and on his boys' faces just as often.

With alarm I realised that Lisette was crying. " 'E 'as changed, Alex. 'E is not my George anymore," she choked out.

Reaching into the back seat for the box of tissues, which I placed on her lap, I struggled for the right words as I negotiated the narrow road appropriately named Long Lane. On the one hand I didn't want to discount

Lisette's feelings by appearing to disagree. In fact, I feared she was right. On the other hand, I wanted to tell her it wasn't so. I settled on the more positive course.

"Lisette, no one can change *that* completely. Of course he's still your George." She had covered her face with the tissue and was rocking in the seat next to me, consumed in hopeless sobbing. I put one hand on her shoulder and squeezed. "He's going to get this out of his system and come back right as rain. Really, he will."

But I heard the hint of uncertainty in my own voice and knew she had, too. If anything, she sobbed harder. I pulled onto the verge and stopped, just in front of the roundabout that would put us on to the M25.

"Oh, Lisette," I said, distressed for her. Cars buzzed past on their way to what I enviously imagined were normal workaday Wednesdays. She sobbed silently, still covering her face, with only the occasional gasp for breath. Five minutes passed, then seven, according to the car's clock. Just as I began to wonder what I should do—I didn't know if she was having a nervous breakdown or merely letting off steam—she seemed to pull herself together. The tissues came away from her flushed face and went down to her lap, bunched in her hands.

"Alex, I'm so sorry." Her face was red and swollen, and mascara had given her American football player's eyes, a little semicircle of black beneath each.

"Don't be—" I started to object, but she broke in again.

"It's just that you are really the only one I can talk to about this." With that she threw her arms round me. I was acutely aware that any of my neighbours driving by—and they all would, eventually—couldn't help but misunderstand the situation. I put that selfish thought out of my mind and tried to think of Lisette. I gripped her solidly, and as I did I realised that I really did love her—like a sister. And a friend.

As I held her there in my car, I felt a wave of guilty pleasure at the thought of Sarah and our fast-approaching wedding, and what an extremely happy life lay ahead of us together. Not for us the misunderstandings and agonies of most married couples. . . . With an effort, I pulled myself back to Lisette's personal tragedy. Just as she began to release her desperate grip on me, I was horrified to hear the toot of a car horn and then to see Helena Hotchkiss's small white BMW in the side mirror. As it screeched to a stop next to us, Lisette pushed me away and sat up straight in her seat, blowing her nose.

"Alex!" Helena purred as her window slithered downward.

"Morning, Helena." I tried to smile, and knew I succeeded in looking guilty instead. She peered past me to Lisette and raised her eyebrows fractionally. As usual, my flamboyant pharmaceutical baron friend was dressed to the nines, all white silk on this particular day, with bright red lipstick. It didn't work well with her skeletal frame; Helena always looked pallid and in need of gaining roughly a stone. Had she been wearing a fur she would have been a dead ringer for Cruella De Vil.

She sensed she had me at a disadvantage in the circumstances and smiled, almost gloating. "You *have* managed to remember tonight, haven't you?"

My face must have looked blank. She gripped the steering wheel with both hands and went on, exasperated.

"Really, Alex. It's been planned for weeks. The County Boundary Committee meeting? Remember? With a little gathering at my place afterwards?"

"Of course, of course." I nodded to make up for the fact that I hadn't exactly been looking forward to the occasion. "Yes, I'm planning on it."

"Well. I know how busy you are." Helena smiled, catlike, and peered past me once more. This time Lisette eyed her back, trying to retain a shred of her dignity. "But we are counting on you. Ta, then."

I lifted a hand in farewell as her window glided up again and she peeled out into the roundabout.

" 'Oo on earth?" Lisette asked.

I put up my window and shifted the car into gear before answering. "One of the former banes of my existence. Helena Hotchkiss. Nearly your neighbour."

Lisette made a face, as if she'd smelled something unpleasant. "Not *that* 'Otchkiss," she said mournfully.

"Oh, yes," I said, merging into the crush of rush-hour traffic. At least Helena had given us something to distract us momentarily from George. "*That* Hotchkiss. The hedge preservation society president. I dated her briefly—awkward teenage years sort of thing. It was a disaster."

I remembered with distaste the way Helena had virtually attacked me in her hunger for sexual experience. She'd also tried to ply me with drugs, something I'd stayed away from. There was nothing at all tempting about cocaine, as far as I was concerned. I rather liked my brain the way it was.

And ever since I'd moved back to the Orchard, Helena had phoned periodically. It was usually when she was drunk or high, I sensed. She was forever suggesting that we get together.

"Isn't she the one who started that organic pharmaceuticals business that just went public—Nature's Chemist?"

I nodded. "She was always interested in chemistry. And chemicals. The environment is another of her passions, thus her leadership of the national Hedges in Transition group." I sighed. "Yes, Helena's done very well for herself."

"Sounds like quite a woman. I've read about that company of 'ers. Something tells me she still 'as feelings for you."

"It's extremely awkward. She doesn't seem to hear me when I tell her I'm about to be married." I overtook a milk lorry and slid back into the middle lane. "Perhaps when she sees the ring on my finger."

"Let's 'ope," Lisette said. We lapsed into silence.

The first thing I did upon arriving at the office was check my voice mail. There was a message from Nigel Charford-Cheney, which I played with what proved to be justifiable dread.

"*Damn it all, Plumtree!*" His voice grated like sandpaper from the speaker. "*Proofs are a dog's breakfast! What in heaven's name are you playing at? Gibberish—utter nonsense. What kind of an outfit are you running over there? Your father will be turning in his grave.*"

That stung. He may well have been. I winced as the vitriol continued.

"*Grandfather too, for that matter. Friend of mine, you know. For goodness' sake, pull your finger out, man, and get me some proofs in* English! *Thought you said this would be a rush job. Weeks away from publication, mere weeks, and I need proofs. Book's the biggest publishing sensation in this nation—in the world—and that hippy woman in Clerkenwell keeps botching the job.*"

I leaned over my desk, expecting more. I heard heavy breathing, then a calmer, more threatening voice. "*Listen, Plumtree. If that girl can't produce a decent set of proofs, get rid of her and find someone who knows how to set a page of bloody type!!*" Bang.

I was completely in the dark. Proofs? Amanda hadn't *had* the chance to run more proofs yet, as far as I knew. She'd been abducted only yesterday; she should still be in bed, recuperating. Besides, if she had run proofs somehow—had Bruce stayed up all night, or something—she'd have sent them to us, not directly to the author.

Sighing, I dialled Charford-Cheney's number. Best to give him immediate attention, then sort out what had happened when I went to visit Amanda. After the first ring, his well-modulated yet harsh tones grated down the line.

"Who is it?"

"My Lord, it's Alex Plumtree. I—"

"Damn it all, Plumtree, what kind of outfit are you running over there?" More breathing down the line. I could hear the air whistling through his nose and decided to concentrate on the multitude of long grey hairs bristling from each of his nostrils as a way to keep a grip on reality. Also as revenge.

"My Lord, we've had some problems. We haven't sent you any proofs yet; the ones you've received must have been some kind of prank. When did you receive them, and who delivered them?"

"Outside the door this morning, weren't they? No idea who brought them."

"Hmm. Well, they weren't delivered by us or the printer, I'm sure. There's been a bit of opposition to your book, as you well know. In fact, our 'hippy' printer, as you put it—her name is Amanda—was abducted yesterday. Abducted, I might add, as she was setting your book for the *second* time—her shop was vandalised the other day. We think the printing of *Cleansing* has been sabotaged several times now, My Lord."

There was more whistling, and I imagined the hairs being swept in the gale of his stertorous breath. "Don't care if the damn woman's been abducted by aliens! Signed a contract. Promised Dexter Moore proofs when I see him next week. Future prime minister asked to see a copy, and you send me gobbledygook! *Gad!*" His voice grew ominously quiet for the grand finale. "Plumtree, if I miss my special appointment as his cabinet advisor, I'll have your head on a platter. Waited my entire life for this."

Well, in the first place I strongly doubted that Dexter

Moore would be our next prime minister. Little did Lord Chenies know that this was precisely what the publication of his book was expected to prevent. Second, it was incredible that Amanda had managed everything so quickly. No hand printer could have done it faster. He had no right to bemoan a lack of diligence on her part.

A sudden fit of humour overtook me, until I reminded myself that this man might soon be crushed by information about his birth. My mirth vanished as quickly as it had come.

"Plumtree! You there?"

"Yes, of course."

"Thought your father taught you more respect than this. Take this book elsewhere if I could." *Oh, if only you could,* I thought as he slammed down the phone.

I tapped Amanda's home number into my sophisticated new system. No answer. *Oh, no,* I thought. *What's happened to her now?* In a panic, I tried her shop in an effort to reach Bruce.

"Amanda Morison," she answered calmly, as if this were a day like any other.

"Amanda! It's Alex. For heaven's sake, why aren't you at home in bed?"

"Don't be ridiculous. *I'm* fine. It's the book I'm worried about." Her voice was wry. "Can you get over here this morning? There's something I want to show you."

"Of course." My job had come to consist exclusively of fighting fires associated with *Cleansing.* Fortunately I had the staff to back me up this year. "As soon as I track down Nicola. By the way, do you know anything about a set of nonsense proofs? Gibberish?"

"What?" Not unreasonably, she sounded totally confused.

"I've just got off the phone with Lord Chenies. He claims someone delivered a set of proofs of his book, but all nonsense, this morning. He doesn't know who or why. I told him they certainly weren't from us."

"What next," she sighed. "Well. See you when you get here. Oh, by the way, thanks—I think—for the security guards. I feel as if I'm living in an armed camp, here and at home, but I suppose it's better than the alternative."

I hadn't even hung up when Nicola breezed in and plopped on my sofa. She crossed her legs, resplendent in a navy-blue suit, with heels to match. She seemed consistently overdressed for our humble offices, as if her motto was to be prepared for a surprise meeting with the prime minister at all times.

Stiffening at the sight of her, I prepared to say something along the lines of *"Listen here, I saw you with Guy Ferris-Browne last night. What exactly is going on?"* But she beat me to it.

"Guy *did* set up the wilding as a publicity stunt. He even arranged for Lloyd Branscomb to come along right after, and for Mimi to get the fast-breaking bulletin during your *Talkabout* appearance. But he swears that Mmbasi Kumba's death was an accident. He claims he has a plan to bring the killers to justice after the election—he knows who they are, of course—but he can't do it before."

"Nicola, how did you—"

"Please—don't ask."

"I'm sorry." I shook my head. "I *must* know." I stopped short of saying that I suspected her of having one foot in the enemy camp, and of asking specifically what she'd been doing at the office of Guy Ferris-Browne, and exactly what her relationship was to him. "I'm ultimately responsible for everything relating to Plumtree Press. Even this mess."

She sighed, staring at the new plum-coloured carpeting, and then met my eyes. "All right. Guy Ferris-Browne is my father."

She let this sink in for a moment.

"He left my mother when I was tiny, and I'll spare you the sordid details. He owes me—more than you can imagine. I just called in an infinitesimal part of the debt."

I thought of the way she had made him stop in his tracks, outside the Palace of Westminster. I remembered his emotion as he tried to embrace her. And I would never forget the way he was left standing as she rebuffed him and stalked ahead of him into the building. Suddenly I was very much afraid of fatherhood.

She stared at me defiantly. "Satisfied?"

"I'm stunned. You went to your *father* over this? I would never have dreamed of asking you to—"

"You didn't ask me, remember? I offered. And if I have a father who is stupid enough to ruin the reputation of my highly ethical employer for his highly *un*ethical political career, well—he deserves what he gets." She sniffed. "In fact, he deserves much more. I told him that if anyone at Plumtree Press or Amanda's Print Shop comes to harm over this book, he'll never see me again."

I was speechless.

Nicola went on, "I'd love to know exactly what Guy's up to this time." The coldness in her tone as she referred to him by his Christian name was indescribable. "He wants to talk to you, you know. He said he'd ring this morning."

I was suddenly terrified of his wrath. He wouldn't be happy that Nicola knew about his involvement in the publication of *Cleansing*, but he had given me permission to tell those trusted few who needed to know. Nicola had been one of them. I hadn't mentioned his name, either; she'd guessed.

But he wouldn't care about those fine distinctions. If Ferris-Browne were to become really angry with me, he'd pull out the big political guns. I had no doubt that he would fight dirty. My name would be mud, even more than it was now; and when he was well and truly finished, I'd be in the same situation as poor Mmbasi Kumba.

For the sake of the prime minister's election, I decided to go along with Ferris-Browne—particularly as he'd promised justice for Mmbasi Kumba's death. And Nicola's threat of not seeing him again was almost certain to keep him in line.

On the sofa opposite me Nicola uncrossed her long legs, took a sip from the coffee cup she'd brought in with her, and said, "So. What's our strategy for today?"

I shook myself mentally and switched gears. It wasn't easy.

"Right. Yes . . . I'm afraid I have more bad news."

"Try me. What could be worse than what I brought you this morning?"

I had to admit this woman could handle anything I threw at her. "It's Amanda. She's all right, but someone attacked her—someone who crept up her own shop's cellar stairs, mind you—and left her chained to the wall at the Clerkenwell House of Detention."

Nicola's face was a blank; I could see that she didn't know what the House of Detention was.

"It's an old underground prison, now just a very authentic and ghoulish tourist attraction. Whoever abducted her took her through underground tunnels that led to the prison—or so she thinks."

Nicola's sangfroid vanished. "We were right. We knew something was wrong!"

"Mmm." I fiddled with a Biro on my desk. "She claims she's okay—I just spoke with her, in fact. She wants to see us this morning; she won't tell me why. Lord Chenies got some *Cleansing* proofs this morning—he claims they're gibberish. *How* he got these proofs I can't imagine: I haven't seen any, and Amanda couldn't have had time to run them. She knows nothing about this extra set of proofs, either. Oh! And our phones have been bugged, though I've had them cleared. Careful what you say till this is over. And you wondered what else could go wrong," I added, trying to smile.

But Nicola was beyond smiling. "I must be a jinx," she said bitterly. "Just look what's happened since you hired me."

"Ha!" I burst out. "No, you don't realise. *I'm* the one. Seriously, I hate to admit it, but people around me find themselves in grave danger more often than you'd believe." I hadn't meant to share such a private thought with her, but she had gone so far as to ask a favour of a father she despised, for me. For her third day on the job, we had reached a remarkable level of shared confidence.

"Looks like we have that in common, too," she said, then, with a sigh, stood. "When do we see Amanda?"

"Now," I said, rising. "All right?"

She nodded. "I'll just get my things." At the door, she hesitated. "Would you mind if we walked? I know it would take a bit longer, but it might—well, it might do us good."

"Of course. Brilliant. Won't take us much longer than the Tube, anyway. And it's one of those days."

"Exactly," she said, and I knew we had hit upon yet another point of understanding. The desire to be outdoors on these days was nothing short of desperation. Perfect weather didn't come often enough in our part of the world to be ignored, and life was short.

Sometimes it looked as if it might be very short indeed.

As I let the heavy door of the Press swing shut behind us, I acknowledged a strong sense of disquiet. It was true that things had an odd way of connecting in the book-publishing world; it has always been an incestuous business. Publishers trade employees, authors, buildings, and equipment without thinking twice about it, and have done for centuries. But I didn't like the way everyone seemed to be related to everyone else here—Simino and Lord Chenies, Malcolm Charford-Cheney and the author himself, and Nicola Beauchamp and Guy Ferris-Browne.

As it happened, I was right to worry. There was far more to this web of relationships than I ever would have guessed.

CHAPTER EIGHT

———◆———

Damn your principles! Stick to your party.

BENJAMIN DISRAELI

As we walked up Clerkenwell Green, all looked peaceful. Sparrows hopped along the pavement, pecking at something only they could see. It seemed wildly incongruous that murders, abductions, and wiretappings occurred here. I nodded and said good morning to the plainclothes security man sipping tea on the street; he winked at me.

But when I swung open the door of the print shop, I found Amanda sobbing next to her Vandercook proofing press. An older man with a balding pate and an olive complexion, whom I instantly recognised as Anthony Simino, had his arm around her. Alarmed, I realised yesterday's events had done deeper damage to Amanda than she'd admitted.

"She's all right," Simino told me quietly, then lifted his eyes to the words that had been added to her Morris quote. "She's just now noticed the vandalism."

"Alex, Nicola—I'll be myself in a minute," Amanda said through sobs.

"I'm so sorry, Amanda." I wanted to go to her, but Simino had her locked in a tight squeeze. Nicola and I stood awkwardly nearby. I tried not to remember the parish book Martyn and I had uncovered, not to think about the fact that I might be standing face-to-face with Lord Chenies's blood relative. I couldn't help but notice the physical resemblance; their large, distinctive noses were identical, as were their dominant grey eyebrows. Simino had a less attractive face than Charford-Cheney, due to scarring from skin problems. And his colouring looked unnaturally dark, as if perhaps he used a tanning salon, whereas Charford-Cheney's was untouched by sun. But his eyes had the same flat coldness as Charford-Cheney's. How could I have missed all the similarities when I'd met Simino months before? But then I'd had no reason to link the two men from such different worlds. Brothers or cousins? I wondered for the twentieth time.

"Anthony, this is Nicola Beauchamp, head of our trade division," I began, social ritual once again rescuing me from an awkward situation. "Nicola, Anthony Simino, head of the Clerkenwell Neighbourhood Association." The two nodded politely to each other. I refrained from mentioning that Simino had been the one to find Amanda in the prison yesterday.

"Okay, okay." Amanda broke away from Simino to snatch a tissue from her desktop. "We're ready to do business." She blew her nose briskly. "Thanks, Anthony. You're an angel."

Simino realised he was being dismissed, but seemed only too happy to do her bidding. "Now remember. Ring if you need me. I'm barely a street away."

She nodded and smiled. No sooner had the door swung shut behind him than Bruce and the security guard entered, carrying a large box between them. To give Amanda time to compose herself, I greeted him warmly.

"Bruce. What've you got there, lead type?"

He grunted as he and the guard manhandled the bulky box over to Amanda's library table. "Feels like it. The deliveryman met me outside; like a berk, I said I'd hump it in."

"Gently, now," the security guard cautioned, as the two of them set the box on the table. "I'll have a butchers. Why don't you all stand back while I check this out."

Amanda, dry-eyed now but flushed, regarded the box quizzically. "I'm not expecting anything. No return address. Hmmph."

I didn't want to come out and say it, but I too suspected the package. Anything arriving at Amanda's these days was suspect—and in London of the nineties a box could just as easily contain a bomb as books.

We all watched as the guard examined the parcel, pressed his ear against it, then delicately sliced open the tape across the top. He opened the flaps of the box as if they were glass.

"Bruce, be a good lad, get us some coffee?" Amanda didn't take her eyes off the box.

"White for this lot, right?" He went off willingly, content to help his mentor.

Bruce rattled milk bottles and mugs by the little fridge as the guard lifted out a bubble-wrapped cocoon and began to unwrap it. We watched as he pulled what appeared to be a tattered book out of the plastic and inspected it, then passed it to Amanda. Her lower lip quivered as she took it from him.

"What is it?" I asked sharply.

Trembling, she held up a tragically ruined treasure: a one-off special edition she had made of the bibliophile's bible, *Books* by Gerald Donaldson. This was a book *about* books that Amanda had treasured. She had carefully unbound it just to rebind it in specially tooled leather with contrasting corner points and spine. She had even created a special slipcase for it—also covered in fine leather, and stamped in gold with the book's title and a custom design of an open book on it.

But now the shredded slipcase looked as if wolves had attacked it. Its peach suede covering had been sliced in strips from the cardboard. The once-remarkable book hung in tatters from a limp spine, its cover grotesquely defaced with what looked like acid.

"I hadn't even noticed it was missing," she whispered.

Nicola spoke, her rich voice calm but firm. "We need to call the police, Amanda. We must stop this harassment before anything more happens to you."

"No!" Amanda cried, with surprising vehemence. Even Bruce seemed taken aback.

"You've no idea how I've fought for this"—Amanda motioned to the shop around her—"and how much effort it's taken from the Neighbourhood Association and Anthony, and . . ."

Her lower lip trembled, and she thrust her chin forward. "Besides. You don't understand. There's something . . . some people . . ."

"What? Who?" I tried to be gentle, but if there was something she hadn't told us . . .

"I can't tell you," she sobbed. I saw desperation, and fear, in her eyes.

Nicola spoke. "But, Amanda, after what happened yesterday, we're talking about your safety. Your *life*."

The guard, meanwhile, was reaching into the box, deep among the polystyrene peanuts. "There's a note," he said, lifting out an envelope, which he passed to Amanda. "And . . . " Hesitantly he explored the packing material, then grasped something. Gingerly, he produced a bottle of clear liquid and placed it on the table for all to see. It was a litre-sized juice bottle, with its label removed and another affixed: WHITE GAS.

He lifted a second bottle out of the box and placed it next to the first; it had the same sort of label but contained a yellowish fluid. As I lifted the now empty cardboard box onto the floor, touching it by its edges in the hope that I could talk Amanda into letting us have the police dust it for fingerprints,

Bruce quietly brought the coffees to the table, exchanging a glance with Amanda.

"Well?" Nicola prompted. "What is it?"

Bruce ran a hand through his technicolour hair and pointed at the yellow-tinged bottle. "That one's acid," he said grimly, "for etching plates. It's powerful stuff. And that one is a solvent for dissolving petroleum-based inks, but also for lacquer, glue, things like that. The solvent's incredibly inflammable. And it's volatile when put in contact with the acid. It's one of the things you learn on a printing course. We use both of these chemicals all the time, but someone's sending us a message, putting them together like this."

So the box *had* contained a sort of bomb, after all.

Amanda looked ill. She still clutched the unopened envelope.

"Shall I?" I said, and reached for the envelope. She nodded. I opened it and pulled out a plain white laser-printed sheet of paper.

"UNPRINTABLE" was all it said, in forty-eight point bold letters, Times Roman, that leapt off the page. The message was terrifying in its starkness. I half-expected Amanda to pluck it out of my hands and hold it up to Bruce as an example of why "less is more" in typesetting.

"Oh, no," Amanda gasped, and sat down, covering her face with her hands.

"Another threat," Nicola said. "Listen to me, Amanda. Surely you'll agree now that we must do something."

The security guard had picked up the phone. "Doesn't matter what she thinks; I'm obliged to ring the police, now we've got hazardous chemicals sent through the post."

We all listened as he gave them the address and told

them what had happened. The guard then set about carrying the two dangerous bottles out to the alley behind the shop—one at a time. Bruce went with him, arguing that they could actually use the chemicals in the shop. The guard muttered something about evidence, and carried on. Nicola and I pulled up chairs and sat with Amanda while we waited for the police to arrive. Amanda was holding up remarkably well, I thought, considering what she'd been through.

"Look, Amanda. It's high time we put an end to all this. Too much has gone wrong. I'm cancelling this book, special edition and all, right now."

"No, Alex, you mustn't. I—I know what's going on here. I should have told you before, I suppose. All this is to do with *me*, not Lord Chenies." She sniffed. "It's no secret that I'm a member of the National Union of Pressworkers—or at least used to be. Well, within the NUP we've formed a group of environmental activists. In fact, Bruce was a member, too."

Bruce, back with us, nodded sadly in confirmation of this.

"This group," Amanda went on, "they—were my friends. But most of them work for the big papers, and they don't understand much about running a business. They don't know that you have to make compromises to stay afloat. I don't agree with Lord Chenies's politics, but that doesn't mean I can afford to refuse printing his book. My friends just can't understand that. They think I've sold out on them by taking on this novel by an arch-Conservative, the kind of person who hates environmentalists and rips out his hedges just to annoy them." She sniffed again, wrapping her arms around herself.

"And this," she went on, nodding toward the alley to indicate the bottles. "I don't mind telling you, this is scary. One night at the pub, after our union chapel meeting, some of the more outrageous blokes were fantasising about getting violent. They were laughing about how quickly we'd get results if we acted more like the animal rights crowd. I thought they were just joking when they asked if I had anything flammable in the shop and if I knew anything about making bombs." She looked me in the eye. "I told them that white gas and nitric acid could be dangerous. Now they want to use it on me."

It took me a moment to find my voice. As I studied her, I thought I could detect the distinctive and detestable odour of a lie.

She tried for a smile, but the result was tragic. "I know you're trying to help, Alex. But let me have a quiet word with my ex-friends in the union. Besides, what's it going to do for my business if the police are always swarming all over the shop? Sweet old Mr. Lovegren from the Order of St. James won't want anything to do with me. Same with the ad agencies and architects round here. They'll go somewhere else."

Gooseflesh rippled up my arms as I knew for a fact that she was lying. How would talking to the union friends who'd got her *into* this mess help? There was something else. . . .

She licked her lips. "I'll make a deal with you. I'll tell my troubles to Anthony Simino, too. He knows everyone round here, and everything that goes on. The man *is* Clerkenwell. And he already knows what happened yesterday, so he's in on my little secret anyway. Would you believe, as a young man he even worked as a printer's devil—like Bruce? He even knew Mmbasi Kumba—gave him some after-school work."

I felt as if she'd jolted me with an electric shock. Simino knew Kumba? Was Simino somehow in league with Ferris-Browne? And Amanda believed he was her friend, or pretended that he was. . . . A myriad of unpleasant possibilities assaulted my brain as the police came through the door.

Two wore plain clothes and directed a group of four colleagues in heavy chemical-protection suits to remove the hazardous bottles. The security guard showed them to the alley. The two officers quizzed us for the next hour. We told them about the abduction, the vandalism, and that morning's delivery as Amanda resolutely denied knowing who had done this to her and why. *The police aren't going to be of much help if you don't tell them the truth,* I thought. But they knew that the emotionally charged public, primed with political hype for the upcoming election, was reacting violently to the stimulus of Lord Chenies's novel. It was reasonable for them to assume that what was happening to the printer of the book was a further manifestation of vehement opposition to Dexter Moore.

"We're becoming better and better acquainted with the terrorist groups in Britain as this election approaches," one CID officer told us, shaking his head. "The Dexter Moore crowd uses their G18 group for wildings in Paternoster Square, and the Lefty crowd uses the National Union of Pressworkers and Trades Union Group for things like this."

I saw Amanda stiffen as he named the union she'd been so careful not to mention to them. Secretly I rejoiced that, despite Amanda's reticence, the police were on the right track.

"Lovely world we live in," he finished. Then, after extracting a promise from Amanda to ring them at the slightest hint of anything peculiar, they left us.

We sat, much subdued, seeking refuge from the awkward moment in our cold coffees. At last Amanda sighed. "All right. We know that someone not only intercepted two good sets of proofs but somehow actually printed rubbishy proofs that at least had *Cleansing* headers— *something* to make Lord Chenies believe they were his proofs." I saw a muscle tighten in Amanda's cheek as she glanced at Bruce, who was carrying the shreds of the ruined Donaldson book to the rubbish bin.

"You'll have to forgive me, Amanda," Nicola said. "I really don't know enough about your sort of printing to understand how that would work. What does making a set of proofs entail?" She was offering a diversion, and Amanda grasped at it eagerly.

Standing, she motioned for us to follow. "Come over to the monocaster, and I'll show you." She flipped a switch on the machine and sat down on a stool as we clustered round. Bruce joined us. I loved seeing his face at moments like this; he was so eager, so in love with every last detail of printing. Some people seemed to catch the fever, and once they had it, it stuck with them for life. My father had had it.

"This is a machine for making type one piece at a time," Amanda instructed. "There's another kind, called a Linotype, which you've probably heard of." Nicola nodded. "A Linotype casts an entire line at once, but it's harder to make corrections that way—you have to reset the entire line. I prefer to cast one letter at a time. That way I can keep sets of fonts when I'm done, too, if necessary. With Linotype, you melt down all the lead after the job, for recasting into more lines of type later."

"I'm with you so far," Nicola said.

"Okay. When I set out to cast the type for *Cleansing*, I put in the matrix for Caslon—heaven knows Lord Chenies wouldn't want a foreign typeface like Garamond or Bodoni or something. Caslon is the supreme English typeface."

Nicola and I looked at each other surreptitiously, remembering the strange phone call she'd intercepted the day before. I made a mental note to mention it before we left.

"Like this." Amanda slid the Caslon matrix out so we could see it. It was a grid of letters in roughly a three-inch square, with a long handle. She slid it back in again. "When I type a lowercase *g* on the keyboard, it makes a paper tape with holes in it. When I feed the tape into the monocaster, the machine shoots hot lead up into the mould, forcing it into a block with the letter on top." She cast one right then and there: in less than a second, the little block of type was ready.

Amanda picked up a pair of tweezers and gripped the tiny piece of metal, then lifted it up for us to see. "This little notch here, at the base, is called the nick. It tells you when you've got the letter the right way round, without looking. Typesetters slot type into composing sticks so fast that they can't actually look at each letter; the nick lets us *feel* when we've got it right. And this," Amanda said, turning the type letter side up, "is the shoulder." She pointed to the flat surface beneath the raised letter. I saw a little round spot there, with a tiny impression of Amanda's mark, an *A* and an *M* intertwined. On every item she printed Amanda added her printer's mark as a tailpiece, at the end of the book. It was one of the perks of being a fine-art printer. I'd seen her mark printed in colour on a specimen tacked up along her wall—she'd displayed her environmentalist's stripes by making the *A* in blue waves, like a river, and the *M* in green leafy texture, like a hedge. Evidently she also put her mark on every piece of type she made.

"Before monocasters came into use," Amanda continued, "type was made by foundries, who poured hot metal into moulds. The punch that shot the bits of type out of the mould left a round circle on the side of the sort, called a pin mark." She reached round and showed us a piece of old foundry type, with the indented circle on its side. "The mark used to just be a blank circle, until foundries twigged to using it to show that their company had made the font. Believe it or not, it used to be a matter of fierce pride—not everyone had the mould for casting every font. For a long time, the Caslon Letter Foundry cast type not far from here, in Aldersgate. They were the only ones who could produce Caslon, for instance. Now anyone can, given the matrix and a caster. I suppose you could say the shoulder mark on my type is the modern private printer's version of the pin mark. Private casters got the idea to use the shoulder for their mark because foundries used to carve little messages there for typesetters, an 'lc' when the lower-case l was hard to distinguish from the number 1, for instance.

"So," Amanda continued with a sigh, "when I cast the type for *Cleansing* earlier this week, I did it in the order of Lord Chenies's prose, then slid it right into the galley trays. I ran the proofs on the Vandercook over there immediately afterward, since all the signatures were ready to go."

She led us over to the proofing press. "I lock the galley tray in here, place a sheet here, and roll the cylinder, like this." She turned a crank and the six-inch-diameter cylinder purred down the bed to the end; she rolled it back again. It obviously took some strength to roll the cylinder, but Amanda did it with grace and finesse. "With this size sheet of paper, fifteen inches by twenty-one inches, I can make an eight-page signature. But of course there are only four to each side, so I have to print both sides. Then a machine folds the signatures, and I bind them. After binding, the folds have to be cut on two sides so they'll open. In this case we won't trim the book, right, Alex?"

I nodded. The look of rough, deckled edges was much preferable for a collector's edition.

Nicola asked, "So someone got in here and either used your caster to set nonsense type or took the bits of type out of your cabinets and set them?"

"Right, but I've checked all my Caslon cabinets. Nothing's missing. And if they used the caster, they completely melted down all the lead again; the trays are empty." She shook her head. "It would require a vast amount of work."

"And a bit thick besides," Bruce said. "If you wanted

to stop someone printing a book, surely there'd be easier ways than intercepting proofs and printing nonsense ones." He shrugged. "In the end, it wouldn't stop the book being printed. Besides, this is just the special edition, right? You're going to have tens of thousands of the things printed in Hong Kong."

"Absolutely," I confirmed. The tens of thousands of copies that would reach the masses wouldn't be out until *after* the election. This had to have something to do with the election, I thought; someone wants to prevent us publishing the book until *afterwards*. Ferris-Browne cared about the election, Dexter Moore, and . . .

In the next instant I was knocked sideways by a horrible thought: the prime minister. Graeme Abercrombie cared about the election and stood to lose more than anyone else. What if Abercrombie was secretly working at *cross-purposes* to Ferris-Browne, trying to keep us from publishing *Cleansing* before the election? The special edition would be all he had to prevent. And he could do that, at this point, by incapacitating us. Not difficult to do, especially as the most powerful man in Britain.

My mind raced. Did Abercrombie think that Ferris-Browne's strategy for manipulating public opinion wouldn't work? Was Abercrombie hand-in-glove with the powerful unions, as Labour was meant to be, and had he promised them the book would never be published? All he'd have to do was prevent the special edition until after the election: after that, there was little they could do. Their votes would be cast.

Or . . . had Dexter Moore's people decided that Ferris-Browne's strategy was all too effective, based on those preliminary polls after the release of *Cleansing*'s first chapter? Could it have been the neo-Nazi terrorist group G18 that had abducted Amanda and sabotaged her printing so far?

I was afraid to publish this special edition—deeply

afraid. But how would we bring justice for Mmbasi Kumba and Amanda, and expose these forces for what they were, unless we saw the publication through?

"We'll just have to be smarter than they are, now that we know someone's out to stop the book," Amanda said, breaking into my troubled thoughts. "We'll deliver all proofs by hand, personally. All right?"

We agreed. Nicola asked, "Who delivered the first two sets of proofs you sent out?"

"Clerkenwell Couriers," Bruce replied. "We always use the locals. I rang them when Dee called to say you'd never received the second set. They swear they made the delivery."

I got a bad case of the creeps thinking about what we were up against. Normally cooperative couriers had become agents for our saboteurs . . . or else someone like Rachel Sigridsson, my own trusted employee, had stolen them. That was, if anything, worse. And people had crept through subterranean tunnels to kidnap our innocent printer. Involuntarily I glanced at the door to the cellar; someone had added a hefty padlock since yesterday.

"You know," Nicola mused, "it's not hard to think of other people besides your NUP friends who might want to stop this book—or even create a bit of mischief to make life difficult for us—as a statement. Off the top of my head, I can think of four or five: activists from the Left or Right; the parents of the boys Lord Chenies used as models for the wilding victims in *Cleansing*; personal enemies of Lord Chenies; and"—she looked at me meaningfully—"his son and daughter-in-law, the original publishers. After all, we've now deprived them of a certain best-seller."

I hated to acknowledge that we had so many enemies, but there was no denying it. I also hated to think that the most likely enemies were at a far higher level than those she had named.

"If we were to continue with this," I speculated, feeling

a need for some resolution, "and I'm not certain we will, we've very little time now to get this thing printed, bound, and slipcased. The contract specifies a release date of April fifth. That's less than two weeks away." I looked Amanda in the eye. "If we decide to go ahead, could you do it, Amanda?"

It came out sounding like a challenge, though I certainly hadn't meant it to. The poor woman had been to hell and back already, trying. I heard her breath quicken, sensed the way she stiffened.

"Yes. Yes, we can. Right, Bruce?"

Bruce didn't look as confident as Amanda sounded, but he was game. "Sure."

Suddenly all of us became very busy with our coffee mugs again. When we all realised it, we set them down at the same time, which made things even worse.

Amanda was the first to speak, doing her best to keep her voice level and calm. "This afternoon we'll reset the book. Bruce or I will print the proofs and hand-deliver two copies to you at Bedford Square by this evening. If you don't mind, Alex, perhaps you personally could take one of them to Chenies on your way home tonight. You said you live quite near the Manor, right?"

"Yes. But wait for my call before you go ahead; I'll make a decision and ring you in the next couple of hours." After I talked to Ferris-Browne again and tried to get some sort of reading from the PM directly, if I possibly could. I desperately needed some answers.

"All right . . . if you do end up delivering proofs to Lord Chenies, perhaps you could let him know that we're on an extremely tight schedule, give him a couple of days, tell him we can't cope with a lot of changes."

"I've heard he's not a last-minute re-writer. If it all looks to be in order, he might phone with the go-ahead tomorrow," I said, trying to be reassuring.

"Good. Then we'll be printing by Friday, latest, and

binding next week. We'll be done before time, Alex." She made another heroic effort at a smile, but it failed. There were huge dark circles under her eyes, and coils of wiry red hair had escaped from the long braid that hung down her back. Her pallor was disturbing. Wryly, she finished, "Ah, the joys of a small print shop."

I hated what I'd done to her for the sake of my little favour to Abercrombie.

The meeting was over. We said our good-byes, urging Amanda to be careful. The guard stood just inside the door, watching the street.

"Oh," I said, turning back again. "When we were here waiting for you yesterday, Nicola answered your telephone and got a rather peculiar message." I looked at Nicola, indicating that she should continue.

"Someone named Bodoni wanted you to know that Jenson was after you, something like that. He said that you should try to leave the country, and that Goudy would have you. It was all quite strange."

The muscle flexed again in Amanda's pale cheek as she received this news. "Thanks," she said stiffly.

Seized with concern for her, and keenly feeling my responsibility for the danger she was in, I said, "Amanda, is this Bodoni business something we can help you with?"

"No, no. I know it all sounds a bit strange, but it's all right." She nearly shooed us out the door.

Bruce told her apologetically that he had to make a quick stop at the bank, and followed us. We heard the guard lock the front door after we left, which made me feel a bit better.

Bruce's eyes were clouded with worry. He looked at his watch. "I don't want to delay getting to work with Amanda, but I need to talk to you both about something. Let's keep moving away from the shop. She'll hate it if she thinks we're talking about her."

"Of course," I said, wondering what little worry bomb he was going to drop next. We kept walking. People who had found excuses to venture out on such a perfect spring day filled the streets, and early drinkers were already entrenched in the outdoor garden of the pub on the green, the Clerk's Well.

"Shall we stop at the pub?"

Bruce nodded. "Inside. More privacy." It didn't seem safe to talk on the street anymore, if even Clerkenwell Couriers might be involved in this conspiracy. Who knew where there were ears?

I took orders and got drinks while Nicola and Bruce found a table at the rear, deep in the smoky interior of the pub. Muted jazz camouflaged our voices.

"All right." Bruce's scowl revealed distaste for what he was about to tell us. "I went to an NUP chapel meeting the other night—Amanda can't show her face there any more, of course. They're rabid," he said, "and it's mostly about this book. *Our* book," he added sourly. "Not that many people know I'm working for Amanda. As far as they're concerned, I'm just at the College of Printing. Anyway, the NUP is planning a march," Bruce said, picking up his glass.

"A *what*?"

"You know—a march, a protest. Against *Cleansing* and in favour of EMU. On Clerkenwell Green."

I groaned.

"We'll have to tell Amanda to board up her windows," Nicola said. "It won't be a friendly crowd."

"And her cellar door," Bruce said pointedly.

I shuddered, thinking of the intruder who had stolen up on her so surreptitiously, and the terror her abduction must have caused her. Softly, I asked, "When?"

"Dunno, exactly." He looked round the pub, though it was nearly empty at this hour. "The NUP activists aren't going to send out word until the afternoon of the march, so the wrong people don't get wind of it. We're all supposed to be ready. Needless to say, I won't be among them.

"There's something else," he continued. "I heard you mention the Bodoni bloke—the one with the Italian accent. Amanda gets those strange calls all the time." Nicola and I exchanged a glance. "She never wants me to answer the phone, but if I do—when she's out—they hang up on me. They'll never leave a message. I'm worried about who she might be involved with. I asked her about it once, but she pretended she didn't know what I meant, so I let it pass."

So there was far more to Amanda's troubles than she was telling us.

"At least no one can get to her now, with the security service there," I said. "And the police know that those radical groups are targeting her; they're on to the NUP, according to the detective. When your union friends ring you to say it's time to march, you might give the Met a quick ring."

"Yeah. I might." Bruce looked at his watch again, thanked me for the drink, and excused himself. We watched him hurry off.

Nicola gave me a grim look over her mineral water. It's even worse than we thought, her eyes told me.

As usual, she was right.

CHAPTER NINE

———◆———

All the wickedness of the world is print to him.

CHARLES DICKENS, *Martin Chuzzlewit*

FERRIS-BROWNE WAS CHAMPING AT THE BIT TO TALK TO me. He'd left half a dozen messages at the office in the time we'd been at Amanda's. Evidently it was all right for him to call me, if not the other way round. With trepidation, I dialled the number he'd left.

"Plumtree," he said, sounding delighted. "What a surprise to find my Nicola working for you. What an astonishing coincidence!"

What a politician, I thought.

"Listen, though, I'm a bit worried that you thought I *arranged* for the teenager to die in the wilding in Farringdon Road. You don't *really* think I'd do that, do you?"

"At this point, I'm not certain what I think, Deputy Prime Minister. A boy's died; there's been yet another wilding; and the printing of the special edition has been sabotaged in the most awful ways. Amanda Morison was abducted yesterday—locked up in the dark in an old dungeon, for heaven's sake."

"Good Lord." There was a moment's silence. "Why didn't you tell me?"

"I wasn't to ring you, remember? 'Don't call us, we'll call you?' You made it quite clear."

"But this *is* a bit much. Those other things have nothing to do with me. And in the first wilding, the boy *died*. I do want to see Graeme re-elected, but I'm not a murderer." He hesitated. "Look, Plumtree. I apologise for involving you in the Clerkenwell wilding. But it was an excellent opportunity for us—for the PM," he added firmly. "I realise you've been through a lot for us, and so has your printer, of course, but I really must ask you to persevere for the sake of the election. The history of *Europe*, not just Britain, is at stake here. Do you really want to see Moore and G18 running the country, with Nazi marches in every city? I *know* my strategy will prove successful, if you'll just stay behind us."

I said nothing.

He sighed. "There are lots of things I *can't* tell you, Plumtree. You'll have to trust me."

"I need to talk to the prime minister before I agree to continue."

"That can be arranged, if absolutely necessary."

"If you want me to publish this book, it is absolutely necessary. I intend to cancel the special edition within the next hour and a half unless he can persuade me otherwise. I never dreamt there would be deaths, abductions, buggings . . ."

"*Buggings?*" He sounded genuinely surprised, then cautious. "You've had them removed, haven't you?"

"Yes, at considerable expense." Incredulous, I nearly pointed out to him that he had glossed over deaths, and abductions, to obsess about buggings. But he was speaking again.

"Well, I certainly didn't put them there, old boy. Good heavens. You really are knee-deep in it, aren't you?"

He thought for a moment. "I will say, though, the PM's security men have been known to engage in a bit of eavesdropping now and again. It's their trademark, rather. But I assure you I have nothing to do with it. I might also mention . . . " Here he hesitated again before continuing somewhat grimly. "Well. There are some things that must remain unsaid, Plumtree. But you may as well know that the PM sometimes goes off on his own, doesn't exactly play by the rules. Are you with me?"

I reeled at the implication of his words. Was he confirming the suspicion that had first occurred to me in the print shop, that the prime minister might be causing these disasters to befall us? Somehow pursuing an agenda of his own?

"I'll arrange that call for you right away, Plumtree. I can't tell you how grateful I am for what you're doing, though I realise our plan has gone slightly awry. The entire nation's talking about the book—just as I'd hoped. Really, I am extremely pleased. Stay with us, Plumtree. We need you. After the election, I promise to have the Kumba boy's murder checked out at the highest levels—no matter the cost to me personally."

"Thank you," I said lamely.

"The election's mere weeks away now," he went on, sounding self-satisfied. "If we can just hang on, all will be well, and I daresay there'll be a little something for you at the end of it."

We rang off. I felt disturbed by the way we'd glossed over such serious matters. And had that been bribery at the end? The little carrot of a reward? No, I wouldn't take his word for it, but I would listen to Graeme Abercrombie. It was Ferris-Browne's job to get what he needed, real means-justifying stuff, and damn the consequences to the little people. But I knew that Graeme Abercrombie was trustworthy. Unless he had changed substantially . . .

But before I had two ticks to think about it, Graeme

Abercrombie's voice boomed down my phone line. "Alex," he said warmly. "Glad we have this chance to talk. I've been thinking of you a great deal, with all that's happened—especially that poor boy dying in the Clerkenwell wilding. I know this can't have been easy for you, with your name caught up in it all, and the family publishing house. But I can't stress to you how very important it is to me—to Britain—that you see this through. I can tell you in all honesty that I know your father would want you to do this. If you can just believe in me and support me in this, you'll see. It'll all come right in the end."

He sounded so sincere, so serious, so completely genuine. And so very worried. My instinct told me I could count on him. I heard myself saying that I would continue with the special edition. And I told myself that if I was wrong about Abercrombie, the world would know by the time I was done. I would clue Max in and get him sniffing round, as insurance.

I rang Amanda and told her we were going ahead, only to learn that she'd already recast eight pages. How could she still be so keen, so willing to see this book through?

I put the issue firmly out of my mind and got on with the tyranny of the urgent. The hours spent lately at Amanda's shop had created a desperate backlog of ordinary work, which would have been far worse if Lisette hadn't dealt with so much of it for me. She was a godsend. I beavered away on the massive pile of belated correspondence and decisions to be made until six o'clock, when Amanda herself arrived, accompanied by Bruce, with proofs for the first half of the book.

I met them in the foyer. "You're amazing!" I exclaimed. "How on earth did you manage it?"

"You can't keep a Morison from printing," Amanda said, thrusting the small parcel into my hands. "Talk to you tomorrow." As she strode off toward Tottenham

Court Road with Bruce, I saw that this was a matter of pride for her. She held her head high, and her thick braid swung with each confident step.

Ten minutes later I was roaring off to Chorleywood with Lisette, the proofs in the rear seat. As if the day hadn't been frantic enough, that evening I had still more commitments—though in this case one of them was fortunate. After delivering the proofs, I'd promised to go to Max's for a quick dinner with him and his wife, Madeline. It would be the perfect time to talk to my brother about my little deal with Ferris-Browne and the prime minister, and get his journalistic help in working out the complexities of who was doing what to whom.

Afterwards I'd have to tear off to the county boundary meeting for seven-thirty. If only I hadn't accepted a call to duty from Hotchkiss to serve on *that* all-too-political committee.

I was preoccupied on the drive home. Guilt assailed me for not having told Lisette about my deal with the devil, as I now considered my promise to publish *Cleansing*. But every time I considered telling her, I realised that she was better off—safer, even—not knowing. A slightly uncomfortable silence reigned for most of the journey, but Lisette seemed not to take offence. She had other things to worry about, I thought.

After delivering Lisette to her door, I raced off to Chenies Manor to personally deliver the partial proofs. As long as Lord Chenies didn't harangue me for too long, there would still be time for the quick early dinner Max and Madeline had promised.

I drove past Martyn's house and Christ Church Chenies, into the forecourt of Chenies Manor. It was remarkably beautiful, I thought, admiring the multiple twisting chimneys on top of the old brick building as I crunched up the gravel walk to the door. The perfect day had turned into a rather gusty, blustery night. I rang the bell and

clutched the box that held the proofs; I didn't want anything else to go wrong with the wretched things.

Charford-Cheney's man, as he called him—actually
his butler—opened the door. I couldn't recall his name.
He looked troubled; his chin quivered slightly as he regarded me.

"Good evening," I said. "I'm Alex Plumtree—here to
deliver proofs for Lord Chenies's novel. Is he at home?"

"No, I'm sorry, sir. I—we—" He licked his lips ner-
vously and seemed uncertain how to proceed. "The truth
is, sir, we can't find his lordship." A tear appeared in his
left eye and overflowed, travelling a tortuous path over
wrinkles until it reached his jaw, where it hung.

"Can't *find* him?" I repeated, disbelieving. Immediately I thought of Amanda's abduction. An elderly man
might not survive such treatment. "Does he often go off
like this?"

"Never, sir. Never." The poor man was in tears again.

"Have you talked to Martyn Blakely, the new vicar?
Perhaps he's seen him."

His eyes lit up. "There's an idea. The vicar might have
seen if he's gone for a walk. His motor is still here, you see.
But he's never missed his tea like this. . . ."

This wasn't good at all. I wondered if Martyn had seen
him. . . . *What if Martyn had told him what we found in the
vicarage attic?* That might have caused Lord Chenies to
disappear—in any number of unpleasant ways.

"Let me see if I can find Martyn—perhaps he's seen
his lordship." I thrust the proofs into the butler's hands
and trotted over to the church, barely twenty yards from
the front door of the manor house. I opened the gate from
the garden into the churchyard and ran round to the
church entrance. The heavy door swung open when I
pulled—a good sign that Martyn was there, since even
Christ Church Chenies had to lock its doors against
thieves and vandals these days. In the dim light, the scent

of musty stone and candles struck me, along with decades of associations. The church was deserted; I walked toward the altar and veered toward the little office traditionally used by the vicar. Martyn was there, hunting and pecking at the keyboard of a portable computer.

"Alex!" he exclaimed, startled. "What brings you here?" He stood at once, perhaps perceiving my alarm.

"Lord Chenies is missing. His butler—what's his name?"

"Wilkins."

"Right. Wilkins seems quite upset. Lord Chenies missed his tea. Evidently it's not happened before. I was just wondering if you'd seen him."

"Er—yes, I saw him earlier. Round two o'clock." Martyn looked nervous.

Uh-oh, I thought. He's told him.

"Martyn, did you—"

"Not now, all right?" He sounded perturbed. "Are you coming with me to the manor?"

"Yes . . . I'll have to ring Max and Madeline, though—they're expecting me for dinner." I picked up the phone and began to dial their number.

"No, Alex—you go on. Let me handle this little parish disaster, if indeed it is one. I'll go have a word with Wilkins, perhaps have a look round. His lordship's probably just gone off on a ramble."

Or on a massive bender, I thought, considering the news you gave him. Although perhaps that was preferable to another abduction.

"Something terrible might have happened to him, Martyn. This book has turned people into monsters." The phone rang and rang at Max and Madeline's; no answer. It frustrated me no end, the way they turned off the ringer when they didn't want to be interrupted. Their answering machine wasn't picking up, either.

"Really, Alex—what can you possibly do here that I

can't?" Martyn argued. "It doesn't take two of us to baby-sit Wilkins. And you can't wait here for Lord Chenies if he's gone off somewhere—it could be days."

As I listened to Max's phone ring, I grudgingly saw the logic in Martyn's words. And with some irritation I acknowledged that Lord Chenies had already done enough damage without my rearranging every last minute of my life. I put down the phone.

"I'll ring you later," Martyn offered. "What time will you be home?"

"I have the blasted County Boundary Committee meeting after Max and Madeline's. Not that they couldn't live without me, but I promised. Should be back by ten or half past, I should think. I'll come round after."

He nodded. We hurried back through the church, locked the back door, then walked briskly together through the churchyard to the manor house. Wilkins stood in the doorway still, eager for the vicar's comfort and help. I left them to get on with it with my good wishes, promising to be back later. Feeling a pang of guilt for fobbing off the problem on Martyn, I hopped in the car and travelled with due speed to Watersmeet, my brother's stately home.

As I piloted the car westward, a powerful wind rocked it each time I emerged from the sheltered, wooded lanes. I had to get out of the car to shift a huge downed tree limb from the middle of the lane just before reaching Max and Madeline's.

"Alex!" Max greeted me with an effusive hug. It wasn't the traditional greeting in our family, but I'd become used to the new mannerisms he'd developed while in treatment for alcoholism two years before. I was so grateful for a healthy brother that I didn't mind the warmth and intimacy that was his new trademark. In fact, Max had taught me a thing or two.

As I stepped into the oak-panelled foyer, Madeline

appeared and planted a kiss on my cheek. "So glad you could come, Alex," she purred. Her long blond hair shone against her black velour dress. After a year of marriage she was no less a double for Cindy Crawford. Since she and Max had moved into this house, Madeline had deprived Christie's of her rare book expertise and started her own firm with Max. He bought and sold; she appraised and advised.

"I know it's a busy night for you. Come in and have a drink," she said, taking me by the arm and guiding me into the library, the room she knew I loved best.

"What a week!" Max exclaimed.

He didn't know the half of it. "You must be glad to be out of the publishing business, Max. Who would have guessed that such violence could come from the printed page?" I shook my head.

Sinking into one of the sofas placed at right angles to the fire, I was grateful for the flame crackling in the grate, and the bottle of my favourite merlot waiting on the table in front of it. Madeline served only the best. I used to worry about having alcohol in any form at Max's house, but they both assured me that it was actually a good idea to have it about.

"Yes, well, as it turns out, I *am* back in publishing in one sense of the word," Max said enigmatically. As he came to sit across from me, and as Madeline poured the wine, I couldn't help but gaze in awe at the floor-to-ceiling rare books in the room. This had once been the home of a friend of mine, a rare book expert named Armand Beasley. When he died he'd left his home—and its books— to me. But as I preferred to live at the Orchard, I'd passed his house and his collection on to Max and Madeline in exchange for the old Plumtree family home.

"Oh?" I said. Max was always full of surprises. Fortunately, these days they tended to be more pleasant than disastrous. "How's that?"

He smiled mischievously. "I've been doing a bit of freelance writing again. Only the things that really interest me, of course." He poured a small bottle of San Pellegrino into a glass. "A bit of information on the water scandal came my way, and I put it to use."

"Good. Which paper?"

"The *Watch*. With their political orientation, they're eager to make mincemeat of all the wealthy water bigwigs. They were thrilled to have it."

"That's wonderful, Max. You're a gifted writer—it would be a shame to let your talent go to waste." And it wouldn't have a chance to, after what I was about to tell him. Out of courtesy, I asked, "What exactly is going on in the water business? May I see your article?"

"Certainly," he said, nodding. "It's not running in the *Watch* till tomorrow. I'll bring it with your dinner." He rose and headed for the door. "Thought we might eat here by the fire, since the timetable's a bit tight," he threw over his shoulder.

"Can't think of anything nicer."

As he disappeared into the hallway, I asked Madeline how the book business was going.

"Remarkably well," she replied. "We seem to have just the right amount of work. And the most fascinating thing has happened," she said, cocking her head to one side. The firelight danced on her blond hair. "Did you ever have the experience in school of studying two things that you didn't know were related, then finding that they overlapped?"

I nodded. Those had been the most rewarding moments in nearly two decades of education.

"Well, Max's research into the water issue has overlapped a bit with the work I'm doing at the moment, appraising a library. Do you know Richard Hotchkiss?"

Madeline had only been in our family for a year or so, and had not yet learned the chapter of Plumtree history that included my ill-fated teenage courtship of Helena.

"Yes, indeed," I answered, deciding to spare her that knowledge. "In fact, Hotchkiss and his daughter are heading opposing sides of the County Boundary Committee. I'll be seeing them tonight at the meeting."

Madeline's bright eyes clouded. "In that case, it's a good thing your meeting is tonight instead of tomorrow. I'm afraid Richard Hotchkiss isn't going to be very pleased with the Plumtree clan after Max's article comes out."

I groaned inwardly. It wasn't the first time Max's journalistic work had reflected badly on me. I hated to see Hotchkiss become an enemy; for years I'd entertained the notion of one day being asked to join the board of directors of my old school, prestigious Merchant Taylors of Watford. Hotchkiss was on the nominating committee. Despite the débâcle with Helena, it had occurred to me that he might suggest me to fill the seat of a retiring board member. Still, I'd much rather that Max find satisfaction in writing again than have a seat on the board. In fact, I'd learned the hard way merely a year before that, depending on the organisation, being a board member for a charity could be just as dangerous as book publishing.

Max re-entered the library carrying a large tray, with some papers tucked under one arm.

"Here we are," he said with satisfaction, setting a steaming plate of what looked like chicken and vegetable pie on the table in front of me.

"This looks wonderful," I enthused, catching the aroma of sage, onion, and white wine. Only Max and Madeline would be confident enough to serve red wine with chicken. "Who's responsible?"

They gazed at each other lovingly. It had taken some time for me to grow comfortable with their public displays of affection, but it wasn't difficult to be tolerant when I recalled the huge difference Madeline had made in Max's life. Sometimes I wondered if Sarah wished I were more open in displaying my affection for her . . .

something else for us to talk about during our weekend together. Endless subjects awaited us; it would take a lifetime to explore them all.

"Max did the crust and the sauce, and I took care of the rest," Madeline said. "Isn't he wonderful?"

Smiling, Max put the other plates on the table, gave out the cutlery and serviettes. He waved his hand at the plate to indicate that I shouldn't wait to start, and then put the papers to one side of my plate.

I forked up a bite consisting of crust, a chunk of white chicken meat bathed in a succulent white sauce, and a carrot. It was so delicious that I actually closed my eyes.

"This is superb," I said, lifting my glass to Max. The red wine complemented the pie well, standing up nicely to the strong overtones of herb and onion. I turned back to the pie and glanced over at the article.

"Mmm," Max said through a bite. "I'll give you a summary, if you like. You can read it later, when there's more time."

"Great."

He drank some Pellegrino and began. Madeline, sitting next to him on the sofa opposite me, put a hand on his back. I could see the excitement in his eyes, and he sat forward on the sofa, clasping his hands. *He must really believe he's on to something,* I thought.

"All right. Until now the water scandal has focussed on excess profit and insufficient investment. But I've got another angle." He rubbed his hands together. "I heard about it when Madeline and I were up at Merchant Taylors, cataloguing the library there. I'd gone to the car with our materials and was waiting for her."

I nodded my encouragement and continued to demolish my pie. I began to hope for seconds.

"Little did I know that Richard Hotchkiss and his cronies from the school's board of governors were standing round the corner, behind that tall hedge as you come out the side door."

I knew just the one he meant. "You sneaky devil," I said. Madeline refilled my wineglass, and I smiled at her gratefully. It was never a chore to come to dinner at Watersmeet.

Max grinned. "It was a journalist's dream. They had no idea I was there. It seemed foolish to make a rumpus to inform them of the fact, so I sat innocently in my car, waiting for my wife," he took Madeline's free hand and squeezed it, "and heard a few things.

"Hotchkiss told Fine that he was going to, and I quote"—Max picked up the papers by my plate to read from them verbatim—"here it is: 'give the public what they want. If they want more investment in the water supply of the future, they shall damn well have it—whether it's necessary or not. You know how the British public like making sacrifices? Well, they can sacrifice their money and feel that they're doing the right thing: investing in the future. But it'll bloody well cost them to be so virtuous, and we'll profit in the end. It's the perfect opportunity to make my little project pay off.' "

"The man sounds positively criminal! What on earth can he mean?"

Max shook his head. "I still don't know what he meant by 'his little project.' That's the one part that's stumped me, but I'm filing it away for later. No doubt when it comes to light it'll make a good story, too. At any rate, the main thrust of my story is what he said about letting the public pay for what it thinks it needs. There's no misunderstanding his point: he's going to bilk them for money to line the pockets of the London Water shareholders, and manage to gain privately as well."

"He's as crooked as they come," I said, incredulous. "And all this time I thought he was a pillar of the community.

Of the nation, even." One by one, my illusions were being shattered.

With a sigh, I regretfully set about shattering a few for Max and Madeline. "I'm afraid I've another story for you, Max—and it's not at all a happy one. But I want you to hang on to this until after the election. I've given my word. All right?"

"Of course."

"I made a deal with Graeme Abercrombie to publish *Cleansing*, because Ferris-Browne thought it would swing sentiment away from Dexter Moore and toward Graeme. I trusted him. Remember how highly Father used to speak of Abercrombie?"

Max nodded.

"Well, the whole thing's got rather messy. Ferris-Browne admitted to setting up the wilding as a publicity stunt, and placing me in the middle of it. He claims he didn't mean the boy to die, that it was an accident. Now someone is trying to sabotage the printing of *Cleansing*. Amanda, our printer, was abducted yesterday, and before that, someone dumped out her entire book's worth of finished galley trays. Even before *that*, two sets of proofs were stolen. Tonight Lord Chenies has gone missing." I wondered how Martyn was doing at the manor, and whether his Lordship had turned up yet.

"Alex, this is incredible! Have the police been notified?"

"Yes, but not of what I'm about to tell you. I've asked myself: who would so persistently interfere with the publication of this book, especially when bulk copies will be released in less than a month? And then it hit me: Max, I think Graeme Abercrombie himself might be sabotaging us. But I'm going to stick with it, as they've both asked me to. It's not just because I promised, but because this way I think I'll find out what's really going on. At the heart of this is a man who might have had an innocent boy murdered. Ferris-Browne claims he'll do the right thing after the election, and own up to organising the wilding . . . though I can't quite picture it. Even if the death was an accident, he's ultimately responsible for setting it all in motion. And both Amanda and the police said something about the NUP being involved. I know you have contacts . . ."

"Of course I'll check it out. But Alex, I—I hardly know what to say. If they—whoever *they* are—*know* that you know this . . ." Max shook his head.

Yes. My life was in danger. What was worse, everyone associated with this project was in danger. I checked my watch. The blasted county boundary meeting. I'd stop in quickly, leave early, and head straight for Chenies Manor.

"Well, I hate to drop a bomb like that on you and leave, but I have promises to keep. And miles to go before I sleep." I tried a smile, but Max hadn't caught the Robert Frost quote—he wasn't big on American poets. And he and Madeline looked grave in the extreme. "Thanks so much . . ."

We said our farewells; I hurried out to my car, buffeted by the wind. A shell-shocked Max and Madeline watched me go.

Just as I started down the drive, Max ran toward the car, yelling, "Wait!"

I stepped on the brake and opened my door. "What?" I called.

He came abreast of me, looking distraught. "Be careful, won't you?"

"You too," I said.

We both knew he was caught in the web with me now.

CHAPTER TEN

‑‑‑‑◈‑‑‑‑

I will but look upon the hedge and follow you.

WILLIAM SHAKESPEARE, *The Winter's Tale*

THE GALE HADN'T ABATED AS I PULLED OFF THE COMMON Road into the car park of the Chorleywood Memorial Hall. Perhaps two dozen cars sat on the gravel, many of them familiar to me: Hotchkiss's Mercedes, Victor Fine's Saab, and . . . With surprise I noted that Helena's white BMW was absent. Perhaps I'd be fortunate and she wouldn't come that evening—and would therefore be unable to host her little party afterward. Now *that* would be a reprieve.

The boundary debate, after hedges, was the closest thing we had to a local controversy, and it had split the town roughly along political lines. The Labour contingent wanted to keep the boundary where it was, along the line of hedges that separated the Orchard property from the adjacent farm, which I leased to my neighbours. Labour wanted to protect my hedges by keeping them in Hertfordshire. They also wanted to keep as much money as possible for the Herts schools, rather than lose rates and pupils to a new Bucks school.

The Conservatives, on the other hand, by and large didn't give a hoot about hedges, and in fact opposed the effort to preserve them partly out of spite. They also felt that good schools should be rewarded no matter where they were located, and if some people wanted a Bucks address, well, that was all right too. But the real issue for the Conservatives was water rights. In exchange for the section of Herts that would be ceded to Bucks in a boundary change, Herts would get a patch of Bucks that contained a spring. And Richard Hotchkiss had had little trouble persuading the local Conservatives that water was power, especially after reminding them of the severe drought several years before. I didn't care much one way or the other which county my hedges and I belonged to, but I came down mildly on the side of the Conservatives.

Helena Hotchkiss, of course, led the faction representing the Labour point of view at these meetings. They'd always been fairly civil, but I couldn't imagine what horrors tonight would hold. At least it was the final meeting before the county referendum: this would all be over in a couple of weeks.

I sat in the car for a moment, looking out into the night, rocked by gusts of wind. How had I got myself into this predicament? I somehow felt my entire life called into question. In fact, what was I doing *here*, wasting an evening of my life? Not only did I have people falling all around me on the sacrificial sword of this reprehensible novel, but my personal life had practically ceased to exist. Having just left Max and Madeline, I was aware of the extreme contrast of our situations. My fiancée was a thousand miles away, and here I was, fulfilling thankless community responsibilities. Max and Madeline worked together, were together all the time. What on earth was I thinking?

The answer came as quickly as the question had. It couldn't be helped that my wedding to Sarah was still months away. In the meantime I was living out the Plumtree tradition: I was a slave to responsibility. Not just in my allegiance to the prime minister and my perceived duty to help him but also in finding myself in this car park at this moment. How many nights had my father felt this way as he drove off, leaving us in the comforting fug of the kitchen doing our homework over cups of tea, as he went to a parish meeting or other town function?

I'd grown up believing it was the right thing to do. My father had rarely refused a call for help—whether from the town, the church, or his publishing charities. And it had seemed right for me to help the town through the county boundary ordeal.

I sighed and climbed out of the car. As I ran for the door, the huge trees surrounding the hall creaked ominously in the wind. Would the little building collapse like so many children's bricks if one of the massive branches fell? Light shone welcomingly from the tall, narrow windows of the Victorian building. I steeled myself for the ordeal to come.

I'd barely blown through the door when Hotchkiss boomed, "Ah, Plumtree! There you are." He and the Conservative contingent were clustered casually in a group, going over our position before the meeting with our hedge-loving friends. Nearly everyone wore a coat; the hall was chilly.

I nodded a greeting, and to my dismay saw Helena wink at me as she stood with her own group in the opposite corner. She was dressed as if for an evening out at a nightclub in London, in a slinky black cocktail dress. It was only just made reasonable for the occasion by a black jacket she'd obviously shrugged on as an afterthought.

"Seen Nigel out there anywhere?" Hotchkiss asked, frowning at me. "The man promised he'd be here."

"No—in fact, he seems to be missing. I was going to ask you if *you'd* seen him."

"Bloody hell, just what we need," he blustered. Hotchkiss seemed surprisingly shaken by this news. I had the feeling he was trying to hide his distress. "If that man can cause trouble, he will."

"As soon as we're done here, I'm going to the manor to see if he's turned up."

A sheen of sweat had broken out on his face, and with fumbling fingers he pulled an agenda out of a folder he carried. I hadn't realised he was so close to Lord Chenies. . . .

Hotchkiss cleared his throat. "Right, we'd better make a start," he pronounced with authority to our little group. The other conversations faded away. "Now, you all know this is our final meeting with our HIT friends. The issue will be settled, for better or for worse, in two weeks' time by the referendum. The leaflets have been posted, the mailings done, and all that remains is the telephone campaign. How did you get on with the poll, Saunderson?" James Saunderson was a wiry little solicitor who had recently moved into the town with his wife and two children, and was trying to be a good citizen.

Saunderson squirmed. I'd noticed that he was eager to ingratiate himself with Hotchkiss; he was also a rather ambitious member of the Chorleywood Conservative Association. "We're in good shape, I think." His tone gave the impression that his real message was *We've duped them into it, all right*.

We all knew that there was another reason why Saunderson and his type were fighting to get their corner of Chorleywood into Buckinghamshire. It wasn't just that the Bucks County Council was offering grants for new schools. Buckinghamshire was the stockbrokers' paradise, while Hertfordshire was—well, Hertfordshire. Delightful but distinctly lacking the cachet of Bucks. These people were all for anything that might bump up their property values.

"Sixty-seven percent of those contacted on my poll said they plan to vote for the change," Saunderson said sonorously.

"Excellent," Hotchkiss said, but gave poor Saunderson no further credit. "And what was your sample size?"

It was Saunderson's hesitation more than anything else that gave him away. "Er—yes—well, I'm not *exactly* sure. . . ."

Hotchkiss, an authority on human behaviour, scowled. "Great God, man. You know how many people you phoned. Out with it!"

Suddenly looking very much the new boy in the second form, Saunderson blushed extravagantly. "Er—I think perhaps a dozen or so."

Hotchkiss exhaled impatiently. "All right, then. Victor?"

Victor Fine said, "Well, you know, Richard, I've been rather busy here with Plumtree and the Left Book Club."

Next to me, I felt James Saunderson stiffen. Most of the people here undoubtedly loathed and detested the Socialist book club, which Fine ran. If the truth were told, I was delighted to have someone, anyone, remember that this year Plumtree Press had published equal numbers of politically explosive books on both the left and the right.

I'd asked Victor at one of these meetings months ago how he'd landed on the Conservative side of this boundary issue, considering that he and his publishing house, Rollancz, were wholeheartedly Socialist. He'd come up with some vague reason to do with water rights, which I remembered doubting at the time. Now I smiled at him, hoping he wasn't still angry about the meeting I'd postponed. He winked back at me.

Victor was yet another of my father's friends, not only because they'd grown up in the same town and gone to the same school but also by virtue of their shared occupation as Bedford Square publishers. Through the years the Plumtrees and the Fines had got together a fair amount, though Victor and my father had never been the best of friends. Politics had no doubt come between them at some point; my father had been strongly, though quietly, opposed to Socialism. I quite liked Victor Fine; he fascinated me as an example of a wealthy, privileged Socialist who seemed to see no hypocrisy in his way of life.

"I should think, Richard, that I'll manage to get a few articles in the regional press before the referendum." Victor's face was acquiring the wrinkles of an apple left to dry in the sun, but there was no mistaking the sparkle in his eye. Fine and Hotchkiss were good friends, and it was obvious that Fine wasn't afraid of Hotchkiss. Even if Hotchkiss were to reprimand him for being slack in carrying out his responsibilities, Fine would calmly smile and make it seem that Hotchkiss was the one out of line.

John Pilkington, a local pub owner who ran to fat, inhaled audibly. "What I want to know, Richard, is who's done the water-testing on the bit of land we'd be gaining from Bucks in the exchange?" he wheezed.

Hotchkiss shot him an exasperated look as if to say, *What on earth are you babbling about?*

Pilkington guffawed, his triple chin rippling grotesquely. "Well, if we were to gain an underground spring, our troubles would be over, wouldn't they? No more water shortage!"

Hotchkiss seethed. Evidently he'd had his fill of working with village idiots after hobnobbing with London's finest on his various boards and at his club. I had no doubt that soon he would be *Sir* Richard, at which point he would probably stop speaking to us all. As it was, Hotchkiss's tolerance had limits. If they were now going to niggle him about water issues, however good-naturedly, I was sure we were in for fireworks.

I wasn't disappointed.

"You ignorant *swine*, Pilkington," he spat out. Breathing heavily, he jabbed one finger into the air immediately in front of the publican's nose. "There's more water bubbling about beneath London—*and* round here—than you'll ever know. If I were to tell you—"

He stopped mid-sentence and reddened, then withdrew his finger awkwardly and cleared his throat. He looked very much as if he wished he could take back his words. I wouldn't have thought much about it if he hadn't reacted so strongly, and if I hadn't just heard Max's news about Hotchkiss. As it was, I made a mental note about Hotchkiss and the water bubbling about beneath London. There were getting to be more and more secrets to remember about more and more people.

"Well. Time to march bravely into battle," he said, suddenly busy pulling out a chair. Pilkington, who had admirably thick skin, merely looked curiously at Hotchkiss as if to say, *Well, what's got into you?* I had never seen the great Hotchkiss so uneasy. Victor Fine studied him intently, as if he might discern the full meaning of Hotchkiss's words by staring at him.

Hotchkiss looked round at us and said, "Anything else I should know before we begin?"

We all demurred, though I'd come prepared to report on my activities for the cause—unofficially, I was to take a barometer reading of those opposed to the shift. In my research I had found Helena's small but very determined faction surprisingly enthusiastic about hanging on to every last scrap of Hertfordshire soil.

When Hotchkiss pulled out that first chair, everyone took it as a signal that the meeting was starting. There was a wave of getting settled, and I saw that we had roughly a dozen people per side. Helena sat at the centre of her contingent, and Hotchkiss was in the middle of ours. Father and daughter faced one another like duelling cowboys.

When the settling-down noises abated, Helena began. "We would just like to point out that according to our polls, we have already won. You may as well give up and go home." She threw me a secretive little smile.

Her father answered, "If you remember, we are meeting tonight not so much to gloat over potential victories as to iron out the items on which we agreed to compromise, regardless of who wins."

Helena waved an issue of the local paper. It was the weekly *Chorleywood Communicator*, just released that day. "My *very* good friend Guy Ferris-Browne wrote an article for today's *Communicator*." She cast a glance at me for a reaction to Ferris-Browne's name, or perhaps to her mention of close friendship with him. I smiled, which I hoped would irritate her no end. Although mildly surprised to hear Ferris-Browne's name in this context, I might have guessed that the two of them would gather together over candlelight to sing the praises of the rain forest. They moved in the same powerful circles.

Helena's lips grew pouty for an instant; then she forged ahead. "It says that even if you win this referendum, he's going to blow the whistle on you for scheming to benefit financially from the spring. He is, after all, minister for the environment. He has the power. A *very* powerful man," she finished pointedly, looking at me again. If she was trying to make me jealous, she was failing miserably.

Hotchkiss was seething at this betrayal by his daughter. She'd never mocked him publicly before. "Your beloved minister for the environment may very well lose his position when Dexter Moore wins this election. Speaking of polls, my dear, Moore's in the lead. He has respect for private industry—those of us who actually bother to supply jobs for the working class and even tolerate their snivelling, opportunistic unions!"

This incensed Hotchkiss's opposite dozen beyond their ability to contain themselves. One woman in wire-rimmed glasses exclaimed, "It's people like you who are ruining this country! You—"

Another stood and shouted, "Nazi-lover!"

I watched in disbelief as the room crescendoed into a cacophony of insults and epithets. Was this the same group of people I met in Budgens on the High Street, inspecting the sterile offerings of the freezer case or selecting their beef joint for Sunday lunch? Hedges and water had turned these normally rational people into raving, hateful lunatics. I stood and waved my arms. "Please! Let's be reasonable. We didn't come here to—"

The woman sitting closest to me, with whom I'd worked on a local literacy committee the year before, stood and sneered. "Piss off, Plumtree." A spray of saliva hit my ear. "Publish any good *hate* literature lately?" Next to her, Wendy Dedham glared at me, her mouth a straight, hard line.

Stunned at their ferocity and undisguised hatred, I abandoned my plea for reason. Hotchkiss chose that moment to rise, shaking with rage, his face crimson. Abruptly he walked out, not five minutes after he'd sat down.

Helena yelled, "Meeting adjourned!" and her group gave a whoop of victory.

In disbelief, my colleagues and I wordlessly agreed that there was no point in staying for further abuse. As we filed out, much subdued, I asked Saunderson how his daughter was faring after an equestrian accident. He obliged with details all the way to the door, where Helena overtook me at last. It was inevitable. She nobbled me at all these meetings.

"Good night, Saunderson," she said curtly. The man couldn't help but understand that she wanted him to disappear, and fast. He evaporated out of the door.

Helena grabbed my arm with fingers like talons. She was surprisingly strong, for someone so scrawny.

"Drive me to my party?" Again, she stood too close. Every time I told her I was going to be married in a few months she only became more aggressive, until I had decided that perhaps she was a bit unbalanced. Either that or some designer chemical scavenged from the rain forest made her behave this way.

I held the door open for her and followed her through. "Helena, I'm so sorry," I said. "But Lord Chenies has gone missing tonight. I must—"

"Oooh!" she exclaimed, as a strong gust of wind knocked her off-balance. Throwing herself against me, she pressed all her significant body parts against mine and clung there for an instant until I could get a grip on her and firmly thrust her away.

"Helena, for goodness' sake."

She laughed. "You won't even drive me home? Some friend you are. Guy Ferris-Browne would drive me home—he's a gentleman. Really, Alex. At least drive me up to the house. I don't have my car tonight."

My irritation mounting, I bit off a terse "All right, then," thinking that at least I might ask her a few questions about Ferris-Browne, and ushered her to the passenger side of my car. I opened the door for her and shut it again after she'd climbed in, exposing as much leg as she could possibly manage. Shaking my head, I walked round the rear of the Golf and thought it odd that no one had mentioned her party at the meeting. Helena certainly hadn't announced it. Perhaps she hadn't included everyone from both sides, and felt it was more tactful this way. She was, if anything, a worse snob than her father.

Turning the key in the ignition, I said, "Helena. You know I'm to be married a few months from now."

She turned a bright smile on me. "Well, I must redouble my efforts, then, and quickly. Mustn't I?"

Despairing, I fortified myself with the reassurance that I wouldn't have to see her again after that night, and piloted the Golf out of the car park onto the Common Road. Her heavy perfume made me feel ill. Despite the howling wind outside, I rolled down my window an inch.

"You know, Alex," she began as I drove toward Heronsgate, "I'm surprised at you. You profess this absolute loyalty to—what's-her-name? Sarah? Yet I saw how it was between you and that Stoneham woman, Lisette—and barely off the road! You've become much more daring."

I longed to let her out right there on the road. But I'd learned a thing or two about village life in thirty-four years. People simply didn't disappear—the bad ones resurfaced time and again like recurring nightmares. It was essential to travel straight through the middle of these personal crises and come out friends on the other side, if I hoped to live happily in the personal and professional world I'd chosen.

With all the inner strength I could muster, I adopted a pleasant tone. "Helena, be reasonable. I've worked with Lisette Stoneham for years. We share the journey to work. She's married to my best friend. She has some rather serious difficulties at the moment."

We rode on in silence.

"You know, I like this, riding in your car," Helena eventually murmured with languor. "It even smells of your aftershave. It's been years, Alex."

I concentrated on driving. As long as she kept her hands to herself, I thought, we'd be all right. "So what's all this about you and Guy Ferris-Browne? I had no idea you two were so close. Though I might have guessed, with your leadership of HIT. I suppose you've pledged the support of your group for the election, eh?"

She looked furious. "In fact," I continued, "I suppose he might have been of assistance in getting approval for your Nature's Chemist imports, with his position in the government."

She sat bolt upright. "Don't you have any idea how important he'll be one day, as president of the European Union?" she said shrilly. "Guy'll be more powerful than anyone in Europe, influencing the courts for all of—" She caught herself and exploded, *"Damn you, Alex!"* as she struck the dash with a fist.

I gave thanks for Sarah's even temperament. How could anyone live with someone as volatile as Helena?

Guy Ferris-Browne, president of the European Union . . . interesting. Our selfless servant of the people had high aspirations indeed for power within the union he championed—the union that was supposed to benefit us all so much. There was a great deal to the man, and not much of it good, that I could see. As if to calm herself, Helena took a cigarette lighter from her purse and flicked its flame to life, watching it burn in front of her. Her habit of playing with fire was one I remembered too well from dating her long ago—she was forever lighting matches, burning scraps of paper or whatever was to hand. She plucked a hair from her head and dangled it over the flame, entranced. The awful smell filled the car.

"Helena, for goodness sake," I said, disgusted. "Put that out." Giggling, she complied.

It was with grave misgivings that I arrived at the Hotchkiss home to find it deserted. "Where is everyone?" I asked Helena, suspicious. I brought the Golf to a sudden halt directly outside the front door. "What about your party?"

Pointedly ignoring my question, Helena smirked as she unfastened her seat belt.

"Come in," she said. "I have something to show you."

"Helena," I said, "please. Not only have I got to get to Chenies Manor, but—"

"No, no, no." She laughed, waving dismissively. "I'm not going to show you my etchings. Or should I say *first editions*, in your case?" She laughed naughtily. "Oh, Alex, don't be so damn stuffy. Don't worry. This is something else entirely."

Sighing, I followed her inside, muttering something about "Only a moment, then." I was safe in the knowledge that at least her father was likely to arrive soon. She removed her coat; I left mine on. She seized the opportunity to brush against me heavily as she threw her coat over a Jacobean-looking coffer. "So what's happening at Chenies Manor tonight? I couldn't believe you agreed to publish that book for Guy. Thought you were smarter than that."

Ah. So Ferris-Browne hadn't kept my complicity a secret, at least not with Helena. "Lord Chenies has gone missing."

"Really! How thoughtful of him. Hope he's done himself in somewhere. The world will be a much better place without him. Drink?" she asked, strutting ahead of me into the sitting room on her high heels. "Or something a bit more exciting? The wonders of the rain forest await you."

"No, thanks," I said, frozen in her front hall like a startled deer. "Helena, where are your other party guests?"

She had already poured herself several fingers of Glenfiddich, neat, and gulped it down before answering.

"Ah, Alex," she sighed, smiling and starting toward me, waving her glass dramatically. "You've never understood. You *still* don't understand, darling. You and I were meant to be. The party *is* us!"

Seeing the look on my face, she stuck her lower lip out in a pout and returned to the drinks trolley, sloshing a goodly amount into her glass—again.

"Daddy'll be gone for hours. He and Victor Fine have some desperately secret business arrangement I'm not supposed to know about. They've been using these county boundary meetings for months as an excuse to get together." She tossed her golden hair and threw back another great gulp of a drink.

I began to think that if I could bear her company, I might be on the receiving end of some rather useful information. But what a price to pay. . . .

"You know, *Alexander*"—she pronounced my full name as if it were something exotic—"you really should be nicer to me. You know why?"

I didn't answer. I was half-considering a bolt for the door.

"I could get your brother into a great deal of trouble." She wagged a finger at me. "He's got very boring now," she sighed, "but we used to see a lot of the same people, Max and I. And I know everything—I mean *everything*—he did."

My stomach churned.

"It would be a shame if all that came out, wouldn't it?" She paused, directly in front of me, only her drink between us. She was clearly enjoying the effect of her words on me. "He's married now, isn't he?" she said, feigning uncertainty.

I tried to disguise my hatred for her, reminding myself that she deserved pity instead.

"Look, Helena, whatever Max did, he's finished with all that now. And it's time for me to go."

Her half-smile faded instantly. "Oh, Alex, I wouldn't leave if I were you. You're the one person I'm going to share my little secret with. Not even Guy . . ."

I turned and headed decisively for the door. "Sorry,

Helena," I said over my shoulder. I turned the doorknob; the door didn't budge. Hurriedly, with my other hand, I worked the lock above the doorknob. It turned; still the door wouldn't open. Then I looked more closely at the modern keyhole above the lock.

A dead-bolt. I was locked in.

This knowledge gave rise to the first faint inkling of panic. Having been buried alive in the walls of the Press at one point the year before, I had developed an intense dislike for closed-in spaces. So far I'd been able to control it, but . . .

Stay calm, Alex, I told myself. I remembered that when we came in, Helena had fiddled for a moment with something at the door. Afterwards she'd slid her hand into the pocket of her dress. I would have to fight her for the key— she'd just love to have me groping in her dress—or find an alternate escape route.

I turned to confront her and found her standing behind me in the hall, empty glass in hand, bent double with laughter. I walked to her, grasped her wiry but surprisingly muscular upper arms.

"Helena. Give me the key."

"Mmm," she said. She looked at my hands on her biceps, then closed her eyes. She was enjoying my touch. I jerked my hands away; her eyes shot open.

"After I show you something," she said almost normally. One moment she was overwhelmed with desire, the next calm and reasonable, the next making vile threats.

"Let me," she pleaded, still reasonable. "Really, I want to help you, Alex. I promise I'll be good. Five minutes in Daddy's study and I'll let you go."

What choice did I have but to humour her, then make my exit as quickly as possible? So I followed her into Hotchkiss's study; I left the door open behind me.

Helena went to a cachepot on her father's desk and plucked a tiny key from it. Lots of secrets in this house, I thought. Lots of locked-up things, including the front door—and from the inside, too. She moved to a cupboard below the bookcase and unlocked a door. As she opened it, a light went on inside the cupboard.

What I saw took my breath away. There were four shelves in all, one above the other, about three feet long. Each held a collection of relics from feudal days that seemed to radiate their own golden light, as very old things do.

There was a jewelled dagger, a frightfully ancient-looking stone pot, two huge golden Maltese crosses inlaid with jewels, a tall, gleaming golden chalice, gold coins—in all, four long, lighted shelves laden with breathtaking antiquities.

"Gorgeous, aren't they?" Helena was watching my face.

"Incredible," I said honestly. "Belong in a museum somewhere, I should think. The Maltese cross. Where did he get these things? Don't they belong to the Order of St. James?"

"Ah," she whispered, smiling, putting her finger to her lips. She poured another triple Scotch before answering, this time not bothering to offer me any.

"Daddy's little secret. But I wanted you to know. Let's say the shared confidence is a little present from me to you, Alex." She drank, and I thought I saw a tear run down one cheek. She swiped it away quickly with the back of the hand holding her glass.

"I know from the papers that you've been doing things round Clerkenwell recently, so you're aware of Daddy's excavation in Farringdon Road."

I nodded. My mind flew immediately to Hotchkiss's comment about the water bubbling beneath London.

"You're probably also aware that in days gone by, the Temple of the Order of St. James was roughly where Daddy's earthmovers are now. Before Henry the Eighth plundered all the Catholic churches, that is."

Then I understood, but all I could do was stare at the gleaming items in the cupboard. Hotchkiss really was a contemptible old crook.

I'd read that builders frequently failed to reveal archaeological finds because to do so brought construction to an immediate and expensive halt. Projects could be delayed for years while archaeologists excavated the site, removing dust from artifacts in situ with toothbrushes as contractors watched millions slip through their fingers.

Still, it was unthinkable that Richard Hotchkiss would have brazenly stolen artifacts from his excavations, relics belonging to the British public, or to the Order of St. James at the very least. A memory flashed past of how close Nicola and I had stood to the fenced-in construction area and how we'd complained about the dust.

"You see?" Helena said. "I thought you should know. Now we'll see what *you* do with the information." She closed up the cupboard again and dropped the key back into the cachepot after holding it up for me to see with a little smile.

"If you marry me," she breathed, "it will all be yours—"

"Speaking of Clerkenwell," I said, desperate to change the subject, "has your friend Guy said anything about a printer named Amanda Morison? Does Guy himself ever set foot in that bit of Middlesex?"

"Ha!" she snorted. "If only you knew about your hippy printer woman."

This was interesting. . . . Perhaps this lurid excursion would be worthwhile after all. "What? Her ties to the NUP terrorists?"

"You think so small, Alexsh." She was beginning to slur her words. "Actually, tha's another flaw of yours. There are much bigger things afoot than Guy's little to-do with the unions. Though there is a man with the French union . . . " She trailed off as her eyes took on a dreamy look and her tongue flicked to the corner of her mouth. She was getting sloppy.

Unions. EU unions. Of course Labour and the unions always went hand in hand. The Trades Union Group, or TUG, right behind us off Bedford Square, was one of Labour's closest allies and a manic supporter of Britain's move toward Economic and Monetary Union with Europe.

"Oh." Helena's skeletal hand flapped in the air. "One more thing." She reached into the bottom shelf of the bookcase and pulled out a brown leather-bound scrapbook.

"Go ahead," she said, holding it out. "Open it." I was standing so far away from her, purposely, that I had to reach to grasp it. Impatiently, eager to be gone, I opened the cover. My full name filled the first page in huge calligraphic letters. I turned the pages. Every newspaper article I'd ever been the subject of was pasted inside. Years and years of articles—twenty years, to be exact. She'd met me when I was fifteen.

"I don't believe this," I muttered. There was a squib from the Merchant Taylors school newsletter, which her father obviously received as an old boy and board member, about the literature prize I'd won at sixteen. An article from the *Tempus* about my M.A. from Cambridge. An article about the sequel to an anonymous book I'd published three years ago, which had caused quite a stir. Another about an automobile accident I'd been implicated in, falsely, that had nearly killed one of my authors the year before. Even articles from as recently as the previous autumn, about my boat from Threepwood overtaking a Leander eight in the Henley Regatta.

When I flipped to the very end of the album, I saw a clump of articles, loose against the back of the scrapbook. Holding the large book in my left hand, I clawed through the articles with my right. My skin began to crawl again: these articles were about Sarah, and each was badly slashed and gouged, as if someone had gone at them with scissors, or fingernails. They were taken from the Boston *Globe* and the Nantucket *Inquirer-Mirror*. Some were photocopies, evidently obtained through library research.

"There," she cried, snatching the book back. "Now you know. You know everything." She came toward me and I prepared to avoid her, but she walked right past me into the corridor.

"Leave, if you like." Placing the scrapbook on the coffer, she walked to the door, pulled the key out of a pocket of her skintight dress, and unlocked the dead-bolt.

"Oh. By the way. Don't lie to me again about you and that Shtoneham woman, Alex. I've sheen your car leaving Chez Lisette at three in the morning." She spoke the slurred words bitterly, particularly Lisette's name.

I was stunned at the implication of her words. Helena had been watching my car or, rather, Lisette's house? The Stonehams' house was three doors down; there was no way she could have seen Lisette's drive from her own windows. Had she been crouching in the bushes, or in the field across the road, at three A.M., watching me as I hugged Lisette good night? It occurred to me that it may have been Helena at the back of my garden the other night. I'd taken her for a largish animal.

"Good night, Helena."

"See you soon, Alexsh," she replied, with deceptive cheerfulness. "Thanks for coming tonight."

And on that bizarre note I took my leave.

I drove straight to Chenies Manor and found that

Martyn had spent the last two and a half hours trying to comfort poor Wilkins. "No sign of him, then?"

Martyn sighed and shook his head. "We went out together and had a look through the garden. Wilkins felt faint, so we came right back in."

"Have you a torch? I could go out and have another look."

"Let me come with you." He stepped back into the sitting room and said, "Mr. Wilkins, Alex Plumtree has come—we're just going to have another quick look round the grounds, all right?"

I heard a muttered response, and Martyn pulled his coat on. He fetched a large torch, and we stepped out into the cold wind and started round the house. Then I stopped short. The gaping hole made by the hedge roots, juxtaposed with the fury of the HIT crowd at the Memorial Hall . . .

"What is it?" Martyn called, trying to be heard over the wind.

I barely heard him. Grabbing the torch, I raced across the front lawn to the hedgerow trench. With a feeling of dreadful certainty, I shone the beam of light on the dark earth, then stumbled down the length of it, Martyn close behind me, until . . .

"Gracious Lord," Martyn murmured, dropping to his knees. Lord Chenies lay facedown in the trench. We both reached in and lifted him out, Martyn at the head and I at his feet, thinking to revive him.

But we were met with a horrible sight. Where Lord Chenies's face wasn't smudged with mud, it was a ghastly blue, and displayed an expression of intense shock and dismay. His eyes stared at us as if he could still see. I let the torch beam fall away from the grisly scene.

Martyn turned away and was sick on the grass. This very human reaction galvanised me into action; I pulled off my coat, threw it over his lordship, and tucked it under him to keep it from blowing away. Then I went to Martyn, on his knees on the grass. "Let's go inside and ring the police." I helped him up, and we stumbled together towards the Manor.

CHAPTER ELEVEN

—◆◆◆—

Love your neighbour, yet pull not down your hedge.

GEORGE HERBERT

AN HOUR LATER, THE SCENE AT CHENIES MANOR WAS somewhere between grim and tragic. Poor Wilkins appeared to be on the ragged edge of shock despite the wool blanket wrapped round him. The butler had insisted upon venturing out in the terrible wind to see his employer. We led the grey-faced man back to the sitting room, coaxing brandy into him.

Several police constables had arrived; they'd deemed Lord Chenies's demise a sudden death—that is to say, not a natural one. The man with the camera round his neck was, I learned, the scenes-of-crime officer; a portly silver-haired man scribbling notes at the dining room table was the coroner.

In the sitting room I stood by Martyn and Wilkins. Martyn had looked haunted since we'd found his lordship. Was it guilt? Again I wondered if he'd told the peer of his adoption.

A tall man, not in uniform, came into the room and stood writing in a pocket-sized notebook. He glanced round, took in Wilkins in his blanket and Martyn in his dog collar. Then his gaze fell on me. Feeling compelled to introduce myself, I said, "I'm Alex Plumtree, Lord Chenies's publisher." The man's expression instantly altered, and I realised that my now ignominious name was familiar to him. *Another suspect*, I imagined he was thinking.

Without acknowledging me, he slid a chair next to Wilkins and sat. "I'm sorry, Mr. Wilkins. My name's Fawcett, Criminal Investigations Department. I must ask you a few questions."

Reluctantly, Wilkins raised his watery eyes to the constable's. I could almost see the detective thinking that he'd better try to get his answers now.

"Our experts estimate that Lord Chenies died at roughly three-thirty this afternoon," Fawcett began. "Were you here at the time?"

The old man's face clouded, as if his employer's death had been his fault. "No," he murmured. "No. I'd gone round to my daughter's in Sarratt; his lordship said he wouldn't be needing me this afternoon." A tear escaped from his right eye; Martyn handed him a handkerchief. Wilkins reached out from beneath the blanket and seized it. "I laid out the tea, as usual, and left."

"Was he going to be alone for tea? Was he expecting guests?"

Wilkins shook his head. "No. Just his lordship. It was such an ordinary day . . ."

Martyn's head snapped up at this, as if he were about to comment. But my friend remained silent. If the detective noticed, he didn't let on.

"Tell me what's happened since you returned from your daughter's, please, Mr. Wilkins."

The butler took a shaky breath. "His lordship wasn't here when I got home about five o'clock to see to his dinner. His tea hadn't been touched. I pottered about the house, tidying up, and at about six Mr. Plumtree, here, came by to deliver something to his lordship. Something to do with his new book."

As the old man continued, I could practically see the detective thinking. *Plumtree Press. Charford-Cheney's book. The Clerkenwell wilding. Now* he *had reason to* . . .

Wilkins soldiered bravely on. "I mentioned to Mr. Plumtree that it wasn't like his lordship to disappear without a word and without having had his tea. . . ."

Detective Fawcett gave me a hard look. "So that's when you really started to think that something was amiss?" he asked Wilkins.

The man nodded miserably.

"Does Mr. Plumtree come by often?"

Wilkins shook his head. I could see all too clearly where we were heading.

"What happened next?" Fawcett enquired.

"Mr. Plumtree asked Vicar Blakely to come over and help, saying he'd return after his other commitments." Wilkins, perhaps aided by the brandy, seemed to recover himself a bit. "Very thoughtful of them both, I must say," he added.

Martyn didn't need to be asked for his tuppence worth. "It was no good just sitting and worrying, so I suggested that Mr. Wilkins and I take a walk in the grounds. I thought perhaps Lord Chenies might have fallen and been injured. But Mr. Wilkins started to feel a bit woozy, so we came right back in. We didn't find Lord Chenies until Alex came back."

Detective Inspector Fawcett nodded impassively. I knew Martyn well enough to be certain that he was hiding something. I was willing to bet he'd told Lord Chenies about our find in the attic, and was scared to death that he'd caused the old man's suicide.

Martyn carried on explaining that I'd thought of looking in the trench that used to house the massive and ancient roots of Lord Chenies's hedges—and there he'd

been. Shaking his head, he added, "I've had two parishioner suicides in my decade as a vicar. Both of them chose
a corner of the garden to—er—do it."

Something like respect passed over the detective's face.
I wondered if perhaps he was realising for the first time
how like his own job Martyn's was: when people got into
trouble, they called him for help. Even when it was too
late to render assistance, the problem still landed squarely
in his lap.

But I felt no such sympathy for Martyn. If he had told
Charford-Cheney about his parentage, the news could
easily have motivated him to take an overdose of pills, or
whatever. I longed to grab Martyn by the collar of his polo
shirt, shake him, and scream, *"I told you it would destroy
him! I warned you!"*

Instead, I remained silent. The detective frowned and
directed piercing green eyes into Martyn's own deep
brown ones. "Do you have reason to believe that Lord
Chenies wanted to kill himself?"

Martyn cast me a brief glance, which the detective
took in with interest. "No," he answered, his face suddenly stonelike. I doubt that many vicars excel at lying,
and Martyn was no exception.

"Hmmm," Fawcett said. "Mr. Wilkins?"

Wilkins had been squirming ever since the word *suicide* had been spoken. "Yes, well, I really do feel I must
speak out about this." He looked at Martyn almost
aghast, as if the vicar had impugned his employer unfairly.
"Lord Chenies most certainly would not take his own life.
It's absurd. He's so looking forward to this book coming
out, despite all the problems with it, and the government
position he's expecting. Never. He . . ."

Seeming to realise that the present tense was now in-
appropriate, he faltered.

"Please, Mr. Wilkins, I meant no disrespect," Martyn

interposed gently. "But in my line of work, I've seen suicide before."

I felt his eyes seeking mine out, but couldn't bear to meet them, now that I knew that he had, in effect, killed Charford-Cheney.

"Government position, you say?" Fawcett was prompting Wilkins for details.

"Yes. He's—" Wilkins flinched. "*He'd* spoken to Mr. Moore himself. Mr. Moore wanted him to serve as an advisor of some sort—I don't know exactly."

Fawcett seemed to come to a decision. "Well. Mr. Wilkins, I think we've troubled you enough this evening. Thank you. PC Bailey here will make sure you get to your daughter's for the night, if you like." Rising, he gave Martyn and me a no-nonsense look. "If I might have a word outside . . ."

Wilkins roused himself and saw us to the door; Martyn told him he'd come round in the morning. We bade him good night and ended up on the windy front step of the manor with the detective inspector. As the elegantly worm-eaten ancient door of Chenies Manor thumped shut behind us, Fawcett raised the collar of his coat. "Where can we go to talk? Can we get into the church?" He spoke loudly to be heard over the gale.

Martyn looked surprised. He leaned toward the detective and shouted, "Er, of course, yes, the church. Or you're welcome in the vicarage. . . ."

The detective eyed us shrewdly. "The church, please."

As we hurried across the manor's gravel drive to the back gate of the churchyard, I thought I could read Fawcett's mind. He saw our relative youth and lack of callous criminality, and judged he'd get the full truth out of the vicar and his friend in the one place where they'd be incapable of lying. I wondered how Martyn would cope.

It was extremely dark in the churchyard, and the mood

was appropriately sombre as we traipsed down the path after Martyn, surrounded by gravestones. Martyn fished out the church door keys, swung the heavy door open with a creak, and switched on the overhead light in his tiny paper-filled office. We didn't stop there, though; he seemed to know that the detective wanted the sanctuary.

The odors of old stone, wood, and books struck us as we entered the chancel. With a vicar's pride in his church, Martyn switched on subtle lights along the walls, a fairly recent addition of Charford-Cheney's. The indirect lighting spotlighted the carving along the walls, as well as the words painted on the arch across the front of the nave, over the altar. The Gothic-lettered words fairly jumped out at us: *"I shall be a father unto you, and you shall be my sons and daughters."*

The words struck me with a profundity, given the situation, that they had not possessed since my own father's death. Seeing them daily would surely have driven Charford-Cheney mad, had he lived to read them with his new-found knowledge. As if to emphasise the drama of the moment, the wind crescendoed and moaned round the old building.

Fawcett could not have engineered this any better. I watched Martyn for a reaction as he surveyed his domain as if making sure it was tidy for guests, but he was already too familiar with his surroundings to really notice the words on the arch.

"Please," he said, "do sit. What can I—"

"I want to know what you aren't telling me," Fawcett said as he sank into a pew, arms crossed.

I suppose I'd expected as much, but Martyn was startled. Too smart to attempt to deny what the detective had sensed, he appeared to compose himself, if not a story.

"All right." Martyn pushed the hair off his forehead with a shaking hand. "There is something." He looked at me guiltily. I returned my best blank look. "But it's confidential. A private matter. I've been asked specifically not to tell anyone but the family."

"Yes?" Fawcett queried, unimpressed.

Martyn squirmed. "It's just that . . . well, I gave Lord Chenies some unpleasant news today. Perhaps he was unable to bear it. Though I must say, of all the people I wouldn't have expected to take his own life . . ."

"Mmm," Fawcett broke in again, settling forward, elbows on his knees. "This news. Can you give me a hint what it was about, Vicar?"

Martyn glanced at me in desperation, but I didn't budge.

"Family," he spluttered finally. "It was about family matters. That's really all I can say." His face was pale, and a thin film of sweat shone on his skin. I felt the first touch of pity for him, and some of my anger dissolved.

I impulsively decided to come to his rescue. "It really is a—er—delicate situation. Martyn is extremely conscientious about ethical issues, including confidentiality, Detective Fawcett."

"Then perhaps I should seek enlightenment from you, Mr. Plumtree. Later, I might have to insist that you tell me what *you're* being so secretive about." There was a grim set to his jaw. "Exactly why did you come round to the manor today? Surely you don't do that for all your authors?"

"No. We've had a few problems with page proofs, and our publication date is fast approaching—hence the urgency. I live nearby, and I wanted to give Lord Chenies the proofs as soon as possible.

He frowned. "Mr. Wilkins said something about 'all the problems' Lord Chenies had been having with this book you're publishing. What exactly did he mean?"

"Well, we've had an extraordinarily difficult time getting his novel into print. In fact, we've decided the printing has been sabotaged. Our specialist printer is virtually under siege; she was kidnapped yesterday—back now safe and sound, fortunately. No doubt you're familiar with the outcry over the novel."

"Indeed I am. Causing all sorts of problems—not to mention this evening's riot in Clerkenwell." He looked at us in turn, meaningfully.

"*What?*"

"You haven't heard? Quite a violent night there—the fringes of both extremes. Fire bombs, busted windows."

My head was whirling. Poor Amanda. How much more could she bear?

I knew what Fawcett was thinking. It was too much of a coincidence for the violent march to have taken place tonight and for Lord Chenies to have died the very same day. Was his death the work of the violent fringe of the NUP?

"Tell me, Mr. Plumtree. Do you think Lord Chenies would have taken his own life? I gather you were privy to this news Vicar Blakely passed on to him, despite the fact that you're not a Charford-Cheney yourself?"

His ironic tone was grating, but I let it pass without comment. The circumstances through which I'd learned of Charford-Cheney's parentage were completely innocent; but the inspector had no way of knowing that. "When I accidentally learned the news Martyn passed on to Lord Chenies, I told him that if Lord Chenies ever found out, the knowledge would ruin him."

Martyn shot me a look as if to say *Thanks a lot, Alex*, then stared at the needlework dove on the seat cushion as I continued. "But I must say, I would never have *thought* Lord Chenies would take his own life. And he had a lot to look forward to just now. . . ."

"Who do you think did it, then?"

"An unbelievable number of people might have wanted to. The hedges group, HIT, really had it in for Lord Chenies—have you seen this week's *Chorleywood Communicator*?"

He nodded.

"Well, in addition to yesterday's abduction, our printer has been the victim of other violent attacks that seem to have come from the NUP. Her assistant thinks so, too."

Fawcett said, "Right," with the ironic twist that probably helped him through the days. He focussed on Martyn. "Now, I know we went through this back at the manor, Vicar. But humour me. At what time did you see Lord Chenies today?"

"It was about three o'clock," Martyn answered miserably. I listened with interest; I'd not heard this part yet. "I'd phoned in the morning, and asked him if I could see him about something rather important. This—*matter*— I had to talk to him about was burning a hole through me. I—it didn't seem right that *I* should know, if he didn't. So . . . " He trailed off.

"So he said to come round at three," Fawcett prompted. "Was anyone else there?"

"No, but as I told you, I had the impression he was expecting someone. He kept looking at his watch and peering through the windows."

Fawcett left a silence as the wind moaned and whistled, sounding as tortured as Martyn looked. Along the west side of the church, branches of an ancient gnarled oak grated against a seldom-used door. Lord Chenies's spirit, I told myself, trying to gain entry.

"But he never actually said he was expecting anyone?" Fawcett asked.

Martyn shook his head. "No. I'm certain."

"And how did he react to the news you gave him?"

Martyn swallowed. "As I said, he blustered at first, denying it. He was very angry indeed. But then I showed him the actual proof, a—a document."

"And did you see him put this document anywhere for safekeeping?"

Shaking his head, eyes closed, Martyn murmured, "No. I'll never forget it. He turned white and let it fall onto the table." Looking at the detective, he practically whispered, "Then he asked me to leave."

"So you were there for how long?"

"Possibly ten, fifteen minutes. No more."

"He didn't offer you tea?"

"No."

"Hmmm."

I don't know why the detective chose to take us into his confidence at that point. Perhaps it was because Martyn looked ready to die of guilt. Or perhaps because he wanted to frighten us. But he sighed and studied the carved rope design along the wall, and mused, "Four cups. There were four cups out for tea. We're having them checked for fingerprints, of course. Wilkins said he put out just one for Lord Chenies. So you were right about the visitors, Vicar. Any ideas?"

Martyn looked surprised at the turn the conversation had taken. "N-no."

I shook my head, but my mind raced to Helena's diatribes in the local press against Charford-Cheney and his disregard for history. Would Helena and her colleagues at HIT have actually *killed* him? Heaven knew, Helena herself was disturbed enough.

"With whom did his lordship usually associate? We have his diary, naturally, and Wilkins to talk to. But who would you guess he'd been seeing?"

"There's the PCC—the Parish Council Committee," Martyn stammered. "He sometimes had them to tea. And the volunteers for when the manor is open to the public, on Tuesdays, of course. And his horticultural experts. That's all that comes to mind."

"I wasn't a close friend of his," I added, "but we did attend church here together all through the years, and we both attended Merchant Taylors in Watford. He was on the board of governors there, and could have been seeing some old boys." I hesitated. "There's also the Chorley-wood Conservative Association. Lord Chenies was supportive of the group, though not active in terms of attending meetings."

Fawcett nodded. "All right. I'll be in touch." He got to his feet tiredly. Still standing in the pew, he squinted at me. "Are you still going to publish his novel?"

"Tempted not to," I replied, perhaps too honestly. "But I'm bound by contract. The document is still valid, despite his death. Malcolm and Hillary Charford-Cheney are suing me, however, for the right to publish the book themselves. Perhaps I'll turn it over to them now."

Fawcett raised his eyebrows at that piece of news. I thought he mumbled, "You'd be well out of it," as he stepped into the aisle. "Thank you—Vicar, Mr. Plumtree. Good night."

Before he'd made it down the aisle, however, we heard the door to Martyn's office burst open. The wind had been attacking the church in angry gusts. Martyn mumbled, "Latch keeps slipping," and hurried after Fawcett to see him out and secure the door. But no sooner had he got to his feet than Malcolm and Hillary Charford-Cheney strode into the sanctuary looking angry as wet hornets, followed by a police constable. Both halted when they saw Fawcett.

"We've just come from the manor. They wouldn't even let us in—said we had to speak to someone by the name of Fawcett in here," Hillary snarled. She eyed Fawcett with derision. "A constable is posted at the manor to keep us *out*, for goodness' sake. What an insult to a grieving family. And it's *Malcolm*'s manor now, if I'm not mistaken. The nerve! What's all this about a murder?" She fairly spat the words. I saw no evidence whatever of grief on the part of Lord Chenies's only living relatives.

Detective Inspector Fawcett watched this performance

with interest, then said quietly, "I'm glad you've come. I'm from CID, here to investigate your father's death. The constable was correct; I need to speak to you. Won't you sit down." It wasn't a question.

There was silence for a moment as it registered with all of us that these two were also suspects, since Malcolm stood to gain through inheritance.

Into the silence I murmured, "Malcolm, Hillary, my condolences." Malcolm glared at me with loathing but said nothing.

"God, what a night. We've just come from the theatre." Hillary moved towards a pew at last. "Everyone was ranting about that horrendous mess in Clerkenwell. And how *dare* you pretend to be sorry, Plumtree, when you stand to make more money than ever off the book you're *illegally* publishing?"

She was right about the money; an author's death always escalates sales of his work. Still, I met her eyes coolly. "Since you mention it, Hillary, if you want the book back, you can have it." Fawcett looked on with fascination.

Apparently I'd knocked her off-balance, though that hadn't been my intention. Her mouth opened. She eyed me suspiciously, as if she thought I was trying to trick her.

Malcolm came to her rescue. "If you don't beat it all, Plumtree. Trying to sneak out of the contract now there's been a death! Scared are you? Let me tell you something: you're going to publish this book if it's the last thing you do."

As well it might be, I thought.

He stabbed a finger at me. "If you try to weasel out of that contract, Plumtree, I'll sue for all you're worth!"

Fawcett's head moved back and forth as if he were watching a Ping-Pong match.

"Do you mean to tell me. . . " But I had the good sense to stop. Now it was obvious: all this pair wanted was money. They planned to sue me whether I published the book or not. My opinion of them plummeted still further. Hours after his father's death, Malcolm could think of nothing but financial gain. He knew that the fastest way to the easiest money was to have Plumtree Press publish Lord Chenies's book now, as scheduled, amid the controversy and sensationalism of the riot and the author's suspicious demise. He had just inherited massive royalties.

"Are you withdrawing your existing suit, then?" I asked evenly.

For a priceless moment they looked at each other; things were obviously happening a little faster than they'd anticipated. All was quiet, apart from the gusts of wind moaning in the eaves, and a branch rapping against a window in the darkness.

"No!" Hillary snarled, recovering. "What do you take us for—*fools*?" She glared at Fawcett impatiently. "Well, what is it that you want to know?"

Fawcett nodded at Martyn and me, dismissing us. As we walked out, Malcolm couldn't resist another sneer in my direction.

Back in Martyn's office, I turned to my old friend and put a hand on his shoulder. Malcolm's furious voice, uttering indistinguishable words, drifted in from the sanctuary. I said, "You must be exhausted, Martyn." This had surely been one of the worst days of his life. He was close to emotional, if not physical, exhaustion. There were purple-black smudges beneath his eyes, and his colour was ghastly. Finding a corpse in the hole where a hedge once grew was bad enough; thinking you were responsible for that body would be a hundred times worse.

"Cup of tea? Toast?" I said, propelling him through his office and out of the door, fastening the latch carefully as we went.

He didn't answer. I got him in the front door of the vicarage and took him through to the kitchen. There was bread in the bread box, so I cut a couple of slices and put them under the grill, then lit the gas. As I hunted for the butter, I saw that Martyn had seated himself at the kitchen table and was staring into space. I filled the electric kettle and switched it on, and as I pulled two mugs from his cupboard I had a thought.

"Martyn."

After a moment he looked up, distracted. "Hmm?"

I leaned back, elbows on the worktop, hearing the hiss of the grill. "Did you see the tea laid out at the manor?"

His eyes drifted off again, and he nodded absently.

"You did?"

"Mmm. Why?"

"I'm curious about something. Did *you* see the four cups?"

Morosely, he shook his head. "No. I remember thinking it quite rude that he should have all the apparatus out when I came, but only one cup. It saved him saying, 'You are *not* invited to tea'."

"Why didn't you say something about it to Fawcett?"

Martyn shrugged. "He didn't ask. And I didn't think about it." Then he frowned at me. "Alex, the man is *dead*. And you're talking about *tea* cups!" Exasperation battled with incredulity in his voice.

"Martyn—don't you see that if Lord Chenies set out the other three cups after you left, even in his state, he was planning to stay alive for his guests? And for tea?"

He looked back at me with the beginnings of awareness.

"*Telling* him didn't kill him, Martyn. But perhaps someone who came after you did."

"It's so horrible." His nose wrinkled.

I pulled the toast out from under the grill and buttered it generously before slathering on a thick layer of blackberry jam. "Come on," I said, nudging the plate toward him. "Believe me. You'll feel better if you eat something."

When he finally focussed on the toast and picked up a slice, I knew he would recover. "I must see about

Amanda," I said, looking at my watch. It was half past ten. "And ring Nicola. Talk to you tomorrow, all right?"

With his mouth full of toast, Martyn nodded and gave me a mute wave of dismissal, and I trotted out to my car. After punching Nicola's number into the mobile phone, I got the car in gear and rolled out of the Chenies Manor drive. On the second ring, her voice came across the airwaves.

"Hello," was all she said, her voice sultry.

"It's Alex. I'm afraid I've more bad news."

She exhaled audibly. "Go ahead," she said, in her businesslike voice.

"Nigel Charford-Cheney is dead."

Silence, except for the sound of the wind buffeting the car as I snaked down the narrow lane towards Chorleywood.

"The police seem to doubt that it was suicide. He was found in the trench where his hedge used to be."

She sighed. "No use asking why. He wasn't anybody's favourite person."

"No."

"When did it happen?"

"This afternoon, probably around three. My friend Martyn, vicar of Christ Church Chenies, visited him just before that. He—um—had to deliver some bad news to Lord Chenies. Private family matters."

I heard rustling on her end, and imagined that she was in bed, or watching late-night television. "Well, I suppose the bottom line is, are we still locked into publishing *Cleansing*?"

"The bottom line is that, according to Malcolm and Hillary—who came round to rail at us after the theatre tonight, by the way—they're going to sue us whether we publish or not."

"Ah. All torn up about the pater's death, are they?"

"About as torn up as I'd be to find this had all been a nightmare."

She chuckled. "I'd love to tell you that was the case." More rustling. No doubt it was Reg in bed with her. I could hardly wait for the day when I could do a bit of rustling myself with Sarah. "Well, what happens next?" she asked.

"On with the show, I'm afraid. Except now it's going to be more of a madhouse than ever—you know about the dead-author law—and a murder investigation into the bargain."

"Sorry if this seems crass, but we will sell loads of books, at any rate."

"Yes." I pulled into my drive and nearly braked in surprise. "I've no doubt . . ."

She must have heard the trepidation in my voice. "What is it?" she demanded.

"Odd . . . I'm pulling up at the Orchard, and all the lights are on." Every last light in the entire house, in fact, upstairs and down.

"Do you want me to ring the police?" Alarm reverberated down the phone. "Alex, you're the publisher of a very controversial book, remember. And—er—not to frighten you unduly, but in view of the deaths . . ."

"Thanks, Nicola. I'll be careful."

"I'm going to ring back in five minutes; make sure you're all right."

"No need. Max and Madeline probably popped in. But—by the way, the next time you do phone me, use my mobile number. Someone's bugged my phone line at home. It's been fixed, but I won't really trust it until all this is over."

"You're joking."

"No. I'm afraid not."

She swore softly, with a where-will-it-all-end sigh. "That means they've probably bugged the office as well."

"Mmm-hmm." I let the car idle in the drive, some distance from the house. So far I'd seen no one move inside.

"There was an odd little bunch installing the new phone system a few days ago. Lisette and I walked in on them. I *knew* something was wrong. But I've had that seen to, as well. The security firm found bugs and removed them."

"I feel as if we've walked into the middle of a James Bond film. But you went through British Telecom for the new phone system, didn't you?"

"Yes, indeed." I took her meaning. Someone had obtained official permission to tamper with my phone lines. Someone quite influential.

Again, she swore—quite imaginatively this time. "If I find out that my father . . . " The threat faded into silence, but I understood completely. I almost hoped, for Ferris-Browne's sake, that he *hadn't* arranged the wiretap.

"Don't think of it now," I told her. "Good night. Talk to you tomorrow."

" 'Night." She sounded disgruntled, and I doubted that Reg's rustling in the bedclothes would come to anything that night.

Switching off the ignition on the Golf with the creeping-flesh feeling I'd had all too often of late, I climbed out and quietly pushed the door closed. Slowly, I walked towards my alarmingly well-lit home. I couldn't see anyone inside, but that didn't mean they weren't there. Surely anyone intending harm wouldn't light up the place like a Christmas tree.

But when I opened the side door, the smell of gas hit me in a powerful wave. I dashed through to the kitchen and switched off all four gas jets. They had been open all the way. Terrified at the thought of a single spark making its way into this fuel-laden atmosphere, I raced through the house, flinging open windows and doors, checking in each room for hidden intruders. Literally every light in the house blazed, and the thought of someone walking through and deliberately switching each one on was somehow as disturbing as the gas.

When I reached my bedroom, I saw that most of my clothes had been taken from the cupboard and tossed on the bed. Even my pyjamas and running clothes were strewn on the floor.

I continued my dash through the house until I had windows open in every corner. Confused, I walked outside, far from the house, and sat in the gazebo, staring at the bizarre vision before me. The smell of the gas was still strong in my nose, and my head ached.

Was this another instance of backlash from the NUP? Or the hedges folk? My brain swam with possibilities. Ferris-Browne and, worse yet, the PM were excellent candidates. I felt some measure of gratitude that they hadn't thrown a match inside on their way out. But why my *clothes*?

Then a wave of nausea swept over me. Helena Hotchkiss had always joked about being a pyromaniac, and was forever setting scraps of paper aflame with her lighter. Once she had even set a little clump of her own hair on fire, at the ends, just for the thrill of it—as she had in my car. It had only burned for an instant before I grabbed it with my fingers and put it out, but I remember her giggle, and how disturbed I was by the episode. If it had been Helena, that might explain the clothes out, as well, since she seemed so desperate for intimacy.

But . . . if she wanted intimacy, why try to do away with me with gas? Why ransack my bedroom? If it had been Helena, she was even more disturbed than I'd realised.

In fact, she was positively dangerous.

CHAPTER TWELVE

———◦◦◦———

Thou hast most traitorously . . . caused printing to be used.

WILLIAM SHAKESPEARE, *Henry VI*

IT WAS ELEVEN O'CLOCK. AS I ROUSED MYSELF TO CLOSE UP
the house and turn off some lights, my thoughts turned
belatedly to Amanda and the Clerkenwell riot.

In the library, I picked up the remote for the television
and snapped the cable news station to life. I gaped in disbelief as news cameras revealed Clerkenwell Green as it
had been several hours before. It was a battle zone. On the
film, mounted police were attempting to control an angry, chanting mob, and as the camera recorded the action,
Amanda's Print Shop could be seen in the background.
The front windows of the shop were shattered, and flames
licked at the wooden panels beneath the windows.

*"Again, in Clerkenwell tonight, an anti-Conservative
rally turned violent. We have footage from the riot earlier
tonight, when Marc Fulbright was on the scene."* The anchor-
woman disappeared, and scenes of teeming crowds in
Clerkenwell dominated the screen. Suddenly, in the foreground, a group could be seen energetically and repeatedly

hitting someone on the ground, while a horse stepped skittishly nearby, the whites of his eyes rolling.

The image changed to a virtual ocean of baldheaded youths, a number of them trying to support a banner screaming "THE NATIONAL FRONT." The camera shifted. An ocean of equal size faced the skinheads: wire-rimmed, long-haired NUP members and anti-Conservatives. They were being held off one another by a three-deep line of riot police in full protective gear.

The reporter shouted above the rabble: *"One mounted constable was severely injured after being pulled from his horse and beaten. Four others have been seriously injured here tonight, and the chaos shows no sign of ending soon. The riot police arrived moments ago and seem to be preventing further carnage . . . I understand that the water cannon is being prepared in an effort to break up the crowd."*

I couldn't imagine how Amanda was taking the disaster, but I knew she would be at her shop, surveying the wreckage. I needed to be there, too.

When I arrived forty-five minutes later, the devastation was stunning. When I was finally allowed through the police cordon, I found Amanda sitting in the burnt and water-soaked remains of her shop. Robert Lovegren sat with her on the remains of the library table, silent. From outside the doorway, which no longer boasted a door, I could see that the windows were in shards on the floor. The stink of charred and wet wood permeated the scene as thoroughly as the sense of disaster. Someone had placed a huge battery-powered torch on the library table, and it cast eerie shadows round the room. In the beam of the light on the west wall I could make out the remnants of the broadsheets she'd tacked up. They'd all gone up in smoke except for one, the survival of which was particularly profound. Smoke-damaged and sodden, the folio hung together, just. She'd set the page in a huge, thick

William Morris–style black letter with the initial capital enlarged and illuminated in vermilion:

> *Meanwhile, if these hours be dark, at least do not let us sit deedless like fools and fine gentlemen thinking the common toil not good enough for us and beaten by the muddle, but rather let us work like good fellows, trying by some dim candle-light to set our workshop ready against to-morrow's daylight.*—William Morris

I shook my head and stepped in as quietly as I could, considering the rubble that crunched beneath my shoes.

Amanda's face was smudged with ash as if she'd been made up as an American Indian for a western film. The deep shadows made her look fragile in the extreme.

"Plumtree," Lovegren said, surprised. He rose to greet me. "Didn't expect to see you here."

"They threw a Molotov cocktail into the shop," Amanda said in a monotone. "Your security guard tried to keep them out, but once the fire started . . . " She trailed off, only to mumble a moment later, "They didn't get the fonts."

Lovegren lifted a hand and patted her shoulder, saying, "Shhh, there, now," as if to a child.

"I'm so sorry, Amanda," I said, aghast. Flames had crept right up the once-pristine cream walls, engulfing all of her lovely pages on the way up to the William Morris quotations, fuelled no doubt by the shelves laden with solvents. Everything that wasn't black looked as if it had been smudged by heavy smoke. The Vandercook press and its antique companion were no doubt salvageable, but their surfaces were blistered, and the ink rollers had buckled in the intense heat. Her printer's cabinets were charred—a good thing type was made of something as indestructible as metal, I thought. Her current jobs and files on the lower shelves round the room were utterly soaked from the firemen's efforts; in the shadows they were recognisable only as piles of pulpy stuff.

"I'm afraid there's more bad news," I continued reluctantly. The last thing I wanted to do was bring further misery, but she deserved to know. "Lord Chenies is dead."

"No," Amanda whispered. "Not after all *this*!" She halfheartedly spread out an arm as if to indicate her ruined premises, then began to sob.

"What's it all been for, then?" she shouted, ending in a cry that must have penetrated all of Clerkenwell. *"All for nothing!"* she wailed.

"Here, now, my dear," Lovegren murmured. He looked at me, and we hurried to take her by the arms, afraid that she would slump to the floor. She stood, racked by sobs. All we could do was stand with her in her moment of utter dejection. Police lights, flickering blue and yellow into the shop, added to the unearthly feeling of the scene.

I vowed to find a way to help Amanda. I wanted to ask so many things. Did she have insurance? Did the Clerkenwell Neighbourhood Association have insurance? Could the machines be repaired?

After a time, Lovegren spoke. "Alex, why don't you go on? I've talked some local chaps into boarding up the place. I'll see Amanda home. There's really nothing more we can do here."

"She's lucky to have you for a friend, Robert." I gave Amanda a hug, and turned to go. But as I moved toward the door, she said, "Wait."

She wiped her eyes with the backs of her hands, further smearing the ashes on her forehead and cheeks. "I'm not going to let the NUP win. I'll print this damnable book if it's the last thing I do. You've a press at the Orchard, haven't you?"

"Yes—a Minerva Cropper hand press and a slightly

larger Vandercook proofing press. But they've not been used for years."

"That's all right. I'll salvage anything I can from here and bring it with me in the morning."

"Amanda, I—"

"Go along home, Alex. I'm just going to gather a few things."

I left her silently poking about the rubble, Lovegren at her side. At least she seemed to be finding some comfort in action. Secretly, I wondered if her idea of printing at the Orchard wasn't a nonstarter; my father's machines had sat without oil or attention for four years.

Firemen clustered round various buildings near Clerkenwell Green, extinguishing the remnants of the blaze. Police huddled near the Marx Library, no doubt reliving the disastrous evening. With them stood Anthony Simino. He wore an expensive sweater and smooth, well-tailored trousers. But his flushed, pockmarked face had the rough look of a man of the streets.

I felt an odd impulse to approach him, and followed my instinct. Simino turned to greet me. "A disastrous evening," he said, shaking his head.

"Poor Amanda's had all she can take." He nodded in agreement, looking sorrowful. "Does the Neighbourhood Association have insurance? Or did she, do you know?"

"That's the really tragic part of it all. The association can't be responsible for what our grant recipients put inside our buildings. We'll be compensated for the building, but Amanda didn't have the money to insure her presses and other materials."

"She's all but ruined, then," I said. This had been my fault. Stupid, stupid idea to play into Ferris-Browne's hands. "Will she get the building back, once repairs have been made?"

To my surprise, his eyes sharpened. I'd never seen eyes as beady as Simino's. His illustrated the term: small, round, and cold. "I'll get the solicitors onto it in the morning, see what's to be done. I'm not certain yet."

I nodded matter-of-factly, but thought it an odd response. Surely as the head of the Neighbourhood Association he knew every last jot and tittle of its rules. Amanda's words drifted back to me: "*He is Clerkenwell.*"

As Simino gazed round his smouldering neighbourhood, I threw caution to the winds. "I hate to be the bearer of bad news, but . . . have you heard what's happened tonight in Chenies?"

Again, his eagle-sharp eyes with their tiny pupils snapped to my face. "What? What other news?" Beads of sweat appeared on his forehead and upper lip.

"The author of the book that caused all of this"— I waved an arm at the devastation—"Nigel Charford-Cheney, Lord Chenies, was found dead this evening. The police think he may have been murdered."

For a moment I thought Simino might topple over. He swayed, and his face took on a ghastly shade of grey. "I say, I'm sorry. . . ." I said, amazed at the intensity of his reaction.

"Excuse me," he mumbled, and set off hastily in the direction of his real estate offices, looking ill.

Well, I'd certainly put my foot in it. I saw Simino stagger as he made his way up the hill. What had I done? *Had* he known that Charford-Cheney was related to him?

Scenes from the eventful evening replayed in my mind all the way home. Lord Chenies in the ditch, with mud on his horribly blue, surprised face; Amanda sobbing disconsolately in the ruins of her shop. I began to wonder . . . why had *they* been the targets of such violent abuse, when I hadn't? I'd paid a high price in terms of my reputation, certainly, but no one had tried to abduct me or dump me lifeless into a ditch. The buggings and gas-

and-light extravaganza had been threatening, but not actually harmful. Was it really just the NUP behind all of this? Between thoughts of Ferris-Browne, the NUP, HIT, and Dexter Moore's G18, I couldn't seem to think clearly anymore. I suspected everyone, but seemed to have no way of proving anything. It was all a gigantic muddle.

Back at the Orchard I trudged from the garage into the kitchen, cracking open a window to dispel the slight lingering odour of gas. I felt a rare craving for neat Scotch. Longing for contact with Sarah, I decided to pour myself a drink and ring her, despite the hour. As I threw my keys on the worktop, I saw a note next to the toaster informing me that the security firm had indeed found a transmitting device in my telephone and that it had been removed. They'd taped the device to the page for me to see. I glanced at it, shook my head, and pressed the playback button on the answering machine before pulling a glass out of the cupboard. A male voice hissed urgently from the tape.

"Alex. Bruce here. The march is tonight." His tone was a forced whisper. *"Eight o'clock, Clerkenwell Green."* Click.

That message might have saved Amanda's shop, had I received it in time. Had Bruce somehow played a part in Amanda's misfortune? Had he even *tried* to prevent the march, if he'd known about it in advance?

The next message was playing. *"Alex."* Something happened to me when Sarah said my name, even over a telephone answering machine.

A pause, as if she were sorry that I wasn't there, and hoped I might be running to the phone. *"Sorry I missed you. All's well here. Love you . . . bye."*

I replayed her message, then went to the library. Stretching out on the leather sofa, I picked up the phone and dialled Sarah. No answer. And it was . . . one-thirty in the morning there. Where was she? We hadn't talked in days, and I sorely missed her.

What a hellish night, I thought, sipping my drink. Its medicinal taste and peaty smell revived me a bit.

The wind howled mournfully, and still-dormant vines knocked against my home. For just a moment I felt very alone and exposed; faint echoes of the feeling I'd had by the pines a couple of nights before raised the hair on the back of my neck. I looked at the dark, uncovered French doors and felt compelled to stand and close the curtains. But before pulling them closed I gazed for a moment in the direction of the barn, and wondered.

Telling myself I was getting far too jumpy, I took another sip of Scotch. But when I tried to set my glass down on the table with a shaking hand, it went over, splashing on to the carpet.

I covered my face with my hands.

My eyes popped open into the pitch blackness; I listened carefully for a moment: nothing, except my heart pounding at an absurd rate. Though I tried to find sleep again, it was gone. I went upstairs and showered and dressed, adding a heavy sweater and warm socks. It was just before six o'clock when I made coffee, and carried a steaming mug out to the barn.

The printing smells hit me immediately when I swung open the squeaky door. They somehow welcomed me, drew me inside. When I turned on the light and saw the presses waiting, I felt glad there would be printing here again. I allowed myself a few moments to walk around, studying the place and trying to imagine it as a printing shop. Would she be able to get these venerable machines running again? I felt a pang of guilt. I should have cared for them better.

Amanda would have to prepare the press, but I could make the place a bit more presentable, at least. I went back to the house for some rags, and used them to clean off every surface I could find—the top of the cylinder press bed, the cabinets and their drawer pulls, the long table against the far wall. Then I made another trip for a couple of tall stools from the kitchen. Nothing said we had to actually suffer physically to print this book.

Back in the barn, I jumped; the door was inching open, creaking as it let the first glow of daylight into the artificially lit room. I grabbed a broom, the only weapon at hand, ready to strike out at anyone who came through the door. *How had they found out we would be printing here? What if Bruce . . .*

It swung open slowly, and just as I prepared to slash the broom down on my intruder, I glimpsed Amanda's red hair. I relaxed my death grip on the weapon, but there was no way Amanda could mistake what I'd been about to do with it.

She started violently, then put a hand to her heart. "Whew! Sorry to frighten you, Alex—I didn't want to wake you so early. I didn't think you'd mind if I came for a look at the new shop."

"No, not at all—fine." My watch said it was now half-past six. "But I'm amazed you're up and about so early, after last night."

"I couldn't sleep." Dark circles bore witness to her words. "So the best thing seemed to be to get on with it." She still seemed a bit shaky, but I knew that what she said was true; she'd go barmy sitting round all day thinking about the destruction. Getting started again was for the best. She stepped in purposefully and went first to the proofing press. "Let's see what we have here . . . ah, twenty-one inches wide. We'll be able to do this faster than I thought—twelve pages to a signature, instead of eight." She applied her muscles to its crank; the cylinder lumbered down the path of the press bed and back again co-operatively. "Nothing wrong with this old girl . . . a little oil, a good cleaning, and we'll be ready to go." She sighed.

"I'm afraid my caster's come a cropper, though. Someone who knew what he was doing smashed it up in all the right—I mean wrong—places. It was more than a random riot; they intended to ruin me for good and all."

"Amanda, do you think it was just the NUP? I was wondering—why were you and Lord Chenies targetted for such acts of violence? Why wasn't I, as the publisher, attacked?"

"I wouldn't complain if I were you. I've no doubt it was the NUP," she said, inspecting the cylinders of the press. But an exaggeratedly casual tone betrayed her.

It was time to do away with subtlety. "Amanda. What do you know about all this that you haven't told me?"

She wheeled and faced me, looking into my eyes with . . . was it fear? "Why don't you just mind your own business, Alex? Be glad they haven't come after you yet."

Stunned by her abrupt, angry words, I managed to say, "This *is* my business, Amanda. If I involve three other people in publishing a book, and one of them dies, one has her shop ruined and is abducted, and another is concussed in a wilding that involves yet another death—I think that deserves some looking into." My cheeks grew hot; I needed to know what she was hiding.

She turned away again and caressed the smooth black cylinders. "Look, Alex." She sounded more weary than anything else. "I'm sorry. I simply can't tell you what you want to know. If you think what *you're* involved in is dangerous . . ."

For a brief instant I wanted to demand that she answer me. Then I came to my senses. I would find out somehow, with or without her help.

Her gaze fell on the line of printer's cabinets, and she moved toward them. "Any idea what your father had in the way of type?"

"No. I wasn't that interested in printing when I spent time out here. Now I wish I'd paid more attention."

Amanda was already pulling open a drawer in the first

cabinet. She stood absolutely still for a moment, then closed that drawer and pulled open the next, then the next, and still another. She exclaimed, "I've never *seen* so much Caslon in one place!" She moved to the next cabinet and pulled open the drawers one by one. "And Baskerville . . . mountains of it." She went back to the first cabinet, picked up a bit of type, and turned it over in her hands, examining it. I heard a little gasp of surprise. "Your father . . . he—" She stopped abruptly.

"Yes?"

"Nothing, nothing," she said, deeply flushed. What could be so earth-shaking about a piece of type in my father's printing cabinet? If she would only stop being so mysterious about everything. . . . Crossing to her, I looked at the letter in her hand. Quickly she turned it over, hands shaking, to the side away from the letter and shoulder. "Did—um—your father have a monocaster?"

"No," I said, picking up a piece of the type myself and studying it. "But I have a vague recollection that my grandfather did. I wonder what became of it." She watched me as I turned my lowercase *p* letter side up. I could see that my grandfather had arranged for his matrix to stamp the shoulder of each piece of type with tiny interlocking *P*'s, but there was something else on the other side of the shoulder . . . an almost microscopic mark. I strained to see what it was, but couldn't make it out. Scratching at it with my fingernail, I felt an indentation.

"He's got piles and *piles* of Caslon," she said, obviously still taken aback. "That's a stroke of luck."

I grinned, forgetting my anger at her in the pleasure of her growing excitement. I put down the tiny piece of type. "You must see this," I told her, and motioned for her to join me at the platen press. "This is what I found when I ventured back into the barn for the first time in years, just a couple of days ago." She followed my eyes to the bed, took in the galley tray: *Welcome, Alex.* "Gave me quite a start."

"I would imagine so," she said, a faint smile playing at her lips. "You know what people say about a printer living on through his press. . . ."

"Mmm."

"Well," she said almost cheerfully, turning back to the cabinets. "Unless I miss my guess, we'll be able to do the job just fine here. We may even be able, with all that type, to set a whole sheet at once. No point in even bringing any type from my shop."

I had never suspected that there was anything extraordinary about my father's printing retreat; now I couldn't help but wonder what Amanda had inferred. Perhaps nothing more than his unexpected wealth of Caslon and Baskerville.

She announced that she was leaving to obtain paper and the requisite supplies, and promised to return by noon. "Perhaps you can get Nicola—and maybe Lisette—to help. I rang Bruce last night, but he'll need to know how to find you. That is, if you don't mind," she said, suddenly realising she'd asked her customer to go to work for her.

"Of course I don't mind—I was the idiot who took on this publication, remember?"

She half-smiled and jotted Bruce's number on a card from her purse.

After she left, I returned to the house and rang Lisette, Nicola, and Bruce, passing on the awful news of Lord Chenies's death and the ruin of Amanda's shop. They'd seen it all in the morning papers, so I didn't stun anyone. I asked everyone to assemble at the Orchard around noon. Finally I rang Dee at the Press and told her where we'd all be for the next few days. "But we're trying to keep this quiet, all right? Tell no one."

"Your secret is safe with me," she whispered in her best secret-agent tones. Dee loved drama. "Oh, by the way, your security bloke was here when I arrived—just thought you'd like to know."

I'd decided the employees at the Press shouldn't be endangered because of my foolhardy agreement to publish *Cleansing*. Now that a second person had died because of the project, I wasn't taking any risks.

A shame Ian was away, I thought; we could have used his calm presence . . . and his hands. Then again, at least one of us got to ski with Sarah. The thought of Ian brought vague memories trickling back of Ian talking with my father in our barn. Once I'd come in when they were both out here, and I remembered noticing that I'd interrupted them. They stopped talking and focussed their attention on me, when I knew they'd been discussing something important. They'd looked so serious. . . .

Amanda returned well before noon, her van laden with huge boxes of paper like the ones I'd seen in her shop— twenty-one by thirty-six inches—and a dozen little tins of ink. "I've arranged for the binding gear to arrive tomorrow," she said, going to work. While Amanda began to clean the cylinder, prepare the galley trays, and assemble everything we needed, I unloaded the supplies. The others arrived on time, surprised to find the unassuming barn the hive of such activity. Amanda was setting the last lines of the first sheet, using a metal composing stick that hung round her neck. I shook off mental allusions to millstones, and watched along with Nicola and Lisette.

We all looked on intently as Amanda's bits of type went *click-click* into the stick. She picked them from their individual cubbies without even looking at the drawer and placed them in the order Lord Chenies had written. When the stick was full, she transferred the lines of type into the galley tray, in position. Her purposeful activity said, *We* will *print this book.* Meanwhile, Bruce inked the roller and prepared the press.

Amanda assigned each of us a task. Bruce ran the press with impressive efficiency, his powerful arms turning the crank all the way forward and then back again every twenty seconds, for a remarkable rate of one hundred and eighty impressions per hour. Nicola passed him a sheet of paper when he was ready; Lisette took the finished sheet and placed it on the table. I didn't have much to do until the other side of the sheets were printed; until then I occupied myself with things like keeping my coworkers stocked with what they needed, and searching for the electric fire to make the barn more habitable.

Once both sides of the first sheet were printed, I was put in charge of the folding machine. Amanda had hired it when she went for the paper. After three hours, all five hundred copies of the first twelve pages were done, and Amanda had the galley trays set for the next two signatures.

We decided we'd earned a tea break, though I'm sure we were all a bit daunted at the thought of producing twenty-four more of the same, times five hundred. I could almost hear the group's mental calculations: *Twenty-four times three hours . . . too long.* Five extremely long work-days, or three entire round-the-clock days. If we did it exactly to that timetable, we would have precisely the one day left required to have the books encased in their boards, leather, and slipcases. If all went well. If no one found us. . .

If so much *sturm und drang* hadn't already gone into the project, I think we would all have enjoyed the actual printing process. There was a certain companionship about it and, now that we'd all been through so much together, a closeness. But I'm sure I wasn't the only one whose thoughts crept back incessantly to Lord Chenies and Mmbasi Kumba. Overall, however, the general atmosphere in the impromptu press was one of emphatic determination.

As we tucked into hot tea and biscuits in the kitchen on our first tea break, Amanda started to say, "I—I just want you all to know how much I . . ."

Lisette knew what was coming. She never received a compliment graciously, if she could help it. "Oh, go on," she interrupted. " 'Ow do you know we won't pack it in after tea?" Amanda just laughed.

We worked on through the next two signatures, stopping for a hasty dinner courtesy of Lisette—typically, she'd picked up the components of a salad and pasta before driving over that noon. We all agreed that in case something went wrong later, we needed to push ahead with all possible speed. That evening we went on for four more hours—another set of signatures done—until midnight. "One-sixth done," Amanda pointed out as we parted. I could see the mixed feelings in the faces of my colleagues. "See you at six tomorrow," she said, and no one dared contradict her.

We soldiered on for the next three days with little variation. We gained an extra pair of hands when Martyn rang on Friday afternoon and heard of our secret project. He couldn't be dissuaded from joining us, and became a dedicated member of the Barn Brigade, as we christened ourselves when we grew punch-drunk late on the first night.

I found myself increasingly worried about Sarah; I rang her each night during the printing operation when we stopped for dinner. She was never in her room, but later, when I was back in the barn, she would ring on my cell phone. I stopped work to find a quiet place and chat with her, but her reactions seemed off to me. Something was definitely wrong.

"Are you all right, Sarah?" I asked on the second night. She sounded weak, and not at all herself. She claimed she was just tired and about to go to bed. I'd had to cancel my trip to Switzerland, of course; surely she hadn't taken that to mean I no longer cared. Sarah wouldn't jump to a conclusion like that—would she? And she wouldn't really be spending her nights in Jean-Claude's room—would she?

I tried to put it out of my mind as best I could, and clung to her promise that she would be home the following weekend. We could sort it out then, whatever it was.

It quickly became apparent that Martyn had more than a passing interest in Amanda. He was glued to her side like a paperback cover. Midmorning on Saturday, the third day of the printing operation, he tore himself away from her to prepare for Lord Chenies's funeral. At one o'clock I abandoned my shift as well to change into my suit and tie and weave the Golf through the narrow lanes to Chenies.

The first surprise was the massive crowd. Half a mile from the church, cars lined the lane so that I ended up parking in the drive of a fellow church member who saw me cruising past. "In here, Plumtree," he called. "The journalists have taken over. The Bedford Arms is fully booked. They've come from all over Europe, and even America! Some famous Conservative personality named Bush Nimbaugh came to pay his respects; they're crawling all over him." He shrugged and walked over to the church with me.

The funeral was to start in fifteen minutes. The entire churchyard was filled with dark-suited people, and I noticed groups of less respectably dressed attendees massing to either side. On one side I saw members of what I thought of as the punctured crowd; most had not one but dozens of piercings filled with rings or studs visible somewhere on their anatomy. I didn't even like to think what they were doing here. On the other side, I saw an equally recognisable group: skinheads in leather and massive black boots. All this was quite unheard of in pastoral little Chenies.

As I made my way toward the church, Martyn hurried out in his robes, saw me, and half-ran in my direction.

"Alex! Thank God you're here. I've rung the police, but they're not here yet. Who'd have thought they'd do this at his *funeral*? Do you think you might possibly . . ." Then he realised. "Oh, no! We mustn't let them catch sight of you. Into the church, quickly!"

We made our way through the throng, and I'd only just secured a seat in the last row when Dexter Moore strode in, surrounded by bodyguards. Fortunately in the chaos he hadn't noticed me. From outside, the shouts of hecklers came from one side of the yard and the cries of Lord Chenies's defenders from the other. Of course, I thought. England's most conservative population would be here en masse to pay tribute to one of their own. The shouts grew louder, until it was obvious the funeral would never commence if this went on. I stayed in my seat, but my friend from the driveway stood at the door and issued reports. "The police are here now. . . . they're trying to get the crowd to disperse. Uh-oh . . . bit of a scuffle . . ."

In short, there was a riot on the grounds of Christ Church Chenies, the likes of which had not sullied the rural complacency of the village since its birth. Reporters from round the world dashed back to their hundred-and-fifty-quid-a-night rooms at the Bedford Arms to file their stories of the riot before the funeral even began. Martyn drifted through the church, passing the word that he would wait to start the service until the problem had been taken care of.

The noise was overwhelming; after ten minutes I gave up hiding and watched with the rest of the crowd from the doorway. A full two dozen police in riot gear now stood between the two angry mobs, and, as I watched, more police cars and vans arrived. Their strategy was obviously going to be to physically remove the troublesome group; they began loading the predominantly male crowd into the vans, separating skinheads from longhairs.

An hour passed as fragile white-haired ladies tut-tutted at the front of the church and the rest of us gazed in disbelief at the circus outside our peaceful little spiritual home. When at last the disturbance had been removed, and no more shouting was to be heard, we directed our attention to the front of the sanctuary. My friend whispered, "I think that big man up at the front is Bush Nimbaugh—sitting next to Dexter Moore."

There was no casket in the centre of the aisle; this was more in the way of a remembrance service, as Lord Chenies's remains were still required as evidence in the police investigation. Flowers cascaded from every possible nook and cranny, filling the church with delicate scent. The Altar Guild had done a spectacular job; the array of funeral wreaths and sprays of gladioli were splendid. The absence of a large wreath emblazoned with the glittering words, *"In loving memory of our dear father. Malcolm and Hillary,"* was painfully obvious. Malcolm and Hillary were in attendance, however, in the very first row. They waited with unconcealed impatience for the whole thing to get on, turning round from time to time with irritated expressions, and hurling angry words at Martyn each time he passed. The newly restored parish book stood near the altar, displayed on a book stand.

At last Martyn gave the organist the cue to begin the first comforting strains of "O God, Our Help in Ages Past," and we rose to sing. Martyn did an admirable job after that of offering a view of death from the Christian perspective; that after a life of dedication to his church and family, Lord Chenies was now enjoying his eternal reward. As he said those words, I saw more than one cynical mourner turn to a neighbour and smile. *Yeah, an eternity burning in hell,* their looks said. Martyn laid out for the congregation what an exceptional benefactor Lord Che-

nies had been to his church, and what a man of faith. I
thought it was especially good of Martyn to point out that
in his final days Lord Chenies had been badly misjudged
by those who had read only the opening chapter of his
book; that those who'd seen the whole thing (namely me)
said it was not a book of hate, but one that recorded instead the fate of the upper class in England.

Then he intoned a tragically appropriate lament from
Psalm Twenty-Two:

> *My God, my God, why hast thou forsaken me? Why
> art thou so far from helping me, and from the words of my
> roaring? O my God, I cry in the daytime, but thou hearest
> not; and in the night season, and am not silent. Our fa-
> thers trusted in thee; they trusted, and thou didst deliver
> them. But I am a worm, and no man; a reproach of men,
> and despised of the people. All they that see me laugh me to
> scorn; they shoot out the lip, they shake the head, saying,
> He trusted on the Lord that he would deliver him; let him
> deliver him, seeing he delighted in him.*

Afterwards it was Malcolm's turn. His painfully lukewarm
eulogy began with the words "My father was far from perfect." As he meandered on through every wrong he could
recall his father inflicting on him and the world, I found
myself fearing fatherhood once again. If a child of mine
ever felt this way about me . . .

I was ready to step in and silence Malcolm myself
when Martyn began to do so, only to have Dexter Moore
rise from the opposite side of the front row and actually
snatch the miniature clip-on mike out of the vicar's hand.

"It is a terrible thing when a man with an exemplary
life is reviled for his political beliefs and ordinary human
failings," he thundered. "Say what you will"—here he
glared at Malcolm—"Nigel Charford-Cheney, Lord Chenies, was a highly intelligent, gifted man who acted

passionately on behalf of that in which he *believed* passionately. Let us not criticise such a life unless we ourselves have done better. *Let him who is without sin cast the first stone.* And if wrongs are perceived, surely the right thing to do is to forgive." With a last furious nod to Malcolm, he seated himself next to the American celebrity as Martyn continued the service, the remainder of which was mercifully uneventful.

I stayed after the service to have a word with Martyn, who made no attempt to disguise his immense relief. "At least you know the worst moments you'll ever have in this parish are already over," I told him.

He brightened a bit more. "Thanks, Alex. I'll join you when I can. Er—by the way, do you know if Amanda is attached to anyone—er, romantically?"

I smiled at him. "No, I don't think she is. She's always struck me as a very lonely person. I must say, you may have found your match in intellectual firepower—and stubbornness."

"I think I'll take that as a compliment," he said cheerfully, and went to change out of his robes. Martyn was true to his word: he did return to the barn shortly, and remained a half-time part of our team—he did have other duties, after all—until the end of the fourth day, when we were well and truly done. Nicola, Bruce, and I sat bleary-eyed over coffee at the kitchen table on the morning we finished. Amanda and Lisette found us there at nine o'clock, having already looked for us in the barn.

"We did it!" Amanda exclaimed, allowing herself a small celebration as she made the rounds and congratulated us one by one. I felt it had all gone too smoothly. The work hadn't been easy, by any means—it had been exhausting but honest work. It's just that it was so calm and quiet out at the Orchard. *Very* quiet. What, no more bombs? Fires? Spies skulking in the shrubbery? The very lack of trouble made me suspicious. But I told myself to think positively and followed the others out to meet the custom-casing man's van.

Amanda spoke as we stood in front of the house watching him depart with our hard-won books, all *five hundred* of them. "Well, that's that, then." She turned to me with a tired smile. "I've a meeting with Anthony Simino in the Neighbourhood Association offices—to discuss what's to become of me and my shop. Wish me luck, Alex." I watched as Martyn barely managed to restrain himself from offering to go with her. He saw me watching him and reddened.

Amanda told Bruce she'd let him know when and where she needed him, and that he should take the day off. Both roared off amid our good-byes, and Martyn left shortly thereafter, looking wistful.

"That's exactly what you all need, too," I said, casting a glance at my weary employees. "A holiday." Nicola had finally let her hair hang loose around her face, and I'd seen her in jeans and sloppy sweaters now three days in a row. Her face showed not a single sign of wear. Lisette looked absolutely whacked, her hair matted, her eyes puffy. "I don't want to see either of you for the next few days," I told them. "And I mean it."

They went off without argument, and I stumbled up to bed with a quick stop at the phone along the way. No answer at Sarah's. My awareness of something wrong there had become a lead weight of certainty. I began to wonder if she still planned to come back with Ian in three days' time. In fact, I began to develop a number of bizarre theories involving Jean-Claude and my fiancée, but as it turned out, none of them approached the truth.

CHAPTER THIRTEEN

———◦〜◦———

England does not love coalitions.

BENJAMIN DISRAELI

TEN O'CLOCK THAT MORNING, A MONDAY, FOUND ME AP-
proaching Plumtree Press as if I hadn't been there in years.
I felt a virtual stranger to the place. As I strolled up to the
door I again had the feeling that things were too quiet.
Where was the flurry of camera-wielding vultures? Where
was my old friend from the book cart, Lloyd Branscomb?
I hadn't expected them to forget the *Cleansing* issue—or
me—so quickly. It wasn't like them. As I introduced myself to the security guard I'd posted outside, I couldn't help
but wonder whose carcass the press had picked clean this
morning.

Dee greeted me with pleased surprise as I stepped into
Reception. "Mr. P! Thought maybe you'd abandoned us."
She glanced out into the hall, then whispered, "For the
printing trade."

"Done with that for a bit. Though I must say it wasn't
all bad."

"You're finished, then? With *the book*?"

I nodded and winked. "My old friend Diana Boillot is

working magic with leather covers on the blasted things even as I speak. Actually, they did come out rather nicely."

"All the same," she said, "I'm glad that's the end of *that*. I'm awfully sorry about Amanda's shop—you'd think we lived in some Third World country, people rioting in the streets, ruining honest businesses . . ."

A tone hummed from her electronic switchboard. She said, "Call for you, your direct line. Want to take it?"

"Yes, thanks."

So began a seamless hour of phone call after phone call. There was the printer from Hong Kong, and our acquisitions editor, Timothy Haycroft, reporting in from his conference up north with suitable expressions of shock and regret about what had happened in his absence.

Ian rang, full of vigour, from the slopes. He was delighted to hear that the book had been printed. "Well *done*, Alex," he congratulated me. "There isn't anything you *can't* do, is there?" Kindly, he filled me full of compliments and encouragement. "Sarah's still on the pistes. She asked if she can phone you late tonight, at home. All right?" I wondered what she had planned for the evening and told myself not to be jealous of Jean-Claude. I debated asking Ian if he thought everything was all right with Sarah; then I decided not to put him in the middle of our personal business.

Max rang to say hello and urged me to come see him and Madeline as soon as I could; there was more dirt on the water scandal. "And something else," he said softly. "You've had your phones taken care of?"

I assured him I had.

"Well," he continued, "I asked someone I trust at the *Watch*. He said that Ferris-Browne is famous for glad handing with the unions. Not only the Trades Union Group here but all over Europe as well. He even told my friend in confidence—foolishly, as we all know there's no such thing as 'off the record'—that he has a plan to create

EuroUnions, a united union across the whole of the EU, in each industry. Can you imagine a Euro-NUP?"

The mere thought filled me with dread. Maybe there was something to Ian's passionate anti-EU sentiments. What Max was saying could actually be on the cards, if we went to true Economic and Monetary Union.

Max went on, "My friend also said he's got the impression Ferris-Browne is mounting a huge PR campaign for himself . . . sort of on the side. And he's thick with Helena Hotchkiss, of all people. Romantically, as well as to capitalise politically on her HIT success."

"At least maybe he'll keep her busy—she'll keep her claws off me." I remembered with a shudder how Helena had threatened to bring Max's lurid past to light and destroy his marital bliss with Madeline if I didn't give her what she wanted. "Thanks a lot, Max. I owe you."

I managed a brief walk round the Press, to find out how everyone was doing in the accounting, production, and academic groups, and found myself back in the office at half-past twelve with the phone ringing again.

The instant I heard Amanda sobbing down the line, her voice so broken that I could barely understand her, the fragile sense of equilibrium I'd achieved shattered into a million jagged pieces. She was in such a state that I couldn't make out what she was saying at all, except for the name Simino.

"Hang on, Amanda—are you at your office?"

That set off a new round of sobbing, and finally I heard Robert Lovegren's voice over the phone. The man always seemed to be there, as if by magic, when she needed him. "Alex? Another little difficulty, I'm afraid. If you've time, we're at St. James's Gate."

Racing downstairs, I called out to Dee that I was on my way to Clerkenwell again.

"Right. Be careful," she warned.

I grabbed a taxi on Tottenham Court Road and was at

the sixteenth-century Gate in fifteen minutes. The Gate was a lovely stone arch that crossed above the road, very impressive, but it was a mere fraction of the massive priory that had once dominated the area. After Henry VIII had dissolved the wealthy monastic orders in the sixteenth century, the gatehouse of the Priory of the Order of St. James had come into use as everything from government offices to a coffee house. The King's Master of the Revels censored Shakespeare's plays while sitting in the room suspended over the road; later Dr. Johnson and Oliver Goldsmith had visited the offices of *Gentleman's Magazine* there. Now the Gate was part of the order's museum.

As the taxi drew into St. James's Close, I saw signs of the riot all around: broken and boarded-up windows; shards of glass on the streets and pavements; scars from licking flames. I hurried into the Gate and asked for Robert Lovegren. The man at the front desk directed me to a door just down the hall.

Robert was sitting next to Amanda, his hand on top of hers, speaking calmly. I noticed that Amanda was wearing the most businesslike clothes she owned: a filmy Indian print skirt and a blouse, topped with a leather waistcoat. She looked up, saw me, and the floodgates broke again. "Oh, Alex," she wailed, coming toward me with red-rimmed eyes. I took her hand and squeezed it. She was too overcome to say anything more, and I had no idea *what* to say . . . this time.

"It's all too much," Lovegren said, shaking his head. "It seems that Mr. Simino, who as you may know owns most of Clerkenwell with the exception of our little corner, has chosen this particular moment to snatch up the print shop property for his own use."

"His *own* use!" I exclaimed.

Lovegren nodded. "I read about an application for planning permission for a hotel on Clerkenwell Green, and wondered where on earth anyone *could* put a hotel there. Now I understand." His expression was wry. "Simino told Amanda this morning. The Clerkenwell Neighbourhood Association can't afford to renovate the three buildings that were worst damaged in the riot— Amanda's and the ones on either side—so he's 'taking them off the association's hands,' no doubt for a song. All the while *they* think he's doing them a favour. 'We must do what's best for Clerkenwell,' he told Amanda. It's not completely out of character, mind you, but it's low—even for him. It makes me wonder if he orchestrated this entire NUP riot, just to snatch up those properties. He does have a printing past, and shares their political ideology. It's entirely possible."

"I—I trusted him," Amanda moaned. "He knew everything about my business. He seemed to *care*."

"Doesn't the Neighbourhood Association see what he's doing?" I asked, outraged.

Lovegren frowned. "Ah. But you see, Mr. Plumtree, Anthony Simino *is* the Neighbourhood Association. Virtually all the grant money for businesses like Amanda's came from him and his property empire. The Association know which side their bread's buttered."

"It's not that this is the only place to have a shop," Amanda said. "It's not the building so much; it's that he said they were even rethinking my grant, given the difficulties I seemed to have in keeping the shop going. He said they'd open other premises for grantees in the area, and I know I can get started again, somehow. But without his grant I'm as good as finished."

Her words hung miserably in the air.

"Amanda, you're not finished. You have friends. You could use my barn until we find you presses and a place of your own. I'll help you get back on your feet again. And when Martyn finds out, he'll be desperate to help."

She let out a little laugh mid-sob.

"In fact, I know Martyn would love to come fetch you and take you out to Chenies with him," I assured her. "I'll ring him right now."

I picked up the phone and dialled the vicarage. Moments later a very concerned and sympathetic Martyn was on his way to Clerkenwell.

Amanda blew her nose and seemed to calm down a bit. "Thanks, Robert, you've been wonderful too." She reached for a much soiled and stained broadsheet that I recognised from her shop. She must have snatched it after her meeting there with Simino. It quoted William Morris again, her favourite printer-poet:

For what and for whom hath the world's book been gilded,
When all is for these but the blackness of night?

I glanced at Lovegren, who looked at me with disconcerting calm and wisdom. Why did I have the feeling that he knew more about the Machiavellian machinations of Clerkenwell under Simino's evil spell than he'd told us?

He promised me he'd wait with Amanda until Martyn arrived, so I walked back to Bedford Square. Even through the uneventful afternoon—as I chatted with my solicitor Neville Greenslade about the spiteful lawsuit under way by the Charford-Cheneys, rang Martyn, and spoke to an author we hoped to sign—I remained preoccupied. Amanda's betrayal by the Clerkenwell Neighbourhood Association belied the surface victory of getting *Cleansing* out; it signalled that far from getting back to normal, events were still tumbling out of control.

At six o'clock I decided it was time to end the day, and switched off the lamp on my desk. But I was uncomfortable knowing that of all the people at the Press, I hadn't yet spoken to Rachel Sigridsson. No doubt she thought Nicola's and my extended absence for printing the book could be written off to a bit of hedonistic cavorting in the countryside. Rachel's disapproving attitude toward me was like an itch that I couldn't scratch.

Standing up, I stretched and set out on my mission round the corner, stopping outside the door of Rachel's office. Rachel was there, beavering away as usual under the light of her own desk lamp, her back to me as she sat beneath her Greenpeace seal poster. The grey mass of her chignon and the sagging shelf of reference books dominated her domain.

"All right, Rachel?" I asked.

She spun round in her desk chair and flew to her feet in the cramped office, apparently horror-struck.

"I'm sorry," I said, taken aback by her reaction. "I didn't mean to startle you."

"Oh, Mr. Plumtree! I—we—I'm so sorry."

I assumed this was her way of expressing regret for Lord Chenies's and Amanda's misfortunes. "I'm sorry for Lord Chenies too," I told her. "He didn't deserve that. I just left Amanda; she's lost her—"

"No, no." Her eyes, her mouth—all pulled miserably down at the corners. She was headed for a spectacular set of jowls in old age. "I mean . . . Oh, do you have a moment, sir? Here." She fussed, motioning me into her office. With the door safely shut, she turned back to me and we stood facing each other like skeletons in a cupboard—quite fittingly, as I was about to see.

"Mr. Plumtree, I've done a terrible thing. A lot of people have. You know the Clerkenwell riot?"

I nodded, baffled.

"We were all sworn to secrecy, but I can't go on this way. You and your father, you've always been so good to me, and I . . . I'm sorry I turned on you." Her eyes brimmed with tears.

"Rachel—"I began, but she cut me off.

"Mr. Plumtree, you know I'm part of the environmental group, Watchlands. I'm also a member of the National Union of Pressworkers."

No, I hadn't known. Watchlands was affiliated with Hedgerows in Transition. The former was an extremely political group, well-organised about getting out the vote for the environmental candidates. By and large it was a left-leaning organisation.

She went on, disconsolately. "And you know I was dead set against *Cleansing*. Thought it beneath you, your family, and the fine trade list you've built."

I'll take that as encouragement, I thought.

"But, sir, I didn't know how far they were going to go. You see, as one of the few people who actually belonged to both HIT and NUP, I took it upon myself to link the two organisations formally. I was . . . er, put in touch with Helena Hotchkiss by my father of chapel in our local NUP chapter. So HIT is hand in glove with the NUP now. And though the union organised that riot, HIT doubled its strength. They were lashing back at you and poor Amanda for that wilding—which of course I know you had nothing to do with—and for printing the book. I've just felt so wretched, sir, knowing that my dues helped pay to destroy Amanda's shop and kept a Plumtree Press book from being printed—no matter *what* book it was—and that I personally talked to Helena about HIT joining forces with the NUP."

She trailed off, too dispirited to continue, and the room fell silent.

"Rachel, you couldn't have known that your group would resort to violent tactics. What they've done is not your fault. I'll be very pleased if you and I can be on friendly terms again."

She wiped at a tear with a closed fist. "Thank you, Mr. Plumtree. I don't deserve your forgiveness. I want to make it up to you, I really do."

I shook my head and reached for the doorknob. "If you felt you could, you might let me know if you hear of further plans on the part of the NUP or HIT."

"Yes, yes, I will. There is one thing Helena told me. . . . She said that Guy Ferris-Browne had plans to galvanise the entire Trades Union Group against Dexter Moore and *Cleansing*. She said that the EU is too important to the NUP and all of the unions to let Moore ruin it all."

"Thank you, Rachel. Let's hope the worst is over, now." Ferris-Browne and the unions again—talking about still more violent action against *Cleansing*. The Trades Union Group, or TUG, carried massive power. Ferris-Browne might even be talking about a national strike. It had been decades since those fearsome, crippling days of national strikes. . . . Then I had a further horrible thought: what if Ferris-Browne succeeded in forming EuroUnions, and all Europe suddenly shut down when one of their lot wanted more money or fewer hours . . . or didn't want to see a book published?

Suddenly I felt every bit of the exhaustion of the last four long days, and the bitter discouragement of the last two weeks. Giving Rachel what I hoped was an encouraging smile, I left, not closing the door behind me.

Dead on my feet, I shuffled back to my office, slumped into my chair, and sat staring at my blotter. Rachel, Helena, Ferris-Browne, and perhaps the entire TUG—all lined up against us. When the phone began to ring it seemed to take a huge effort of will to pick it up.

" 'Ello, you. What are you still doing there? You would live there if people didn't lure you away. I am calling to see if I can persuade you to come to dinner with me and two boys who are desperate to see you."

"Lisette, you're an angel. I'd love to." I didn't want to be alone that night.

"Good, because otherwise I would have a mutiny on

my hands," she laughed. "For Uncle Alex, they can stay up a bit late on a school night."

"Wonderful. I'll be on my way, then." Cheered by the mere thought of companionship with my good friend, and horseplay with her boys, I rang off and dashed off to the great northwest.

Later I would consider it unfortunate that we'd chosen that particular evening to comfort one another.

"One more each, then it's time for bed."

Lisette stood, arms akimbo, and watched as the boys and I did what we did best. I flung Edward onto his mother and father's bed, head over heels, as he squealed with delight. "I never understand 'ow it is that they don't break their necks." She laughed, shaking her head.

I tossed Michael, who had grown large enough to be a challenge, and said, "You worry too much." I was instantly sorry: without thinking, I had quoted George's stock reply to her accusations of excessively rough play. The boys, following tradition, attacked me, desperate to wring five minutes more out of the evening.

"Boys, boys!" Lisette clapped her hands to get their attention. Both had climbed onto me, were hanging from round my neck and waist. "I said that was it. Now clean your teeth and get your pyjamas on. If you are ready by the time I count to twenty, Alex said he'll put you to bed."

They raced off down the hall, and Lisette smiled. "They adore you," she told me. "Thank you so much for giving them some attention." Sighing, she led me back to the sitting room, where a fire blazed in the grate. She sat and stared at the flames: I sank into a chair opposite her.

"Have you heard from George?" I asked.

"Not a squeak. What do you hear from Sarah?"

We made a pathetic picture, I thought, each separated from the one we loved.

"She's finishing up with the film in a few days. It seems she's been gone forever."

The boys came pounding down the hall just then, and with a wink to Lisette I ran to meet them. They were so vulnerable, so full of happy expectation. It was unthinkable to disappoint them. I read them a story, then a chapter from their children's book of Bible stories. It never failed to amaze me that the stories in that ancient book were still the most captivating tales I'd ever read.

Then, as usual, we talked. And talked. "I have a question" was the signal for the long discussion to begin. It was part of the fun. "Why did Daddy stop loving us?" Michael's small hand clung to my arm as I sat on the bed; its warmth penetrated my shirt.

Golly, I thought. But they never started off with the easy ones. I'd noticed long ago with the boys that at bedtime, in pyjamas and with only the night-light on, a magical transformation took place. The carefree little faces grew serious, and all the really knotty issues leapt instantly from the depths of their souls.

"Michael, he hasn't stopped loving you. He *never* will. He needs to help some other people for a while, people in faraway places who don't have doctors. He knows you need him, too. He'll be back."

"But if he loves us, why did he go away in the first place?" Edward's blue eyes were earnest. He had a precise duplicate of Lisette's mouth. He would be chased silly by girls in his teens; I could see it coming.

"Well, Edward, he knows that his commitment to you is forever." I nudged a lock of curly brown hair off his forehead. "He just wants to take a tiny scrap of time, from his whole life, to help the kids who have never even seen a doctor before. You know the kind of things your daddy's doing for them, don't you?"

This was a rhetorical question. I'd heard Lisette going on and on about all the kids who would be able to run and play again after the heart surgery their father was performing, how those kids would now live to get married and have families themselves. She always painted George as a larger-than-life hero to their children.

"Are you going away too, Uncle Alex?"

"No. I'm never going away—at least not for very long. Just for a couple of weeks when I marry Sarah this summer. I'm not as noble as your father. Besides, I can't leave your mum to run Plumtree Press all by herself, can I?" I smiled. "Now, it's really, really late, and I promised your mother I'd not keep you up too long—"

Immediately Michael piped up. "Can you stay with us till Daddy gets back?"

"I'm afraid not, Michael. I have to live in my own house. But I'll always be just down the road." I kissed each of them good night, closed the door of the cupboard that they swore housed the most vicious monsters, and made sure the hall light was on just the way they liked it. "Good night."

" 'Night, Uncle Alex," they chorused.

I walked back to the sitting room, where Lisette sat forlornly in front of the fire on a flokati rug. She'd poured two snifters of brandy and now held one of the glasses, swirling the amber liquid in it as she studied the flames. As I picked up my own, I saw that her shoulders were shaking.

"Oh, Lisette," I said, sitting beside her. "You'll get through this."

She sniffed. "It's not just me and George. It is *all* so unfair. I begin to doubt everything sometimes. . . . I begin to suspect that the world is *completely* evil, that there is nothing good anymore, anywhere. That someone might have killed Lord Chenies for 'is politics . . . " She wept bitterly. I moved over and put my arm round her shoulders, squeezing her.

In the midst of her emotional crisis, I thought I heard something at the window behind us, the one looking out on the back garden. Lisette and George never closed the curtains in their new house; they felt there was no need. The back garden was so heavily wooded and private that no one could ever see inside from a neighbouring house. I'd warned Lisette, since George left, that she should really draw the curtains in case there were prowlers or Peeping Toms. But she steadfastly ignored the advice, and now the dark wall of windows stretched behind us across the back of the room. I turned to look, and thought I saw a dark shape retreat into deeper shadow.

"Lisette, don't look now, but there's someone at the back of the house." She tensed under my arm. "When I say 'go,' grab the phone from your bedroom, lock yourself in the boys' room, and call the police. I'll try to chase him off. All right?"

But before we could leap into action, the back door burst open. I leapt to my feet at the sudden noise, marvelling at how quickly he'd got in. Then I saw who it was.

"*George!*" Lisette exclaimed, thunderstruck. Her brandy spilled into the rug as she scrambled to her feet. "You—you—"

I stared at the man who banged the door shut, his face twisted in rage. "My *friend*, Alex Plumtree," he said, each word a caustic drop of acid. "So this is what friends are for. Taking advantage of lonely wives!"

"No, oh, no, George!" Lisette was aghast. "Alex was just—"

"I'm not stupid," he spat. "I can see what was going on here. You've all but moved in, have you, Plumtree?" His face was extremely dark from working in tropical climes, his hair almost completely white-blond. He'd lost weight. He was so unlike my easygoing old friend George Stoneham that I could scarcely believe it was the same man.

"George, you've got the wrong end of the stick completely. Lisette and I—"

Out of the corner of my eye I saw the boys advance to the end of the hallway and peer into the sitting room, their eyes wide, their faces horror-struck. My heart ached for them.

"How *stupid* do you think I am?" he demanded. His mouth was twisted in an ugly snarl. "I finally came to my senses, realised I've my own family to care for, and this is the greeting I get. My welcome-home party is a cosy little tête-à-tête by the fire—only I'm not the one there with my *wife!*" He looked at us with unspeakable loathing. "You can have her, Plumtree. I'm off." He turned dramatically and started through the door.

"George. The boys." I pointed to where they cowered at the edge of the room.

He stopped, stared almost hungrily at them, and no doubt saw the fear and distrust in their young eyes. Anguished, he cried, "Now I'm not even welcome in my own home!" he fled. I raced round to the front after him. A car crunched on the gravel, buzzed out of the drive, and took off at high speed down the lane.

When I stepped back inside, Lisette had gathered the boys in her lap by the fire. Both seemed too stunned and disappointed to speak. She rocked slowly back and forth, patting them and smoothing their hair. I closed the drapes, too late, and locked the back door as she began to sing, *"Lully, lullay, lully, lullay, the falcon hath borne my mate away . . ."*

What to do to help them now? Under the circumstances, it hardly seemed right to stay.

I touched Lisette lightly on the shoulder. "I'd better go," I said, my voice soft. She nodded slightly. I let myself out.

I felt as if the world had ended. How could it be that all I wanted to do was *good* in the world, but instead I seemed to precipitate disasters. For my friends, authors, employees, printers . . . and even strangers.

I drove the five minutes home and checked my phone messages. Nicola had left a gleeful one, saying "the packages" were ready. She'd been unable to reach me on my cell phone and so had spoken in a sort of code, remembering that the line had once been bugged. She also said that she was going to observe the first delivery at nine o'clock. Did I want to join her? She said she'd be at the office at eight the next morning.

At least that had gone right, I thought. Tomorrow the cursed tomes would go out to the shops, according to the complicated allocation system we'd arranged. The books were so hotly controversial at the moment that private individuals had been ringing us at the Press to reserve copies. We'd instructed Dee to tell everyone that all of the books were promised to the shops already, but they could be purchased at the following stores on Tuesday. . . .

Tuesday was now tomorrow. I shook my head. If only the public knew about the wildly unconventional production process for the first edition. Someday, perhaps, it would make a good story, when time had dissipated the miasma shrouding the project.

At my desk in the library, I picked up the phone and tried Sarah's number, although I knew she'd be ringing later. As I listened to the endless ringing of the phone in her hotel room, I wondered where she was and why she wasn't in her usual scented bath . . . yet again. Perhaps she was attending some raucous Hollywood-style party. Though I trusted Sarah to the ends of the earth, I felt another sharp twinge of worry that all was clearly not as it should be.

I hung up and dialled Detective Inspector Fawcett at the Buckinghamshire Constabulary. I hadn't heard anything about the official cause of death of Lord Chenies. The detective inspector was there and more than willing to talk about it.

"We did find something unusual," he confided, "but not deadly. We discovered surprisingly large amounts of a root extract in his bloodstream, one of those homeopathic remedies by Nature's Chemist, that was supposed to stop aging. Took us quite some time to work it out, I can tell you—our forensics experts don't come up against obscure plants like that every day."

Nature's Chemist . . . Was it a coincidence that Helena's company had supplied something found in excess in Lord Chenies's body?

I thanked the detective and rang off, promising to keep in touch. Sighing, I began a long letter to George—though even as I wrote it, I realised I would not know where to send it. Would he return to the Medecins avec Avions headquarters in France, or communicate with them?

At eleven, Sarah rang.

"Alex!" She told me about the film project and how it was all going. Her voice seemed strained.

"Are you all right, Sarah?"

"Of course," she replied, but she sounded as if she'd been caught in a lie. I knew her so well. "Why not?"

I hesitated. "I care about you," I said, my imagination reaching for the worst possible situation. She and Jean-Claude had been out that night, and he had proposed? Had she accepted? "I miss you horribly and hope everything's all right over there. If only this mess hadn't happened . . ."

She assured me that everything was just fine, to stop worrying, and that she and Ian would be back in just a couple of days. We rang off. It hadn't been a satisfactory conversation. *You're tired, Alex,* I told myself. *Things always look wrong when you're tired.*

Yawning, I took out my contacts and stretched out on

the long leather sofa in the library. I unfolded my green woollen blanket with the large white *D* for Dartmouth on it and pulled it up to my chin.

When I woke up, I felt somewhat better. I fought off recollections of George's surprise appearance the night before, and the worrying phone call with Sarah, and told myself to try to be positive. With the special edition of *Cleansing* on the streets at last, no one had further reason to bother with us. I gave a rueful chuckle at the extremely unorthodox fact that I hadn't even seen a cased book yet, and wouldn't until the shops did. It was a strange feeling, as if even my books had now been torn from my control.

Lisette and I arrived at the office at exactly eight o'clock, having driven in our usual car pool. The journey to Bedford Square was made in companionable but miserable silence. Lisette had emerged from her house in huge sunglasses, the ones she always wore when she'd been crying. I couldn't begin to imagine what torture the night had held for her. The two boys stared out through the front window, subdued, in the nanny's care as we drove away.

At the Press, Lisette retreated directly to her office. Nicola was already in, raring to go, full of high spirits about the victory the day represented. "Shall we watch some books hit the street?"

"Yes, let's."

"I brought the car in, to take you in style. All right?"

I nodded and we made our way into the March sunshine. It was going to be a stunning day, I thought, as I swung into her low-slung sports car. Not a cloud in sight—yet. She sped round the square and into Gower Street. "Where exactly are we going?" I asked. "Your message was nicely veiled last night."

She smiled. "I rang the distribution company yesterday. Would you believe, the first stop is Harrods? It's an unusual outlet, I know, for special editions, but evidently they're branching into collectibles now."

I felt oddly cheated, as if it should have been Quaritch's or Hatchards, or at the very least Foyles, Waterstones, or Dillons. Still, mine was not to wonder why. We drove through the traffic-choked city, first down Gower Street to Shaftesbury Avenue, then through Piccadilly Circus and along Piccadilly to Knightsbridge.

I looked out at the familiar sights of Eros, Green Park, and Hyde Park Corner along the way and reflected on how very much I did love London. There was no place like it on earth, and I told myself I'd done the right thing to keep the Press in Bedford Square instead of moving it out into the countryside.

"Alex . . . " Nicola let the car drift to a stop in the slow-moving traffic along Knightsbridge. "Tell me you don't see them. Tell me it's not true."

The massive structure that enjoyed the reputation of the world's favourite shopping paradise towered before us, its pavement clogged with sign-bearing protesters. "Oh, surely *not*," I said, despairing.

Don't pollute! Stop Cleansing, one read. *NUP against Fascists,* said another.

Staring at the spectacle, I remembered my feeling that the production of the special edition had gone too easily. There hadn't been a single attempt to sabotage us at the barn. I should have realised that our enemies hadn't needed to; they were a step ahead of us. They'd just thwart the deliveries. Of course they'd rung our supplier, probably masquerading as a bookshop clerk, and found out the delivery timetable.

It had just gone nine o'clock, and as we advanced opposite the store I caught sight of our distributor's van. It bore the name Bookdrop, and I glimpsed it turning down Sloane Street to reach the rear delivery door.

"Ring the police! Meet me at the back!" I said, and hopped out of the car. I saw Nicola's stunned face, but she zoomed obediently away as I raced across the one remaining lane of traffic between me and the store. I tore down the pavement opposite the store, praying that no one would recognise me. But they had to look at something, and a man madly dodging traffic and racing down a street past them was too tempting a sight.

"*That's him! That's Alex Plumtree!*" A general hubbub of excitement, action, and movement ensued, and I sensed a massive shift of the protesters in my direction. But I didn't look back. I kept running, way ahead of them. Sadly, by the time I rounded the corner, my worst fears had already come true. As I arrived, gasping, at the delivery van, I saw the driver, now out of his van and facing a circle of sneering attackers. A thin stream of blood ran from his nose. He reeled, but stayed on his feet.

"*Stop!*" I bellowed. The four thugs attacking the driver froze. All were equipped with knuckle-dusters and coshes. "It's me you want. If you want a fight, come and get me!" A human barricade of equally unsavoury specimens blocked the delivery bay. Too terrified to intervene, the store's staff watched the spectacle from the loading dock. Why hadn't the crowd out at the front attracted the police?

The poor delivery bloke scrambled into his van to lick his wounds, slamming down the locks, front and rear. The leading lout squinted, strutting close enough to spit at me—though he spared me that. He was thick and squat, like some stupid, slow-moving animal. I towered over him and his cronies. The NUP had clearly massed its burlier members—or hirelings—here. Perhaps I was facing down the bodybuilding corps of the entire TUG. They looked the sort who munched steroids for snacks.

When would Nicola get the police here?

"You're Alex effing Plumtree," said the lead thug, with a surprised laugh. "Mates, look who's here! It's the publisher gent!" He eyed me with relish. "Never thought I'd get this chance—though I can tell you, I've been longing for it." He moved one step closer, breathing hard, and the unmistakable smell of alcohol drifted over me in a stale cloud.

"You know that this is illegal," I said with a pleasant calm that was calculated to irritate him. "Rather like killing and abducting people, destroying private property in riots, and tampering with a private press. Where do you think it'll get you?"

He sneered at me. "You toffs think you can win every time. Exploit the working class and the foreigners and keep the spoils for yourself. Well, you've gone far enough. The entire country's going to see, there'll be hell to pay if Dexter Bleeding Moore comes anywhere near Number Ten. Wait till the unions are exploiting *you*!"

At that point he tired of invective. With surprising speed, he swung one arm up and caught me on the side of the head with the knuckle-dusters. I heard the hollow sound of hard object hitting skull, and flew back against the van. "Mmbasi Kumba!" he yelled. "Rajahandra Gupta!" another voice brayed. A crowbar hit me squarely in the upper arm. I wondered if it occurred to the thugs that *they* were committing a wilding—the very crime they claimed to be avenging.

It hurt. My head buzzed. I stayed hunched and ran straight into them, hoping to knock them off-balance for long enough to get on the offensive or at least put up an active defence. My plan failed. These fellows were stout as brick walls. Running into them like a human battering ram was like trying to breach a steel door with a tooth-pick. They piled on top of me like players in a rugger scrum, each falling to the task at hand with his weapon of choice. I was just getting fuzzy about the edges when I heard the wail of a police siren. My attackers slowed, and the leader mumbled something. Before I knew it I lay alone on the concrete, and they'd bolted.

The first tentative movements were the worst. But I'd had my share of knocks before. There wasn't anything too

gruesome about this set of souvenirs. My body was accu-
mulating an admirable collection of scar tissue, I realised,
increasing with every problematic book I published. I'd
just got to my feet when several PCs arrived at a run,
closely followed by Nicola. I heard her mutter an oath;
then one policeman wordlessly ushered me to a waiting
ambulance as others moved to deal with the driver of the
van. Two more advanced on the riffraff who still stood
stupidly on the loading dock as a physical blockade.

They faded into the background, and Nicola swam
into the foreground as I sat heavily on the bench inside
the parked ambulance. "Mind if I cut your hair?" a medical attendant asked, wielding a small pair of scissors and
gently probing the gash on the side of my head.

"No," I said, and began to laugh. Something about
the contrast of being asked permission to cut my hair after
the incivilities I'd just suffered seemed overwhelmingly
hilarious. I laughed so hard it hurt. The poor man said
with not a little pique, "Really, Mr. Plumtree, I know
you've been through quite a lot, but do you think you
could just . . ."

Nicola, who'd been watching with a sick look on her
face, was suddenly overcome too. The ambulance man
tut-tutted in disgust, resigning himself to make the best of
it. Nicola bent over, rocking silently with laughter, then
came up for a breath and caught my eye. She pointed at
my haircut, which I knew sported a new bald spot over
my right ear, and howled. Then she pointed at my left eye
which had nearly swollen shut, sending me into another
paroxysm of hilarity.

As we moved from one spasm of silent, choking
laughter into another, the medical attendant said, sounding worried, "All right, let's just calm down now," and
"Really, let's get a grip, you two." His utter seriousness
only made it worse. We'd attracted an audience by that

time. Several police and more bystanders were gaping at us through the open rear doors as if we'd lost our minds.

"I've never seen anything like you two." The ambulance man winced as he inspected my head. "You should have stitches in this. But I've used a plaster to hold it together for now." He handed me an ice pack for the swelling eye, and swabbed with a sterile alcohol pad at the cut edge of my lip. "You'd better put some ice on this one, too." As he handed me a second pack, Nicola giggled, pointing at my face, now nearly obscured by ice packs.

A police constable approached. "Mr. Plumtree? PC Tiffin. It begins to look as if your driver will need a police escort for his deliveries today."

"Yes, I'd say so. And I'm going to be in his passenger seat. Moral support, you know."

"Right," the policeman said, with a glance at the ambulance man. "Do you wish to press charges, sir?"

My smile faded. "Not much point, is there? No."

He acknowledged this by raising one eyebrow. "All right, then. We've got the crowd under control here. Your driver has delivered his box. He shared the rest of his timetable with us, so whenever you're ready . . ."

So it happened that Nicola and I found ourselves bumping down the road in the company of John Pitkin, delivery van driver. Aside from a colouring bruise on his cheekbone and a wild look in his eye, he seemed all right. He was silent, though I couldn't blame him—who wanted passengers who'd nearly got him killed once?

The NUP had, in fact, made a meal of delivery day. They were waiting in impressive numbers at Quaritch's, Hatchards, Waterstones, and Dillons. Nicola and I personally entered each of the stores, leaving John locked safely in the van, guarded by the police. I carried the single box of books allotted each store directly to its manager.

At midday I took everyone to lunch, coppers and all,

at Pizza Express. We were quite a spectacle, with such a large knot of police, not to mention my haircut and John's technicolour face. Two PCs stayed with the books in the van, and I personally delivered their pizza.

"Ta, sir," one of them said, and I felt a small amount of pleasure that we were actually getting the books delivered. We had done it.

My good humour faded only when we reached Foyles in Charing Cross Road at a little past two o'clock. Nicola and I took the books in and spoke to the bookshop owner personally. It was quite an honour, as she was a notable figure in the world of books. She eyed us as if we were utterly mad, and shook her head. "You know what they're going to do, don't you," she asked rhetorically.

"Mmm? What's that?" I asked, with a sinking feeling.

She picked up the phone and handed it to me. "Ring one of the shops you delivered to this morning. See how many copies they have left."

I found the number for Dillons on Holborn and pushed the buttons with dread. "Yes, hello, Patrick," I said. "What's happening with the books?"

"Do you want the good or the bad news?"

"Both."

"The good news is, all the books have sold."

"Wonderful." I hadn't actually worried about that at all. "And . . . ?"

"The customers, er, evidently didn't buy them to read them."

"What do you mean?"

He hesitated; I knew he didn't want to tell me.

"*Please*— what is it?"

"I'm sorry, Alex. The NUP crowd is burning your books, which they bought in the space of about five minutes after you left. They threw them in a metal dustbin on the pavement and poured petrol over them, then threw in a match."

Burning them? With their leather covers and stamped gold spines? Mmbasi Kumba had lost his life for that bonfire, as perhaps had Lord Chenies. And Amanda had lost her shop. I couldn't believe it was all for naught.

I dredged up a "Thanks" and rang off.

The blond eminence of the bookselling world nodded sagely. "You didn't know, did you?" she said. "They'll stop at nothing."

Too right.

We finished the deliveries halfheartedly, and the police deposited us back at Nicola's car at Harrods around five o'clock. We accepted PC Tiffin's offer to escort us back to Bedford Square. Nicola got her car into gear and pulled out ahead of him as I switched on the car radio.

We were all over BBC Radio Four's P.M. news programme. It was the stuff of which juicy broadcasts were made: massive crowds, protests, Harrods, assault. But we looked at each other in surprise when we heard the angle the commentators were taking on it.

"Andrew, I understand you were on the scene at Harrods today, and later at some of the other bookshops where Cleansing *was delivered. Can you tell us what happened?"*

"Well, Brian, today was a bleak day for those who fight censorship everywhere. As a single van delivered the handprinted leatherbound copies of a special edition of the controversial novel *Cleansing* at Harrods, the van was attacked by a violent mob openly identifying itself as the NUP. Other unions, we know now, may also have been involved. First the van driver and then publisher Alex Plumtree himself were attacked and beaten in an effort to prevent the books' being delivered. In recent history, Brian, we've never seen such a betrayal of human rights by a group that *claims* to defend them. The irony is stupendous."

"Yes, indeed it is, Andrew," his partner of the airwaves responded. "What's been happening in the shops?"

"Well, Brian, no sooner were the deliveries completed

under police escort than mobs of NUP activists swarmed into the shops to buy out the stock, paying for the books with union funds. We've been informed that they've made a bonfire of most of the novels on Clerkenwell Green, though other fires were seen throughout the day."

"What sort of political reaction has come out of all of this?"

"The American Civil Liberties Union wants to be involved," Andrew continued. "They claim that it's an injustice to people everywhere. The political effect is absolutely fascinating, Brian. The way I saw it, with an election looming, the public's reaction to that first chapter of *Cleansing*, published serially, was delivering votes to the prime minister. As was the hue and cry over Plumtree Press publishing the full book. But now I think the general public is so appalled by the behaviour of these union activists—*terrorists*— that they're running straight into the arms of the alternative government, and as you know, that's Dexter Moore."

"Well, Andrew, Moore's been saying for some time that something like this was bound to happen, that the pendulum had swung too far. That it was fine to have foreigners residing in our country, but ridiculous for them to receive preferential treatment when seeking jobs, and even to have jobs created for them with our money. He's also pointed out that it was fine to cooperate with the nations of Europe, but we didn't have to give up our currency and our own way of doing things. I must say, I used to think him a bit skewed. Now I think perhaps he saw something brewing before the rest of us."

"The Campaign for an Independent Britain has taken out adverts in all of the papers for tomorrow, I'm told, spelling out the consequences of economic union. It's quite astonishing, Brian—the things that have been swept under the carpet by the last few governments. They warn of EuroUnions with sweeping power, and actually jobs *lost* instead of gained. There's also talk of the way the European Court has taken precedence over the English courts; they've overturned English decisions now on a number of cases—one of them in favour of an IRA terrorist. The most bizarre of these points against the EU is an alleged plot to turn all of Europe into a Roman Catholic state. Supposedly the European court in Strasbourg is . . ."

Nicola exhaled loudly. Her father's political machinations had backfired. She turned into Bedford Square's oval road, sliding into a parking place toward our end of the street. "What a bizarre twist," she murmured, shaking her head. "And his beloved EU is getting quite a black eye."

We had to brave a front step full of reporters. Our private security guard ran to the car to escort us into the building. The cameras followed my face as the questions began to fly. I ignored them all until I had reached the top step, and then, with my hand on the door, I said, "Censorship in any form is a very bad thing. This violence and *killing*—no matter who does it—must stop." I retreated inside with Nicola and locked the door.

Lisette ran down the stairs to meet us. "*Mon Dieu!* All over the news! Alex, Claire is upstairs managing the deluge." Claire was our freelance public relations consultant; we called her in only for special events. Our entire business, it seemed, had become a special event. "The *Mehrer Newshour* wants to know if you will speak with them tonight; there is a studio 'ere in London they use. Claire 'as a whole stack of interview requests, television and print, English and foreign. She is positively salivating over them, keeps saying she 'as never seen a press coup of this magnitude."

Aches and pains dogged me as I climbed the stairs. Things were rapidly going from bad to worse as the hours passed.

The *Mehrer Newshour*. The ultimate in-depth journalism television programme in the United States.

McLein/Mehrer was the only news I watched during my four years at university there. I couldn't believe it. I walked into Lisette's office and surrendered myself to Claire.

"These cuts and bruises are perfect," the publicist enthused. "Alex, you couldn't have planned this any better!"

I had proved it beyond all doubt: truth is stranger than fiction.

CHAPTER FOURTEEN

———·———

I can hear, underground, that sucking and sobbing, . . .
The small waters seeping upward.

THEODORE ROETHKE, *Cuttings Later*

I SAT AT MY DESK, DAZED AFTER FOUR HOURS OF NONSTOP interviews, with Claire and Lisette for company. The security guard had driven me first to the studio the *Mehrer Newshour* people had specified, and I'd given them their pound of flesh. After that, there had been dozens of others on the phone. I was in a fog.

The words of America's most-respected news anchor floated through my mind. Immediately after introducing me, Jim Mehrer had attempted to summarise the issues associated with *Cleansing* for the American people. He had done so extremely well, in the placid drawl that the world loved.

"In a nutshell, Alex Plumtree, you've published a book, *Cleansing*, that the public perceived from its first chapter as being pejorative of the underclass in England. But as I understand it, the title actually refers to the purging of the long-line aristocratic families from England. As we can see on our monitors, you've taken a beating for publishing this book—figuratively as well as literally—

and the author, Lord Chenies, has died what the police are calling an unnatural death. All in all, an unprecedented response to a novel. But the political ramifications have been just as surprising. The National Union of Pressworkers has claimed responsibility—not only for a riot that ruined the shop of *Cleansing*'s printer, but also for the handiwork on your face and for the immediate burning of all the copies of *Cleansing* produced and delivered today to London's bookshops. Yet because of this violence and instability, informal polls taken in London today reveal a shift to the right, toward ultra-Conservative, isolationist Dexter Moore and away from moderate, pro-Europe Graeme Abercrombie. The British public evidently senses that the Labour Party, traditionally the champion of unions in Britain, has lurched toward anarchy rather than moderation. The Campaign for an Independent Britain is said to be revving up to capitalise on this lack of faith; they're accusing the Labour governments past and present of having tricked the public into acquiescing to Europe. Alex, what do you have to say to all this?"

Now, I couldn't remember *what* I'd said. I hoped I'd managed something halfway intelligent.

As I drove away from the square, I'd wished my mother and father could have seen the *Mehrer Newshour*, during which the kindly news host had painted me as a hero of free speech, defending the world against "intellectual terrorism," as one of the other pundits on the show had called it. And another sound bite is born, I thought. I couldn't help but wonder what my father would have done if his friend Graeme Abercrombie had asked him to publish *Cleansing*. I think he would have done it. But what would he have done now, about the utterly out-of-control political situation?

"Come on," Lisette urged me. "You are the most pitiful case I 'ave ever seen. Enough, Claire, enough. I am taking 'im 'ome. I will drive, Alex." She came round the desk as if to pull me out of my chair, but as she did so, the phone rang yet again.

Claire picked it up. "Plumtree Press." Her eyes narrowed; a suspicious smile spread across her face. "Yes, the hero of the free world is here. . . ." She looked at me and raised an eyebrow. "What did you say your name was?" She shook her head in frustration. "Sorry, I can't make out what you're saying."

I reached over and took the receiver as Claire mouthed the words, *"Totally pissed."*

"Alex Plumtree here."

"Alexsh," came a whisper. *" 'S me. 'Manda. Couldn' tell her it was me, could I? Please, you* must *come down here, Alexsh. I mean 't. There's someone in my—Shmino's building, inna cellar . . . inna tunnels."*

"Hang on, Amanda. I'll be over." *What on earth?* I wondered.

I stood, feeling stiffness in every muscle and joint, and pulled the car keys out of my pocket. "I must go and help a friend. Thanks anyway, Lisette. Can you catch the train home?"

"You know jolly well I can. But if you ask me, it is time you let your friends 'elp *you.* Look at yourself."

Actually, I felt better than might have been expected. That blasted book was off my hands, at least. I stepped over to Lisette and gave her an affectionate hug. I hoped she read into it everything I couldn't say in front of Claire: *I understand what a horrible time you must be having because of last night; I'm sorry this latest turn of events hasn't left us time to talk about it. I care.*

"I'll ring you when I get home, Lisette. Claire, thanks for everything. It seems the tide has turned—for Plumtree Press anyway. Now if we can just avoid more riots and killings . . ."

Claire, energised by the sudden intensive press activity, beamed. "I think you've made people stop and think. You've saved the day, Alex."

I wasn't so sure. I waved good-bye to them both and went with all due speed to the Golf. What was Amanda on about, I wondered? It was *most* unlike her to be inebriated. Camomile tea was the farthest I'd seen her venture into the beverage line.

As I buzzed eastward, I thought longingly of my comfortable bed at home. The positive turn of public perception was a relief, though it showed just how fickle people could be. Condemned one week, exalted the next. Book publishing was the strangest and most wonderful of all professions.

And I wouldn't recommend it to anyone.

Not a single light shone from the building when I screeched to a halt in front of what used to be Amanda's Print Shop. I pushed the car door closed softly and ducked in through the unlocked front entrance. Someone had hung a temporary door at some point after the riot. The shop had an abandoned, forlorn air; all of Amanda's equipment but the charred printer's cabinets had vanished. Perhaps Simino was keeping those to restore for his new hotel—they were much in demand as antiques. My footsteps echoed as I crossed the floor, wondering where I'd find Amanda—and in exactly what state.

"Up here," came a whisper from behind an open door at the back of the shop—the one through which Amanda had been abducted. I hurried to the door and pushed through it, and in the dim light saw a flight of stairs to my left. I climbed, putting my hands out to catch myself in case I tripped in the near-total darkness of the staircase.

Amanda whispered, "Quiet, he's shtill down there."

I reached her at the top of the steps. The upper storey appeared to be disused, judging from the bare wood floor and total absence of furniture. Besides Amanda, there was nothing but a small nearly empty bottle of whisky on the bare wooden floorboards. No wonder she was imagining mysterious intruders in the cellar.

Amanda motioned me closer. She smelt like one of the old distilleries that had made such good use of the river Fleet wending its way beneath Clerkenwell. "Sho glad you came," she slurred, draping an arm round my shoulders. Jerkily, she pulled away and hiccuped. "Down . . . there." She pointed down the stairs. "Inna cellar. Clinking round with shumming. I came here to"—she collected herself to enunciate the word—"ruminate"—a proud smile—"on the abshurdty of the human condition. It is *sho abshurd*, Alexsh. Been here f'r a while"—she looked significantly at the bottle on the floor—"I heard 'm come in."

She continued in an intense, confidential whisper, the words spilling over each other in a sloppy muddle. "I think there' shumming shtrange 'bout Shmino and 'is building. Lovegrensh right. Shmino wanted me out for his own shelfish purposheses."

With that pronouncement she hiccuped again loudly. To be honest, I had my own questions about Simino. I put a hand on her shoulder. "Well, Amanda, there's only one thing to do."

"What?" Amanda asked, swaying towards me perilously, wide-eyed as a child.

I smiled at her alcohol-inspired innocence. "I'll go down and see what sort of mischief is being done in the cellar. Even if it *is* Simino's building by rights. But I hope you'll agree—you're in no condition to join me. Stay right here; I'll be back."

She protested, of course. But when she tripped at the top of the stairs and nearly tumbled headlong down, her fall broken only because I was two steps ahead, I said sternly, "Amanda. Please. You'll do yourself an injury."

Grumbling, she acquiesced. She plopped down heavily on the nearest step. "I'll wait here, then."

"You do that." I reached the bottom of the stairs and

started down the flight that descended into the cellar. It was pitch black, and I didn't know what I was heading into. When Amanda had been abducted through that door, she said she'd passed through a tunnel on the way to the House of Detention. I hadn't thought much about it at the time, thinking that perhaps she'd merely *felt* as if she were travelling through a tunnel.

But now, as I descended step by steep step into the cellar, I felt the hair on the back of my neck prickle. Subterranean London was nothing if not an inch-by-inch archaeological feast. So many incarnations of the city had been built on top of one another that you never knew what would be found under this or that old building. It was possible that there was a network of tunnels beneath Clerkenwell, especially because of the Fleet and . . .

Ah, I thought. Eureka! The Order of St. James.

Continuing down the steep, narrow stairs, manoeuvring by the awkward method of foot Braille, I reflected that the Order of St. James had been an impressive and extremely wealthy religious order. The crusading knights had held lands throughout Europe and the Middle East since the twelfth century. Their well, the Clerks' Well, was barely a hundred feet from here, and they might have constructed a series of escape tunnels running from their church to their residential buildings. Like all religious orders, they'd faced jealous opposition from the kings and queens of England over the centuries—especially King Henry VIII in the sixteenth century—and had no doubt planned for the inevitable day they'd fall out of favour.

I stepped onto the stone floor of the cellar at last, my nose detecting the strong stench of mould and damp. It wasn't surprising; the river Fleet ran in a murky stream through the cellars of many of the buildings in Clerkenwell. I stood, willing my eyes to adjust to the inky blackness. My night vision was wretched even in twilight; in complete darkness like this I was twice as blind as anyone else.

As I stood pondering, I glimpsed a dim line of light at the bottom of what I assumed must be a door leading from the cellar. My heart beat faster. Something *was* afoot here.

An underground door? Out of the cellar? Into . . . exactly what?

I stepped toward the light and listened. There was the distant sound of someone splashing deliberately in water, then a muffled four-letter curse that resounded in an eerie echo. I felt for a doorknob, but my fingers closed instead around an old-fashioned latch mounted low on the door. All such old doorways were far short of my height, and I found myself ducking frequently in ancient structures. It was quite possible that the cellar had been there three or four times as long as the Victorian building above it.

I pushed the latch down gently, not wanting to announce my presence. It clicked loudly, and I held my breath. The intermittent noises—scraping, clinking, and splashing—continued uninterrupted from the distance. I took them as reassurance that I hadn't been heard.

The door swung open, miraculously without a squeal, revealing an awesome spectacle. I stood and gaped. In weak light filtering through mist I saw primitive-looking stone walls and ceiling, five feet high. Amanda had been spot on. There was indeed a tunnel here. But whose? And why?

I stepped cautiously forward, crouching uncomfortably as I entered the tunnel, and was immediately rewarded with cold water seeping into my shoes. Walking like the Hunchback of Notre Dame, I advanced slow step by slow step so as not to splash, toward the light and sounds. Amanda had been correct: the tunnel curved, snaking in the direction that would eventually lead to the House of Detention. I couldn't see more than twelve feet ahead. Awestruck, I looked at the stones surrounding me as I slogged forward. Who had placed them so carefully together? And in what century?

Down the tunnel, glass clinked against metal. I inched forward, still rounding the curve toward the light. Suddenly an astonishingly large black creature darted right between my feet, scuttling and splashing through the darkness. Rats. I shivered.

Chilled, I sloshed forward resolutely into the brightening light. But my trepidation grew with each step. At last the tunnel straightened, and I caught a glimpse of a huddled form in a yellow overall. His back was to me, and he wore a yellow hard hat as he crouched over the water. He dipped something into the water, then seemed to hold a sample flask of it up to the light of his battery-powered work lamp.

After a moment's thought, I decided to go back and wait for him to emerge at the top of the cellar stairs. But before I could move, I perceived packing-up-to-go signals—grunts, regular splashes, and movement of the light. Swiftly I went through the door, closed it, and ran to the top of the cellar steps.

Amanda was watching from upstairs. "Well?" she demanded.

"Shhhh." I put a finger to my lips. "Stay there. He's coming."

Footsteps mounted the stairs. I dashed to the light switch. When I heard his footfall on what had been Amanda's domain, I flicked the switch. It was hard to tell what frightened the newcomer more, the sight of my grotesquely swollen and discoloured features, or the shocking blaze of light. The hand holding the lamp shot to his eyes.

"Please," he said, looking utterly terrified, "I'm only taking water samples. See?" He held up a rack of flasks, the kind used in chemical tests.

"Water samples for whom? Why?"

He hesitated and looked at me sideways, lowering the flasks as if preparing for a fight. "What's it to you?"

I glowered at him and took a step closer. He was a foot shorter than I, and slight. Looking at my puffy eye and lip, he must have surmised that I wasn't afraid of a fight.

"All right, all right. Look, I just work for London Water. Mr. Hotchkiss wanted some samples taken from the new water source, that's all."

The new water source. Hmm. "Is it normal procedure for London Water to take samples in secret, at night?"

He shrugged. "When the head of the board says so, anything's normal. Now if you don't mind—"

The head of the board: Richard Hotchkiss.

"Oh, but I *do* mind." I eyed him with all the artificial animosity I could muster, to keep him chatty and obedient. Intimidation wasn't my normal tactic, but in this case it seemed easiest. "Where does that tunnel lead?"

"I don't know, do I? I just take the *samples*."

I'd got what I needed, anyway. "All right, go ahead," I said, and waved him out of the building. He stepped past me with a look of bitter resentment, pulling his tattered dignity round him like a cloak. After loading his samples in the back of his van, parked several spaces behind my car on the street, he revved the engine to life, switched on the headlights, and shot off with an excessive show of speed.

I looked at my watch: eight-thirty. "Amanda. He's gone."

She crept toward me, looking somewhat more sober. "New water shoursh? Down there?"

"Intriguing, isn't it? Let's get some coffee. Have you had anything to eat?"

She shook her head, looking ashamed, and I ushered her out. I switched off the light and took her up Clerkenwell Green to the Well. The pub, of course, had escaped damage in the riot of the previous week. This was not as miraculous as it may seem, since I knew the NUP held its chapel meetings upstairs.

"Why *me*, Alex?" Amanda asked as we walked. She

had passed from the animated stage into the maudlin one. "Hotels, water battles, tunnels . . ."

I shook my head in reply and opened the door to the pub. Light, warmth, and a reassuring buzz of voices and laughter spilled out into the street. "It's been rotten for you, Amanda. But everything will be all right now. Mark my words." Being industrious and intelligent, Amanda would get her business back on its feet somehow, I was certain of it. And as the book was out now, I was confident that no one had reason to trouble Amanda further. As for myself, I resolved that from this moment on I would keep no more secrets—not for Richard Hotchkiss, not for Guy Ferris-Browne—not even for Graeme Abercrombie. I had to tell Max everything as soon as possible, so he could help me find out the truth.

I ordered coffees and dinner, raising my eyebrows slightly at the announcement of the day's special—a trendy goat cheese ravioli in lobster sauce. Dragging a correspondingly inflated number of bills from my wallet, I reflected that perhaps Clerkenwell was becoming a bit *too* posh.

As I joined Amanda at the table she'd found, she looked so forlorn and vulnerable that I felt rising anger toward Hotchkiss and Simino. It incensed me that those two felt they could trample all over her to get what they wanted. Were they in league? I wondered. I looked round the pub; Simino did, of course, own the place. It was quite possible, even probable that he might be there at any given time. Come to think of it, with the water board offices only streets north of here, it was conceivable that Hotchkiss might make an appearance, too. But I saw no sign of either Hotchkiss's imposing presence or Simino's swarthy, well-dressed one.

"You know, Amanda—thank you," I said, looking up at our waiter as the steaming plates, and then the coffees, were set down before us. Amanda tucked into her ravioli greedily, but kept her eyes on me, as ravenous for reassurance as she was for food. "I can see how Simino benefited from reclaiming your print shop, property being what it is here." The stylish crowd assembled in the pub was surely capable of paying several hundred thousand pounds for a house there, not to mention eight quid for pasta in a pub. The street outside was lined with expensive cars.

I picked up my fork and stabbed it into a pillow of pasta, twirling it in the red sauce. "But what I *don't* see is why Hotchkiss is involved, sneaking samples by night from the water in the tunnel—through Simino's building." I put the bite into my mouth and chewed, closing my eyes briefly as the goat cheese, lobster, and pasta blended serendipitously on my tongue. Definitely worth the eight quid. "This stuff's rather decent," I said, forking up another bite. Amanda nodded; hers was nearly gone.

"Surely people can't go about taking water from beneath London and calling it their own. . . ."

Then it came to me. What had Hotchkiss said, at the county boundary meeting? That there was *"more water bubbling about beneath London than anyone would believe."* And he'd instantly looked as if he wished he could take his words back. I well remembered his odd expression of remorse, because any lack of confidence was unthinkable in the baron of the road construction and water industries.

Suddenly I felt something akin to fear sweep over me. I had a bizarre image of Hotchkiss assembling a subterranean kingdom, with his road construction excavations, the watery tunnels, and Amanda's cellar linked together in a sort of evil empire. Did the London authorities even know about these tunnels? Had the man in the yellow uniform been on official London Water business? Or on Hotchkiss's *private* business? Perhaps Hotchkiss wanted a water supply of his own. . . .

I ate, deep in thought, as Amanda sighed and sat back.

"Much better," she said. "Thanks, Alex. Food works wonders on a liquid stomach." She picked up her coffee cup and sipped. "You know what I want to do?"

I shook my head.

"I want to perform a printer's ritual, and I want to do it tonight." She looked thoughtful; I waited. "One of the greatest English printers, Cobden-Sanderson, of Doves Press, threw the special font he'd designed for his ultimate masterpiece into the river Thames."

"Why on earth would he do that?"

Amanda smiled as if she had a secret. "Because he didn't ever want anyone else to duplicate it, or use it again."

"Ah. A symbolic gesture. You don't want anyone to go through what you have for *Cleansing*."

"That's the general idea. I'm going to put it all in the past—including Simino. Except I'll throw my set of Caslon—the one I cast for the original typesetting at my shop—into the Clerks' Well. Come with me?"

"How fitting, for a Clerkenwell printer." After all we'd been through, I couldn't say I looked forward to a further expedition to the well that night. But it seemed important to her, and I couldn't bear the thought of her performing such a melancholy task alone. The way she'd felt earlier that evening, she might decide to throw herself in, too. "Of course I'll come with you."

I drove to Amanda's nearby Islington flat and waited while she dashed in and picked up the font. She returned to the Golf with an open cardboard box—very unassuming for such an elegant set of type—and I piloted her back to Farringdon Lane and the well. A sense of quiet jubilation permeated our little outing, as if in this way she could declare victory over Simino and her ex-friends at the NUP.

Amanda led the way to a modern glass door and began to rattle with her keys.

"The well's in *here*?" I asked, noting the name of a magazine firm on the door.

"I know—you'd never guess," she said, and stuck her key in the lock.

"How'd you get a key?"

"Simino lent me one and never asked for it back." She pushed open the door, and we stepped into a vestibule that contained *another* glass door. Amanda applied her key to that lock, and we were in. She switched on the lights. I saw that the well had been enshrined in a small room of its own, with large posters and facsimiles of old maps mounted all round to tell its story. The well itself was down a short flight of stairs, which we duly descended.

"It never ceases to amaze me, the difference in the level of the top of the well and present-day London," Amanda told me. "At pavement level, we must be six feet above the top of the well. Six feet of difference between the surface of ancient and modern London, built up over as many hundred years. Think how many bombed-out buildings, roads, graves, and other relics of humanity it took to add *six feet*." We both regarded the rather unassuming well—recognisable only because of the wooden circle that covered it. It was perhaps three or three and a half feet in diameter—by no means huge.

The Well was once the water supply for the Order of St. James and the other religious orders located outside the City of London, I read from the placard. "The Clerks of the Priory held their passion plays here during Lent—thus the name Clerkenwell. Hmm. Hard to believe this place was ever considered countryside." For the first time I understood why the surrounding streets had names like Saffron Hill and Herbal Hill. The monks had gardened there.

Amanda shrugged. "Outside the City's square mile, but not by much."

"Here, let me open the lid for you." As I bent down to

do so, I heard rattling at the door. I'd flipped one half of the heavy wood-plank lid open when I straightened to see Simino and Hotchkiss entering the outer vestibule.

"Oh, no!" Amanda hissed. "I don't want to see *him*!"

"No way out now," I muttered, and bent over to open the other half, slightly curious as to the appearance of the water in the well.

Amanda looked cornered, clutching her cardboard box.

"Well, hello, Amanda!" Simino boomed. "It's my girl. 'Evening, Plumtree. We saw you from outside and thought you'd like to hear the good news." He advanced until he stood down at our level, and came to Amanda, putting an arm round her. Amanda closed her eyes, as if steeling herself for the ordeal.

"Plumtree! The man of the hour!" Hotchkiss proclaimed, following Simino into the room.

"Good Lord—what's happened to your face?" Simino asked, viewing my injuries with distaste.

"Slight accident delivering Lord Chenies's special edition," I replied.

"Isn't he something?" Hotchkiss beamed. "That's a Merchant Taylors man for you. *'A little accident.'* The story's all over the airwaves, about the NUP thugs roughing you up! Simino here caught me at the end of a late meeting at the water company—more political fracas, I'm afraid—and asked me to come and celebrate with him." Suddenly he seemed to realise that he hadn't met Amanda. "I'm sorry," he said. "Richard Hotchkiss."

Amanda was tongue-tied. She looked relieved to have a reprieve from Simino, but still stood stiffly in place.

"Amanda Morison," I answered for her. "Amanda was our printer for Lord Chenies's special edition."

Hotchkiss's eyes showed he was aware of what this meant. He shook his head. "You've been through a great deal, Miss Morison. I'm sorry. Damned bleeding hearts."

Amanda looked away. She was actually one of those

bleeding hearts. Or *had* been until they'd ruined her life and livelihood.

"What is it that you're celebrating?" I asked Hotchkiss and Simino, trying to be civil.

"It's a great day for Clerkenwell!" Simino's reply echoed off the walls and ceiling in the small room. *Great day . . . great day . . . for Clerkenwell . . . for Clerkenwell . . .*

"In fact," he continued, "it was *so* good, I decided to stop by after Hotchkiss's meeting and tell him. We're off to the pub in a moment—perhaps you'll join us?"

"Thanks, but we've just come from there—it's been a very long day, I'm afraid, for both of us. What are you celebrating?" I asked again, hoping the subject change would get us off the hook.

"Oh, yes—the National Trust has just raised the well to National Landmark status. You know what that means," Simino said, clearly chuffed. I'm sure Amanda and I merely looked blank. "No? It means that Clerkenwell will receive funds to improve the tourist entrance to the well here. There will be so many more visitors passing through—it's a boon for the entire community, not to mention a long-deserved honour for the Clerks' Well. A real silver lining of the damaging riot. A terrible tragedy for poor Amanda here, but ironically the neighbourhood will be better off for it. Lots of insurance money and improvements, don't you know."

My wild suspicion that Simino had orchestrated the riot for his own gain was beginning to seem more and more realistic. I was incredulous that he had the gall to elaborate on it in Amanda's presence. The man displayed a total lack of sensitivity.

For some reason, it hit me only then that Hotchkiss's water was directly beneath Simino's 'hotel' property. Of course . . . they had to be partners. Hotchkiss needed Simino to have complete control of the *land* to grant him rights to the water.

"I have a plan to re-create the Lenten plays by the well," he continued, "just as the Order presented them hundreds of years ago. It'll be an attraction for people round the world, like the Passion Play at Oberammergau or the Mozart Festival in Salzburg."

Amanda stiffly said, "Alex, we should go. I need to get back."

I understood. It had to be agony for her, thinking of a hotel going in at the site of her print shop—all to service coaches full of cultural pilgrims from America. "Right," I said. "It's been quite a day. Lovely to see you, and—er, thanks, Richard."

"Oh, no, don't go just yet. I see you've opened the cover," Simino said, stepping closer.

"Yes." I saw my chance to ask them about the water in person. It should be safe enough; Hotchkiss didn't know I'd seen the man taking samples. "I was wondering . . . does London Water manage this water now? How does that work?"

"Interesting question." Hotchkiss nodded. "And my historic speciality. It used to be that people owned water that ran on, or under, their property. But of course that's all changed these days—brave new world, you know— aside from a few antiquated loopholes in the law." Here he exchanged a casual look with Simino, which nonetheless seemed loaded with meaning. One of those antiquated loopholes no doubt applied to the tunnel that led from Simino's property.

"This"—Simino gestured toward the well—"techni- cally belongs to London Water now. But in the monks' day, it was absolutely theirs. Incidentally, the water is only about five feet below the surface in the well, which if you think about it is rather interesting." He gazed at us expec- tantly, as if at any moment we would grasp the signifi- cance of this fact.

We didn't.

"Tube stations in the area are, as you know, *much* deeper than that. The water level is almost dangerously high in London now. It's a well-kept secret that certain Tube stations must be pumped clear of water every morning before opening—or City gents would have to wear their wellies to work. You see, now that the distilleries, paper factories, and other water-dependent businesses have moved out of London, there's a *surfeit* of water. Ha!" He laughed, as if to mock those who worried about water shortages.

His comment about water bubbling about beneath London now made more sense than ever.

Amanda blurted, "I must go. But first . . ."

She leaned forward, hurling her metal bits of type out of the box. Before they'd even hit the water, Simino, perhaps believing that she'd accidentally dropped something, or had stumbled, was grappling with her. She uttered a cry of horror. I watched in disbelief as Amanda pitched forward into the narrow black hole of the well. I reached for her but was too late. She'd disappeared. We couldn't make out anything through the murky water; Amanda was nowhere to be seen.

Simino and Hotchkiss stared in horror, neither moving. When she didn't immediately reappear, I plunged in after her. In my former life as leader of flotilla sailing holidays, I'd rescued plenty of people who were better drinkers than they were sailors.

I heard Hotchkiss cry, *"Plumtree! No!"*, his voice receding as I plummeted downward, feet first into the narrow hole. The undisturbed mould of centuries found its way up my nose as I splashed down, instantly engulfed in icy putrefaction. The water stung in the cuts on my head and face. My forehead grazed the side of the well, and my feet struck Amanda underwater. Struggling to reach her in the narrow space, I grabbed a handful of her blouse and kicked madly to propel us upward. Amanda seemed limp;

she'd probably hit her head on the way down. I popped up and got Amanda's head above water, only to feel it fall back limply. I held her face above the surface, struggling to tread water.

Hotchkiss's horror-stricken face appeared in the circle of light at the top of the well. "Hang on! We're going for help!" he bellowed. I was a strong swimmer, but nothing prepared me for the sudden darkness that descended on us. The lights seemed to have gone out . . .

Had they left us for good? And turned off the lights as they'd gone?

The darkness was more terrifying than the well.

Surely . . .

My outrage at Simino and Hotchkiss was overwhelmed only by my instinct for self-preservation. Suddenly I found myself fully occupied saving myself from Amanda, who had come round and was hysterical. *"I can't swim! Can't—"* She kicked against me as best she could in the claustrophobic cylinder, screaming as she tried to scratch at my eyes with her nails. She sank her fingers into my hair and pulled.

"Listen to me!" I bellowed. *"Calm down!"*

But she was too panicked to hear me. She lashed out at my head with her arms and fists, twisting out of my grasp, while I struggled to clutch a bit of her clothing anywhere. We would both go under, I feared, if she carried on like this.

Finally she wrenched free of my grip, sinking like a stone in the slimy water. I felt her against my legs and groped blindly after her. My fingertips brushed the end of her braid. I gripped the thick plait and pulled, but in the slimy ooze it slithered out of my grasp like an eel. Running out of air, I went deeper, desperately reaching. I got her head in my hands and pulled her to me, then grasped her tightly round the waist with one arm and kicked us both toward the air—again.

Amanda struggled feebly, coughing up water and gasping for breath. I held her close to me as I treaded water, keeping my movements economical, breathing in a steady rhythm. As the moments passed, she settled into an exhausted, shuddering deadweight. Flashes of claustrophobic panic struck as my feet hit the edges of the well with each kick. *One more minute, one more minute,* I told myself in a hollow litany. My arm muscles began to shake from the effort of holding Amanda. I could continue for a good long while, but not all night.

Where were Hotchkiss and Simino?

CHAPTER FIFTEEN

⚓

I read the newspapers avidly. It is my one form of continuous fiction.

ANEURIN BEVAN, BRITISH LABOUR MP

THINGS COULD BE WORSE, I TOLD MYSELF. WE COULD already be dead, for instance. But to have come so far— through the book's sabotage, Amanda's abduction, Lord Chenies's death, vilification by the nation's press, the eventual printing of the book, and then acclaim—it didn't make sense to die *now*. Simino would no doubt profit from our death, using the story of our demise to titillate the coaches full of tourists. *"A controversial printer and publisher accidentally drowned in the well, and ever since, if you listen carefully, you can hear moaning. . . ."*

It was growing harder by the minute to sustain Amanda's weight and keep us both above water. As the moments passed, I knew I had to do more than maintain the status quo. I had to find a way to get us out. And yet escape seemed impossible.

At that moment, when I had despaired of help ever coming, the lights flashed on again. My rage at their ever having been extinguished rose again, mixed with immense relief. I heard shouts, and bright lights shone directly into the well. For the first time I actually saw the murk in which we'd been submerged. The water wore bits of green froth, globs of which Amanda and I sported grotesquely. Within moments a collapsible wooden ladder was lowered into the water next to us, and a fireman clad in waterproof gear began his descent. He was with us in mere seconds, asking Amanda if she could manage the climb herself. I thought she was past it, but she nodded.

"I'll help you," he said. The sweetest three words—well, almost—in the English language.

The fireman got Amanda between himself and the ladder, and between the two of them, she got to the top. As I climbed up the ladder, I heard Amanda say through chattering teeth, "Keep him away from me!" I knew she was talking about Simino.

I hoisted myself out of that evil pit, shivering uncontrollably. Someone wrapped a blanket round me and suggested that we go along to hospital. I heard myself say that all I needed was to go home, thank you very much. Hotchkiss was right there, repeating how sorry he was this had happened and what a fine Merchant Taylors lad I was.

Amanda's face was a pasty white as she sat near the lip of the well, wrapped in her own blanket. I watched as Simino advanced toward her. She shrilled, "Stay away from me!" He backed off, looking wounded. She clearly believed that he had pushed her into the well. I wondered.

Hotchkiss knelt next to me. "Really, Plumtree, most extraordinary the way you dived in after her. Let me drive you home."

"Thanks, Richard," I said. "But I'm fine. Thanks for bringing help."

Amanda wanted the police to take her to a friend's house, though I offered a room at the Orchard. They took her off, and as I staggered to the door, my arms and legs felt like overcooked pasta. I kept the blanket and revved the heat up to high for most of the journey to Chorleywood.

Along the way, I was beleaguered by deeply disturbing thoughts. *Had* Simino pushed Amanda? Now that I knew how ruthless he'd been over the hotel property, I could see that it wasn't out of the question. But why should he want to kill her? Perhaps he suspected she knew . . .

I felt a creeping uneasiness about Simino, Hotchkiss, Ferris-Browne and his unions, and Abercrombie himself. If the special edition had prompted killings and riots, what would the days immediately preceding the election bring? Now *those* were big stakes.

Upon arriving at the Orchard, I threw every scrap of sodden clothing in the rubbish bin. My shoes alone survived; I left them outside. God only knew exactly what bizarre life-forms lurked in that water, and no doubt it was better that way. Upstairs, I took out my contact lenses, which had survived miraculously, and put them in the case to soak. Then, after fiercely showering every last bit of muck off, I ran a deep, hot bath with my last ounce of energy and relaxed in the steaming tub. I doubted I'd ever be completely warm—or clean—again.

Grabbing the phone from the edge of the tub, I rang Sarah. Again, no answer in her room. No answer in Ian's room. And it was midnight. What on earth was going on there in Switzerland?

I rang Max, only to get his machine. I left a long message detailing what I'd learned about Simino's Clerkenwell land (and how he'd obtained it), Hotchkiss's water and his private collection of artifacts. Then I closed my eyes.

At three in the morning I woke up in an extremely unpleasant bath full of cold water. I towelled off, dressed in warm pyjamas, and descended to the kitchen. While I heated some milk, I listened to my phone messages, one of which was from Max. It was disturbingly intense.

"Alex, I need to talk to you." Pause. *"Look, I just want to apologise in advance for intruding on your business—however peripherally. We're about to go out for the evening, but ring me when you get a chance. Until then you must believe that I only wanted to do the right thing."* He rang off.

With dread, I contemplated what his message might mean, but found I had little imagination left. I drank my milk, climbed the stairs, and fell into bed.

The morning dawned achingly beautiful, the sun casting a warm, bright rectangle on my duvet. In the first instant of awakening, I knew there was a dark cloud overhead, a reason I was supposed to be miserable. In the next moment, the stench and slime of the well, and the vision of Amanda falling, came back to me. Oh, yes—and Max's phone message. Not to mention Sarah and the rest of it.

I closed my eyes again and recalled that it was April first—April Fool's Day.

After coffee and toast, I dressed and drove straight to Lisette's. She hurried out to the car in her heels, smiling bravely as she climbed in. A characteristic wave of floral perfume drifted in with her.

By the time we reached the bottom of her drive, I'd told her about Amanda's and my little excursion into Clerkenwell's latest historic landmark. She clucked like a mother hen and wrapped me in a hug that was as much for me as for Amanda. I stopped there for a moment, unable to drive with her arms around me. "It is a good thing that Sarah is coming to take care of you, yes?" Tears streamed down her cheeks, and I thought, *If only George would come home to take care of you.* Her emotion, always close to the surface, threatened to make *me* lose my composure, too. Abruptly, I slammed the floodgates closed before they could be breached.

It was inevitable, I suppose, that Helena Hotchkiss should be leaving her home at precisely the same moment, evidently back from the Euro-Enviro Summit in

Verbier, Switzerland. She screeched to a halt, blocking the drive.

"Oh, Alex—have you talked to Sarah lately?" She eyed Lisette, smirking.

I didn't answer.

"Maybe you should." She waved snidely before moving on.

"Cow," Lisette said, one of her favourite insults for women she disliked. "I wish she'd stayed in Switzerland." I looked at Lisette and saw twin rivulets of mascara painting her face, like a tragic clown. She took a shivering breath as I pulled my handkerchief from a pocket and daubed at her cheeks.

I handed Lisette the handkerchief, patted her knee, and pulled out into the lane. Moments later I steered the Golf into the roundabout feeding onto the motorway, past the *first* place where Lisette and I had stopped on another tearful morning. Helena really had a nerve to accuse us of roadside snogging.

There was no space for the Golf in the square that morning; I had to park on Bedford Row. As Lisette and I passed a newsagent's on our walk to the Press, I caught a glimpse of the Watch. I stopped dead in my tracks as I glimpsed its headline: "LONDON WATER CHAIRMAN USES POSITION TO CREATE RIVAL BUSINESS." And a subhead within the story: *"Historic artifacts stolen from excavation site."* My jaw dropped when I saw the byline: Maximilian Plumtree.

Max worked fast.

In a trance, I stepped inside the newsagent's and bought the *Watch*. Lisette read over my shoulder as I drank in the copy. Max's phone message made sense now. An unnamed source was quoted throughout the article. A separate editorial called for Hotchkiss to come forward with the relics for the sake of history and science, and also demanded the introduction of laws preventing builders and excavators from hiding finds to keep projects on schedule.

We walked to the corner, past the Trades Union Group's great white box of a building. As we passed it, I saw a young man come out the front door and hesitate. He seemed somehow startled to see me there, and—guilty, perhaps. Muscles bulged beneath his light grey business suit, and he sported a thick shock of dark, wavy hair. In the next moment he turned and walked nonchalantly in the opposite direction from us. Who could *he* have been, and why had he been so surprised to see me?

Back at the Press I took refuge in my office, but should have known that there could be no refuge, anywhere, from the forces unleashed by my brother's journalistic prowess. I'd wanted him to investigate, but I wasn't sure I'd intended for him to reveal everything immediately. A bit of quiet sniffing round was more what I had in mind.

Skimming another article under the headline, *"Sir Richard Hotchkiss Asked to Resign,"* I saw that Richard had indeed lost everything. But equally fascinating was an article a bit lower on the page. *"Clerkenwell Property Mogul Simino Brother of* Cleansing *Author."* Max had gone on to say that an unidentified source—there he was yet again, I noticed—had learned that Simino, while pretending to be a champion of fledgling Clerkenwell businesses, actually did his best to ruin local businesses and their property. This allowed him to purchase their land for less money, or receive permission to rebuild on a site that otherwise would have been protected. The *Watch* had learned that Simino's financial backers had withdrawn their support for the hotel development in light of the scandal over how the property was obtained.

I began to wonder how many of Amanda's misfortunes had been caused by the man she'd thought was her friend, Anthony Simino.

I reached for the phone and dialled. "Max. I've just seen the papers."

"Alex. I don't suppose you're terrifically pleased with me."

"I'm not angry—perhaps a bit surprised. I didn't know you'd go public with everything so quickly."

"But, Alex, you're not going to believe this. . . . I've known this stuff for more than a week. When you rang last night and left a message saying exactly what I'd got from another source, I couldn't believe it."

"Hang on . . . you *already* knew?"

"From my source."

I felt an unreasonable anger with him for not having told me earlier, but I did my best to keep it out of my voice. "Who," I asked, "is your source?"

Max sighed. "Alex, this is very important: my source is a good man. He doesn't deserve to be ruined by the mess around him."

Cruelly, I said, "I'm not the one who reveals the secrets in this family."

After a moment he sighed. "Right. Fair enough. But I'm trusting you not to drag this mess to his door. No one else knows, not even my editor at the paper. I was able to substantiate it all from other sources, once this man gave me the story." A reluctant pause. "His name is Robert Lovegren. He's with—"

"—the Order of St. James," I interrupted, surprised. "I've met him."

Max continued. "He knew that the road construction was going on through a site that was thought to have been the mausoleum of the order, ages ago. He'd been watching the construction from the very start, without attracting attention—who notices a little old man in a flat cap watching the earthmovers?—and saw some of the artifacts being removed from the site.

"Instinct told him big things were afoot, and he saw Hotchkiss arriving not much later at the caravan that served as the construction team's site office. So he took a

stroll behind the caravan and overheard a discussion between Hotchkiss and the job foreman. He heard
Hotchkiss say to 'keep those things under wraps,' that
stopping for a team of experts would 'suck the profits
right out' of the job. Then my source"—I noticed he still
preferred not to call Lovegren by name—"saw Hotchkiss
walk away with a closed box. He guessed Hotchkiss was
going to keep the treasures for himself."

"He guessed right. I saw them in his house. How did
you get on to Lovegren, for goodness' sake?"

"I didn't—he got on to me. Rang me one day, roughly
the time your troubles started. In fact, just a couple of
days before you came to dinner that night. I didn't want to
tell you then, because I hadn't checked it all out."

"And how did you find out about Simino and Lord
Chenies?"

I could picture Max at home at Watersmeet, flipping a
pencil between his fingers as he spoke. He could make it
travel round his hand with surprising speed, transferring
it from between his index and third fingers to the next,
and on round his hand in a little wheel. Such dexterity, I
thought—manual and moral.

"Well," he said, "this was the part that trespassed onto
your patch ever so slightly, because it pertained to Chenies. I had no idea the rest of it would mean anything to
you, when I wrote it." He sighed. "My source told me. It
was in the Order's records of all the local affairs. At one
time it was the charter of the Order in Clerkenwell to
place unwanted children and orphans in homes. The
neighbourhood wasn't always so prosperous, you know.
All those prisons, and the brothels and slums of years gone
by—lots of opportunity for Christian ministry and knightly
chivalry toward unwanted and orphaned children.

"I asked your friend Martyn Blakely—great to have
him back in our quarter, by the way—to corroborate from
the parish record, as there were no official birth records.

He looked at me as if I were the Antichrist, and asked how I knew about the record. That was all a bit odd—I thought *all* parishes had records. Anyway, I saw from his face that it was true—our Lord Chenies was really a Simino of Clerkenwell. Martyn couldn't bluff his way out of it, and later he even showed me the record. He seemed greatly affected by it all, I suppose because he was there when they found Lord Chenies's body."

I sat in silence, struck by the fact that it was another book—the parish record, of all things—that had set this particular lethal machine in motion. Inevitably, when books contained uncomfortable truths, the Almighty set forces in motion to chip away relentlessly until the truth was revealed. It had happened three times now to me at the Press in as many years. The power of the written word, indeed.

Suddenly I felt so tired that I thought the phone might drop out of my hand. I told Max I'd talk to him later and rang off.

At ten o'clock my telephone rang.

"How could you *do* this to me, Plumtree?" Hotchkiss's voice boomed, with the full force of his fury. It was actually a bit frightening to have such a powerful person so angry with me. "I save your life, and this is how you repay me? By jumping to unfounded conclusions from a workman taking samples?"

I could hear him breathing like a bull in heat on the other end of the line. "And listen, Plumtree, you were taken into my family's trust, through a very vulnerable, unstable daughter, I might add"—I nearly choked at this—"and you've abused that trust at every turn. *Publicising* my private collection of artifacts. Helena probably showed them to you. And to think that I was going to offer you a seat on the board of directors at Merchant Taylors this very month."

"Why did you switch off the lights last night at the well when you went for help?" My voice was deadpan.

There was a pause. "*What?*"

"The lights in the little vestibule, at the well. You turned them off when you left. You knew we were in the water."

He made a high, exasperated sound. "Damn it, man! What do lights have to do with anything? They're on a bloody *timer*, aren't they? Simino showed me once. So they aren't left on for days at a time. What does it *matter*?" The enormity of what I was saying hit him at last. "Good Lord, Plumtree, you don't think . . . !"

I said nothing.

He blustered. "That's preposterous," and with fresh vitriol went on to tell me that not only had I caused the borough of Islington to cancel his contract for the road construction project, but I'd caused his new water company to perish. The council had already been on to him that morning. "Simino cut me out of the deal, which hinged on access to that ridiculous little print shop property. It was all perfectly legal. When I think of what I've lost because of you . . . He says he can't afford to be associated with me. You—your brother—painted me a villain in these newspaper articles. Simino says he won't sully his hotel and other developments with any connection to me. It must be convenient, having a direct pipeline into the *Watch*. You've well and truly ruined my life, Plumtree. But you'll pay. Wait and see."

As I heard him slam the phone down, I didn't doubt it.

The mention of paying for other people's mistakes reminded me of the lawsuit. I rang Neville and asked how we were faring. He said he hadn't heard a squeak in response to his letter, but that was a well-known tactic. The cagey old solicitor said he still had a few tricks up his sleeve, not to worry. I thought briefly of asking him about the legality of a private spring under real estate in London, but decided there was no longer any point. Hotchkiss's plans were up the spout.

The rest of the day passed in a comforting deluge of details. There were cheques to sign, contracts to approve, and end-of-the-month financial reports to inspect.

At teatime, Nicola popped in with a cuppa. I accepted it gratefully.

"I have good news, of a sort. Advance copies are in." She whipped a copy of the trade paperback of *Cleansing* out from where she'd hid it in her lap. I reached out and took it, studying the cover.

If I looked at it objectively and pretended it was just another book that hadn't cost lives and untold misery, I could appreciate it. The cover art was a photograph of a waterfall our art director had found at a picture library. The huge stream of water poured furiously off the edge of a dizzying precipice, dashing the rocks below. The title, *Cleansing,* was printed in tall, elegant white upper- and lowercase letters, in the grey sky above the waterfall. Simple. Eloquent. Perfect.

But in no way worth what it had cost.

"It's fine," I said, after a moment. "But I never should have taken it on."

"I know."

"Nicola, I'm just a bit worried about something. I wondered if you might consider helping me."

"Of course."

"I'm afraid that—" I didn't quite know what to call Ferris-Browne in front of her. Her father? Guy? Ferris-Browne? "I'm afraid that Guy Ferris-Browne will be planning something far more momentous than the publication of *Cleansing,* now that our little scheme to re-elect Abercrombie has failed. At this point I've heard from a couple of different sources that he has ties to unions all over Europe and wants to organise them into a European super-union. That makes me wonder if he had a hand in organising the Clerkenwell riot, which was largely made up of NUP members and his friend Helena's HIT members. I also understand that he has high ambitions for himself within the EU. I don't quite know why I think this, but something is niggling at me that he might be responsible for Lord Chenies's death."

She regarded me steadily. "And you want me to try to find out what he's planning next."

I nodded.

"I'll do it, but I don't think I can go to him many more times over this."

"Of course not. And if you'd rather not . . ."

"No. It's no problem."

"Thanks, Nicola."

My watch said it was half past four; a good time to call Sarah. But again I was disappointed. No answer at all. Now my disquiet was overwhelming.

But in the next moment I was pleasantly surprised when the phone rang and it was Sarah. "Good evening, my love," I began with some trepidation. "I just tried to ring you—you must have only just got in."

"Oh—yes."

I tried not to jump to conclusions, though only a fool would fail to see that she wasn't staying in her own room anymore, and making no attempt to hide it. "I've been desperate to speak to you, darling; we've had a bit more excitement round here."

"Oh, no," she said. "I'm sorry. What *now*?"

"I'll tell all someday."

"You're all right, though?"

"Of course."

"Good, because I've been dreaming of an idyllic holiday starting tomorrow at a quintessentially English country house called the Orchard. It's quite charming, really, with the sweetest man who owns it all. And it has some very famous hedges."

She sounded herself again, which was encouraging, though I groaned inwardly at the mention of the hedges. "So . . . the wedding's on?"

I could picture her smiling in the pause. "Oh, Alex. The wedding is *so* on." She hesitated for a moment. "You've got all those nutcases locked up over there now, haven't you?"

"I assure you, you will be perfectly safe." I hoped she didn't notice the lack of a strong answer in the affirmative. Hotchkiss and Simino were still out there somewhere, along with the entire NUP. No, the nutters weren't locked up. Chances were they never would be. "I'll defend you with my life," I said with mock drama, but meant it.

Besides, I asked myself, what more could possibly happen?

With a bit of peace and quiet at last, I made my way out to the barn and had a go at my bulging drawers of Caslon. The shoulder marks Amanda found on my type had piqued my curiosity; I was certain they meant something. I yanked open the door and pressed the switch for light. The barn was illuminated in all its earthy charm and comfort, along with the row of printer's cabinets. I stepped across the chilly concrete to the cabinet Amanda had used for *Cleansing*, and slid out the drawer. Pulling up a stool, I picked up my father's magnifying glass and took the lowercase letter *a* in my hand. A tiny number 4 peered up at me, magnified, on the flat surface below the character itself. I went next to the rectangle containing the lowercase *b*'s, and found that each of them bore a microscopic *e*. I continued to pick up the pieces of type one by one, certain that a pattern could be found there. After *g* I resorted to jotting down the shoulder-mark letters with a pencil on a scrap of paper, but all I found was gibberish. After the letter *l* the letters began repeating themselves: I decided I'd been mistaken about a pattern, or wasn't clever enough to figure it out. The case stared up at me like a giant, hopeless jigsaw puzzle.

That done, I pottered about creating a welcoming broadsheet for Sarah. What were the most suitable words of love . . . ah, yes—Elizabeth Barrett Browning's finest would do. I decided upon *"How do I love thee? Let me count the ways . . . "* and set to it. I was awkward at placing the type in the composing stick; my large fingers, callused from rowing, barely felt the tiny letters. Actually picking them up and aligning them in the stick was a bit like grasping grains of rice and standing them on end with woolly gloves on. Feeling terrifically clumsy, after an hour I'd set the entire sonnet and began locking it into the chase, along with an italic *"For Sarah"* at the top and *"From Alex"* at the bottom. I decided against fancy patterns round the edges. Setting the type had been triumph enough. Now to see if I could actually ink the press. . . .

I found a container of soy ink and poured a small amount into the automatic inking mechanism, which sat on top of and to the left of the Minerva Cropper handpress like a little chimney. It would take several impressions to get the ink distributed and the poem printed properly, I speculated. I set a piece of the fine, thick rag paper waiting on the back table into the press and began to work the treadle. The press swung into motion, the two halves of its clamshell-like mechanism moving together, clasping the paper, and then releasing it. On the first impression, I didn't have enough packing behind my paper, and the impression was far too faint. No emphatic kiss at all. That would never do for Sarah.

I tossed it aside, slid several extra sheets of paper behind the tympan so the type would bite more deeply into my paper, and reached for a fresh sheet. This time it came out a bit better, though still much too faint; I admired it for a moment before fingering yet another sheet. The black letters were lovely in their simplicity and starkness on the plain white page; they screamed their message in the beautiful curves and lines that Caslon had designed hundreds of years ago. Actually, I corrected myself, it was the spaces *between* the letters that spoke so eloquently; that was what the eye actually saw, or so my literacy tutor had told me. With confidence I set another sheet in the press and pumped the treadle. This time the product was perfect.

Feeling inordinately pleased with myself, I admired the warm glow of the lights in the house as I traipsed back through the garden carrying my trophy. The house was ready and waiting for Sarah; it was almost as if it, too, anticipated her arrival with an expectant air. The smell of imminent rain was all around me; the perfumes of a damp night on the sceptred isle were intensified by the mist: coal smoke and fresh, wet vegetation.

I went in through the library doors, then locked them behind me.

I still had work to do in the kitchen: I wanted to prepare my speciality, vegetable soup, for Sarah. The potatoes boiled and bubbled as I chopped carrots, broccoli, onions, and took chicken broth out of the freezer. I opened frozen packages of corn, green beans, and peas and added them to the mixture. When I knew that the flavours had blended, I turned off the gas burner and let it all cool before ladling it into several small containers for the fridge and freezer.

I had no misgivings, no instinctive feeling that I shouldn't let her come. After all, what more could possibly happen?

CHAPTER SIXTEEN

———◆———

Unkempt about those hedges blows
An English unofficial rose.

RUPERT BROOKE, *The Old Vicarage, Grantchester*

I SLEPT FOR TEN HOURS THAT NIGHT AND WOKE UP
feeling more refreshed than I had in weeks. I plucked the
Tempus out of the potted bay laurel on the front porch
with a smile. What did it matter if the delivery boy threw
it there? Plodding contentedly back to the kitchen table, I
shook my head, marvelling that I could ever have been
disturbed by such an insignificant detail.

I tucked into my coffee and toast over the paper, taking my time. I had declared a day's holiday for myself, anticipating Sarah's arrival later that day. The *Tempus* had
picked up the stories about Hotchkiss and Simino from
Max's lead. In amazement I read that mild-mannered
Robert Lovegren had already purchased the three buildings Simino had planned for the hotel, including the
building that had housed Amanda's Print Shop. The article explained that Lovegren planned to offer the buildings
for charitable use, primarily to health-oriented organisations that would complement the St. James ambulance
men's work. His hope was to acquire as much Clerkenwell

real estate as possible on the priory's original site to restore it to the original service of the Order: helping people.

I idled away the next hour, pottering about the house, making everything just so for Sarah. At the linen closet, I lifted out the coverlet my grandmother had embroidered with many-coloured varieties of roses, all punctiliously labelled with their Latin names. I carried it to the room that I still thought of as my parents' and laid it out on the bed. Gazing round the spacious room, I reflected that it would be Sarah's and mine after the wedding.

Sarah had always stayed in the guest room when she'd visited before, and I hoped our new room would please her. It was the largest in the house, with a king-size bed and an ultramodern adjoining bathroom with the centre-piece of a claw-footed bathtub. But the bedroom's most noticeable feature was a huge bank of windows overlook-ing the back garden. I swung one open to let the mild air into the room, enjoying the expanse of the garden with its gazebo and gone-to-seed grass tennis court. Standing in the warmth of the sunlight, I turned back to the room to give it a final inspection.

My mother had decorated it shortly before her death, using an elegant deep green paisley fabric studded with dusty pink roses. An antique desk stood in one corner, its leather top glistening with the gloss on which Emily, the old friend who cleaned the house, prided herself. My eye fell on the empty bedside table. *Books.* I needed to put some special books out for Sarah—something she'd like. I ran down to the library and plucked out an attractively bound volume of poetry by Rainer Maria Rilke, and a fac-simile of *The Fleuron*, one of the books about the art of printing that Amanda's great-uncle had published. Sarah liked to learn about specific areas of publishing I encoun-tered in my work; this month, it was definitely typogra-phy and printing.

The crystal water carafe with its glass rested next to

the lamp; I'd fill it with fresh, cool water when she arrived. The only thing missing was flowers. I would find some at the airport and greet her with them.

On the drive to Heathrow I reflected how different life would be with Sarah living at the house. Not just now, before the wedding, but forever. When she visited, the place changed completely: she brought new life to old rooms, a fresh light that seemed to illuminate them. I loved hearing her voice drift up the stairs and down the halls; loved seeing her sitting on the furniture, in the kitchen, searching through the fridge.

At the airport I waited outside customs just beyond the door, clutching a dozen long-stemmed pink roses that perfumed the air around me. I was just sticking my nose into them for another whiff when I saw a leg in plaster, propped up on a wheelchair, come through the door. Some poor devil run amok on the pistes, I speculated. But in the next moment I saw that my beloved fiancée was attached to the unfortunate leg, pushed by a porter in my direction. I was struck, at first sight of her face, by how extremely well she looked—long, dark hair shining, mouth curved into a breathless smile.

I finally recovered enough to call out her name, duck under the rope, and hand her the roses.

She looked up in surprise, her eyes flashing with high spirits. "Alex!" She grinned as she took the flowers, the characteristic roses in her cheeks deepening in colour. I stooped quickly to kiss her, and saw her studying the contusions on my face. Thanking the porter who had got her safely this far, I traded a tip for Sarah's carry-on bag and wheeled her out of the stream of arriving passengers to a quiet corner. As I walked behind her chair, the sight of what I knew to be a phenomenally gorgeous, lithe, muscular long leg enclosed in the plaster cast was tragic. *Why hadn't she told me?*

Having reached the most secluded recess of Terminal

Two available, I knelt on one knee and took her face in my hands. "Sarah. What happened?"

"I might ask the same of you," she said, studying my battered face.

"My NUP friends," I explained. "But come on—tell me."

She put her hands on mine. "It was bound to happen sooner or later. But please don't worry—it doesn't even hurt anymore."

"How did it happen? *When?* Why didn't you tell me?"

"I lost control on one of the takes—some crazy person skied right in front of me while I was on the slalom course. As I see it, I'm lucky. It might have been far worse than a broken leg." She shrugged. "It happened last Tuesday. Ian was there to help me. We didn't want to worry you with it—it seemed you were barely keeping your head above water."

That was certainly accurate. Suddenly I thought of the strange feeling I'd had on my way to the barn, roughly a week ago, of tumbling through the air, and the scream. I had known the moment of her accident. Belatedly I thought of the times I'd rung when she hadn't been in her room, and the odd tone of her voice. She hadn't been coping with a lack of love for her fiancé; she'd been coping with a broken leg. In hospital.

"Where's Ian?"

She shrugged. "He said he had some business in Paris. He'll probably be home in a couple of days."

I never knew what Ian was up to. One moment he seemed the soul of predictability and goodness; the next he was involved in some mysterious business in Paris that I knew nothing about.

"Oh, Sarah." I embraced her, loving the feel and scent of her. She held me tightly in return.

In the car, on the way home, a peculiar silence fell. I knew well enough that this always followed a lengthy separation; we'd come to expect it and not worry. Eventually Sarah broke the awkward silence as she told me incidental bits of news, and I did the same. We'd missed so much of each other's lives during her absence that there was a daunting amount of information to exchange. By the time we arrived at the Orchard, we were perfectly comfortable together again. Would we still pass through this ritual as a married couple, every time we were reunited after an absence?

After I'd ensconced Sarah in a cocoon of pillows on the library sofa, and after a cup of tea, we did nothing for the rest of the day but sleep. I carried her up to my parents'—*our* room, and put her gently on the bed. After getting all the cushions just right under her leg and head, I climbed in next to her.

"Heaven," I breathed, stroking her hair, watching her face directly opposite mine. Her mouth curved deliciously at the corners, and her almond-shaped eyes, intriguingly green, slanted up the tiniest bit at the ends. Her mahogany hair fell in a blanket over the pillow, and I smelled a trace of the spicy, complex perfume that was synonymous with Sarah.

We studied each other, perfectly contented, wanting nothing more than to be together. Carefully, I wrapped my arms around her and held her. She put her hand on my arm, and we fell asleep entwined on the bed.

It was five-thirty in the afternoon when I awoke, arm still draped over Sarah, to see her smiling at me. "You must have been exhausted," she said. "You need to tell me what's been happening here."

"I will. Thank God, the worst is over," I said drowsily, snuggling my head closer to hers. The afternoon had grown gloomy. The temperature had dropped in the room. I frowned. "Have you been warm enough?"

"Of course. I've had a highly efficient heater here in bed with me. You must promise to stop fussing, Alex. If I get cold or hungry or whatever, I'll either take care of it myself or say something. I'm not totally helpless, all right?"

"I know," I said, "but now I've got you here, you can't blame me for wanting to pamper you a bit." I kissed her and roused myself with difficulty, sitting on the edge of the bed for a moment. I slid my specs onto my nose, pushed the hair off my forehead and stood to close the window. After fastening it shut, I padded sleepily to the bedside table and switched on the lamp. "I still can't believe you're here." I perched on the edge of the bed and caressed her hand. "You'll never believe this, but for a while I thought . . . when I couldn't reach you in your room . . ."

"You think I wouldn't *tell* you if something were wrong?"

"I think you'd wait until you were here."

She looked at me in disbelief. "You're not going to rest easy until August twenty-ninth, are you? For goodness sake, Alex. Have a little faith."

"Right." I fetched the crutches from downstairs at her insistence, and rolled up the rug in the hall, so the rubber tips of her crutches would have better purchase on the wood floor. When we reached the top of the stairs, I walked down just ahead of her, but backwards, to catch her in case of trouble. She made it look easy, but I knew from having been on crutches once myself how difficult the early days were. "An admirable job," I said. "Only you could do it with such panache."

She pulled a funny face and said, "Don't make me laugh! I'll fall," and safely completed her descent. I got her settled in the library, laid a fire and lit it, and asked her if she wanted to see the news while I got dinner. "Good idea," she said, trying not to let on that she was exhausted from the journey downstairs on her crutches. I noticed her breathlessness, saw the sheen of sweat on her face from the effort. I loved her dignity, her bravery. The cupboard that housed the television was recessed in the bookshelves. I swung open the TV cupboard doors and passed Sarah the remote, kissing her as I went to the kitchen to warm up the soup.

The phone rang as I put a pot on the burner and lit it.

"Alex. It's me," Max sounded worried. "Are you still angry?"

How could I say yes when he put it like that? Besides, with Sarah here, the tawdry little issues of political books, hedges, and water had faded into relative insignificance. "No," I said, tucking the phone into my shoulder as I reached for a loaf of dense brown bread. "In fact, it was quite a story, Max. Congratulations."

He seemed taken aback; there was a pause before he answered. "I don't deserve you."

"I think it's the other way round. You've solved a lot more problems than you've created. Besides, it's always right to expose the truth, isn't it?"

"Thank you," he said quietly. "So," he said after a moment, suddenly all brisk and cheerful. "Are you going to keep Sarah all to yourself, or do we get to see her too?"

"Of course. Can you come round for lunch on Sunday? Or no, wait—that's the Clerkenwell Fête. How about the next Sunday?"

"Love to. Thought you'd never ask."

I laughed and cut four thick slices off of the loaf, then gathered them into a cloth-lined basket. "Great. One o'clock, then, Sunday week."

"Good. I won't ask what you're up to this evening."

"Just as well." I grinned. "Oh, and Max?"

"Yes?"

"I'm proud to be your brother." I'd never actually said such a thing before, being of the actions-speak-louder school, but it seemed appropriate. Max's transformation from a wasted, self-centred bully, drinking himself to death, into a committed, married crusader for justice was one of the great wonders of my world. And that was leaving out his sudden proficiency at enviable domestic skills, such as his contribution to savoury chicken pies. There was, I thought, an advantage in having sustained losses over the years: everything *good* stood out in spotlighted prominence.

"Me too. Sometimes it's hard to believe that things have gone so right."

You paid a high enough price for it, I thought.

"And things will start going right for you, too," he continued. "They already have."

We said good-bye on that positive note, and soon afterward the soup began to bubble aromatically. I fixed a tray for Sarah, setting it with the good china and a linen napkin with an embroidered *P* on it. After all, what was the stuff for if we didn't use it? I poured her a glass of burgundy and ladled soup into her bowl, then put a large pat of butter on her bread plate. As I carried the tray in, a tea towel draped over my arm for effect, I said, *"Mademoiselle, votre dîner."*

She smiled distractedly and sat up a bit taller to receive the tray. "Listen to this, Alex," she said, with a nod of her head toward the telly. She had it tuned to BBC One News. It was a report on the effort of the Government to speed the revamping of the House of Lords. They hoped at least to eliminate the right of hereditary peers to vote, if not do away with them altogether. I couldn't help but think of the meal Eurosceptics and Conservatives in general would make of this. *Further evidence that our government is bent on destroying the England we know, and doing away with every last bit of Conservatism. Socialist conspiracy!*

The broadcast held further news of interest, unfortunately. A snippet of film showed Dexter Moore, speaking to a group at the Institute of Directors. "No-one could illustrate my point better than the publisher who's been so much in the news lately, Alex Plumtree."

No. This can't be happening. . . .

"It is a sad day when an honest Englishman going about his own business is attacked by the media and union thugs. When an honest Englishman going about his own business has to worry about Socialist terrorists destroying his printer's shop. This has gone far enough. We must make Britain safe from militant unions. We must make Britain a safe place to publish books. We must make Britain a safe place to *print* books. And above all, let's keep Britain *Britain*, not part of the United States of Europe."

The clip over, the news announcer went on to say that informal polls showed the nation leaning dramatically away from remaining in the European Union; now only forty percent of people polled were in favour, and only sixty percent of that minority wanted Economic and Monetary Union. Moreover, Moore had jumped ahead in popularity over Abercrombie by several points in the last twenty-four hours. With the election a mere week away, this was extremely bad news.

I groaned. "Now I'm Dexter Moore's poster boy! Is there no *end* to this?"

Sarah was indignant. "To think that he can use your name, and everything you've been through, to his own advantage—and without even *asking* you! There should be a law . . ."

"My name's only just been dragged out of the rubbish bin. I'm right back in again." Really, the fast-paced mood swings of this turbulent political period were almost comical.

I leaned over to switch off the ringer on the library telephone. Within moments I'd be inundated. *Are you working with Dexter Moore on his election campaign? Was* Cleansing *a publicity stunt?* I could hear them now.

The television news moved on to coverage of union uprisings across Europe, calling for Britain to stay in the

EU. The Greens in Germany were up in arms, claiming it wasn't fair for England to have more lenient environmental restrictions than the Continent. Politicians in the various countries were doing their best to placate these militant groups, which had in the past been inclined toward terrorism. The consensus of Europe's political leaders, regardless of their leaning to the left or right, was that it was time for England to step up and take its rightful place in Europe of the twenty-first century. Reference was made to the amount of money invested so far in working out the problems of the Euro and other issues of European unity, and that it wasn't ethical to back out now.

Abruptly the news reader switched to the story of an aeroplane disaster in India. Sarah switched off the set. "What do you think's going to happen?"

I shook my head. "I can't believe someone like Dexter Moore is more attractive to the people of England than Graeme Abercrombie. Something tells me we're in for more surprises."

"I really don't understand a lot of this, Alex. Why are the unions, and the environmentalists, so interested in whether England stays in the EU, and goes to full Economic and Monetary Union?"

"Darling, I could fill your ears for days on end about accusations of Socialist conspiracy, peers awakened by visions that the EU is satanic and dedicating their fortunes to fight it . . . you simply can't imagine. Everyone's gone a bit mad on this one. But I did see a fairly reasonable article about it in the *Economist* just recently. If we remain in the EU, and go to Monetary Union, it means more power for all of the unions. Just imagine: if something goes wrong for the brothers in Manchester, all of Europe would strike to support them. Imagine how much pressure would be brought to bear on that factory owner to end the strike— in fact by all the leaders of Europe. Really, it would give the unions *lots* more power. And, in the terms of pay, holiday, and benefits, suddenly the country with the best package becomes the European standard. No one wants to see people underpaid, but eventually it reaches a point where businesses are being milked for all they're worth. Many are barely surviving. And as far as the environmentalists are concerned, Britain will have to live by still more rigid emissions and other standards. Everyone under one thumb, so to speak. No one to oppose them, except the other continents."

"I see." Sarah frowned. "Suddenly it's difficult to remember the advantages of the EU."

"I know what you mean. If some of the more radical elements would only calm down . . . but frankly, the thought of Dexter Moore in office makes me squirm, too. The NUP and the rest of them aren't going to take this sitting down. What worries me most of all is what Guy Ferris-Browne will do."

Sarah caught my eye and smiled. "Come over here. I need to erase that frown before it becomes a permanent fixture."

Erase it she did.

The next morning, I left Sarah happily ensconced on the library sofa with the *Tempus* crossword and enough reading material for a week. I still tasted her kiss as I climbed into the Golf and set off for Lisette's.

Lisette asked endless questions about Sarah's accident, and asked when she could see her. When she was satisfied about Sarah, she told me some extremely disturbing news. "I almost rang you last night," she said nonchalantly. The casual tone usually belied important information. "I thought I 'eard someone outside the 'ouse again. I got away from the sitting room windows and stayed by the phone, but"—she shrugged—"it must 'ave been an animal or some such thing."

I suppressed a shudder at the thought of Helena creeping about behind Lisette's house, given her hint that she'd been Nosey-Parkering about there. Then I wondered if it could have been George, reconsidering and trying to get a glimpse of his family again. I supposed he had every right to creep about his own garden, peering in his own house, but . . . it was crazy. I shook my head. "Lisette, promise you'll ring me next time. What if it had been someone who wanted to harm you? You know what's gone on with this book."

"I know, but that's over now."

"No, I have a feeling this isn't over until the election. Promise me you'll ring me next time."

"All right, *all right!*"

When we arrived, Claire was fluttering about inside the front door in a state. "Alex! What's wrong with your phones? Where've you been? I've been trying to reach you. Everyone wants you. *Everyone.* You have the BBC at ten o'clock—"

"Claire, I think the time has come for me to stop all this. I'm not a news commentator; I'm a book publisher. Sorry, you'll have to ring them with my apologies."

She stared at me openmouthed. "But—but—you can't *make* opportunities like this, Alex. People would kill for this kind of exposure. When it comes, you have to . . ."

But I was firm. People *had* killed for this sort of exposure. That was the problem. Somehow the fact that my meeting with Victor Fine had been rearranged for that morning made the decision easier. All this trouble had begun when I'd cancelled my meeting with him the first time and run off at Ferris-Browne's beck and call. It was about time for a rocket from him, I thought, about the backfired impact of *Cleansing*. But I wouldn't go in search of a tongue-lashing, or worse. Ferris-Browne could come for me, if he had the nerve.

And come he would . . . in his own way.

The phone was ringing as I stepped into my office. I'd asked Dee to screen my calls. "Alex! It's Amanda. You'll never believe what's happened." She sounded elated.

"Try me."

"I know it's just a publicity stunt, to try to earn back the respect of the community, but Simino's given me back the print shop building—for as long as I want to use it. And he's *also* found some old shop that no longer wants its Albion handpress and Vandercook proofing press—not to mention a monocaster! I'm back in business!"

I tried to put it out of my mind that the publication of *Cleansing* had been a publicity stunt as well. I only hoped that this time the stunt would be harmless.

"Amanda, that's fantastic! I'm really happy for you. And while you're on the line, I have a proposal for you."

"Oh?"

"You remember the printing journal, *The Fleuron*."

"Remember—how could I forget it? It was my family's claim to fame."

"Exactly. How would you like to continue publication of *The Fleuron*?"

Silence.

"And how would you like to print it for me?"

"Alex, that would mean a great deal to me." She paused. "I've wanted to carry on what my family started . . . and you can't imagine how many things I've longed to tell the printing world—not just stories about the Pelican Press and Nonesuch but current trends. New fonts, new methods . . . everything! And I know loads of people who could contribute."

"Why don't you jot down a few ideas and bring them to lunch Sunday week? Around one o'clock? Martyn will be there."

"Really? I'd quite like to see him again. Well! Thanks very much, then, Alex. One o'clock next Sunday."

I sighed. It was lovely to make people happy. It was one of the best parts of publishing . . . though of course there *were* authors one could never satisfy. Smiling, I vowed not to publish any more miserable ones.

Glancing at my watch, I saw it was nearly ten o'clock. There was still time to prepare a few notes for my meeting with Victor Fine.

Nicola stuck her head in my office. " 'Morning, Alex."

" 'Morning. What's up?" I wondered if she'd had a chance to speak to her father yet.

"Just wanted to let you know that the rollout of the trade edition is going very smoothly. We have enough orders already, prepublication, to guarantee the best-seller list. For what that's worth."

I thought of poor Lord Chenies, and how he would have loved to see his novel's success. "Well done, Nicola. You've really taken hold quickly, and not under the best of circumstances."

"I love my job. And"—she lowered her voice—"I spoke with my father. He handled me just as he did the last time: looked incredibly sad and denied nearly everything. But I did *see* something interesting."

"Oh?"

"The head of the Trades Union Group himself was on his way in to see Guy as I was leaving."

Yes, that was interesting, I thought. "Thanks, Nicola. I'm sorry to have put you through that again."

"Not at all, Alex. Actually, seeing him in this light, since I've come to work for you, has really helped me. The very thought of him used to trouble me a great deal more than it does now. Now I just see him as a tragic politician—a lying and cheating one—with whom I have no real tie. In fact, let me reassure you: a predisposition to lying was *not* one of the genetic gifts I received from my father. Though it's certainly dominant in him."

She smiled and turned for the door. "Oh—by the way, you heard all the union uproar on the news." I noticed she considerably refrained from mentioning Dexter Moore's appropriation of my fate for his own purposes. "I just heard on the radio that some union bigwig in France, the head of the union consortium coming together under the EU, issued a statement. He asked all of his union brothers not to use force to keep Britain in the EU; that it would be achieved by peaceful means. I thought that was encouraging. Now if the NUP will only listen . . ."

"Right. God willing, we've had enough of them." I stood and grabbed the jacket it seemed I'd only just hung on my coatrack. "I'm off to speak to Victor Fine about starting a bibliophile's book club."

I stopped in reception to tell Dee that I was off across the square.

"Mrs. Khasnouri just rang with a message for you. She'd like to come for her tutorial next week as usual." She beamed at me.

I beamed back. "Thanks, Dee." Somehow that one bit of news cheered me more than anything else could have. Life was indeed going back to normal.

I stepped out of the door into the grey day, and crossed the road outside our door. Victor Fine's company, Rollancz, was almost directly across the oval of Bedford Square. That meant I had the luxury of walking along the curve of the park that sat at the centre of the oval like an emerald on a ring. As I walked, I peered through the high wrought-iron fence at the utterly empty park. It made me long for late spring and summer, when we would picnic there on fine days, and the park would be filled with laughter from all the buildings round the square. Smiling at the thought, I stepped into the street on the other side of the park.

One moment all was quiet. The next moment there was an ominous revving of an engine behind me and the sound of a throttle fully opened. Its roar seemed to come from roughly an inch behind my neck. I dived at the kerb and could have sworn I felt the rush of air from the bumper against my ankle. Having landed none too gently, I picked myself up and saw a large black Mercedes screech round the curve. I couldn't make out its plate by that time; it was too far round the corner. My hands stung; they were not only scraped and bloodied from landing on the pavement, but shaking. I no longer believed in coincidence.

Where had that car come from?

I shook my head, brushed myself off, and crossed the pavement to Rollancz's doorstep. As I let myself in, Victor advanced from his office. I knew he occupied the front room on the ground floor; he enjoyed his view of the square and didn't want to have to climb stairs continually. He half-walked, half-shuffled toward me, obviously deeply upset. His mouth was open in an *o*, and his unruly white eyebrows bent deeply down at the bridge of his nose. "Plumtree! Are you all right?"

"Yes, thanks, Victor. It was a near thing, wasn't it?"

He looked me up and down in amazement. There was a hole in my trousers; my knee smarted where it had hit the pavement. "I *saw* it . . . I *saw* that car drive straight toward you!" It seemed to be a greater shock to him than it was to me.

"Yes, well, fortunately I heard him coming. Extraordinarily bad driver. How are you, Victor?"

"I'm not the one who was nearly run over in the street. I'm fine. But I am worried about you. Don't you think it's a bit odd?"

"Victor, everything's gone berserk ever since I agreed to publish *Cleansing*. A close call in the street is nearly normal."

He smiled at last and ushered me into his office. "Tea?

Coffee? Or perhaps a Scotch, since you've just seen your life flash before your eyes?"

"Nothing, thanks. But I do appreciate you seeing me, and postponing from the week before last."

"Not at all, not at all. You've become quite the political sensation. In fact, I half-expected to see you making the rounds of the news programmes today instead of being hard at work. No one believes that you're in Dexter Moore's camp for half a moment, don't worry. At any rate, I suppose you're ready to put all that behind you."

Too right, I thought.

"Tell me exactly what I can do for you. You know I'll do anything for a Plumtree. Your father helped me through plenty of rough patches."

"Thanks, Victor. As you know, I'm an admirer of your Left Book Club. I know it was started long ago, when Rollancz himself was actually running the company. But is it a separate line? Are your titles available to non—club members in the same edition . . . ?"

And so we launched into a rewarding transfer of information, right through lunch. But as usual, the most important information came as we chatted after the pudding.

"You know, political book publishing is a truly fascinating enterprise. Imagine a rectangle of paper and boards, infuriating or engaging the most powerful men of the day. There've been times when the government was *furious* with us for publishing one book or another." He looked at me directly, his grey eyes sparkling. "That's why I've been watching you, and Nigel's novel, so closely. But I'll be damned if I can work out what's going on."

"That makes two of us. And how the NUP managed to turn it all to the advantage of Dexter Moore, I'll never understand."

"The boys in the union went too far. They're young; they don't listen to us any more. We could save them a lot of trouble, but they think we're past it." He chuckled. "But I'll tell you who knows what he's about; your friend Ferris-Browne. I don't think we've begun to see what's up his sleeve. A true political operator, that one."

I didn't dare comment. Silence reigned for a moment as he watched me.

"I see you're wearing your Merchant Taylors school tie, Victor."

"Yes, oh, yes, indeed. Quite a few memories there, don't you know, Plumtree. Your father among them. He was the only decent prefect we had. Always honest; always did the right thing. Unlike certain other students I could mention." He shook his head. "Nigel Charford-Cheney was horrible, you know—making fun of anyone weaker than he was. He couldn't make fun of your father— nothing to poke fun at—but you can imagine how he tormented me for being a Jew, and Simino for being a scholarship student. Astonishing news about his being Lord Chenies's brother, wasn't it? After all this time . . . And Nigel even laid into Hotchkiss, if you can believe it, for being, well, less than manly."

"I had no idea you'd all been to MT at the same time." Somehow I hadn't placed Hotchkiss, Fine, Simino, and my father there all at once. Again I had the feeling that everyone knew everyone else in our corner of the world. Victor stood, signalling the end of lunch. We ambled amiably back to the square, and I crossed to the park and eventually to my doorstep.

"Mr. P!" Dee called out, as I waved on my way upstairs. I retraced the bottom three steps and leaned into Reception. "Did you hear the news?

"Some bloke tried to kill Dexter Moore—with a gun, outside his campaign headquarters. Didn't succeed, unfortunately." She winked, ever tongue-in-cheek.

"Just watch, it'll turn more people in his favour. They'll feel *sorry* for him."

"Wouldn't surprise me," Dee said, tidying her desk. "This country's become a three-ring circus."

The afternoon passed all too quickly after that, in a flurry of telephone calls and a frenzy of long-neglected paperwork. Lisette had begun to forge my name on letters, a practice with which I was very happy. But today there were contracts, which I always like to check over when possible, and expense forms to sign. The spring catalogue was ready to be printed, and tradition dictated that I look over the final proofs. If nothing else, it was useful to evaluate what we were publishing and how it all looked when we listed each of our titles. The backlist was always a vote of confidence. I looked at it twice a year, spring and autumn, and allowed myself to gloat. *We published these books.*

Except this time I thought there was one book we might strike from our backlist rather quickly. . . .

Lisette stuck her head round my door at six o'clock. With a twinkle in her eye, she said, "Sarah's waiting."

We were out in a flash, and this time travelled to our corner of Hertfordshire—soon possibly Buckinghamshire—uneventfully. With a sense of relief I stepped through the garage door into the house, and called out to Sarah. It wasn't until her cheery hello wafted down the corridor that I wondered if it had been very clever to leave her alone all day.

Kicking myself, I vowed to place a guard at the house for her the following day.

CHAPTER SEVENTEEN

The plum survives its poems.

WALLACE STEVENS

"DARLING," I SAID, PLANTING A KISS AND SINKING ONTO the sofa next to her. "You got on all right?" I wrapped my arms round her.

"Of course. I heard loads of news, talked to Mom about the wedding plans, caught up on my reading. I still can't believe someone tried to kill Dexter Moore."

"No." I moved in for another kiss, relishing her closeness. We stayed wrapped up in one another for a few delicious moments, until I heard the building creak ominously. I lifted my head to listen. "Wow. Sounds like we're in for a big one."

I pulled away from Sarah to look out the windows. In a premature twilight, black clouds scudded across the top of the beech wood beyond the garden, propelled by an angry wind.

"Good night to be inside by the fire," I said. The fire was already laid in the grate; in a moment it was crackling to life. I watched it with satisfaction, enjoying the golden glow it cast on Sarah. "Glass of wine?"

She nodded. I went off to the kitchen to get it, feeling fortunate. Who could ask for more? A stormy night, a fire in the grate, a glass of wine, Sarah in my arms. I snuggled close to her on the sofa, my arm around her. We listened contentedly to the flames and the howl of the wind, enjoying the moment. The ancient plum tree outside the library doors tapped against the glass, and I got up once more to close the heavy curtains against the cold and near-dark, checking the locks on the French doors.

A glass of wine and half an hour later, I was famished. "Fancy some dinner?"

"Sounds wonderful," Sarah said. "Thanks."

As I hurried down the hall to the kitchen, I heard a noise upstairs. I stopped and listened. There was nothing more than the wind's peculiar howl in the chimneys. I hoped they'd stand firm through the storm; we'd lost one several years before, along with a stone pediment over the front door.

Ten minutes later I brought trays for us both, and sat on the floor at Sarah's side. We ate contentedly, while she told me about some of the wedding arrangements her mother had made back in Massachusetts. She sipped her wine. "Mmm, that was wonderful," she said, and leaned back.

"Here, let me take that for you. More wine? Water?"

"I'd love some water." She thought for a moment, her head cocked to one side in the attitude I loved. "Do you know, that's the one word I can't even pretend to say with an English accent?" She smiled. "Would you teach me how to say 'water' like a true Briton?"

I laughed. "Of course. I'll just fetch it first." Shaking my head in amusement, I trotted back toward the kitchen. Sarah did this occasionally, chose a typically English word that intrigued her either with its meaning or with its sound. We'd been through "peckish," "flummoxed," and "dogsbody" in her early days in London, and she was now moving on to the subtleties of pronunciation. After years of working here in England, her speech had been polished into what might be called a mid-Atlantic accent, a softened American sound. She had no inclination to deliberately change her speech, seeing that as an affectation she despised in more pretentious Americans. But she was fascinated by the many differences in our common language—pronunciation in particular.

"Water," I mumbled to myself. Then I said it again with an American accent, which I could do without flaw, if I did say so myself, thanks to four years of doing my best to blend in at university. "Wahder." The British version had three syllables, almost, rather than two, as one would think. And it was more . . . well, mellifluous.

I poured Evian out of a chilled bottle into a glass for Sarah, then stopped cold. I could have sworn a latch had clicked inside the larder just off the kitchen, where the circuit-breaker box hung on the wall. Instantly, all my senses were on alert.

Pulling open the knife drawer as silently as I could, I slid out the biggest one I could find and crept toward the larder. After listening round the corner for a moment, I flung myself into the narrow cupboard lined with shelves, hitting the light switch as I went. No one; nothing. I looked out the door at the end of the tiny storage area, but no one could have escaped through it that quickly without my hearing.

Had I begun to imagine intruders? My heart galloped wildly in the aftermath of a massive adrenaline surge. Trying to slow my breathing, I replaced the knife, wiped a sleeve over my perspiring forehead, and picked up Sarah's glass. I stepped over to the larder once more to turn off the light, and frowned at the fuse box. It was closed, as always, and as I left the kitchen I warned myself against seeing gremlins behind every door. The ancient house always shifted in a gale. Strange noises were bound to result.

Once a roof tile had come loose in just such a storm and blown right through the kitchen window.

When I saw Sarah on the sofa, glancing through a copy of *Hello!* she'd bought in the Paris airport, my misgivings faded. I was just so worried that something would happen to her, my mind was playing tricks on me. I placed her water glass on the coffee table, within her reach. "How would you like a nice massage with your elocution lesson?"

Her eyes narrowed mischievously. "Ooh, I thought you'd never ask."

"Do you think you can lie on your stomach?"

"Yes, I think so, if you can just help me lift this . . ."

"I'll do more than that," I said, and picked her up, princess-style, as she called it. She smiled at me, her arms around my neck. She was so close . . . the smell of her . . . I eased my lips slowly toward hers, and the kiss lingered. At last our lips parted, and we looked at each other, eye to eye, with ill-concealed desire.

"Marriage—I mean, massage—first," I said with a grin, and saw that her eyes had the misty, heavy-lidded look they always got when she was—er—interested. No doubt she sensed all the signals in me, too.

Our intimacy had been enhanced by the fact that we had not yet indulged in the ultimate thrill. We had resolved to wait until marriage. I was convinced that the tantalisation of that one apple we hadn't plucked had made it more special, and that our future together would be all the more delicious. This was no fleeting thrill we were contemplating; it was marriage for a lifetime.

"If you can just stand for a second," I said, lowering her feet to the floor gently, "I'll take care of the rest." I picked her up again with her stomach on my forearms, and replaced her on the sofa, backside up. The full skirt she wore stretched tightly over her buttocks. "Very nice indeed," I said, and placed a hand on her briefly before shifting the cushions round, throwing several onto the floor. She lifted her head from the pillow and threw me a look.

"Are you quite comfortable?" I asked. Her leg was flat on the sofa, not elevated as it had been since she'd arrived.

"Mmm. Fine."

"Okay," I said, as I peeled up her blouse. "You really do have the most breathtaking back," I said, caressing it gently. "Strong." I bent over and kissed it in half a dozen places, slowly, relishing the feel of her smooth skin on my lips. Clearing my throat, I sat up. "Right, then. Here we go. Water," I said deliberately, kneading the first handfuls of her shoulders.

"Ohhh," she said. Then she collected herself. "Woh-tuh," she tried.

"Not quite. Too staccato. Think of a stream flowing." I said it again, drawing out the first syllable with a little up-down in it. "Woh-oh-tuh."

"Woh-oh-oh-tuh," she said, overdoing it, then burst into laughter. "I can't do it. Maybe you have to be born with a British English-speaking gene."

Rain began to pelt against the windows and doors with great force, blown in sheets by the wind. "No, try again. Woh-oh-tuh."

It was at that moment that the lights went out. I swore under my breath. "Stay here," I whispered needlessly to Sarah. What did I think she was going to do? Run away? With a sick feeling I realised how extremely vulnerable she was.

In a room lit only by firelight I crept over to the desk and reached for the phone. No dial tone. The phone *and* the lights out? Storm or no storm, it seemed too much of a coincidence.

I had to move fast. "The phone line's cut" was all I could say as I ran to Sarah, gathered her in my arms. "Someone's here. He'll be coming from the fuse box." I set her on her feet inside the French doors at the far end of the room. As she steadied herself against the wall, I ran back to the sofa. Hurrying back to her with her crutches and my big green blanket, I pushed aside the curtains in front of the doors, unlocked them, and quietly opened one side.

"Go," I hissed, draping the blanket over her shoulders. "You'll be safer." She bowed her head to the slanting rain as she hobbled outside. The hard-driven drops cut like knives.

Hurriedly I fastened the French doors shut again. When I turned, a figure stood across the room, in the doorway from the hall. By the flickering firelight I could see that he wore a ski mask. Before I knew it, the eerily featureless man had lunged in my direction. In the second or two it took him to cross the room, I glimpsed the thin white cord wrapped round one gloved fist.

I backed round behind my desk and crashed into the chair, seizing my silver letter opener. The man was lightning-quick. When I saw him coming for me over the desktop, I dashed for the door to the hallway. He threw his arms around my shins and yanked me off my feet. Stunned, I slammed to the rug with a *whump*.

As I struggled to kick free, he crawled right on top of me: I felt a rush of air as he silently whipped the cord round my neck, wrenching it tight. One hand still clutched the letter opener; I could only spare two fingers to force crucial space between my neck and the garrote.

I rolled sideways, trapping his body beneath mine. The garrote tightened round my neck; if I let go, it'd be the end of me.

The garrote dug into my left hand at my throat as I moved the right one down, got the sharp end of my weapon facing out. I thrust the letter opener into his leg with all my might. My attacker gasped, but the pressure didn't slacken on the cord round my neck. Was he impervious to pain? I barely had time to pull the instrument out before he forced me over again, back onto my stomach, this time pinning me with his knees. He was incredibly strong for his size.

I felt the sticky warmth of blood on my fingers as he maintained deadly pressure on the cord. I pulled the letter opener back under my body and let go of it, my right hand clawing desperately at the cord on my neck. My position was vulnerable in the extreme; I had to do something, fast.

I struggled, getting my knees under me, with the attacker literally hanging from my neck. I put one foot on the ground, then the other. Backing toward the wall, I rammed him into the bookshelves with all the force I could. I heard an involuntary "oof!" on the first go. Struggling over to the doors, desperate to be free, I rammed him against the solid glass panel of the door. The glass shattered and he bellowed in agony; still, the pressure didn't let up on the blasted cord.

He yanked the garrote still tighter. I grunted as I felt it rip into the flesh of my hands, and smashed him into the second panel of glass. It shattered, and the doors banged open. The storm raged and pelted us with stinging, icy spears of rain, sped by the howling wind. I was growing desperate, feeling his strong legs wrapped round my torso like tentacles. *Go, Sarah, go,* I prayed, hoping she'd found a hiding place.

My tormentor began to squeeze powerfully with his legs, like a human boa constrictor. I grunted, gasping, blindly struggling but losing . . . losing. . . .

Desperate, I sank to my knees, vision wavering as I began to black out. Dimly, I heard a *clonk!*—the sound of metal striking something hard. The cord miraculously loosened round my neck, and my attacker fell away. I yanked off the narrow nylon rope and turned to see the balaclava-clad man sprawled on the wet paving stones. Sarah stared at him wide-eyed, the heavy garden spade still raised in her hands. I whipped the face mask off the unconscious man; I'd never seen him before. Running to Sarah, I held her as the rain blew against us in sheets.

She'd saved my life.

I felt her trembling, and gently carried her into the house and laid her again on the sofa. Not wanting to leave her, I forced myself to the desk for a roll of sticky parcel tape, which I used to bind the man's wrists and ankles. I rang the police on the mobile phone and then carried Sarah upstairs.

"Alex, wh-what is it?" she asked. "You h-haven't said a word. You're all right, aren't you?"

I closed my eyes briefly, full of shame and remorse. "I can't believe I've done this to you—again. Sarah, I love you so, and all I seem to do is bring you into these monstrous situations. Thank you for saving my life."

"R-rubbish. You can't b-blame yourself for this. You stand for good, and there are b-bad people in the world. And you have to admit it . . . you never run from them."

I lowered her onto the edge of the bath and turned on the water. Sarah began to strip off wet layers of clothing as I lowered a step stool into the tub to hold her leg out of the water. It was pure punishment to see her bluish lips.

"You'd b-better go meet the police," she said. "But give me a kiss first." She smiled. Feeling like a cad, I bent and kissed her, then left to keep an eye on the intruder until the police arrived.

It wasn't long before several of them took charge of the man. The constables pulled him to his feet, and he shook his head as if to clear it. He had small, intelligent eyes that studied me with intensity, and fine features that made him look ridiculously out of place in thug's clothing. His balding head was slick with rain; it struck me that he looked the sort of person who would be more at home in the Stock Exchange than strangling me on a dark and stormy night.

"Take him to the car," one of the officers said to his men, and they immediately started toward the driveway. With relief I saw Detective Inspector Fawcett arrive; he and I retreated from the tempest into the library, which was only slightly warmer than outside, thanks to the wind and rain blowing in through the broken doors. "You'll want to get those fixed," Fawcett said, and I nodded. "Those, too," he added, wincing as he looked at my hands. For the first time, I saw that they were covered with blood—not just my attacker's, but my own, from where the cord had bitten into them. I picked up a serviette left on the coffee table and wrapped it clumsily round the left hand, which had borne the brunt of the burden.

Fawcett asked me to relate what happened. I told him, finishing with Sarah clobbering the attacker with the garden spade. Despite myself, I smiled, proud of Sarah and her bravery under duress.

"You've had some rather exciting times, here, Mr. Plumtree. What do you think this man was really after?"

"There's no question: he wanted to kill me."

Someone wanted to keep me silent in the parish graveyard forever, but who? And why? What threat did I pose to anyone at this point? Surely Ferris-Browne knew I wouldn't tell his secret, about asking me to publish the book; it would make me look too bad. If not Ferris-Browne, it could be anyone who was unhappy about *Cleansing*—or, for that matter, it might be Simino, Helena, or even Hotchkiss.

"The book again?" Fawcett asked, as if reading my mind.

"Somehow. It could well be one side of the political spectrum or the other, still unhappy about it. Or some sort of personal grudge." I didn't want to send them straight to anyone's door. "Needless to say, I'm through with anything that might remotely be construed as political publishing."

He gave me a sad smile. "By the way, I've been meaning to ring you. I thought you'd like to know that Lord Chenies's death has been declared a murder, and Malcolm Charford-Cheney is the chief suspect. His debts alone . . . " The detective whistled. "But this assassin might shed new light on the case." He asked if he could have a look round before interrogating the intruder at the station.

"Mind if I check on my friend upstairs?" I asked.

He shook his head. "I won't be a minute here—we won't be needing anything more from you. I've got your statement. I'll ring you when we know something."

I hastened upstairs, stepped into the bathroom, and was relieved to see that there was colour back in Sarah's cheeks.

I knelt next to her.

"Don't look so worried, Alex," she said, reaching a dripping hand out of the bath to stroke my cheek. Everything's all right now. Hey," she said gently, her eyes tender, "the wedding's still on."

I closed my eyes and bent my head to touch hers.

Then I rang the security company and waited up until one guard arrived for the interior of the house, and another for the outside. I wasn't taking any more chances with Sarah.

CHAPTER EIGHTEEN

※

Walls have tongues, and hedges ears.

JONATHAN SWIFT

THE NEXT MORNING, A SATURDAY, DAWNED CLEAR AND lovely. I'd gone downstairs to prepare a late breakfast in bed for Sarah when the phone rang. "Alex Plumtree?"

"Speaking."

"Detective Inspector Fawcett here."

"Yes, sir." I'd recognised his authoritative voice.

"I have some information for you. About last night." He sighed. "I can only tell you so much, Mr. Plumtree; sorry. But I think you've a right to know that the man we took from your house could be with one of the . . . er . . . government agencies."

"Government agencies?"

"You know—special assignments, that sort of thing. Special *clandestine* assignments." He let the extraordinary words hang in the air. Then he dropped the real bombshell. "The prisoner was—um—mysteriously taken from our custody en route to the jail. By some sort of blond giant, and very cleverly indeed."

My worst fears had been confirmed. The prime minister's office was involved . . .

"Ah," I said, doing my best to remain outwardly calm. Graeme Abercrombie, my father's dear and trusted friend, now the most powerful man in the world, had taken the final step: he wanted me dead. The thought made my blood run cold.

"Right. Well, thank you, Detective Inspector. I do appreciate it."

"Not at all. By the way, I thought you'd like to know that we've taken Malcolm Charford-Cheney into custody." His voice was grim when he said good-bye, and he ended with a word of caution. "Be careful, won't you?" Perhaps he thought I didn't stand much of a chance, with enemies like the garrote-man.

Immediately, before fear could gain too much ground, I rang Max. To my great frustration, he wasn't home; I talked to Madeline and asked if she'd mind letting the phone ring when I rang back, so I could leave Max a long answering-machine message. The only way to save myself now—and those around me—was to go public with what I knew about the prime minister. I hadn't wanted to do it, out of loyalty to my father's friend, but now there seemed no doubt that Abercrombie was the bad apple.

"Max. The prime minister's the one behind everything, from the Mmbasi Kumba murder to the Clerkenwell riot. I knew it but didn't want to believe it; last night he sent a government man to kill me. You've got to help me and get this in the open before he succeeds. Thanks, Max—ring me when you can. Bye."

Sarah's dark eyebrows were raised in a question as I entered the bedroom. After putting the breakfast tray across her lap, I leaned close. "The police officer from last night rang. He thinks our visitor was from some government agency—MI5, I'm assuming, though he wouldn't say. They're the blokes who deal with internal affairs."

Her eyes widened.

"Exactly. It isn't good, Sarah—it means the prime minister wants me dead." I told her I'd just rung Max and laid it all out for him.

"You'd better lie low until Max breaks this open in the national press."

"Don't worry, I will."

Ian came home later that day, surprised to find two guards on duty at the Orchard, and oddly closemouthed about his activities in Paris. As we munched scones by the fire late in the afternoon, feeling a bit like prisoners, I told him about our garrote-wielding friend and his source.

"You were wise to hire the security company, Alex. People are getting desperate over this election," he said. "You'd best watch your back till it's over."

The subject eventually turned to Verbier, and Ian exclaimed, "I nearly forgot! Jean-Claude gave me a video they made from the film—it includes all of the ski sequences. Even your accident, Sarah. Would you like to see it?"

"I'd *love* to get a glimpse of that idiot who skied right in front of me, in the middle of the racecourse." She shook her head.

"Me too. Except I'd like to clobber him."

"Her," Sarah said. "I'm not sure, but I think it was a woman. Jean-Claude told me that someone in the film crew skied after her, but lost her in the trees."

Ian returned with the video, pressed Play, and we were treated to the sight of Sarah tackling a steep piste peppered with moguls. She skied aggressively, her legs pumping like pistons, riding the bumps as if her knees were shock absorbers. The next few sequences were of Sarah racing Jean-Claude on a steep race course, both of them in bright helmets and body-hugging Lycra racing suits. I could hear the bleak rasping of their skis on the sheer ice of the course, and dreaded seeing the fall. European ski resorts didn't pamper their customers with overly groomed pistes, and their racecourses were no exception. They let nature take its course. As a result, skiing in Europe was a great deal more dangerous than in the States, where they babied skiers not only by grooming the pistes but by making snow and moving it to bare or icy spots.

Suddenly Sarah's body tensed, and I realised we'd come to the accident scene. As the camera followed Sarah and Jean-Claude down, carving their way expertly from one gate to the next, a slender figure dressed in black shot into the picture from the edge of the course. No fence or rope had been erected to keep her out, and she zoomed across the course at high speed directly in front of Sarah. Something flashed through my mind about her posture—there was something familiar about the woman.

Jean-Claude, farther up the course from Sarah, was thrown out of control for an instant. But the skier's threat was not as immediate for him, and he had time to recover and slow down. Sarah, on the other hand, missed the sleek skier by what looked like mere inches. In the effort to avoid a collision, my noble Sarah caught an edge of her ski in the rut left by other racers. She flew through the air dramatically, one ski flying off immediately, then bounced and rolled down the mountain, tragically limp, like a rag doll. The cameraman kept his lens trained on her until she lay motionless at the bottom.

Still wincing from the horror of her body-crunching fall, I snatched up the remote. "If you can bear it, Sarah, I need to see that again. There's something about that woman . . ."

"It's all right; I'd like to watch it again too," she said. "It's extraordinary, seeing it as a spectator."

I rewound the tape and started it again, letting it run at normal speed until the black-clad newcomer came into the picture. Using the remote, I touched the pause button to stop the tape at one-second intervals, in order to inspect the woman more closely. It was the way her shoulders joined her neck, with a bit of a hunch forward. . . . The second time I saw the woman ski into view, I had a sick feeling.

"That's Helena Hotchkiss!" I remembered Helena stopping in her car at the foot of Lisette's drive, asking if I'd spoken to Sarah lately, remembered her gloating look. And the clippings at the back of the scrapbook, horribly defaced. . . . *She'd meant to kill Sarah.*

Had she done it to prevent me marrying Sarah? Or was this some favour for Ferris-Browne? Except that I knew now it was Graeme Abercrombie who'd turned against me, and not Ferris-Browne. . . . Perhaps someone believed that if Sarah were injured, I would flee the scene in Britain and go to her. But she and Ian hadn't told me of her injury, hadn't let me fall into the trap. Which made me wonder if Ian knew something. . . .

I looked at him, and he met my eyes coolly. He shook his head ever so slightly, once. I knew him well enough to know that he meant we shouldn't discuss it in front of Sarah.

I felt tortured by shame, guilt, and anger. Heaven knew I'd put Sarah through enough horrors over the last four years, in the perils of Plumtree Press. Would I some-day be responsible for her death?

As if from a great distance, I heard my love's rich voice ask, "You mean you *know* her? Who's Helena Hotchkiss?"

I pulled myself back to earth. "I dated her when I was a teenager. She seems to be stuck in adolescence—and for some unfathomable reason, stuck on me. At the same time, she's very closely associated with Guy Ferris-Browne, the deputy PM. You probably know he's also minister for the environment. Helena was at the environmental summit at Verbier with Ian." I told Sarah about Helena's environmental activism in her leadership of Hedges in Transition, and her success with Nature's Chemist.

Sarah looked confused. "I've heard of that company. But why would she want to—"

"Sarah, I'm so sorry." I gripped her hand tightly. "Looking back on things that she said, I can see now that she was threatening you. But I never dreamed she'd try to hurt you—it's so bizarre. She's a very troubled woman." I thought of the night Helena had filled my house with gas. She was a loose cannon. I wished I knew where she was at the moment. Perhaps if I took the video to the Hertfordshire Constabulary, it would prove that Helena had purposely tried to injure Sarah . . . but all she could be held responsible for was skiing in front of her. That didn't prove premeditated intent to harm, and in the European resorts, skiers were left to take care of themselves. No one told reckless skiers to slow down, nor did anyone confiscate lift tickets. Helena wouldn't be prosecuted for her offence.

Ian spoke, his eyes troubled. "I'd guess this has something to do with what Guy Ferris-Browne wants. Alex, haven't you had your suspicions about him, and about his use of violence, of late?"

How did *Ian* know that? He seemed to have a direct link to everything that happened in my life, regardless of whether he'd been in the country. If Ian hadn't been such good friends with Graeme Abercrombie, I could have confided in him; I could have told him that no matter how much I respected the prime minister, it seemed he'd gone out of control in his effort to win this election, and had even instructed the garrote man to get rid of me.

"Yes—yes I have," I said lamely.

I had another word with the security guards after that, feeling the sword of Damocles suspended directly over the Orchard.

Somehow we survived the evening with bodies intact. My sense of well-being, long severely diminished, was now utterly shattered. I'd come much too close to causing Sarah's death. Knowing that, and knowing that it had happened more than once before, was it right for me to marry her?

After Sarah was safely upstairs in bed, I went quietly down the hall to Ian's room and knocked on the door. He opened it as if he'd been expecting me.

"Please—answer one question for me. Is the prime minister involved?"

He sighed. "Alex, you must trust me. There are some things I can't share with you at the moment, but I will—I *promise* I will—one day soon. You know that you're a son to me. A father always does what's best for his son, though the son might not like it at the time."

I knew, as a son knows a father, that he was watching me closely for a reaction. Cruelly, I shuttered my face and denied him one.

He continued. "But you should also know that Sarah realised how fraught things were here, and *asked* me not to tell you of her injury. It was difficult, believe me. I knew how frustrated you were that you could never reach her in her room. I understood your suspicions."

I felt about Ian at that moment as I had about my father: frustrated that he was always so *right* . . . so good . . . so blameless.

And ashamed that I wasn't more like him.

Not knowing what Ian knew cast a dark cloud over the next few days. As luck would have it, that particular Sunday was the long-awaited Clerkenwell Fête. I had no desire to go; Simino and Hotchkiss would almost certainly be there, along with Victor Fine. But Ian wouldn't take no for an answer. "Your boxed sets," he said. "You and Victor

Fine *produced* them for this occasion. Everyone will expect you there. Really, Alex, you must go."

In the end, it was for the best that I did attend the fête. I left Sarah having coffee late Sunday morning with a security guard and Lisette, and rode southeastward with Ian. I was silent, miffed at Ian's continued refusal to confide in me.

It was a shock to see Anthony Simino cavorting and glad-handing as if nothing unseemly had happened a mere three days earlier. I still hadn't worked out whether he really would have, *could* have pushed Amanda into the well. As Ian and I arrived at the fête, he was delivering a speech on top of a soapbox in the middle of Clerkenwell Green. The entire neighbourhood had been cordoned off into one great pedestrian walkway for the fête. I saw from the banners strung across the main roads that various performers would be acting, singing, and dancing throughout the day.

Ian and I approached the already sizeable crowd, where festivities had just got under way. From his podium, Simino said, "And as the president of the Clerkenwell Neighbourhood Association, I pledge to you that Clerkenwell will continue to grow, in keeping with its origins. We're all here to have a good time today, and to celebrate Clerkenwell."

I turned to Ian and raised my eyebrows. Looking at me sideways, he gave me a sad smile. "Some people always seem to land on their feet," he said.

"Hmph."

"May I introduce Robert Lovegren of the Order of St. James," Simino continued, "a man who has a stirring new vision for our community." Robert Lovegren, stepping up onto the soapbox as Simino relinquished it, was greeted by a tide of applause. When it finally subsided, Lovegren thanked the group modestly and began a well-prepared exposition of the Order of St. James and its role of training ambulance men since the First World War. Lovegren was saying that now it was time for the Order to expand into more modern areas, such as charitable foundations to fund health research, when I felt a tap on my back.

It was a smiling Victor Fine. He greeted us both, then said, "Have you seen the boxed sets, over where the crafts and food are being sold?" We shook our heads. "You can be proud of those books. So attractively presented. I'm glad our little co-publishing deal came off so well, Alex. I understand you've sworn off political books, or we might do it again. Did I tell you I've already received more than seven thousand orders for the William Morris book through the Left Book Club?"

"It was a pleasure working with you, Victor," I said. "I'm pleased with the book, too. And thanks again for your help the other day."

"Any time, any time," he said, and wandered off again.

"A decent man," Ian said. "Always liked him, though we've learned to avoid politics in conversation."

"Mmm. He's been advising me on the bibliophile's book club. I learned something from him the other day at lunch—did you know that my father, Victor, Richard Hotchkiss, and Anthony Simino all attended Merchant Taylors at the same time?"

Ian shook his head, as if to say, *Small world.*

By that time Robert Lovegren had finished speaking, and Ian and I drifted toward him as the crowd broke up. "I'm very happy about what you're doing," I told him when we finally got through his admiring public. "It's a fine purpose for the neighbourhood."

"I'm glad you think so," he said kindly. "I know that the newspaper article caused you a bit of trouble, or so your brother thought. But it needed to be done."

"Absolutely. I agree," I said.

He turned to Ian. "Will you be at the book club meeting this week? I've an illuminated book of Psalms, recently found by a member of the Order in France. He's sent it to us for the museum. I thought I'd bring it to show the group."

"Yes, I'm planning to be there," Ian replied, and then the crowd swept in to congratulate Lovegren on his latest act of philanthropy.

"Ian," I said as we walked in the direction of the boxed-set book display, "is there anyone, anywhere, you *don't* know?"

He smiled. "You're wondering how I know Lovegren. Alex, I've been telling you for years, you really must come to the club more often. The Athenaeum isn't one of those snobbish places at all. In fact, it's a bit of reverse snobbery on your part *not* to come."

"*Lovegren* belongs to the Athenaeum?"

Ian nodded.

"I think I've been persuaded," I said, once again in awe of my father's old friend.

"I hate to bring up uncomfortable subjects, but I really must see the infamous Clerks' Well," Ian said. "Don't suppose you want to join me."

"No, thanks. Maybe I'll get something to drink," I said. "Meet you at the bookstalls in half an hour?"

"Good," he said, and took himself off toward Farringdon Lane. I turned up the green, walking past Amanda's shop. The well, the tunnels leading from Amanda's cellar . . . this neighbourhood was full of places I'd rather not visit again.

Stepping up to the pub called the Clerks' Well, I saw that the hostelry had outdone itself for the fete, producing an early May Day atmosphere with wreaths of greenhouse flowers and a festive outdoor drinks bar. A folk musician with a guitar serenaded customers as I ordered a coffee to take away and left the crowd to walk up the road toward St. Mary's Church. Feeling pensive, I reflected that this

fete felt more like a time to remember the disastrous publication of Lord Chenies's special edition than any kind of
celebration.

I turned down a side street toward the churchyard,
where there were nice wooden benches for sitting and ru-
minating, and made for an empty seat sheltered by the
churchyard wall on two sides. With relief I sipped my coffee, glad to be away from the crowd. Then I heard a voice I
recognised, coming from over the wall, and soon after
caught a glimpse of Hotchkiss and Simino strolling past
together. Though they weren't exactly hurried, they were
purposeful in their walk, as if intent upon arriving somewhere on time.

Hotchkiss and Simino had certainly healed their rift;
what were they up to now? After they'd passed, their backs
to me, I rose quietly, dropped my coffee cup in a dustbin,
and followed them. I clung to a tall hedge as they rounded
a corner and made for a walled courtyard to one side of St.
Mary's. Trying to press myself into the shrubbery, I waited
till they were out of sight again, then peeked out of my
hiding place. I was about to step up to the edge of the
courtyard for a listen, when I saw Victor Fine approach
from the other direction along a footpath. He wore the
same purposeful look Simino and Hotchkiss had, and carried a bottle of champagne and plastic cups. Why were
they meeting here . . . in this quiet and isolated place?

After Victor joined the two men in the courtyard, I
crept closer. I was still hidden in the hedge, round the corner from their entrance in case they left suddenly.

They spoke in hushed, excited voices.

"By heaven," I heard Victor Fine say, "we pulled it off.
Even better than we intended." The cork popped, and I
pictured Fine splashing bubbly into their cups.

"After all these years!" Hotchkiss exclaimed. "To
revenge."

"Sweet revenge," echoed Fine and another familiar

male voice, to the accompaniment of clinking plastic. There was silence as they drank. I stood in fascination in my hedge, not daring to move. I could hear them perfectly, every nuance.

"And no one's the wiser," Hotchkiss gloated, sounding like the proverbial cat who'd swallowed the canary. "Malcolm's been taken in and charged. It's too glorious for words."

"I must say, I feel a pang of regret for our boy Plumtree," Victor Fine said, serious again. "We used him rather badly, I think. And he found the old goat."

They were talking about Lord Chenies!

"He's young, he'll get over it," Hotchkiss said.

"Well, *'Yid,'*" Hotchkiss said with ironic emphasis, "you've come out of all this quite well." He chuckled.

"And you, *'sissy,'*" Fine responded. I could hear his smile.

"Not to mention you, *'scholarship boy,'*" Hotchkiss added.

Then I heard Simino's voice.

He sniggered. "He really was a miserable old sod. All that money he extracted from us, over all these decades. A pity I didn't know he was my brother while I was at school . . . when I think how I might have tortured him with it!" Simino sounded almost wistful at the thought. "The great Cheney heir, the future *Lord* Chenies, brother of a *scholarship* student! I would have loved to see his face."

They all laughed nastily at that. I took a stumbling step backward, my footfall covered by raucous laughter, as the truth sank in. Of course . . . Merchant Taylors . . . they'd been there together. How dense of me! And Chenies had bullied them there. And it sounded as if Chenies had blackmailed them, too, threatening to tell their secrets if they didn't pay him. But what secrets? And . . .

They'd killed him? Was that what they were saying? But what about Malcolm?

I blindly stumbled back toward Clerkenwell Green, as bits and pieces came together in my mind. It wasn't that I thought any of the men were saints, exactly, but the unfathomable evil in their souls chilled me from the inside out. To *laugh* and rejoice over someone's—anyone's—death . . . and to have *planned* that death . . .

What to do? Ring the police? I needed to talk to Ian.

When I reached the bookstalls, I found that Ian was already there. "What is it?" he said, after one look at me.

"I need to talk to you. Mind if we walk, away from the crowd?"

He came solicitously, to my side, resting a hand on my back briefly as encouragement. I led the way toward Farringdon Road, now deserted. My plan was to cross it and climb Herbal Hill opposite, a steep slope rising out of the Fleet Valley. It, too, was deserted on a Sunday afternoon.

"Ian," I said when we'd crossed the road and trekked slowly up the hill Mmbasi Kumba had raced up barely two weeks before, in the last few moments of his life, "I've just learned the most extraordinary thing. I was walking toward St. Mary's, to drink my coffee in the park. Suddenly I heard Victor Fine, Anthony Simino, and Richard Hotchkiss talking. I followed them and listened. . . . They were celebrating the fact that Lord Chenies was dead—that they'd pulled it off, sweet revenge, and Malcolm had been charged."

Ian said nothing. He never commented until the speaker concluded. And he always, always, took time to think before opening his mouth.

I went on. "And then I found out why: Charford-Cheney had bullied them at Merchant Taylors. They said something about blackmail as well. . . . Ian, I think they killed him."

He didn't stop walking, but he turned and gave me a long, hard look.

"I can't believe it," I went on. "Someone who hated

his book—that I could accept. Even Malcolm or Hillary Charford-Cheney, eager for his money and title. But Hotchkiss, Fine, and Simino?"

We turned left into Hatton Garden, the gold and diamond merchants' street.

"There is no proof, of course," I admitted. "If I were to tell the authorities what I heard, Hotchkiss, Fine, and Simino would deny having said anything of the sort."

I fell silent, and we plodded past shop after shop filled with gold chains and diamond rings. At last Ian said, "I believe a tip from you might point the Criminal Investigations Department in the right direction to find evidence, if it's there," he said obscurely.

I knew I would have to call Fawcett and tell him. I'd never felt so disillusioned. "I just don't understand it, Ian. Why would they sacrifice all the respect and success they've achieved, their good names, for a vengeful act of pride? How could they be so stupid?"

Then it hit me. I stopped dead in my tracks. Ian stopped too. *"Riceyman Steps,"* I said. "You know how I've told you that I sometimes feel as if I'm being toyed with by Himself, when bits of various classics we published become real life?" He nodded but didn't smile indulgently, as other men might have. My bizarre experience with literature was no joke to him.

"This spring it's the boxed set. So far I've seen the passage from *Oliver Twist*—the Farringdon Road bookstall episode with Mmbasi Kumba—and the Clerkenwell riot à la William Morris, and I've been wondering when a scene from *Riceyman Steps* would occur. I couldn't work out how I'd be miserly enough to resemble that old bookseller in any way, but it wasn't the meanness. It was *pride*." I shook my head. "Pride got me into this mess—wanting a Charford-Cheney best-seller, wanting to be owed a favour by the prime minister. And Hotchkiss, Simino, and Fine succumbed, too."

Ian said, "You are very perceptive, Alex. If you feel you've learned something from all this, don't torture yourself. Accept it and carry on."

I stared blankly at the building ahead of me. Then the name of the street, hung on a sign on the building's wall, registered. "Good Lord," I said. "Look where we are."

The sign attached to the side of the building read, GWYNNE PLACE.

Ian looked startled. "Isn't that the real name of the square Arnold Bennett wrote about in *Riceyman Steps?*"

I nodded.

Ian began to chuckle, a rare event, and I was surprised to find that I too was able to see the humour in the situation. Staring at the sign, I felt a little in awe at the help I'd have been given in figuring out the last piece of the puzzle, if I hadn't worked it out in time.

We made our way back to the fete to see how the boxed sets were faring for the neighbourhood coffers. I sincerely hoped that we wouldn't run into the murderous trio of Hotchkiss, Simino, and Fine, but in my three-plus decades I had learned a thing or two. It wasn't possible to escape bad apples. If those men were never proved to be murderers, I would have to work with them year after year, no matter how painful. They were woven into the fabric of society, like slubs in silk. To avoid Fine, I'd have to avoid publishing. To avoid Hotchkiss, I'd have to move away from Chorleywood and cut all ties to Merchant Taylors. To avoid Simino—well, I might just be able to manage that.

Fortunately the gruesome trio were not anywhere near the stall. "The boxed sets are selling like hotcakes," Robert Lovegren, who was taking his turn selling the Neighbourhood Association's wares, reported. "It's these wealthy young people moving in. They've the education to appreciate this sort of thing. An entirely different type of person than in the past." He smiled. "Thank you again for doing the special set for us, Alex."

Ian and I wordlessly agreed to make our way back to the car and return to Sarah. I felt like a dog retreating to lick its wounds. As I drove, the mobile phone rang in my jacket pocket. I handed it to Ian.

"Ian," he answered. "Yes! Hello, Sarah." Ian's face always lit up with a sort of reverent awe when he saw or spoke to his granddaughter. He listened for several moments, then said, "I see," and glanced over at me. "We're in the car at the moment, on our way back. I'll tell him." Another pause. "All right. See you soon. Bye, m'dear."

Ian placed the phone in the console. "Well, there's been an interesting development." He sounded bemused. "Malcolm Charford-Cheney's been taken into custody to 'help the police with their enquiries,' regarding the sudden death of his father."

"Yes. Detective Inspector Fawcett told me yesterday. If I hadn't just overheard Hotchkiss, Fine, and Simino, I would think it consistent with Malcolm's motivations—the title, the royalties, the seat in the House of Lords, and the manor house. Not to mention his frustration with his father for reneging on their publishing contract. But how does that fit with what I just overheard at St. Mary's?"

Ian shook his head. "Sarah said that Neville Greenslade rang. He said you could phone him at home today, if you like."

"More and more interesting. Perhaps Malcolm's decided to drop the suit."

I was joking, but when we arrived back at the Orchard, I phoned Neville and found that was exactly what had happened. "He's a bit unclear on his reasons." Neville told me. "I think he's just trying to make himself look better—less vindictive—now the police are scrutinising him. At any rate, worry no more."

Next I squared my shoulders and rang Detective Inspector Fawcett. "I don't like to tell you this, but you've got the wrong man for Lord Chenies's murder."

"Why, what have you got?" he demanded immediately.

I told him what I'd overheard.

He said, "The teacups—at last," with a sigh of satisfaction. "I'll look into it. Thanks, Alex." It was the first time he'd called me by my Christian name. I took it as an immense compliment; I'd grown to like the man.

Taking my place by Sarah, I held her in my arms while Ian built up the fire. Lisette sighed, visibly reluctant to leave adult companionship, and mumbled something about getting back to the boys. She said her good-byes and departed for Chez Lisette.

Ian, having tended the fire, announced he was going to boil the kettle for tea, and would I like some? I said absolutely yes, and a few chocolate digestives if there were any, thank you very much. He departed to see to it.

"So how've you been?" I asked, snuggling next to Sarah. "You look marvellous."

"Flattery," she purred. "It never fails. You're very convincing."

"I speak only the truth. Wedding still on?"

She put one hand on either side of my head in a very pleasant vise grip, and pulled my mouth towards hers with urgency. My lips sank into hers and melted there.

"Does that answer your question?" she asked with an impish smile. Her eyes shone. I pictured her as the definitive radiant bride on our wedding day.

"I know what you're thinking," she said, eyeing me. "You've got that wistful, 'I want to elope' look about you. Believe me, I feel the same way. But the big wedding means so much to my parents."

"I know," I said. My lips brushing hers, I murmured, "I wouldn't want to disappoint them. Besides, we'll have the rest of our lives . . ."

"Here we are," Ian said briskly. He came through the door with a fresh pot of tea and all the trimmings. I sat up quickly. "Alex, for goodness' sake, I was young once, too," he said nonchalantly, putting the tray down on the table. "You don't have to pretend round me. Otherwise I shall start to feel quite uncomfortable here. Have you told Sarah what happened at the fête?"

"No," I said. I looked at her shining eyes, and almost hated to tell her how evil the hearts of men could be. But I did relate the whole sordid tale.

"How awful!" she exclaimed. "These are men—well, two of the three—you've known for years. Who would ever think that they'd—"

The telephone rang, and I plucked it out of the litter of tea things on the table.

"Alex." It was Lisette. "The boys and I 'ave a surprise for you. I know I only left a little while ago, but would it be too much trouble if we popped over?"

"On the contrary. You know I always love to see the boys—and you."

"See you in a few minutes, then," she said, sounding positively girlish.

True to her word, she and the boys were on our doorstep before ten minutes had passed. The three of them stepped in, grinning, and in unison said, "Ta-da!" Stunned, I saw George step into the doorway. His eyes glittered with tears, and he suddenly wrapped me in a bear hug. Flabbergasted, I put my arms round him, too.

"I'm so sorry." He spoke over my shoulder. "I only hope I'm in time to make it up to them. And to you. It was your letter that brought me back, you know. What you said about the boys and Lisette. And when I read in the French papers about what you'd been going through, I realised that the place I was *really* needed was right here. Besides, I can't leave you without a partner for Henley."

I clapped him on the back. "You nearly left it too late,

but I think I'll take you back. No, really, George, I can't tell you how pleased I am. My oldest friend has—well, it's as if you've come back to life. This calls for a real celebration. Come in, come in, everybody."

I ushered them all into the warm library, then dashed to the fridge for the emergency bottle of bubbly. It was a strange day, I thought, when you overheard a murder plot *and* welcomed your long-lost friend home with champagne. I also found a bottle of fizzy apple juice for the boys, and carried a tray of glasses and the bottles into the library. George was speaking to Ian, his arm round Lisette's shoulders. The boys exclaimed over Sarah's plaster cast, fascinated.

"Wow! Can we touch it?" Michael asked.

"No, silly, you'll hurt her," his older brother said.

Sarah laughed. "You can rap on it—see how hard it is. And would you sign it for me? Or draw a picture?"

"Yeah!" the boys said in unison, descending on the coloured pens on the table with greedy fingers. With the incredible adaptability that characterises children, they'd already accepted their father's presence and were getting on with life as usual. And they were helping all of the adults do the same.

The telephone rang again as I was pouring the champagne. Ian stepped in to take over while I picked it up. "All go, isn't it?" I said, smiling at him and pushing the On button.

"Alex! Martyn here. Just got some news, and thought you'd like to know. D'you have a minute?"

"Of course, of course. Actually, I've some news for you, too. But you first."

"Well. You'll never believe who's come forward with information in the case of Lord Chenies's sudden death."

"You'll never believe what *I* heard about that today— but come on, out with it," I said.

"Hillary Charford-Cheney."

"*What?*"

"Exactly what I said. Malcolm's devoted wife decided she'd do better to have his money and not be tied to his heinous crime—she told the police that Malcolm killed him with some sort of organic potion of Helena's from the rain forest, acquired by Richard Hotchkiss. But there's more."

"I'm all ears."

"When the police confronted Malcolm with all this, he broke down. He started wailing about how it hadn't been his idea to start with, that the others had got him to do it. Had *blackmailed* him into doing it."

"What others?" I asked, certain that I already knew. All was coming clear now, though it was nothing if not a complicated mess.

Martyn said, "He claims—difficult as this is to believe—that the brains behind the operation were Richard Hotchkiss, Anthony Simino, and Victor Fine."

"That's exactly what I was going to tell you next. At the Clerkenwell Fete today, I overheard the old boys gloating over the fact that they'd succeeded, wasn't revenge sweet, and how super it was that Malcolm had been taken in for the crime. It seems that Lord Chenies used to bully them mercilessly in school. They've held a grudge all this time, and they finally did something about it.

"And as Detective Inspector Fawcett said, it explains those three extra tea cups," I added. "The three old boys came round for a visit, and Malcolm followed."

"That's positively *pathological*," Martyn said. "I've never heard of such vindictiveness."

"Mmm." I paused, switching gears. "Can you come for Sunday lunch after church next week? George Stoneham's back. I thought we'd have a good old-fashioned day together, on into tea later. Max and Madeline are coming, too, and Nicola and Amanda. All right?"

"Yes, thanks. Sounds like great fun. Wonderful news about George!"

We rang off, and after Ian went to pick up Chinese food, the rest of the evening was spent in games with the boys. I could almost, but not quite, forget that I was a marked man.

CHAPTER NINETEEN

I was in a printing house in Hell, and saw the method in which knowledge is transmitted from generation to generation.

WILLIAM BLAKE, *The Marriage of Heaven and Hell*

AT SEVEN THE NEXT MORNING, THE BEDSIDE TABLE PHONE rang. I answered, still sleepy.

"Alex. Guy Ferris-Browne here. Would it be convenient for you to stop by Amanda's Print Shop on your way in this morning? Something's come up; we need to have a chat."

What *now?*

"Nine-ish all right?"

"Fine."

"See you then." *Click.*

An hour and a half later I'd spoken with both security guards who would stay with Sarah for the day, delivered Lisette to the Press, and found a parking place on Clerkenwell Green. I climbed out of the car and saw that Amanda's windows were covered with paper from the inside. The unlocked door swung open easily as I turned the knob.

Once I'd entered and run the gauntlet of printer's cabinets, freshly sanded to rid them of char, I saw why the windows had been masked. A tremendous amount of work had been done. The place had been thoroughly cleaned and repainted. The "new" antique presses stood in place of the old ones. Once Amanda had restored the William Morris stencils, the shop would look like its old self.

But, strangely, the print shop was deserted. Amanda and Bruce were nowhere to be seen. I looked round, puzzled at first, then suspicious. Suddenly the PM's white-blond giant stepped into the room, and two burly bodyguards converged on me. One of them was the dark-haired man I'd seen in front of the Trades Union Group offices.

My stomach twisted in fear; I understood immediately what they intended. I bolted back the way I'd come, but they were expecting that. Before I could get through the door, the TUG man and his friend caught me roughly. They yanked my arms behind my back and twisted my hands upward. The giant walked slowly to the door and locked it.

My cell phone emitted a muted trill from my jacket pocket. *If only I could get a signal to someone at work . . .*

I decided to gamble. Looking the giant in the eye, I said as calmly as I could, "If I don't answer, my office will know something's wrong."

I saw him thinking this over, wondering whether to believe me. The other men looked to him. Clearly he was the brains of the operation. Luck was running with me.

"Answer it," he commanded, pulling a gun from the holster under his jacket. "But if you say anything out of the ordinary . . . " Holding the gun an inch from my nose, he removed the safety with a menacing click.

I nodded and reached for the phone. The giant held up a hand for me to stop. *He* reached inside my pocket and drew out the phone. The men released my arms, which were growing numb, and trained their weapons on me as the giant passed me the device.

I pulled up the antenna and punched the phone to life, extremely well aware of the three guns pointed at my head. "Yes," I answered. Surely the caller would hear my heart pounding.

"Alex. Don't say a word. This is Nicola. Yes or no, are you with them now?"

How did she know?

"Yes."

"Where are you?"

"I'd say go ahead with the printing."

"Printing. The print shop! Am I right?"

"Yes."

"Okay. Get out of there any way you can. My fiancé Reg found out what's going on from one of the PM's assistants—they don't intend to let you leave alive. As soon as you hang up, I'm ringing for help."

"Right. Okay. Thanks, Lisette." I rang off, pressing the power button and sliding the phone back into my jacket pocket.

The big man eyed me suspiciously, then snatched my phone and pocketed it himself. "Let's go." He strode purposefully to the rear of the shop and opened the door to the cellar. What were they going to do? Shoot me and dump my body down the stairs? They didn't seem to have torches, so surely we weren't travelling through the tunnels. . . .

The other two seized my arms and began to pull me roughly toward the door. I didn't have to be a genius to figure out that they were preparing to shoot me without wasting too much time. I cooperated so they wouldn't grip my arms too tightly. As we were about to pass through the doorway, I made an all-or-nothing effort, twisting out of their grasp and through the doorway. I plunged down the stairs toward the tunnels, but slipped on the narrow, steep steps. My feet flew out from under me as a shot whizzed past my ear. I tumbled onto my back, feeling the sharp edge of a step in my left kidney, then bumped painfully down the staircase. Even before I hit the bottom I scrambled for a footing and ended up madly scrabbling on all fours toward the tiny door to the tunnels. All around me, bullets smacked into wood with sickening finality.

Thank God for subterranean Clerkenwell! As I clawed at the latch on the door to the tunnels, their footsteps were loud on the steps behind me. I heard the subdued whine of a silenced bullet, heard it fly into the old wood in front of me. It was only a matter of time before one of them hit its mark.

Hurry, Alex! Faster!

I blundered through the door and banged it closed again, though there was no latch on the other side to stop my pursuers. Crouching in the tunnel, I scuttled forward into the darkness, sloshing through the icy water, hands groping for the sides of the tunnel. I heard the men race behind me through the door; one of them swore and yelled something about a torch. I stumbled on in the pitch dark, using my sole advantage of having seen the tunnel and its curve before. The men splashed along behind me, but I knew they had to move more slowly. They didn't know what was ahead.

An inhuman squeal rent the air; one of the men cried out. He'd encountered the tunnel wildlife. I hoped it had bit him.

My right hand suddenly hit space instead of clammy stone wall. Panting, I stopped and agonised, feeling about in the inky blackness. I found walls that matched the ones behind me: a fork in the tunnel. This was a crucial decision; if I took this branch, it might lead literally to a dead end—mine. Or it might lead to the House of Detention, or even the Order of St. James. I hoped for the latter. To the best of my knowledge, this tunnel led toward St. James's Gate. On the other hand, if I went farther, I might come to a branch that would lead to the House of Detention. Should I carry on straight, hoping to find a tunnel that would lead there, or take this fork to the right?

The advancing men forced me to choose quickly. I splashed out to the right, praying I'd chosen correctly. Their shouts echoed ominously down the tunnels. After a moment I heard the giant swear venomously and yell, "Quiet! Listen!"

I stopped mid-stride, trying to calm my breathing. The eerie silence of the tunnels, their claustrophobic height, gave rise to the beginnings of panic. I dared not move while they waited for me to reveal myself. My back begged me to stand upright.

"You go that way, we'll go this way!" I heard finally.

I plunged ahead, knowing that now I had a better chance—one adversary instead of two. I imagined the third was trying very hard to lay his hands on a torch. But then I heard the giant cry, "He's here! This way!"

A shot pinged off the wall to my left; I recoiled, only to hear one on my right. He was shooting wildly, blindly, hoping to hit me by chance. His odds were good. In the low, narrow tunnel he was likely to hit me. The passage curved gently, like the section I'd seen the other night. If I only managed to stay far enough ahead, I might be beyond range of his bullets.

Concentrating on speed, my back screaming from the effort of remaining doubled over, I came to what I thought at first was another branch in the tunnel. But it was just a niche, like the recessed places in train tunnels I'd always speculated about.

If I could hide in the niche while they ran right past me, all the while shooting up ahead . . . I decided to gamble. Pushing myself back against the wall as best I could, I felt cold slime on my neck and repressed a shudder. My muscles cried out. The men came together now, not speaking, the only sounds their feet through the icy water. I imagined them feeling their way along the tunnel as I had, arms extended.

Please go past, please go past. If they didn't, I'd have to fight them hand to hand, two on one. Perhaps this wasn't so smart after all, I thought . . . but it was too late. They were five feet away now, four . . .

Then it happened: a hand touched my shoulder. In the split second before he reacted, I swept my arm down. From the height of his arm, I knew it was the TUG thug. His weapon discharged, then splashed into the water. As he bent to retrieve it, I came down with both hands together where I thought his head would be. I made contact and his body went limp, splashing to the tunnel floor.

The giant had been ominously silent. I knew he would be training his weapon on me. I dived for his knees—or where I imagined them to be—just as the *ping* of a shot rang off the tunnel wall.

The giant and I fell in the ankle-deep freezing water, grappling for the gun. I was scared silly by this man; there was something inhuman about him. And I wasn't used to being smaller than people; his hugeness was terrifying. I groped for the gun, actually stuck my finger *in the barrel* while searching for it, then pulled it out again an instant before he squeezed the trigger. The shot miraculously missed me. I latched on to his hands on top of the gun, and hung on. But he knew his advantage. He got to his knees, shoving me sideways with brutal force. My head hit stone. Reeling from the blow, ears ringing, I clung to the weapon and his hands as he knocked me over. Twisting my neck to keep my mouth and nose out of the water, I clung to his hands and the gun like a dog to a bone.

Think, Alex. Think fast or die.

But the giant was thinking too. He sprawled on top of me, using the powerful advantage of his size and weight. I panicked for an instant, particularly as I thought of him forcing my mouth and nose into the muck. I had to move, and fast. I gathered myself and, with all my will to live, smashed my arms and the gun up into him. At the same time I let out a subhuman roar and rolled, scrabbling with my toes on the slippery floor for purchase. Somehow I succeeded in forcing myself out from under him. Now he was on *his* side on the ground. I had to use my advantage, and quickly. But before I could get on top of him, he'd scrambled to his knees, cursing. I threw myself blindly at him, at the same time fighting desperately to train his weapon away—I felt it pressing straight into my gut. Fighting for my life gave me strength born of pure, desperate fear. I summoned all my fury and strength and drove my shoulder into him like a pile driver. He went over backwards.

This is your last chance! Don't let him slip away!

Before he could elude me again I crawled right on top of his chest. Focussing all my strength on the weapon, slick now with muck and slime, I managed to get it pointing at the tunnel wall just as he squeezed the trigger. The shot pinged off the wall and ricocheted off the other side. He battled to get the little black muzzle pointing in my direction again; I wrenched it back. He succeeded in aiming it at my shoulder; before I could push it away again he squeezed the trigger. The shot whistled past my ear, terrifying in its proximity. I threw all my weight on one knee, pressing it against the gun, forcing it down onto his chest. Pinning the gun sideways against him, I pulled back one arm and hit the oversized bully as hard as I could in the face. He was on his back in the four-inch-deep water; it came up to his ears. He lifted his head up in an all-too-human reaction, and when I hit him yet again, his head cracked back against the tunnel floor. He struggled no more.

I climbed off him, panting. For an instant I was the only one moving in the tunnel. Then I heard distant splashing and knew that the third man had finally found a torch. I picked up the gun from the unconscious giant beneath me; I didn't want to shoot anyone.

A faint, bobbing glow came from the last branch of the tunnel behind me—the man with the torch. I felt I had no choice but to continue the way I'd been going, toward St. James's Gate. If only there were some way up to street level there . . .

I ran on and on, glancing back from time to time. Dim light in the distance, round the endless curves of the tunnels. It was while I was looking over my shoulder that I ran headlong into something, nearly knocking myself silly. I found myself sitting on the floor of the tunnel in the water, head spinning. Groping with my hands for information about what I'd blundered into, I found that it was a smooth wooden door with no latch or handhold on my side. I banged on it—pointlessly, I knew. I was trapped.

There was noise down the tunnel; perhaps Number Three had found his companions and revived them. I heard voices, the giant's among them, as they splashed toward me. I took my despair out on the door, banging with desperate fists. Damn, damn, *damn*! What an idiot I'd been. A fool to think I could outrun the prime minister's professionals. I kicked at the immovable wall, my death sentence, then threw myself against it, hoping to knock it down before I had to start shooting blindly. It did not budge.

Then a distant noise like a tinkling bell sounded behind me. For a moment I thought I was losing my mind.

Then I realised the sound came from the other side of the door. A sound not unlike that of keys . . .

Incredulous, I turned and watched as the door swung open into a lighted room, up a step from the tunnel. A group of stunned tourists with cameras round their necks gaped at me. I stepped up and out of the tunnel, blinking as my eyes adjusted to the blinding light.

"Plumtree!" Robert Lovegren gazed at me incredulously. "For heaven's sake, I'd have *given* you a tour of the crypt if you'd only *asked.*"

The tourists gaped at my drowned-rat appearance and obvious desperation as I told Lovegren that armed men had pursued me through the tunnels. He locked the door hurriedly, and I rang the police from the Order's reception desk. I feigned ignorance as to who was involved and why, just that three men with weapons had attacked me in Amanda's Print Shop and were now in a tunnel leading from the shop's cellar door. I was informed that a police unit had already been dispatched. Of course: Nicola said she'd rung for help. By now the police knew that the unions and the general population to the left of centre had it in for Alex Plumtree.

"Alex! Thank God! I saw the police at the shop, and those men they dragged out . . . " Amanda ran breathlessly into the Gate's reception area.

Lovegren put an arm round her shoulders. "It's all right now, Amanda. Alex took care of himself quite well."

I studied them. There had been times when I'd questioned Amanda's loyalty; now I found myself questioning it again. Had she been some sort of spy for the PM all along?

Amanda was clearly upset. Well, so was I.

Lovegren looked at me through his kind, wise eyes.

"Alex, you'll have to trust us. Both of us. We can't tell you everything now, but we will. Soon."

Of course I did trust Lovegren, and I wanted to trust Amanda . . . what did he mean, "we"? *They* worked together somehow? That would explain their closeness and his continual protection of her. . . .

It was inconceivable to me that this secret web of relationships existed, had been there all along. I had only seen the people I *thought* I knew. And the one person I trusted in the government, the most powerful person in that government, had arranged to have me killed.

I asked them to leave me in peace while I rang Max. I told him the whole story, which he punctuated with emphatic exclamations.

I told him I had to go to Amanda's shop to deal with the police, and gave him the number there. When he rang me back there twenty minutes later with the news that his editor had torpedoed the story before he could even write it up, I knew we were in trouble. But I should have known. Any Labour PM worth his salt would have the *Watch* well under his thumb.

When the police had finished with me an hour later, I got in my car and drove. I couldn't go home; that was the first place the next wave would come looking for me. If I went home, I might endanger Sarah further. I rang Sarah, told her I was all right and loved her, and asked her to put me on to the security guard.

"Listen," I told him. "People at the highest levels of government are coming for me. I won't come near the house, of course, but I'm worried for Sarah. Ring Detective Inspector Fawcett at the Herts Constabulary, tell him I've been attacked and that I suspect they might come to the Orchard looking for me." I only hoped the police weren't under the PM's thumb as well. *"Do not leave Sarah alone at any time,"* I finished with emphasis.

"They'll have to get me first, Mr. Plumtree," the guard said. From past work with the man, I'd learned he was as good as his word.

At least Sarah was relatively safe for the moment. But I felt cold and sick with disillusion. My clothes were wet and filthy from crawling round the tunnel. The prime minister was a criminal, and I'd willingly done his bidding. In the process, Mmbasi Kumba had died, as had Lord Chenies. Sarah had been injured.

Not only that, but Richard Hotchkiss and Anthony Simino had been exposed as murderers, not to mention cheating businessmen. And now Robert Lovegren and Amanda were in on something terrifically secret together. As if that wasn't enough, Ian seemed to be in on it too.

I decided to go to a hotel to clean up and take stock—some place no one would look for me. I drove dejectedly to the Langham at All Souls Place—no need to suffer privations as well as manhunts—and paid cash for a room. The clerk, to her credit, barely acknowledged my remarkably pungent clothing. Locked in my fifth-floor room, I sank onto the bed and suddenly realised I'd never rung Nicola to thank her for getting onto the PM's plot and calling for help. I phoned her at the Press.

"Alex! Where are you?"

"Why do you want to know?"

A moment of silence told me I'd hurt her. I knew an apology was in order but was unable to offer one.

"I heard what you've just been through," she went on. "Amanda said you left as if you hadn't a friend in the world. So I suppose what I have to say will be good news."

I waited.

"Would you believe me if I told you that just

moments ago, my father and Helena Hotchkiss fled the country in Helena's private jet?"

"What, for a holiday? Now? Just before the election?"

"No. For good. And I feel more pride at being associated with you, who exposed him, than I do pity for him."

"*Exposed* him? For what? *I* didn't—"

"You forced him to play his hand too soon, Alex. He had everything set up to betray Abercrombie and move into Number Ten himself, but you got in the way. You stood up to the protesters, you gave interviews calling for peace, you galvanised your brother and me into action, questioning things. Finally, incredibly, you survived his assassination attempts and phoned the *Watch* with the stories. Only it wasn't Abercrombie—it was Guy all along. Abercrombie has announced now that he *knew* Guy was about to betray him, and only hoped the man would hang himself before Abercrombie had to do it for him. Where are you—I mean, are you somewhere near a TV or radio?"

"Yes," I said guardedly.

"Turn anything on—the story's taken the nation by storm."

I used the remote to switch on the television. News had overtaken regular programming. The anchor intoned, "*. . . and in one of the most sensational turns of events ever in the history of British elections, Guy Ferris-Browne has flown to France with his mistress, pharmaceuticals expert and environmental activist Helena Hotchkiss. The prime minister announced moments ago that he owes a debt of gratitude to Alex Plumtree, the book publisher so much in the news lately for his publication of* Cleansing, *for helping him expose Ferris-Browne's plot.*"

I stared at the screen. On the phone, Nicola said, "See? I'm not making this up."

"But I didn't . . . thanks, Nicola." Distractedly, I

rang off. I hadn't exposed Ferris-Browne . . . *had I?* I'd groped around for information, yes, but why wasn't the PM furious with me for trying to get stories in the *Watch* that he was a murderer? It didn't make any sense. Unless . . .

If the PM had suspected Ferris-Browne, even on the day I'd joined them for lunch at Number Ten, and had used me to play out his deputy's ill-starred plans . . . could that be it? I supposed I had inadvertently turned up the heat on Ferris-Browne by turning the nation's anti-*Cleansing* sentiment into an anti-union, anti-protester sentiment. Thanks to Jim Mehrer, the world had awakened to the mindless violence of British politics. But I didn't see how the PM could have planned that. . . .

The anchorman continued. "*. . . nation is stunned today by the betrayal of the prime minister by his deputy, Minister for the Environment Guy Ferris-Browne. The prime minister has told us that allies from various walks of life warned him of his old friend's treachery, but until he had proof he could do nothing. It does seem clear that Ferris-Browne had laid plans to discredit Prime Minister Abercrombie just before the election and to step in to the top office himself.*

"*The PM spoke to us just moments ago, saying that he is greatly saddened. He said he hoped the country would realise that the wildings and riots of recent weeks were in fact orchestrated by Ferris-Browne and were not in fact the true feelings of the British people.*"

Allies from various walks of life warned the prime minister of his old friend's treachery some time ago. . . . Ian was an old friend of Graeme Abercrombie's, had known him through my father. And Ian had first suggested to me, weeks ago, that Ferris-Browne might be using me and shouldn't be trusted.

"*Ferris-Browne's plans to initiate a European Union–wide strike of all the major trade unions would have crippled*

*the continent, and focussed a spotlight on Ferris-Browne
as the only man who could gain the cooperation of the
renegade unions. Coupled with a disinformation campaign
against Prime Minister Abercrombie, evidence for which
is in the possession of the PM's office, Ferris-Browne hoped
to discredit Abercrombie and step in as prime minister
himself.*

*"But those plans were put off when an unknown negotia-
tor, acting on the prime minister's part, secretly arranged for
the French equivalent of the NUP to opt out of the strike. It
was the first breach of the dam, and the other unions gave in
soon after."*

Suddenly I thought of Ian's unexplained business
trip to France. Plumtree Press didn't have business in
France at the moment. But since when had Ian become
the PM's secret negotiator with militant foreign trade
unions?

The anchor's face gave way to footage of Helena's
plane from earlier, happier occasions, and then to
Graeme Abercrombie's comfortable and comforting face.
He looked overwhelmingly tired. *"This has been a great
ordeal for the British people. We can all be grateful that it's
behind us now. When I think what my once-trusted deputy
put our nation through . . . I can only express my deepest ap-
preciation to the people who exposed Ferris-Browne for what
he was. We now have evidence, through my former colleague's papers, that he arranged for the wilding that ended
in last month's murder of Mmbasi Kumba. We also have evidence that Ferris-Browne feared the power of the Campaign
for an Independent Britain, a small but powerful lobby
which advocates staying out of Economic and Monetary
Union and even withdrawing from the EU. I am sorry to
say that we have evidence that Guy Ferris-Browne arranged
for the murder of Nigel Charford-Cheney, Lord Chenies, because of the latter's secret leadership of the Campaign for an
Independent Britain. Interpol is tracking down Guy Ferris-*

Browne even now, and he will be brought to justice for his crimes."

I leaned back against the headboard, closing my eyes for an instant as the news anchor droned on with further details. Then I lifted the phone and dialled Sarah.

"It's over, my love. I'm coming home."

CHAPTER TWENTY

———❦———

Smile at us, pay us, pass us; but do not quite forget.
For we are the people of England, that never have spoken yet.

G. K. CHESTERTON, *The Secret People*

THE SERVICE AT CHRIST CHURCH CHENIES THE NEXT
Sunday morning was more sombre than usual. The
hedges surrounding the churchyard still showed the rav-
ages of the bizarre riot; the unruly crowds at Lord Chenies's funeral had snapped quite a few branches. It was
likely to be some time before everything seemed normal
again. Lord Chenies was gone forever, and his heir had re-
nounced the title.

One thing that *was* perfectly normal was my plan that
day for an old-fashioned Sunday lunch, with all my
friends and family gathered round. As I left Martyn at the
church door, greeting his flock, he said he'd be along in a
bit. When the last chatty parishioner had done with him,
he meant. Judging from the gaggle of people queuing up
to greet him, not to mention Amanda lingering in the
wings, he was in no danger of being rejected by his congregation. I winked at him as a diminutive white-haired
lady wearing a pillbox hat approached him with rosy

cheeks and expectant eyes, taking his hand in both of hers. Chuckling, I went home to help prepare the lunch.

Lord Chenies would have been pleased, I thought, motoring happily down the lane. If the actual outcome of the election had disappointed him, he'd at least have been cheered by one of its by-products. Graeme Abercrombie had prevailed, but not Ferris-Browne's rampant pro–European Unionism. Our esteemed prime minister had decided that if the nation was in such an uproar over the whole issue, there had to be a national referendum. It had been fascinating to watch: it was as if the prime minister had made public my own thoughts on the matter. He'd publicised in detail, using the major newspapers, how the Common Market had somehow become the European Union without the people's approval, until now we stood at the point of entering into a federal superstate along the lines of the United States. Our defence treaties and loyalties were about to change to European ones instead of NATO, again all without our approval. The more the prime minister talked about it, the more convinced many of us had become that this was not something we wanted. The prime minister's referendum was scheduled for May, barely a month away. I was quite looking forward to placing my vote. I thought of Guy Ferris-Browne seething in his gaol cell, furious at the thought that he'd missed his chance by so little. If he were ever released from prison, I thought, I'd have to start watching my back again.

Hours later, as I sat contentedly with Sarah, Ian, Max, Madeline, Nicola, Martyn, Amanda, George, Lisette, and the boys over the pudding, the telephone rang. "Sorry," I said, and stood to answer it. I left the dining room, crossed over to the library, and picked up the phone.

"Alex? Richard Hotchkiss."

I looked out of the windows into the garden. "Hello, Richard."

"Listen, Alex. I just wanted you to know I harbour no grudge against you for ringing the police about the three of us." To my infinite surprise, it had emerged that Simino, Hotchkiss, and Fine had coerced Malcolm Charford-Cheney into administering one of Helena's rain-forest remedies to his father, but only as a cruel practical joke. Malcolm had put the stuff—some sort of anti-free-radical, youth-preserving vitamin—in a massive dose in his father's tomato juice, knowing he had a glass each day before tea. The vitamin, in excessive doses, gave the symptoms of a heart attack—pain in the jaw, the left arm, and chest—without causing the real thing. Lucky for them they hadn't frightened the man to death, I thought.

But the real surprise had been that another of Ferris-Browne's secret government agents had murdered Lord Chenies with a tiny pinprick of poison, nearly untraceable, through a dart in his neck. The pinprick went unnoticed until after I'd reported to Fawcett on what I'd overheard at the Fête, causing the investigation of Lord Chenies's death to be reopened with vigour. Then Ferris-Browne had scarpered, causing still more suspicion. It was frightening to me that Ferris-Browne, clued in by Helena, had so adeptly used his knowledge of the cruel joke Hotchkiss, Simino, and Fine planned for Lord Chenies. Malcolm had very nearly spent the rest of his life in prison for a murder he hadn't committed. Perhaps Ferris-Browne had felt more threatened by Lord Chenies and the CIB than any of us had realised.

"I've wanted to explain a few things to you, Plumtree, not that it excuses anything we did." A sound of exasperation and frustration travelled down the line. "You see, Victor Fine, Anthony Simino, and I were all at Merchant Taylors with Nigel. . . ." Hotchkiss proceeded to catalogue the offences I'd overheard at St. Mary's Clerkenwell, ending with "and there were . . . er . . . other things." He paused, and I thought of the ghastly things boys had been known to do to each other at English boarding schools.

"I know what we did sounds unforgivable," he went on, "but we never forgot the torture he put us through. And we finally decided to play a little trick on him, which we let Malcolm in on. You might say Malcolm was a member of our little club who couldn't bear his father." He sighed.

"Now it sounds horribly cruel, but if you only knew . . ." His voice faded away. "We had no idea we'd never see the old blackguard again."

Hotchkiss, who was now nationally despised because of his daughter's collaboration with Ferris-Browne, cleared his throat briskly. "At any rate, I, ah, was reconsidering that board of directors seat at Merchant Taylors, Plumtree. I thought perhaps you might like to join us after all."

"I'll have to think about it, Richard."

"Fair enough," he said, sounding surprisingly collected. "Talk to you another day, then. Oh, by the way," he said as an afterthought. "Did you hear? We won the vote."

"Sorry?"

"The boundary vote. The line will be redrawn officially in three months' time."

"Ah. Well." I'd forgotten all about the county boundary issue—hadn't even read the latest *Chorleywood Communicator*.

"If you're interested in investing in a new water company . . ."

I demurred and rang off. No matter how things changed, everything stayed the same.

On the desk in front of me was a document Martyn had brought with him. He said he'd found it among the piles of paper in his new study. It looked frightfully intriguing and ancient, and I couldn't resist a quick glance at it before rejoining the others for coffee. It was a chilly, rainy day, and before unrolling the yellowed paper I pushed the door to the hall mostly closed to conserve heat from the dwindling fire. Returning to the desk, I gently slid the purple ribbon down and off the roll. As I did so, the door that I'd just pushed closed swung open ever so slowly. I looked up, expecting someone to walk into the room. But no one did. The nearly dead fire in the fireplace, however, flared to life as if someone had taken an energetic bellows to it. A draft at the door, I thought, pushed it open and fanned the fire back to life.

But goose pimples immediately covered my arms, travelling up my neck into my scalp. There was no one else in the room, nothing but an odd *feeling* that someone was there. I decided that my vivid imagination was acting up yet again, and unrolled the paper on the desk with a flourish of brisk, normal activity. My eyes widened at what I saw on the paper before me: it was a map of the Plumtree land, our total of two hundred acres at the top of Old Shire Lane in once-rural, now-suburban Chorleywood.

It was as if I'd lived on a river my whole life, but had never known its winding path. The map included the hedges on our property, and to my amazement, I saw that the now-infamous Plumtree hedges had been planted in the pattern of interlocking *P*'s, four to a square, with twenty acres per square. There were, therefore, fifty squares of four *P*'s. The half-circles on the stems of the *P*'s divided up the fields into nicely sheltered small areas. In fact, it rather resembled the layout for printing a book, with the signatures divided into pages. The farmer to whom we'd leased most of the property over the years had asked if he could take some of the hedges out. It would allow his machinery to move over the fields more efficiently, he'd said. But we'd held firm, to the gratitude of the local HIT squad.

My mind boggled. This large pattern had been the outline of my happy world here, and I'd never known it. How could I *not* have realised that those long straight lines of hedge with the curves at one end were giant *P*s? My ancestors had used the interlocking *P*s as their first device for headpieces and tailpieces when they began Plumtree Press. I'd seen it in the early books. But of course the hedges were medieval, so that meant the colophon had been taken from the hedges, not the other way round.

I shook my head. My father had never told me that Plumtrees had actually planted our hedges—I'd always assumed we'd moved here *long* after the Middle Ages, perhaps the early nineteenth century. Why hadn't he told me? I wondered what further discoveries lay in store about my ancestors; they were an apparently endless source of intrigue.

As I looked up towards the wall containing the fireplace and bookshelves, lost in these thoughts, I found myself staring at a panel of interlocking *P*s in bas-relief. There was something about the way that section fitted into the wall just there. . . . I stood and moved slowly toward the panelling surrounding the fireplace. There was a razor-thin line round the panel; it had no doubt been carved elsewhere and set in place after the framework of the shelves had been completed. I reached out to touch the *P*s. To my surprise, as my fingers caressed the wood, the panel popped out to reveal a space behind it, reaching deep into the wall. I peered in to the dark area, and saw—what else, in this room, in this house?—a book.

Carefully, I reached out for the leather-slipcased volume and took it in my hand, glancing round the room as if to see if anyone had come into the room. I *did* have the sensation that someone was there. It was most strange . . . yet I was not at all afraid. Rather like the first night in the barn . . .

I slid the book gently out of the case and saw that the upper centre of its cover bore only interlocking *P*'s stamped in gold into the tan leather. I opened it carefully and saw that my father had inscribed it to me.

To my beloved son, Alex Plumtree, esteemed partner in the printed word, in admiration. I sense a printer in you; I always have. This is my legacy for that yet-unwritten chapter of your life, and the handpress in the barn. Give it a try.

> *Your loving father,*
> *Dad*

As I flipped to the first page, I saw that this was a fully hand-printed and hand-bound book. It had been printed with my father's Minerva Cropper. Though the spine bore no title, the title page read, "Notes from one printer to another" in my father's beloved Baskerville type, with twining plum-bearing branches wreathing the page. His printer's mark, the interlocking *P*'s, was again at the bottom of the page.

I was turning to the next page when Ian came through the door. "Ah!" he said. "Good. You've built up the fire. We were getting worried about you."

He studied me, no doubt sensing something of the odd presence in the room. The door moved a bit behind him, silently, and he took note of it. He looked me in the eye, saw the book in my hand, and said, "Hmm. I'll see to the fire."

I have never doubted that Ian fully understood what was happening in the library on that damp afternoon. He has what I would call a sense of the eternal. If he had placed the book there for me to discover one day, having been entrusted with it by my father . . . well, to me that was the same as my father putting it there.

When the crowd traipsed in from the dining room,

Sarah looked at me questioningly on top of her crutches, but smiled with her usual enthusiasm. I went to her, the book still in my hand. Max and Madeline bade us farewell, saying they needed to get home. I had lived with them long enough here at the Orchard to know exactly what they were going to do. I winked at Max and gave him a hug. "Thanks again for everything, Max. I know it was asking a lot."

"Not at all. Anything for my little brother. Besides, my stock's gone up no end at the paper. The managing editor is convinced I've a direct line to all the big stories."

Lisette went round the room switching on lamps to counteract the dim, drizzly afternoon. "Why are you 'ere in the dark, Alex?" she reprimanded me. "It is not good for the eyes."

"You're right," I said. "It's only just got so dim, really." Normality and the comfort of everyday voices and activities took over as I helped Sarah into her spot on the sofa and placed her crutches on the floor within her reach. The boys dashed directly to the cupboard where the games were kept and pulled out their favourite, Monopoly. I saw Sarah's eyes light up. As an ex-banker, and as Jean-Claude Rimbaud's fund and foundation manager, she loved nothing so well as a rousing competition involving money. The boys, George, Lisette, and Sarah ended up at the coffee table dealing out money in the first throes of that endless game which I frequently call Monotony, just to gall the others.

Nicola, Ian, Martyn, Amanda, and I spread out on the floor with our much-preferred game of Scrabble. As Ian and I did so often, we placed the large Volume One of *The Compact Edition of the Oxford English Dictionary* on the floor to serve as a turntable, with the board on top of it. We each drew our seven letters. Ian drew the *A* to start first, of course. He *always* seemed to get the *A*, and he nearly always won.

"You keep score," he said, and handed me the pad of paper and pencil.

Contentedly, I glanced round the room, taking in all the happy, animated faces, revelling in the lively chatter. I didn't want to dwell too much on what had happened that afternoon, if in fact anything had. But I knew I would never forget it.

When I looked back down at the board, Ian had placed his word. SUPER. I wrote down his score, seven points times two for the double word score.

Then I looked at my own collection of letters. "I don't believe it," I said. "This is a first!"

"Oh, no," Martyn groaned to his team mate, Amanda. "I know that look. He's got something incredible."

Smiling, I began to pick letters off my wooden tray. It read "TRUANLA." I took the *N* first, placing it after the *R* of Ian's SUPER. Next came the *A*, then *T, U, R, A, L.* "Let's see," I said, trying to sound matter-of-fact. "That's a fifty-point bonus for using all seven letters, and fourteen points for the word—times three for the triple word score."

Ian looked up at me, eyes sparkling, and laughed a deep belly laugh that resounded through the room. Sarah looked over, curious and pleased at her grandfather's un-usually mirthful outburst. Ian said, "I think you've al-ready won the game, Alex."

Martyn, Amanda, and Nicola eyed one another for-lornly. Nicola said with a smile, "I *knew* I should have chosen Monotony."

Lisette said, "What's the matter over there?" and came to have a look. "May I?" she asked Nicola.

"Be my guest."

Lisette set down HOME, using the *E* of Ian's SUPER.

"Perfect," Nicola said.

Martyn twiddled his thumbs for a few seconds, then laid down ABSOLVED, using the *A* of my NATURAL.

I smiled.

◆   ◆   ◆

The Stonehams trundled home at about seven, with the boys grumbling that they didn't want to go to school the next day anyway. Martyn wanted Amanda to show him more about printing, and urged us all out to the barn. He'd an idea to start a series of facsimiles of parish books from the churches round England, and was quite excited about it.

"Seriously," he exclaimed. "Everybody'd buy a copy to look up their uncle Ebenezer. Proceeds could go to Feed the Children." But the real motivation for this idea, unless I was mistaken, was the desire to spend a great deal more time very close to Amanda.

Sarah was eager to see the inside of the barn herself; I'd never taken her there before. Ian led the way with Nicola, followed by Amanda and Martyn, who couldn't seem to tear their eyes off one another. I came more slowly, with Sarah.

As we approached the barn, I noted that Ian switched on the light with an oddly familiar, proprietorial air. As Amanda crossed to the Albion to show Martyn how the platen press worked, I glanced at the galley tray in the bed. Expecting to see the now-familiar *"Welcome Alex,"* I was very much taken aback to see *"Baskerville is born"* instead, with a border of interlocking *P*'s, the old Plumtree Press device. At the bottom was the newer Press logo, a small leafy plum tree hanging ripe with fruit. I was a bit puzzled as to the meaning of the phrase, but Ian had come to stand behind me, laughing and putting an arm round my shoulders after I pointed it out to him. I wondered what he'd say if I told him that it had mysteriously appeared over the last few days.

"Now this, Martyn," Amanda said, picking up my father's composing stick, "is what you use to set type. You slide the type in and lock it up, upside down. Alex, if you'll bring over a job case . . ."

I went to one of the printer's cabinets and pulled out a drawer of Caslon. The rectangular drawer was subdivided into small sections, one for each character, so the type wasn't jumbled together. It contained the set of type I'd studied for letters on its shoulders but had been unable to make sense of. I vowed to ask Amanda about it tonight.

Amanda took the tray from me and placed it on the table next to her. "All right. One of the first things a printer learns is the layout of the case. Each little rectangle in this tray holds a different character. Any printer worth her salt knows where to reach for a character without looking at the case." She demonstrated as we watched, Martyn gawking with admiration not only for Amanda but for her art as well. Her hand flew back and forth as she rapidly assembled the type in the composing stick.

She took us through the further steps of locking the type into the chase with same decorative fleurons, suitable furniture, and quoins, then inking the platen, and finally printing a sheet. It said, very elegantly, "Printing holds the secrets of the ages."

As we admired the imprinted paper, I spoke. "Do you mind if I ask about the little letters on the shoulders of the type?" I reached into the case and took out a lowercase *a*—originally known as lowercase because of its position in the lower rack of the case, or drawer. "One night I tried to piece together what the letters mean—because they don't correspond with the bit of type they're on. For instance, this *a* has an *m* imprinted in its shoulder. When I laid out the whole alphabet, the letters added up to nothing but gibberish."

Ian and Amanda exchanged a significant look. Ian lifted his chin and said, "How curious. Perhaps you could show me a bit later—I'd like to see what you found." I knew him well enough to know that he was saying, *Not now, Alex. Later.*

Sarah wanted to try the handpress. "I'd like to know what it feels like," she said. Amanda asked her what she'd like to print, and her eye fell on the "Baskerville is born" chase. Amanda showed her how to lock it in place on the press bed, then where to put the paper and how to use the wheel—at least temporarily, the treadle would be too difficult for her to manage. It took Sarah two tries to make an impression she liked, but beaming, she held it up for us all to see.

"Have Alex tell you about the kiss sometime," Amanda said with a smile.

"Kiss?" Martyn said. "Tell me more." He ushered her out of the barn, and our little group broke up and wandered back toward the house. As I followed Nicola and Sarah out, Ian turned out the light, shut the door, and said softly in my ear, "Let's talk out here later, all right?"

I nodded.

Our guests went home shortly thereafter, with profuse thanks for the meal, tea, and the evening, and Sarah went up to bed, yawning. I told her I'd be up in a while, and met Ian in the barn.

"My boy, your father was a very fine printer." He sighed. "He hoped that one day you might carry on the family tradition. And in his case, that might mean a bit more than you think. What I am about to say you must never tell another soul, unless you feel you need to tell Sarah. I don't know if your father ever told your mother. Someday you may wish to tell a child of your own. Why don't you sit down?"

I pulled a stool up next to the Minerva; Ian leaned against the Vandercook. He took a deep breath and began. "In the seventeenth century, printers were also publishers. They didn't become separate entities until much later. Ever since Gutenberg, printers have known that they possessed great power. Their influence was so great, for instance, in printing the Bible, that the Crown sought to control this by *licensing* the right to print. Only those printers known to be trustworthy and loyal to the Crown were granted a license.

"Over time a group of printers decided to join together and fight all such controls. Would you believe, a printer still had to be licensed to print a Bible in the UK in the first half of *this* century? Printers, who were by their very function the repositories of vast stores of information, turned their knowledge into power. They recorded information about people of stature and influence in a place only a *printer* would know existed—the pin mark, and later the shoulder mark."

The light dawned. I'd wondered when he'd get round to the shoulder mark.

"Printers traded fonts regularly; one was known for his Caslon, another for his Garamond, and so the most delicate and dangerous messages passed back and forth over the oceans and mountains safely. Much of the information was never publicised, but was used to barter with royal or government officials, depending on the century, for better conditions for workers, more lenient licensing of printers, and so forth. The system was so safe because only printers knew how to read the messages; only they knew about pin marks and shoulder marks, and how letters are ordered in cases."

Aha, I thought. They're ordered in a way I couldn't figure out, because I'm not proficient at setting type.

Ian continued, "If you wanted to read a message, Alex—for instance, the one on this set of Caslon—you would take the letters not in alphabetical order, but in coded order, if you like. The first row across the side of a case consists of the odd order of ffi, fl, ', k, e, l, 1, 2, 3, 4, 5, 6, 7, 8, $, pound sign, j, b, c, d, e, i, s, f, g, ff, ,0, A, B, C, D,

E, F, G, ?, h, 0, !, l, m, n, h, o, y, p, w, ' and so forth. There are many more. So this is how the letters would read, taken in printer's case order: p, h, i, l, b, y, i, s, a, s, p, y."

I stared at him, aghast. "That's on *our* Caslon?" I asked.

"You know your father went to Cambridge. This was one of the bits of information that eventually became widely known. I should explain that these days, we mostly trade information to protect freedom where it seems threatened. If that sounds trite or idealistic to you, consider the situation in Britain one week ago. Our country had embarked upon a course of compromise, and no one seemed to be concerned. But we printers were concerned. Over the past few years we've become affiliated with Campaign for an Independent Britain, because we didn't want to be restricted by some European Council on Printing, or something. Your father saw this coming, Alex, and was one of the first to act upon his suspicions. In fact he spoke to Sir John Silversmith about heading a Referendum Party, and—you know the rest."

"You mean my father was anti–European Union when it was still called the Common Market?"

"No. It was the Maastricht Treaty in 1992 that frightened him. At any rate, back to the present, it was Garamond, our French member, who was able to tell us that Ferris-Browne was agitating the French unions and garnering their support for his *own* bid for prime minister, and eventually 'president of the European Union,' which is all a joke. It's a figurehead position, not one of any authority at all. As you know, Ferris-Browne was going to blackball Abercrombie, then claim he was the only one who could manage the unions. He'd lined them all up behind him, promising to deliver England to the EU as well as environmental concessions. The EU is a Socialist effort, and the trade unionists are very much behind it. One of the idiosyncracies of current politics is that many of the unions are now hand-in-glove with environmental activists. Ferris-Brown had HIT, Watchlands, Greenpeace, and all of them tied in with the unions—he had a nice little machine going until we got on to him."

"You—you exposed Ferris-Browne?"

"We couldn't have done it without you."

I struggled to take it all in. They—and my father—had been part of an international network of printers who traded in dangerous information. Was there anything my father *hadn't* done, *wasn't* a part of? I would never live up to his standard.

"Um, Ian—who's the other 'we' you keep mentioning? Or are you using it in the royal sense?"

He chuckled. "No. I suppose I use the word rather loosely. There are a number of us. I've known Amanda for years, of course, ever since your father died. She's carried on for him, with me."

My jaw dropped. "You've known Amanda for years, and you never told me?"

He raised his eyebrows at me. "Her great-uncle, Stanley Morison, was one of us. One of the great Renaissance men of printing in the twentieth century. I couldn't tell you, Alex, because there was quite a lot at stake, as you can tell by what happened to Lord Chenies. Not to mention Amanda—her abduction, the ruin of her shop. People got on to her through one of our French members, who turned informant for the EU maniacs like Ferris-Browne. It was Ferris-Browne himself, of course, who knew that Lord Chenies was a leader of the Campaign for an Independent Britain. Some of those people would do anything to see Britain go all the way to Economic and Monetary Union. I was afraid harm might come to you if I told you. And I hope I did the right thing by waiting until you became interested in printing of your own volition. I didn't want you to do this out of a sense of duty alone."

I didn't feel it was time, quite yet, to ask what it was exactly that I was supposed to do . . . but I knew it was coming.

"You've quite a treasure trove of fonts, here, Alex—your ancestors were printers, too." My eyes were drawn to the ranks of printer's cabinets, and their waiting drawers. What shocking secrets would I discover in those grubby, dusty wooden cases?

"So Bodoni, Garamond, Caslon, Goudy—they're all members of this group?" I was catching on.

"That's right," Ian answered. "You're Baskerville, if you so choose. That's the name your father intended to give to you. Amanda and I have only been carrying on for you until the time seemed right. We could remain as Caslon if we're needed."

"Who is Jenson?"

"Jenson was a French friend who went a little crazy; the others are all right. He was wrapped up with the equivalent of the NUP in Paris; Ferris-Browne had promised him a lofty position in the EuroUnion bureaucracy. When Dexter Moore crept into the lead because of *Cleansing*, Ferris-Browne of course tried to dispose of everyone involved with the novel."

"So Amanda's little story about her friends in the NUP being angry with her was just a front for all of this?"

He shook his head. "Not at all. It was the absolute truth . . . they pied her trays, they sent the early proofs astray and garbled others—they even spray-painted her walls. She just didn't tell you the *whole* truth."

"I don't mean to seem disrespectful, Ian—obviously your group of fine printers has turned round a disastrous situation—but isn't it a bit difficult to work in tiny letters on type shoulders? Why metal type? Why not something easy, like E-mail, or some sort of coded written communication?"

"Alex, you should know that E-mail is one of the least private means of communication that exists. I would no more send a private message via E-mail than I would shout it from my front garden. Believe it or not, our method is surprisingly secure. No one thinks to look at metal type anymore; people think it's a quaint antiquity. But printers all over the world still order various fonts from one another, so type has reason to move around quite a bit. There's also a lot of trading fonts amongst hand printers." He shrugged. "It works. We haven't been involved in anything this volatile in some time, though."

As Baskerville, I prayed that we wouldn't be involved in anything so volatile again for a very long time.

"Thank you, Ian. Sometimes I think there's no end to these secrets you and my father shared."

He waved off my thanks. "Your father was lucky to have a son willing to carry on in his tradition. Not every man is so fortunate."

"Nor is every man so fortunate as to have a true friend."

He put his arm round me, and we left the barn, knowing that we still had much to discuss—over many years, I hoped.

Forty-eight hours later, Sarah, Ian, and I sat at the prime minister's table at his victory party, feted like heads of state. Graeme Abercrombie was speaking to his friends and supporters from the centre of the dais. "And tonight I want to thank everyone who has made my re-election possible. I am aware of the personal sacrifices you have made for the sake of this election. I will always be deeply grateful." He looked down the table to where Ian, Sarah, and I sat, and smiled.

After he'd finished speech-making, the formal part of the evening gave way to celebration. Couples filled the dance floor. Sadly, Sarah and I were not among them, but we were delighted to be together—and alive.

Abercrombie found me as I went for a fresh drink for Sarah, and steered me over to a corner. "Plumtree, I couldn't have won this election without you. If your publishing project hadn't exposed Ferris-Browne, I wouldn't be in office. Labour unions and environmentalists would be running the nation, and the people of Britain wouldn't even realise they were ceding greater and greater sovereignty to the European Union."

"I'm honoured to have been of help, sir. I'm only sorry Ferris-Browne cost so many people so much."

He nodded sadly, but his expression in the next moment said, *Life goes on.*

"I hope you'll join our little group at the Athenaeum— it's only once a month, and I've found a back entrance to use, so there's no hullabaloo."

Wait a moment, I thought. Ian had never said *Graeme Abercrombie* was one of his book group mates. . . .

It was obvious from the prime minister's expression that he knew exactly what I was thinking. "For years now I've been asking Ian when you'd join us; he keeps telling me he's invited you and you'll come when you're ready. It's just a few of us—Ian, Lovegren, and a few others. Lord Chenies used to join us occasionally, but we did grow tired of his railing against foreigners. Do join us next time, Alex. Oh! And if I were you, I'd look forward to a rather special honour in the new year. The Queen is naturally grateful that England has retained its identity for the time being." He clapped me on the shoulder, and went off to work the crowd.

An honour in the new year? Good heavens, he couldn't possibly mean the New Year's List. . . .

Sir Alex?

Grinning, I snatched several champagne flutes from a waiter's tray and wove through the crowd back to Sarah and Ian. I'd keep this my little secret, but I couldn't resist one small indulgence. "Lady Sarah—your bubbly."

She beamed, and held her glass up in a toast. Everything was going to be all right.

NOTE TO THE READER

When I began researching the issue of the UK's European Union membership and Economic and Monetary Union (EMU), I thought I'd have to manufacture a conflict. But as I delved into EU matters more deeply, I learned that there were surprisingly strong (albeit quiet) factions for and against. Half of my trustworthy informants here and abroad tell me it's a no-brainer; it was inevitable that the UK would become part of a European consortium. The trade benefits are huge, and it's ridiculous to think that the end of NATO matters. One British friend laughed aloud when I brought up NATO. Why all the fuss?

The other half are alarmed that a succession of prime ministers have taken them down a road they never sanctioned, aside from a national vote in favour of the European Economic Community (EEC)—very different from the EU—more than twenty years ago. They are worried about a European superstate, and the billions of pounds it is costing the UK annually to simply remain a part of the Union. They don't see any benefits, except for a loss of sovereignty and a mountain of additional costly regulations. They are not at all comforted that the European Court in Strasbourg has the power to override decisions by the British courts, as it already has—most notably, the overturning of a conviction of an IRA terrorist. And they see the end of NATO as an unnecessary risk—if it's not broken, why fix it? They also point out that the UK's strongest financial and political alliances have always been with non-European nations: Wall Street and America in general, Hong Kong, Tokyo, Australia, New Zealand. Finally, they express displeasure with the massive, expensive bureaucracy in Brussels.

When I became aware of the quiet but intense conflict in England over the EU/EMU, I was even more intrigued and made it a central issue in the novel. Considering how the EU changes the world balance—financially, politically, and even militarily—it's disturbing that few Americans know or care.

Will there always be an England?

Finally, a caveat: where it helped the story, I have changed certain facts—relatively insignificant ones, I hope—such as the dimensions of the Clerk's Well (it's really less than three feet wide and only twelve feet deep) and certain geographical realities of Clerkenwell, Chorleywood, Chenies, and Heronsgate. The entire book is fiction, including *all* its characters and organisations.

The fiction is, however, often grounded in reality. There is an Order of St. *John* in Clerkenwell, for example, that trains ambulance-men. There is no real network of tunnels beneath Clerkenwell (though there have been rumours that they existed for transporting prisoners from the House of Detention to the Middlesex Sessions House), but there *are* tunnels beneath much of London that have nothing to do with the underground. (For a fascinating look at the subterranean city, see Andrew Duncan's *Secret London*.)

If you happen to visit London, it is possible to take a walking tour of Clerkenwell featuring the well, the arch and Museum of the Order of St. John, the House of Detention, the Marx Library, and Clerkenwell Green. While

I was writing *Unprintable* the pub on the green helpfully changed its name from the Thomas Wethered to my fictional one: the Clerks Well. If you're visiting, and imbibing, the City Pride is another fine Clerkenwell pub—my local when I worked in Farringdon Lane.

ABOUT THE AUTHOR

JULIE WALLIN KAEWERT, a graduate of Dartmouth and Harvard, worked for book publishers in Boston and Bedford Square before beginning her writing career with a London magazine. She is the author of three Booklover's Mysteries featuring Alex Plumtree and the Plumtree Press—*Unsolicited*, *Unbound*, and *Unprintable*—and is at work on the fourth, *Untitled*. She now lives near Boulder, Colorado, with her husband and two daughters.

The text of UNPRINTABLE is set in Garamond 3.

If you loved the adventures of publisher
Alex Plumtree in **UNPRINTABLE**,
you won't want to miss any of the
books in Julie Kaewert's tantalizing
Booklover's Mystery series!

Look for the next *Booklover's Mystery*,
UNTITLED, coming from Bantam Books
in Fall 1999.

For everyone who loves Jane Austen...

STEPHANIE BARRON'S
~ *Jane Austen Mysteries* ~

Jane and the Unpleasantness at Scargrave Manor

Being the First Jane Austen Mystery... Jane is called upon to save the reputation of her friend, the newly wed Isobel Payne, from the scandal looming over the suspicious death of her husband—the Count of Scargrave.   ___57593-7 $5.99/$7.99

Jane and the Man of the Cloth

Being the Second Jane Austen Mystery... On a family holiday, Jane investigates a captivating new acquaintance, Mr. Geoffrey Sidmouth. He may be responsible for a recent murder. Worse yet, he may be the notorious criminal known only as "the Reverend."
___57489-2 $5.99/$7.99

Jane and the Wandering Eye

Being the Third Jane Austen Mystery... While on holiday in Bath, Jane alleviates her ennui by shadowing the fugitive Lady Desdemona. But this harmless snooping leads to a grave investigation, when the Lady's brother is alleged a murderer.   ___57489-2 $5.99/$7.99

GRACE F. EDWARDS

If I Should Die

A MALI ANDERSON MYSTERY

"Excellent . . . Edwards expertly creates characters who leap to instant, long-remembered life."
—*CHICAGO TRIBUNE BOOK REVIEW*

"This girlfriend really cooks!"
—*MYSTERY LOVERS BOOKSHOP NEWS*

"A gorgeous, sassy heroine and a plot that doesn't quit . . . V. I. Warshawski look out!" —*WOMAN'S OWN*

HARLEM HAS NEVER BEEN HOTTER!